Dangerous Friends

CHUCK MCCRARY IS A WISECRACKING FORMER GREEN BERET turned private investigator with a special genius for helping people in trouble—especially if they can pay him for his efforts.

MICHELLE BABCOCK, the granddaughter of South Florida's legendary restaurateur and Chuck's friend, Hank Hickham, has disappeared. She wakes Chuck with a 4:30 a.m. phone call, desperate for help. James Ponder, her drug addicted boyfriend, has involved her in a double murder that could put her in prison for life unless Chuck can find her a way out.

Michelle only expected free tutoring in college chemistry when she slept with James Ponder, a graduate student obsessed with global warming protests, who has a talent for ecoterrorism. Instead, she is sucked into an unhealthy circle of friendships surrounding an amoral professor whose secret agenda has yielded him millions of dollars with more loot to come. Michelle is swept up in a nightmare of political corruption, terrorism, and mega-million-dollar crimes.

In helping Michelle, Chuck uncovers a conspiracy involving arson, murder, and the Chicago mob. A mysterious millionaire has masterminded a string of mega-million-dollar stock market scams that reach back for five years. The mastermind intends to cut his losses by murdering anyone who can lead the cops back to him. That includes Michelle, Chuck, and the conscienceless professor, who becomes Chuck's unwilling ally.

ONE REASON WE KEEP TURNING PAGES in Dangerous Friends is to watch the gripping character of Chuck McCrary. The skill with which he handles clients, police detectives, mob assassins, and FBI agents—all while controlling the outcomes of the case—is as remarkable as the clues he uncovers. Chuck seeks justice without regard for the legalities involved and tries to leave the world just a little better than he found it.

by Dallas Gorham

Dangerous Friends

*A Carlos McCrary, Private Investigator,
Mystery Thriller*

By Dallas Gorham

ISBN-13: 978-1517482787

ISBN-10: 151748278X

20021901

Cover art by Michael By Design www.MichaelByDesign.com.

Edited by Marsha Butler www.ButlerInk.com

Dangerous Friends

A Carlos McCrary, Private Investigator, Mystery Thriller

Chapter 1

THE BURNER PHONE RANG FIVE TIMES before James Ponder fumbled it out of his pocket to answer.

"What took you so long?" the familiar raspy voice asked. "You think this is a hobby or something, Lamp Post?"

"No, no, no, Mr... I mean, Redwood." Ponder caught himself in time. *Use code names over the phone. Or at least over this phone.* "No," he finished lamely. He knew that Redwood would reject any explanation and he couldn't tell him the truth. "Sorry."

"Are you high again?"

"No, no. I haven't had a hit all day." Ponder inhaled, held his breath, and admired the beauty of the swirling smoke that rose from the hand-rolled joint.

"*Hmph.* You must stay clear-headed. Millions of dollars are at stake here, not to mention the future of our planet. The package is *en route* and should arrive tonight. The schedule is fixed. I've completed the arrangements from my end. Don't fail me again, Lamp Post."

Ponder released the smoke from his lungs. "What time do we... make the delivery?" Quickly, he muted the phone to cover his cough from the acrid smoke.

"I'm waiting to hear from my other source. I'll call Kinetic with the time. You have the present ready, right?"

"It's ready. We're waiting for the, uh, package to arrive. I have good news. You know how I complained that we needed more dedicated volunteers. I may have another recruit for the, uh, the real work we do." He sucked in another hit. *Man, this is good shit.*

"I told you, Lamp Post: Three people are adequate. The more people involved, the trickier the security gets."

"This girl is different, Redwood. She's smart, she's dedicated to the cause, and she comes from a rich family." *And she's been screwing my brains out since that party last Halloween.* "I've worked her around for five months, bringing her along. She's a perfect addition. I think it's time we brought her in on the operation."

"No. We planned this too long to bring in an unknown quantity. She'd be a wild card. Leave her out. Observe her reaction to the operation. Then you'll know if she's as dedicated as you think."

"Well, uh, there's a little complication…" He paused, waiting for his unseen boss to prompt him. Redwood remained silent. Ponder hated that about him. When the boss wanted an explanation, he didn't ask the question like a normal person. No, he waited and let Ponder stew.

"She already knows about the operation. I swear she'll be all right with it. She's a true believer, man. Besides, I told her it would be a peaceful protest." Ponder didn't tell Redwood that he had bragged about the upcoming operation while he snorted cocaine with her. When she had asked for details, he'd invented a harebrained explanation.

"What kind of protest did you tell her it was?"

"I told her we would drape a banner across the front of the package with our message on it."

Redwood sighed. "It can't be helped. That train has left the station." He laughed at his little pun. "You realize that your impetuosity has placed the whole project at risk—again."

"Yes, sir, but it will be all right. I swear."

"You realize that if you're wrong about her, there will be repercussions—serious ones. For both of you."

"She's on board with us. I'm certain of it. She's coming over here later to wait for Kat—Kinetic's call."

"Remember, Lamp Post. Clear-headed. If I find you've gotten high again, I shall be… disappointed. I don't want anyone injured or killed this time; it causes too much backlash. You remember how much I hate to be disappointed, don't you?" The line went dead.

Ponder's stomach knotted. He rubbed the stump of his left little finger. Years earlier Ponder had accidentally killed a night watchman during a mission. Redwood had sent two thugs after him. One had held his wrist while the other cut off his little finger with a hacksaw. "Follow orders next time," the man with the hacksaw had told him. "Redwood don't like you to improvise."

Closing the flip phone, Ponder giggled and inhaled one last drag on the joint before crushing it in the ashtray. The girl would bring Oxycodone to keep him happy after the marijuana wore off. And later *Ka-BOOM!* He would witness the carnage and feel the adrenaline rush, and Redwood couldn't blame him for the deaths.

Chapter 2

THE GIRL PICKED UP HER PHONE AND PUNCHED *REJECT*. "I feel kinda bad sending Daddy's calls straight to voicemail like that."

James Ponder wrapped his arm around her waist and stretched toward her phone. "Why don't you turn it off? You're an adult for crissakes. This isn't the nineteenth century. Your father doesn't own you. You must assert your own personal identity." He spoke with the certainty of long practice and much repetition of well-memorized slogans. "You don't have to be defined by your subservient role to a patriarchal paradigm. You deserve your privacy. *We* deserve our privacy." Ponder rubbed her breast with his chin, tickling her nipple with his beard.

She rolled onto her side, took his hand, and kissed the palm. *James has such a… a…* facility *with words*, she thought. *If only he weren't such an adrenaline junky.* "I know, James, but… Daddy's gonna be worried, you know?" She leaned backwards and laid the phone on the battered nightstand. "Besides, Katherine or Steven might call."

She wrapped Ponder's arm around her waist and rolled onto his chest, straddling his body. He was a more persuasive speaker than she was, but she was better at persuading with her body. She wiggled her hips, giggled, and nuzzled his neck under the beard. "That got your attention. I feel that." She ground her hips against him.

Ponder wrapped both arms around her waist. "Omigod, that feels good."

She nibbled his earlobe. "It could feel even better." She rolled off and reached for her purse. "You'd better slip on a condom. I brought some."

He lay there with his eyes closed. "Not this time. What are the odds, just this once?"

"We discussed this. We won't bring children into this world yet. Not until we clean up some of the pollution." She nibbled on his earlobe.

"I'll use a condom, if you turn off your phone. Don't worry, we have my phone. I don't get as many calls as you."

"What if Steven calls me instead of you?" she asked.

Ponder's eyes narrowed.

"What, you're jealous? That's so bourgeois." She hoped she had used the unfamiliar word right. She'd learned it in her poli-sci class the week before. "You know how pissy Steven gets if we don't answer his calls no matter what we're doing. Or whom." She smiled.

"Screw Steven."

"Oh, I do and I will." She stroked his beard. "James, you said the project will happen soon, maybe tonight. We have to be ready and available. Are you that easily distracted?" She blew in his ear. "Speaking of being ready and available..." She ran her fingers down his chest. "I'll bet I can keep your attention, even if the phone does ring."

Chapter 3

JOHN BABCOCK CARRIED HIS COFFEE INTO MY OFFICE, his hand shaking. He seemed nervous as a nudist at a church picnic.

"Sit down, John," I said. I'm Carlos McCrary, owner, president, and sole employee of McCrary Investigations. "You said on the phone that you had a family emergency. What happened?"

"Mickie's in trouble, Chuck."

"Your daughter, Michelle, right? I met her at Hank's Super Bowl party."

"Yeah. She's a freshman at the University of Atlantic County."

"What's her full name?"

"Michelle Teresa Babcock."

My heart twanged when John said her middle name. I'd once dated a woman named Teresa. It had not ended well. I wrote it down anyway. "What's her major?"

"Environmental studies."

I wrote that down too. "How can I help?"

John's chin dropped to his chest. "Mickie's disappeared. I called Hank, and he told me to call you. Said you helped him out of a tough spot a while back."

Good old Hank. He was John's father-in-law, and he'd sent me several clients in the last year. "Disappeared how?"

"She doesn't answer her phone. I emailed and texted her. She doesn't reply."

"How old is she?"

"Eighteen. She'll be nineteen this summer."

"When's her birthday?"

"What difference does that make?"

I shrugged. "Maybe none. It's the way I work. I get lots of facts. When's her birthday?"

"Geez, I don't know. Sometime next summer—June, I think. Penny keeps up with birthdays, anniversaries, and such." Penny was Hank's daughter and John's wife.

"Never mind. I'll get that later. Where does Michelle live?"

"At home. She commutes to school."

"What's your address?"

He told me and I wrote it down. "How long has Michelle been out of touch?"

"Since Saturday morning. I think something bad has happened to her."

"What does Penny think?"

His lips twisted in a half smile. "Her maternal instincts tell her that Mickie's okay. Penny thinks maybe she skipped out with a boyfriend. She reminded me that we did that when we were in college."

"But you don't think she's with a boyfriend," I said.

"No. She doesn't have a steady boyfriend."

"Sometimes parents don't know their kids as well as they think." I smiled to soften the comment. "Deal with it, John. Legally, Michelle is an adult. There are things you and Penny don't know about her. She has a right to her privacy even if she does live at home."

"Mickie may be eighteen, but she's not really an adult. When I was her age, I didn't have a lick of sense. Frankly, she's naïve about the real world." He lifted his coffee. "Maybe Penny and I've been overprotective. Okay, maybe *I've* been overprotective. You'll understand when you have daughters." He nudged his cup a millimeter to one side, then back.

"When's the last time you heard from her?"

"Saturday morning. Last Friday night at dinner, Mickie said she and friends from the university planned to build houses for Habitat for Humanity during spring break. Penny and I said that was a good way to give back something to the community—especially since Mickie has never shown any inclination like that before. Penny thought the college exposure was helping her mature into a responsible adult." He shook his head. "If we'd known…" He moved the coffee cup again.

"Known what?"

"That Mickie was lying to us. She told us a local motel in west Port City would house the volunteers so they wouldn't have a long commute through rush-hour traffic. She packed a bag and left Saturday morning. We haven't heard from her since."

I consulted my wall clock. "If they were going to build houses all spring break, you wouldn't have heard from her anyway. It's two-thirty Monday afternoon. Why come to me so soon?"

"This morning I had business out near the Everglades. I called Habitat for Humanity and got the address where they're building this week. I was gonna drop by and surprise Mickie. Treat her and her friends to lunch."

"Good for you." I smiled. "A great way for Dad to check up on his little girl."

He shrugged and grinned. "When I arrived at the job site, she wasn't there. She hadn't been there at all."

"So, she played hooky today."

John squeezed his cup so hard that his knuckles turned white. "She wasn't there Saturday or Sunday either. She hasn't ever worked for Habitat for Humanity. She's not on their volunteer list."

Chapter 4

JOHN MET SNOOP AND ME AT HIS DOOR. "Penny would be here if she could. Her spring break is a different week than UAC, so she's at work." He cut his eyes to Snoop.

I tapped Snoop's shoulder. "John, this is Ray Snopolski. He's a retired Port City police detective who works with me from time to time."

Snoop shook John's hand. "Everybody calls me Snoop."

"You gonna help Chuck find my daughter?"

"Yes, sir."

John gestured us in. "Her room's down this way."

Michelle's bedroom was the second door on the right. The heavy perfume scent hit me before I switched on the light. When I did, it looked like her closet had exploded. "Did burglars ransack her room?"

John shrugged. "What can I say? Neat, she ain't."

A jumble of shoes and sandals were piled against the wall beside the door. Textbooks and notebooks littered the bed; more were stacked in a corner of the room. A television had a string of Chinese paper lanterns hung across the corner of the screen. Bras and a swimsuit were piled into another corner, surrounded by a herd of blouses and pants in various colors. One corkboard displayed photos, a sparkly bow made of translucent red ribbon, posters, two blue first-prize ribbons, and assorted medals on tiny chains. Wildlife pictures in idyllic settings covered another corkboard.

A neat stack of clean clothes sat on the floor by the closet. I knew they were clean because they were folded. I figured

Penny or John had laundered them. Two thermal glasses, half-filled with amber liquid, sat abandoned on a nightstand next to a one-liter carafe filled with seashells. Two half-burned scented candles filled the rest of the crowded top.

I faced John. "We won't do a thorough search. It takes hours to search a room properly." *And this one could last days*, I thought. "If Michelle's in trouble, we can't afford to spend that much time. Snoop and I will do a quick-and-dirty for clues to where she might be. Why don't you wait in the living room?"

He left and I winked at Snoop. "You have two daughters. Why would any woman need three hair dryers?"

"Small, medium, and large? Your guess is as good as mine."

I smelled the liquid in the thermal glasses. Some sort of cola diluted with melted ice from the last Ice Age. It must have been diet cola; otherwise, there would have been mold growing in the glasses. "My god, how can anyone live like this?"

"She's a teenager. You should see my girls' rooms. They're almost as bad. Maybe it's their hormones."

I smiled. "First go through the pockets of every piece of clothing in the closet. Then search the clothing scattered across the room. After you examine a piece, hang it up so we can keep it straight. I'll start with the bookcase."

A four-shelf bookcase was crammed against one wall. The top shelf bent under a stack of *Mother Earth News* and another of *Rolling Stone*. The next shelf held dozens of CDs of songs by groups I'd never heard of and a portable player. Michelle would have transferred the CDs to an iPod or smartphone or whatever teenagers use to listen to music nowadays. The third shelf groaned with the weight of a half-dozen textbooks. My eye caught *Global Sustainable Energy: Past, Present, and Future.* I perused the book jacket. "Students will explore the global history of energy sources, both renewable and non-renewable. Renewable energy sources will be investigated and environmentally sound solutions to future needs will be analyzed." I remembered the tortured prose in my own college textbooks. I flipped the pages. Nothing hidden inside.

The next book was *Forests for Florida's Future.* The book jacket promised "Examination of current environmental issues impacting community decisions regarding Florida forest resources. Each issue will be examined within a framework of human behavior, policy options, and media messages. Students will learn to understand key issues and analyze major ecological variables." Nothing hidden in its pages either.

I was getting woozy from reviewing the covers. I didn't read the rest, merely flipped through the pages. The next to last book was marked with a sheet torn off a lined pad with a handwritten note: *James 55-22-16*. Not a bible verse, maybe a combination to his school locker? I stuck it in my pocket. Rule Six: *You never know what you'll need to know.*

The bottom shelf held more shoes, a stack of coloring books from her pre-school days, and a bunch of journals. I made a note about the journals; we could examine them later if necessary. I peeked inside the shoes; found a penny in one. I finished the bottom shelf, moved to the bed, and searched the books there. I arranged them on the shelf as I finished. "Snoop, there's plenty of room on these shelves for these books she's thrown on the bed. Why doesn't she shelve them?"

"I already told you, bud: She's a teenager; they don't think like humans." He grabbed more clothes off the floor and searched the pockets. "Whoa, what's this?" He extracted a three-pack of foil-wrapped condoms from a pair of cargo shorts. "Well, that answers that question. John ain't gonna like this." He snapped a photo, then replaced the condoms where he'd found them.

I picked the shoes off the floor and dumped them on the bed for an easier search. I found her stash in the toe of an old pair of sneakers. "Snoop, have a gander."

Snoop opened the baggie and stuck his nose in. "Pretty good quality weed." He snapped a picture and handed the baggie back to me.

As I finished each pair of shoes, I stuck it in an empty shoe rack on the closet floor. "She has shoe racks. Why doesn't she use them?"

"You know my daughters. Teenagers are a different species."

Halfway through the shoes, I found a yellow pill bottle stuffed in the toe of one. The prescription label had been peeled off. The bottle held six pink pills with *OC* on one side and *20* on the other. "Snoop, I'm no expert on prescription drugs, but these could be twenty-milligram Oxycodone tablets." I handed him the bottle.

He opened the childproof cap and dumped a tablet into his hand. He photographed the tablet and the bottle, then put the pill back. "I've seen enough, Chuck. You seen enough?"

"Yeah. Even if she hasn't run away, she's in trouble. Sex, drugs, and rock-and-roll. Let's go talk to John."

We found John in the kitchen. "Want coffee, guys?"

"A little cream, no sugar for me."

Snoop drank his black.

"John," I said, "we found things in Michelle's room that you need to know about."

He swallowed. "What things?"

"Snoop, show him the first photo."

Snoop had transferred the photos to his laptop, which he opened on the kitchen table. He rotated the screen toward John.

John gazed at the screen. "Is that a pack of condoms?"

"It is," I said. "Those condoms are sold in boxes of six. There are three left."

John frowned. "I don't know what to say."

"It is what it is. Snoop, show him the next photo." He did.

"What's in the baggie?" John asked.

"Marijuana. Snoop, show him the last picture."

"Is that what I think it is?"

"Oxycodone," Snoop replied.

"Jesus H. Christ." John held his face in his hands, elbows on the kitchen table.

"John, is Michelle's phone on your family plan?" I asked.

"Yeah."

"Let me pull up your account on the phone company's website. Let's see what numbers she's been calling."

John gave me his login and password.

I positioned my laptop across from Snoop's. "She called three numbers a lot the last week. Texted them too." I recited the numbers.

Snoop wrote them down. "I'll do a reverse lookup." He punched his keyboard. "Katherine Shamanski is the first one."

I pivoted to John. "You know her?"

"Nope."

"No problem," Snoop said. "That's why Al Gore invented the internet. She's a student at UAC. I'll review her Facebook page... Shamanski's a senior and she's majoring in environmental studies like Michelle."

"Shamanski could be a classmate, but there aren't many classes that seniors and freshmen would both take. You got an address, Snoop?"

"Yeah. I'll check it on the map... She's got an apartment near campus. Here's her picture." He rotated the computer toward John. "You ever see her with Michelle?"

John studied the screen. "No."

"Okay if I use your printer?" Snoop asked.

John gave Snoop his printer password. "It's in my home office. You print it and I'll get it."

Snoop tapped his keyboard. "I'll print off a copy. The next number is a James Ponder."

I glanced at John. "The name familiar?"

He shook his head. "I don't know him either."

Snoop indicated the computer screen again. John shook his head.

"Maybe he's the James on this note." I showed John the scrap of paper I had found in Michelle's room.

"Could that be a bible verse?" he asked.

"Bible verses have two numbers—chapter and verse. I don't know what this is. Maybe a locker combination. That's why I kept it."

Snoop punched keys. "Ponder is a graduate teaching assistant in, wait for it... environmental studies. My god, his picture could be a portrait of a Taliban terrorist, except he's wearing a peace symbol on a chain instead of carrying an AK-47."

Snoop printed the photo. "Ponder is twenty-nine years old."

"Maybe he's a professional student," I observed. "Where does he live?"

Snoop punched the keyboard. "A house near campus. Okay, the next number belongs to Steven Wallace... That's *Doctor* Steven Wallace, a tenured professor. Teaches environmental studies at UAC. Michelle called him several times a day for the last four days."

"John, it sounds like Michelle hangs out with an older crowd. Does that seem like her?"

"In high school she had lots of friends her own age," he said, "but I don't know any of her college friends."

"Oh, wait, some calls were Dr. Wallace calling her," said Snoop.

I asked, "Why would she telephone a professor on the weekend? Especially the weekend before spring break? And why would a tenured professor call a lowly freshman student? Classes aren't scheduled for another week."

John set down his coffee. "Could we be talking sexual exploitation here?"

Chapter 5

"MICHELLE, THIS IS CHUCK MCCRARY. I'm the private investigator you met at your grandfather's Super Bowl party. Call me please. Your parents are worried." I disconnected, then texted the same message. "That's all I can do, John. Her phone rings at least once, so it's on. The screen shows who the caller is, then she rejects the call. If her phone were off, it would go straight to voicemail without ringing."

"She obviously doesn't want to talk to either one of us," John said. "Oh, geez, look at the time. Penny will be home any second, and it's my turn to cook."

"Okay. I'll go find Michelle." I grabbed the slip of paper. "I have three names and addresses near campus. She's likely at one of those."

"Should I call those three other people?" asked John. "Ask if Mickie's with one of them?"

"If Michelle won't answer, they might not talk to you either," I responded. "Something smells like three-day-old fish. I understand Michelle being friends with a senior in the same major. Maybe they belong to the same student club. Maybe Shamanski's a mentor. But adding an older, male graduate assistant to the mix, it gets a little hinky. The guy's practically my age. And don't get me started about a tenured college professor who gives his phone number to a freshman female."

"Maybe Mickie's in a student club with him."

"A student organization fits the bill," I responded. "Ponder or Wallace might be a faculty sponsor. Otherwise, what interest would a tenured college professor have in a freshman woman?

Unless he's a dirty old man. If he's tenured, he's old enough to be her father. This is rarified air for Michelle to be breathing."

I swiveled to Snoop. "When you get home, research everything you can find on Shamanski, Ponder, and Wallace." I grasped my briefcase. "I'll visit these three addresses."

John shook my hand. "Bring her home, Chuck."

"Don't expect too much, John. Legally, she's an adult. I'll make sure she's okay, and I'll ask her to call you, but I can't make her come home if she doesn't want to."

WALLACE LIVED NEAR DOWNTOWN. I decided to begin nearest to the university. Shamanski's apartment was a mile from campus. I cruised the parking lot for Michelle's car—her father had given me the license plate and a description. No joy.

I found Michelle's car parked in the driveway at the second address I called on. A *Save Our Seas* specialty license plate was on a very used Honda Civic. A bumper sticker proclaimed *Today's Environmentalists Are Tomorrow's Heroes*. At least she believed in something. Maybe she wanted to be the campus poster child for political correctness.

Ponder's address was a two-story, shingle-sided Craftsman-style house that must have been a hundred years old. It appeared every bit of its age. A wooden shutter on the second floor hung by one hinge. Behind it, the original dark brown color of the siding was evident. The rest of the siding had weathered to a hopeless beige. The exposed roof rafters were moldy where the paint had peeled. The composition roof was on its last legs, judging from the number of patches. Square wooden posts supporting the porch roof had warped and split. The front steps had been replaced with concrete ones, now cracked and settled with a large split down one side. Weeds lay dying in the bare earth where a lawn had thrived decades before.

Gentrification had not hit this neighborhood.

I wanted to find Michelle, but part of me hoped she wasn't inside this ramshackle heap. The bright, sunny girl I had met at Hank's Super Bowl party shouldn't be in this miserable excuse for a house, even for a short while.

I had driven my anonymous white Dodge Caravan, one of a bazillion other white minivans. I parked seventy-five yards up the street and observed the house.

My stomach growled as a ragged old woman pushed a wobbly grocery cart down the block. Two black plastic garbage bags, containing all she owned in the world, hung from the cart. She stopped the cart, straightened up, and rubbed the small of her back with both hands. She stretched, then pushed aside the overgrown branches of a neglected Ixora bush to retrieve a faded aluminum can hidden among the discarded plastic bags and scraps of paper. She tossed it into the cart and trudged listlessly along the sidewalk.

I got out of the van when she moved closer. "Ma'am?"

She peered at me warily.

"What brand of can did you find?"

She fished in the cart and held up the faded can. "Diet Coke."

"I'm a collector. I'll give you twenty dollars for it."

"It's worth a dime."

"I'll give you twenty dollars for that can."

She shrugged and handed it to me.

I handed her the twenty, returned to the van, and tossed the can in the litterbag. Maybe she could have a good meal tonight even if I couldn't.

Another hour passed and the street remained deserted as a ghost town. I missed the old homeless woman. My stomach complained again.

After sunset, lights came on in the rear windows on the second floor of Ponder's house.

I parked behind Michelle's Civic and climbed the concrete steps. The entire first floor was dark. The doorbell was the old-fashioned type that you twist like winding an alarm clock. I twisted twice and waited. I felt faint footsteps vibrate through the porch floorboards, but no one came to the door. I twisted the bell again. Same vibrations. I heard an upstairs window scuff open and then close. Someone had peeked out at the street. They must have noticed my Caravan parked behind Michelle's Honda, but no one came to the door.

I tested the screen door handle. Unlocked. I rapped on the wooden doorframe. It rattled like it was barely fastened to the jamb. "Hello. Anybody home?"

Floorboards creaked upstairs, but no one appeared.

I swung the screen door open and stepped inside. I wasn't breaking and entering; the door was unlocked. I shined a Maglite around the square foyer. Dark-stained, Florida heart pine floors scratched and worn with age. Double-wide pocket doors opened onto a parlor. A wide wooden staircase climbed up one wall of the central hall. I flicked the light switch at the bottom of the stairs. "Hello. I'm coming up. Anybody home up there?"

I'd ascended halfway up the stairs when a shirtless man banged open a door at the rear of the second floor. He blinked in the hall light. He was rail thin with sunken cheeks visible above his beard. I could have counted his ribs. Eyes sensitive to light. The clues spelled *junky*. A peace symbol on a chain around his neck peaked out from behind a scruffy beard.

Snoop was right. In real life he seemed even more like a Taliban. He shut the door behind him and stood by the window at the rear of the central hall. He spread his feet apart, swaying. He steadied himself with one hand against a side wall.

"Who the hell are you?" he asked, too loudly.

I held out a business card and continued up the stairs.

He wore ragged cut-off jeans. Not fashionable cut-offs, but worn-out pants like a homeless person. He didn't act like any graduate assistant I had met when I attended the University of Florida.

"I'm Chuck McCrary. I'm here to speak to Michelle Babcock, please."

"There's nobody here by that name. You're trespassing." His brown eyes were wide and darted back and forth. I wondered what he was high on. Then I wondered why I wondered; it made no difference.

"When will she be back?"

He cranked his voice volume up a notch. "I don't know any Michelle Babcock."

Michelle's name flowed easily off his tongue, even high as he was. He was familiar with the name. I was in the right place.

I reached the top of the stairs. "Are you James Ponder?" I extended my business card toward him. He ignored it.

"Don't know anybody by that name either."

"Is James Ponder in?"

He balled his hands into fists. "Who wants to know, asshole?"

"You always this polite to strangers?" I reached the top of the stairs.

Dirty bare feet completed his ensemble. He brandished his fist. "You're trespassing. Get the hell outta here."

"I'll leave after I talk to Michelle."

"You'll leave anyway, asshole. I'm gonna call the cops."

Mister Hospitality has a limited vocabulary. "Go ahead, call them. I'll wait." I sidestepped to the center of the hall, staking a claim to his space. I leaned against the banister and crossed my arms.

He seemed a little perplexed.

"If you're not James Ponder, who are you?"

He didn't reply. His gaze flitted from side to side across the hallway, passing over me each time like a searchlight.

"I'll call you Whiskers. Go ahead and call the cops, Whiskers. Or we could be civil to each other. Either way, I'll wait here until I know that Michelle is okay."

"Shit, I'll throw you out myself, asshole." He thrusted off the wall and gathered his balance.

Maybe he was used to the Taliban beard and the wild eyes scaring people off.

"Don't be stupid, Whiskers. The drugs you take make you belligerent. I don't want to hurt you. I merely want to ensure Michelle is okay."

He doubled both fists and charged like a berserk bull.

I sidestepped and he slammed into the banister, smashing his groin. I'd witnessed people so high on drugs that their pain receptors shut off. His balls would be sore as a boil after he came down off his trip. As high as he was, if I had been at the top of the open stairwell when he charged, he would've tumbled down the steps.

I positioned my business card on the stair rail. I wanted this idiot to remember who I was. I stepped away. "Where is Michelle?"

He rose to his hands and knees. He struggled to his feet, stepped toward me, and swung his right fist.

I caught the swing on my left forearm and hit him in the solar plexus with my right. I pulled the punch. I didn't want to send him to the hospital; I merely wanted to stop his attack.

He crumpled to the wooden floor and curled into a ball.

The door at the rear clicked opened. "James, what's going on out there?" Michelle stepped into the hall. "Hello, Chuck. I got your text earlier. I thought it might be you."

Chapter 6

MICHELLE HAD CHANGED SINCE I HAD MET HER at Hank Hickham's Super Bowl party. Her hair was a little longer, and she wore it in a single braid. She wore a peace symbol necklace identical to Ponder's. Her green tee-shirt trumpeted, "Mother Earth does not belong to us; we belong to Mother Earth" in gold letters. Trained observer that I am, I noticed she was not wearing a bra. I was careful not to leer. Inspecting a tee-shirt is not leering. Her preppy shorts were a fashionable white raw silk. The gold-trimmed leather sandals revealed that her feet were clean, unlike her boyfriend's.

"What're you doing here, Chuck?" She didn't seem happy I'd come.

"Your father went by the Habitat for Humanity building site today to take you to lunch. When you weren't there and wouldn't answer your phone, he hired me to find you and make sure you're safe. He's worried."

"How did you know where I was?" She crossed her arms. The tee-shirt's thin fabric stretched more tightly across her breasts.

I carefully held my gaze on her eyes. No leering allowed.

"Did you tap my phone? That's the sort of fascist trick I would expect from a police state."

"Nothing so dramatic. I found you with routine detective work. Your privacy was not violated." *Not much anyway*, I thought, *since your parents pay your cellphone bill.*

She still didn't act happy to see me, but at least she uncrossed her arms.

"Tell Daddy I'm fine." Her eyes were very bright, very wide. I stepped closer and whiffed the stink of marijuana from the room behind her.

Is she high too? I waved toward Whiskers. "I presume that Mr. Congeniality here is James Ponder?"

"Yes. Have you two met?" She gazed down at Ponder, who was having trouble getting to his knees.

"Briefly, when he attacked me."

"You'll have to forgive James. Sometimes I think he gets off more on adrenaline than he does from having sex with me."

If Michelle was attempting to shock me, it wasn't working. "Are you okay?"

"Sure. How did you know his name?"

"Same way I found you; I'm a private investigator. Finding out things is what I do. I know more than you might think."

"I'm an adult. I can do what I please with anyone I choose." She gave me an up-and-down look that made me feel like a cut of beef she was inspecting in the supermarket meat case. She licked her lips. "Anyone."

"Yes, you can, but your parents are worried about you. Would you please call your dad or your mom? Use my phone if you like." I held out my phone to her.

Ponder struggled to his feet and stepped between Michelle and me. I let him.

His eyes blazed. He stuck his arm out to block Michelle. "She'll do no such thing, asshole. She's a liberated woman. You can't tell her what to do."

"But you can forbid her to call home? Somehow, that doesn't seem fair."

"You can't force Michelle to go with you," Ponder said.

"I never said I wanted to take Michelle with me, and nothing about forcing her."

Michelle frowned and half-stepped toward the door. She seemed ill at ease. She grasped her braid in her left hand and twirled it, let it go, twirled it again.

I sidestepped so I could talk to her without looking through Ponder. "Michelle, please call your parents." I held the phone out again.

She crossed her arms again, not focusing on me. "Daddy will insist that I come home. He won't listen to reason, because he doesn't understand me." She struck a pose. "He doesn't understand what motivates me now that I'm grown up and think beyond the mentality of the middle class."

Oh, brother. I wonder if Whiskers taught her that. I didn't want to argue, so I stayed quiet.

Ponder stepped between us again. "Michelle has a higher purpose than short-sighted, middle-class reactionaries like her parents could ever understand. She cares about the future of the entire planet." He spoke like he was on a picket line at an oil refinery. "She's a true friend of Mother Earth."

I seized Ponder's beard with one hand and jerked his head down, bending him over. "I've had enough of you, Whiskers. I'm talking to Michelle, not to you. Step between us again, and I will throw you to the other end of the hall. Interfere after that, and I'll toss you down the stairs." I yanked on his beard and forced him to his knees. "That's the last warning I will give you. Now sit down like a good little boy."

I focused on Michelle. "Can we go downstairs and talk where we won't be interrupted?" I glanced at her boyfriend.

She frowned at him. "Go inside, James. I'll be back in a flash."

James glowered at me, hatred in his eyes. He started to struggle to his feet, collapsed onto his back, and groaned.

Michelle led the way downstairs into the parlor. She switched on the light and walked to the center of the room. "Now what?"

After noticing the filthy, dilapidated furniture, I was glad she hadn't invited me to sit down. "Maybe you can give me a message for your parents."

She contemplated the ceiling as if she could observe Ponder sprawled on the floor upstairs. "Daddy doesn't understand that I am motivated by caring for the future of the entire planet." She said it like she was quoting scripture. "We—all of us—we're tomorrow's heroes. Since I came to the UAC, I see the bigger picture, a worldwide picture. My parents are entrapped by the bourgeois world-view of the middle class."

Cute; she talks like a protest sign. I let it pass. "You're here of your own free will?"

She scoffed. "James tutors me in chemistry. He's really not that good a lover." She gave me the meat market look again.

So young, yet so cynical. Apparently, part of Ponder's attraction was economic: Sleeping with him was cheaper than paying for tutoring.

"Will you at least call your parents?" I tried to hand her my phone.

"Daddy will lecture me with middle-class dogma. He talks *at* me, not *with* me. I'm involved with an important project this week—important to the whole planet. Tell Mom and Dad I'll be home by the weekend. They can lecture me then."

"That's five whole days, Michelle. You know they'll worry." I handed her my business card, one without the logo of a knight on a white horse. Maybe my card needed a logo of Don Quixote tilting at a windmill. I felt about as effective. "If you need someone to talk to... someone who won't lecture you..."

She accepted the card and stuck it in her pants pocket.

I gestured toward the door. "I hope your boyfriend's all right. I told him I was here to make sure you were okay, and he charged me like a bull—twice. I didn't hit him hard."

"Don't worry about him. James has more balls than brains."

"Call me if you need anything. Day or night, okay? I don't do lectures."

She laid a hand on my arm. "I'm all right, Chuck. I really am. I know what I'm doing."

Yeah, right.

Chapter 7

PONDER FLINCHED WHEN MICHELLE SLAMMED THE BEDROOM DOOR behind her. "James, you idiot, were you born stupid or did someone drop you on your head?"

"What—what do you mean? That asshole attacked me. I had to defend myself." He moaned as he rolled onto his side on the bed and clutched his stomach with both hands. He glanced up. *Is she buying it? Nope.*

"Don't make me laugh. Compared to you, Chuck McCrary's a Boy Scout. He took it easy on you, or you'd be on your way to the hospital." She stepped toward Ponder and he recoiled on the bed. "Sometimes, you act like... like..." She stomped a foot and clenched her fists. "I simply don't understand you, James. When the adrenaline hits you, you're a different man—one I don't even know. McCrary was Special Forces. You know, the Green Berets? He could kill you with his bare hands." She twisted away. "Forget it."

She picked up her cellphone. "Katherine or Steven should have called by now. Do you think they're okay?"

Ponder sat up on the bed. "They may be a little later than we'd planned. They have extra stuff to do before tonight." He wouldn't meet her gaze.

"Extra stuff like what? Is there something you're not telling me?"

Ponder's eyes narrowed and his lips pressed into a thin line. "They've planned a little extra surprise for the Earth killers."

Michelle's face lit up. "Sounds like fun. What kind of extra surprise?"

"A big one. You'll see." He peered at his phone. "Since we have time to kill…" He slid his hand up the inside of her thigh. "You have another condom in your purse?"

PONDER'S PHONE VIBRATED AND MICHELLE ROLLED OFF. She snatched the phone from the nightstand before it rang. "Hello, Katherine." She switched the phone to speaker.

"You sound out of breath."

Michelle winked at Ponder. "James and I were… killing time while we waited for your call."

"Ha, I'll bet you were. Is sex all you two ever think about?" She laughed. "You're making me jealous. I'm having a dry spell."

"I could loan you James after I'm through with him."

"His beard is too scratchy."

"That's not why you called."

"Are you and James ready for action? Or should I say, *more* action?"

Michelle smirked at Ponder. "We were born ready."

"James, are you there?"

"Yeah, Katherine. Go ahead."

"I want you both to come in separate cars. Michelle, you park on Seventh Street at least a block east of the park. James, you park on Fourth Avenue a block north of the park."

"Why not park in the parking lot?" Michelle asked. "At night there should be plenty of spaces."

Katherine paused so long that Michelle wondered if the call had dropped. "Katherine? Are you there?"

"Yes. Park where I said."

"Okay, but why?"

"That will become clear later. Michelle, now that you're in the Four Musketeers you must be a team member. Just do it."

Ponder touched Michelle's elbow. "We will, Katherine. Separate cars, a block away from the park. We'll be there in an hour—separately."

"Michelle, did you pack a hoodie and a baseball hat like I told you?"

"Yes."

"Both of you put on your hoodies and baseball hats before you open the car door."

"Okay."

"One more thing," Katherine added.

"We're listening."

"Remove your cellphone batteries from your phones before you get out of the car."

Michelle's stomach clinched like a fist as she disconnected the call. "Why does she want us to wear hoodies and hats?"

"Michelle, you're smarter than that. It's for the security cameras in McKinley Park."

"But why remove our cellphone batteries?"

Chapter 8

"ACCELEROMETER'S AT MINUS THREE. Delray Beach four miles ahead." Harold Greenleaf had been an engineer with the East Carolina & Florida Railroad for twenty-eight years.

Dan Smith, the conductor, noted the reading in the train log. He eyed the speedometer. "We should hit twenty at the city limits." He glanced at his watch. "I make it 10:31 p.m."

Harold consulted the clock on the instrument panel. "I concur."

Harold and Dan rode in the lead General Electric ES44C4 locomotive that controlled the mile-long train. Two additional ES44C4s hauled from the front followed by 108 freight cars carrying coal for Port City Power's Everglades generating plant. Two more locomotives drove the 15,444 tons of coal from the rear. A single one-hundred-eighty-pound man controlled the 22,000 horsepower of all five locomotives.

The wheels rumbled and clicked their hypnotic rhythm. Harold yawned and swiveled the upholstered driver's chair. "I'm gonna hit the head and fix more coffee. You want a cup?"

Dan grasped the dead-man switch and replaced Harold at the controls. "Yeah, thanks."

The lights of Delray Beach paraded sedately by. The clanging bells of the grade crossing rose and fell in volume while the locomotive rumbled past the flashing red lights on the crossing arms.

Dan moved the throttle one notch as the speedometer hit twenty miles per hour. The five locomotives at either end of the 108-car string automatically adjusted all thirty driving axles.

The coal cars between the leading locomotives and the trailing ones paid no attention to the electrical commands that travelled through their innards to the back of the train. They were content to carry the coal that would fuel the Everglades power plant for a little over thirty hours.

By 12:07 a.m. the coal train had crossed the New River Bridge in Fort Lauderdale. At 12:52 a.m. Dan announced, "Twelve minutes to the Everglades switch. I'll take a leak before we make the curve."

Harold rolled his shoulders to relieve the tension in his neck as he sat at the instruments. It had been a long day and he was tired. *I'm getting too old for this. Two more years and I'll retire. Maybe the missus and I will live on a boat in the Keys. We can get an old clunker trawler with enough cabins for two or three grandkids to visit at a time. Then we can go visit them up north at Christmas and enjoy the snow.* The green lights of the Seetiweekifenokee River Bridge grew larger on either side of the double-tracked rail line.

A flash of billowing orange smashed the windshield and enveloped the green lights. Thunder shook the three-hundred-ton locomotive like a baby's rattle. A giant bird's nest of steel girders hurtled into the air spinning on either side of the engine.

"Holy Mother of God!" Harold slapped the Head of Train Device sending wireless signals to all five locomotives and 108 coal cars to apply their brakes. Hitting the throttle with his other hand, Harold slammed all sixty drive wheels into reverse as the locomotive tumbled off the shredded end of the rails and nosedived into the inky water of the Seeti River.

The steep downward tilt of the engine threw Harold forward. Black water rushed through the shattered windshield. Harold pounded on the toilet compartment door beneath him. "Dan! Dan! You've got to get out of there." Water flooded through the side windows, sweeping the engineer away from the toilet door. The steel locomotive slammed into the river bottom, smashing Harold's head into the metal wall and knocking him unconscious.

The cool water rose to fill the cabin.

Inside the toilet compartment, Dan was thrown to one side as the lights went out. He struggled to his feet in the dark and felt for the door above his head. The cabin lights flicked to red as the emergency power snapped on. Dan crouched where the front wall met the metal floor, now tilting at a steep angle. He twisted the doorknob and lunged with his shoulders against the door. The knob turned but the door didn't budge. He didn't know that thirty feet of water pressed on it from the other side with twenty-eight tons of weight.

Water seeped through the cracks at the edges of the metal door and pooled around his feet. The locomotive settled on its side. Water sloshed up the wall and rose relentlessly toward Dan's head.

Chapter 9

MY PHONE WOKE ME AT 4:30 IN THE MORNING. My chest tightened. *Nothing good happens after midnight.* The Caller ID said *Michelle Babcock.*

"Hello, Michelle."

"I need to talk to you."

"Okay. I'm listening."

"Not over the phone." She sounded breathless. "People can listen on the phone. We need to talk in person. I didn't know who else to call."

"Okay. Are you at the house where you were last night? I can come get you."

"I'm not there anymore."

"Where are you?"

"Not over the phone; someone could be listening." Her voice broke. "Something terrible happened. I'm scared, and I don't know what to do."

"Where are you?"

"Not over the phone. We have to meet."

"I don't read minds, Michelle. Tell you what—don't say the name of the place, but do you remember our conversation during the Super Bowl halftime about pie? We compared places to find good pie."

"Yeah, I remember."

"Do you remember my favorite restaurant for pie?"

"I don't remember the name."

"It's open twenty-four hours a day. Don't say the name, but tell me whether you remember now."

She paused. "Yeah, yeah, I think so. Yeah, I do remember."

"Do you have a way to look up the address? Maybe on your phone? Say yes or no."

"Yes."

"Yes or no: Do you have transportation?"

"Yes."

"I'll meet you there in an hour."

"It'll take me two hours."

"Two hours then. I'll be there."

"Chuck, one more thing."

"Yeah?"

"Don't tell Mom and Dad you heard from me. I don't want them involved, especially Daddy. I can't be seen with anyone, so I won't go inside. I'll meet you in the parking lot. Don't let anyone follow you. Can I trust you? This must be an absolute secret. You okay with that?"

"No, I'm not okay with that, Michelle, but I'll do what you ask. This will be our secret."

I PULLED INTO THE PARKING LOT of the Day and Night Diner an hour later. Plenty of time to eat breakfast, then wait in the van for Michelle. The diner had a handful of customers. I sat at the counter and waved at my regular server, Veraleesa Kotanay.

Veraleesa was on the night shift until seven. "Hey, Chuck. Is this a pie run, or do you want breakfast?" She deposited a steaming mug of coffee on the counter for me. Veraleesa had worked at the diner since God's dog was a puppy. We met when I worked the neighborhood on a previous case. The Day and Night had the world's best pie.

"Good morning, Veraleesa. I'll have breakfast."

"The usual?" She was already writing it up. After she relayed the order, she stopped across the counter from me. "You're kinda early. Don't usually see you until after sunrise."

"Early to bed, early to rise. That's me." We chit-chatted about my unofficial foster son Clint until my order was ready.

I finished breakfast and waited in the van. I watched her park her Honda Civic a half block up the street in a dark spot between streetlights. She locked the door and walked back to my van. When she peered in the passenger window, I motioned her in. "Okay, Michelle, what happened?"

She seized her braid with one hand and twirled it around her fingers. "I'm sort of involved in an accidental death."

"Begin at the beginning. Tell me everything."

"You know that railroad bridge next to I-95 across the Seeti River?"

"The automatic one? The one with no attendant?"

"Yeah, that one."

"What about it?"

"He blew it up. *Boom!*" She made an expansive gesture with her hands then tugged her braid again. "There was this big explosion, and the train fell into the river." Her voice broke. "The conductor, or engineer, or whatever you call him—the radio station said he's dead. I think he drowned." She hid her face and burst into tears.

I wondered if the tears were real. I handed her a tissue and waited for her to calm down. "How are you involved?"

"We were going to snag a protest banner across the locomotive as it passed to plaster the train with our message. The banner declared, *No more coal-fired plants.*" She swept her hand through the air like she was spreading the banner. "That train hauls coal to the Port City Power generating plant. They sneak it in during the middle of the night so no one sees it."

A simpler explanation might be that the trains came in at night to avoid disrupting traffic several times a week, but then I don't imagine conspiracies everywhere. Who's to say she wasn't right?

"That train helps the power company poison our air. We wanted to stop it. We *had* to stop it." Her eyes flashed. Maybe it was self-righteous indignation; maybe she was used to parroting people like James Ponder. "People like them are killing the planet."

Oh geez, does she ever stop? This was not a great time to debate energy policy, especially since I knew as much about energy policy as I knew about women—practically nothing. "How are you involved?"

"We... we got to the railroad bridge in a boat." She sniffed.

I figured Ponder was one of the "we," but I didn't interrupt. My questions would wait.

"We tied the boat under the bridge where no one could see it from the highway. We climbed the riverbank carrying bamboo poles to hold up the banner from either side." She wiped her nose with the back of her hand like a little girl, forgetting the tissue. "The poles were fifteen feet long. The banner was twenty feet wide. We were going to hold it up like a football goal post and let the train run through it."

"What about the explosion?"

"The train came rolling down the track on the north side of the river. James and I hoisted the banner in plenty of time, like we planned. Then…" She caught her breath. "Steven said, 'Watch this,' and he held up an old-fashioned flip phone. I recognized the small screen glowing in the dark. I remember wondering about that. Steven has a smartphone like everybody else, and I'd never seen him with a flip phone." Tears gathered in her eyes. "Anyway, he held the phone like it was a magic wand, and he tapped it with his other hand." She twirled her braid as the tears spilled down her cheeks. "The bridge—it exploded. *Boom*. A bunch of twisted metal flying through the air. It was awful. The first few train cars fell into the river." Now she was sobbing.

"Did you know Steven intended to blow up the bridge?"

"No, no, no. You gotta believe me." She seized my arm. "He told me we would hang the banner. That's all. No one was supposed to get hurt."

"The bomb was in the boat?"

"I didn't know it at the time. The banner covered it. After we removed the banner from the boat, I saw a big canvas pulled over something bulky. I asked Steven what was under the canvas, and he said it was nothing. He said it was *nothing*." She stared at me with pleading eyes. "Oh my God, what do I do now?"

Great. I didn't say what I was thinking. I didn't tell her that her radical friends had embroiled her in a felony murder. That it was a federal crime to interfere with a train. That she was a principal in a terrorist act that carried a death sentence at both the state and federal level. I didn't say that she was a naïve knucklehead whose dangerous friends had thrown her into a cesspool, or that she was in way over her head.

I didn't say any of that; I'd promised—no lectures. I bit my tongue instead. "Let me see what I can do."

"Will you help me?"

"You may be beyond help, Michelle. But I'll do my best."

Chapter 10

"Can I stay with you tonight? I'd feel safer with you."

Michelle might feel safer with me, but I wouldn't feel safer with her.

She appraised me like a cut of beef again. Some women offer their body to any man who can help them. Sleeping with James Ponder, even if they hadn't been fellow travelers on the progressive political train, was a prime example. Even though she was frightened, Michelle viewed me as the knight in shining armor coming to her rescue. She might offer herself to me to cement my support.

If it's true that "Hell hath no fury like a woman scorned," then I wasn't about to get involved with Michelle for more reasons than I could count, but turning her down without insulting her was beyond my limited understanding of women. I didn't dare create a "woman scorned." Then I thought of being charged as accessory after the fact, harboring a fugitive, and a host of violations of the Patriot Act or some other law I'd never heard of.

I shook my head. "You should go home."

"I don't dare go home. Mom and Dad will kill me. I know it. You should let me stay with you. You'll be glad you did." She gave me an expression I couldn't decipher. Longing? Lust? Fear? Like I said, my skills with figuring out women are practically nonexistent.

"Michelle, how long since you've eaten?"

"I... I... I had a pizza with the others last night, I think."

"Let's go inside and get you some breakfast."

"But someone might see me." She twisted her braid again.

"You can't hide under a rock until this goes away. Besides, nobody's looking for you... yet. I'll try to keep it that way. Come on, let's get you fed." I didn't wait for her to argue. I popped my door and walked toward the diner.

She followed and sat across from me in the booth, situating her cellphone beside her napkin.

"You expecting a call?"

"What?" She gaped at the phone like she was surprised it was there. "I always set my phone there."

Veraleesa walked over with a coffee pot and two mugs. She set one in front of Michelle. "You want coffee, hon?"

Michelle nodded, and Veraleesa filled the mug. The other mug was mine. She filled it without asking. Setting the pot down, she pulled out an order pad. "What'll you have, hon?"

"What's good?"

"I usually order the *huevos rancheros*," I said.

She smiled at Veraleesa. "I'll have the *huevos rancheros* and whole wheat toast."

"You want the toast in *addition* to the tortillas or *instead* of?"

"Bring both," I interrupted. "I'll eat what she doesn't."

Veraleesa grinned. "You were born hungry, Chuck, and you been hungry ever since." She walked away, laughing at her own joke.

"Aren't you eating?" Michelle asked.

"I got here before you did. I already had breakfast." I poured a little half-and-half in my coffee. "Michelle, let me explain why you need to go home."

She dumped two packets of sugar and a healthy dollop of half-and-half in her coffee.

"Your parents hired me to find you and ensure you were okay. I finished that assignment last night and reported where you were and that you were there of your own free will. You follow me so far?"

She bobbed her head, eyes wide.

"Your folks had a problem: They didn't know where you were. I solved that problem, and they paid me for that solution... or they will when I send them the bill later today. That's what I do for a living—I solve people's problems. Your parents' problem was pretty simple, and I solved it in a few hours."

She blew on her coffee and sipped. "I know where you're going with this."

"Where am I going with this?"

"You won't help me unless I pay you." She narrowed her eyes. In her own way, she had already offered to pay me by spending the night with me.

"That's almost right. I would help you get home safely in any event, because it's the right thing to do, even if your father wasn't a client and your Grandpa Hank wasn't my friend. But you need a lot more help than an escort home. You have a serious life-and-death problem that requires someone with serious life-and-death skills. Solving problems like that is what I do for a living."

"I don't get it."

"I'll help you get home safely regardless of anything else, so don't worry about that. But to give you more help beyond that, I've got to get paid. I'd go broke if I worked for free."

She peered down at her lap and seemed to shrink into herself. "I don't have any money."

"I know. That's why you need to go home. Don't worry. I'll follow you there, and I'll explain your situation enough so your folks will want to help."

Her lower lip trembled. "What if they won't hire you?"

"Your folks love you more than life itself. They'll move heaven and earth to help you, believe me. Most parents are like that."

She gazed into the distance and smiled.

"What are you remembering?"

"When I was sixteen, two girlfriends and I decided it would be cool to stay out all night and skip school the next day. We switched off our cellphones and went to an all-night movie theater. The next day around noon, we realized that our parents would be so mad that we'd be grounded for the rest of eternity. Then I was afraid to go home and face them." She clammed up when Veraleesa came over.

Veraleesa delivered Michelle's order. She gave the toast to Michelle and the tortillas to me, along with a glass of ice water. "I'll bring the salsa. You want water, hon?"

"Yes, please."

Veraleesa left and Michelle continued. "I finally decided to go home, let myself in, and wait for them to come home from work." She forked a bite of *huevos* into her mouth. "Boy, these are good. I didn't realize how hungry I was."

"Food always helps."

Veraleesa brought the salsa and ice water and left.

I spooned salsa on a tortilla. "So, what happened when your folks got home?"

"That's the funny thing—they were already home. They never went to work. They spent the night on the phone calling hospitals, the police, all my friends' parents. Everyone they could think of. They thought I'd been abducted or something. They were so happy I was safe that they cried." She nibbled a bite of toast. "Dad said, 'Someday you'll have children, and you'll understand.' They grounded me, but only for a week."

She smiled at the thought. "Yeah, they'll hire you."

I finished off the first tortilla and slid a notepad from my jacket. "Then let's get to work."

Chapter 11

"WHERE DID YOU GET THE BOAT?"

"It was tied up at the dock at McKinley Park, a mile up the river from the bridge."

I wrote that down. "Was the bomb already in it, or did you stop somewhere to load the bomb?"

"No, we went straight from the park to the bridge."

"Close your eyes." I waited until she did. "Now observe the boat in your mind. Is the tarpaulin there?"

"No, the banner is there. It's folded over once and laid in the center of the boat. Yeah and there's a heap or lump of something bulky under it." She opened her eyes. "I had to step around it to get to my seat."

"Good. We're making progress." I noted *bomb already in boat.* "How did the boat get to the park?"

Michelle shook her head. "I don't know. It was already at the dock, like I said."

"How many of you were in on this?"

"Four, counting me."

"What are their names?"

She frowned. "All our environmental defense actions are confidential. We took an oath not to discuss them outside the group." She attacked her eggs again.

I wanted to shake her until her teeth rattled. Instead, I regarded the ceiling and breathed slowly. Michelle was an eighteen-year-old woman. Legally an adult, yeah. She acted like a full-grown woman wearing that braless tee-shirt, but she had never bumped up against the real world until now. Since birth, the toughest decisions she'd made were which expensive prom dress would her parents buy her and which college to attend. Her wealthy parents had swaddled her in an ivory tower of privilege. Then she moved to the different ivory tower world of UAC. Any resemblance to the real world of crime and punishment was purely coincidental.

I gazed at her until I had her attention. "Michelle. Read. My. Lips. The U.S. Attorney will say that the oath the four of you made was evidence of criminal intent. That you knew that what you were doing was wrong, and the four of you agreed to hide your criminal activity."

She pressed her lips together and crossed her arms under her breasts. I focused my eyes rigidly on the bridge of her nose. "Michelle, you think these people are your friends, but they are not your friends. They lied to you—or at least the guy who detonated the bomb did. They involved you in a federal crime that carries the death penalty. Like that idiot brother who bombed the Boston Marathon."

She caught her breath and lifted a hand to her mouth. "I remember that. It was all over the news."

Finally, I'd gotten her attention. "The FBI and Homeland Security will be after all four of you like a pack of dogs chasing a fox. If you want me to help you, you'll have to tell me everything."

"No one was supposed to get hurt."

They never are, I thought.

She peeked over her shoulder and lowered her voice. "They *promised*. It was a plastic banner. That wouldn't hurt anyone. We wanted television coverage—that's all."

Well, you sure got it. I didn't say that either.

"Did any of your friends video the…" I searched for a word, "…protest?"

"James was supposed to. He was supposed to upload it to YouTube and email the link to the television stations." She scooped up a forkful of food.

I wrote myself a note: *Search YouTube for other protests.* "That would be the guy who attacked me last night? James Ponder?"

"Yeah. Him." She stuffed the rest of the toast in her mouth.

"Who is this Steven guy you mentioned?" I figured he was the college professor Michelle had telephoned several times, but I wanted to see if she would level with me.

"Steven Wallace. *Doctor* Wallace. He teaches environmental studies at UAC."

I already knew that, but I wrote it down for Michelle's benefit. It was important that she know she was helping me. If nothing else, it made her feel more in control of her situation. "You mentioned a Katherine…"

"Katherine Shamanski. She's a senior in environmental studies. We belong to the same student club."

"What's the club's name?"

"Defenders of the Earth."

"You mean like the kid's cartoon program?"

Her lips curled a little. "We figured it was ironic."

"Didn't the program's producers complain about you infringing on their copyright or trademark?"

She shrugged. "They don't know we exist."

"How many in the club?"

She thought for a moment. "Maybe twenty or twenty-five. About fifteen regulars. We have our own Facebook page."

I made a note to look it up.

"Any of them or anybody else at the railroad tracks?"

"No. The three others are sort of the club leaders."

"Why did they include you in this, uh, project?"

"James wanted to recruit me into an inner circle. He said they were making me the fourth musketeer."

"Wallace is a professor. How can he belong to a student club?"

"He's not a member; he's the faculty advisor. When we met this weekend, they said the Three Musketeers were now the Four Musketeers. They made me the fourth musketeer last week." Tears spilled from her eyes again.

"What about the planning? Anybody other than the four of you involved in planning the protest?"

"I wasn't involved in the planning. I learned about it less than a week before Spring Break."

"Any of the other club members know you were going to do it?"

"We didn't tell anyone." She stopped. "That's strange… Usually Steven or Katherine suggests projects at club meetings, and we discuss them with the whole club and ask for volunteers."

"But not this time?"

She shook her head. "In fact, this time Steven met with the three of us at this place above a pizza parlor. He specifically told us not to discuss it with anyone outside that room."

"Where was the pizza parlor?"

"I don't remember. James drove. It was a crummy hole in the wall in Uptown. Not a good neighborhood. If James hadn't been with me, I wouldn't have gone there."

The ivory tower again, I thought. "You remember the pizza parlor's name?"

"Something Italian. I can't remember." Her eyes were moist. "But it's important isn't it? I can't remember…" Tears rolled down her cheeks again. She wiped them with her hands. "Wait, the building had a pawn shop too. Does that help?"

"Maybe." I wrote *Above pizza parlor, something Italian in Uptown. Pawn shop*. "Who piloted the boat?"

"James. He told us where to sit to balance the weight."

"How did you get to McKinley Park?"

She sipped her coffee. "We drove in separate cars, parked on nearby streets, and met at the boat ramp. That way we could split up after the protest."

"Whose idea was that?"

"Katherine's, I guess. She's the one who told us where to park when she phoned James and me at his house. I don't remember some of this stuff." The tears welled in her eyes again. "I didn't realize that all this detail would be important."

I patted her hand while she calmed down. "So, all of you parked near McKinley Park?"

She spread strawberry jam on the second slice of toast. "Yeah, a block away in different directions." She chomped a giant bite.

"How did you get back to your car with your boat destroyed?"

"I ran down the tracks away from the river," she replied. "The tracks cross a street a quarter mile south of the bridge."

"I know the area."

"From there I walked."

"Were the others' cars still near McKinley Park when you got there?"

She clinched her fists. "Chuck, this is hard. I was so shook up I didn't notice anything. I didn't know where the others had parked when I got there. Afterward, when I found my car, I must've been sort of dazed. I drove to the beach and parked while I thought about what to do." She finished the toast, wiped her fingers on a napkin. "Can't you call the cops and explain that I was there under false pretenses?" Her voice climbed higher. "I thought it was going to be a peaceful protest."

I motioned her to keep her voice down. "Michelle, you don't realize the depth of the trouble you're in. We are talking a federal crime here. Even if your protest had gone off the way you thought it would, you violated several laws." I patted her hand, waited for her to calm down again. "You trespassed on a railroad right-of-way; that's a crime. Even tying a boat to the fender under a bridge is illegal. There's a sign that prohibits docking there. If you had succeeded with the banner, it would have been a federal crime of interfering with interstate transportation." I glanced around the room. No one paid any attention to us but Veraleesa, and she was out of earshot. "You are guilty of felony murder."

"Murder? I didn't kill anyone. And I certainly didn't *intend* to kill anyone."

"That doesn't matter. The law says that if a death occurs during the commission of a felony, the persons who conspired to commit the felony are guilty of murder—all of them, even if they didn't pull the trigger or, in this case, push the button. It doesn't matter whether you intended to kill anyone. It doesn't matter if the person killed was one of the perpetrators. What matters is that you were committing a felony and there was a death."

She leaned back in the bench. "Holy crap."

"Yeah. Holy crap. Did you call me from the park?"

Before Michelle responded, Veraleesa returned. She refilled my mug. "You hungry for a piece of pie, Chuck? My shift is over in a few minutes, but we made fresh pecan pie. It's firmed up and cooled some, but a scoop of butter pecan ice cream would cool it off more."

"A scoop of butter pecan ice cream improves any dish. You know me too well, Veraleesa. And bring a piece for Michelle."

Michelle smiled at the tall black woman. "Oh, I couldn't hold another bite."

Veraleesa returned her smile and refilled her cup. "Don't you worry about that, hon. Chuck will eat it if you don't." She walked off cackling.

"Where were you when you called me?"

"North Beach," she retorted. "There's a big off-street parking lot there where nobody could see me."

"I know the spot. I used to have a girlfriend that liked North Beach."

She smiled. "That's the topless beach."

I ignored the remark. "Was your phone on the whole time you were in the boat and waiting for the train?"

"No. Katherine told us to remove the batteries from our phones before we got out of our cars." She jerked her head. "Oh, my God. She knew that the police could trace the phones after the explosion, didn't she? I've seen them do it on TV cop shows."

"Yes, they can."

Her face fell. "That's proof she intended to set off a bomb, isn't it?"

"Yes. There's one other thing you need to think about. You're in danger." This would be a tough subject to broach.

"I know that. That's why I called you."

"I don't mean from the cops or the FBI or even Homeland Security. You're in danger from someone else."

"Who?"

"Katherine, Steven, and James knew about the bomb. You didn't."

"That's what I want you to tell the cops."

I lifted a hand. "Let me finish. You're the one person who can identify them and testify against them."

Michelle's eyes widened.

"They committed two murders," I said.

"Two? The radio said the train's engineer."

I shook my head. "There's a second person in the engine. Safety precaution. They killed two people, and you're the only witness."

"Omigod. What am I gonna do?"

"You have to go into hiding until I handle this situation."

"Should I unfriend them?"

"What?"

"On Facebook. Should I unfriend them on Facebook?"

She was serious. I thought about it a moment. "No. Unfriending them would be suspicious if the Feds examine your Facebook history—and they will. It would indicate that you knew they were involved and wanted to distance yourself from them. But, since you mention it, stay off Facebook and all other social media until I give you the all clear. No posting and no logging in."

"What about school?" she asked. "Spring Break is over next weekend. Can you finish before school starts?"

"No way. It can't be helped. You have to keep your head down for a while."

"But I have mid-term exams coming up."

"Michelle, listen to me. This is not UAC; this is the real world. The world I live and work in. A world where good people are killed for being in the wrong place at the wrong time. This is not a news story on the local television. This is real life and *death—your* life and death. Forget about getting an education right now; I'm trying to keep you alive. These are not peaceful protesters you've gotten involved with; they're stone cold killers."

"Omigod." She stared into the distance, but I think she was obsessed with an image in her own mind.

I gave her a moment for that to sink in. "Now tell me: When did you switch your phone back on?"

Michelle shook her head as if waking from a bad dream. "I got in my car near McKinley Park. I tried to call you, and I realized my phone was off. That's when I put the battery back in. Then I decided to get away from there. I drove and wound up at North Beach."

"Hand me your phone."

She shoved it across the table.

I popped off the back and removed the battery and SIM card. I jiggled the pieces in my hand and considered my options.

"Will that stop them from tracing it?"

"It will from now on, yeah. With the battery out, it's off the grid." I stuck the phone and its parts in my coat pocket. "But the phone company keeps records for every second it's connected to the network. The cops can access them, and they will find out that you were near McKinley Park before the explosion and after the explosion. But that's a mile from the bridge. You might slip under their radar."

"And they'll know the same thing about my three friends, won't they? They're bound to know I was with them."

I shrugged. "Can't do anything about the other three. Maybe I can figure out a way to keep them separated from you with the cops, maybe not. Sometimes you get lucky."

Veraleesa appeared with two pieces of pecan pie *a la mode*. "Chuck, can I give you the bill? I get off at seven."

"Sure, and thanks." I handed her a credit card and she left.

"What are you gonna do with my phone?"

"Throw it in the ship channel in forty-five feet of water." I didn't want the cops to find it on Michelle. For now, all I could do was make it invisible to the cell network. Of course, it had been on until a minute ago and it was right next to my phone. Odds were that Michelle would hear from the Feds in due course. So would I.

Veraleesa brought my bill and credit card. "Thanks, Veraleesa. See you again soon."

She patted Michelle's shoulder. "Honey, I don't know what you and Chuck are talking about, and I don't need to know. But I can read you like a large-print book from clean across the room. I'd bet my next paycheck that you're in big trouble." She held up a hand. "Like I say, I don't need to know. Believe me, you have the right guy in your corner." She patted us both on the shoulder and walked away.

Chapter 12

I HAD MICHELLE STOP IN THE PARKING LOT of an all-night discount store on the way home. I had her wait in her car while I went inside. I bought her a new burner cellphone. Paid cash, of course, although the store had security cameras.

The sun had risen by the time I parked at the curb in front of John and Penny Babcock's house. Michelle curved into the wide driveway and parked on one side.

John Babcock opened the door. He was dressed for the office in a pin-striped suit, cotton dress shirt, and striped tie. "Good morning, baby. Good morning, Chuck. Come on in." He hugged Michelle and kissed the top of her head.

Penny was pouring coffee into China cups in the dining room. She was dressed like the schoolteacher she was. She had laid four place settings with Danish pastry, sterling silver utensils, and linen napkins, as if she expected important company. I could tell she'd been crying. She squeezed Michelle tight but didn't say a word.

John gestured me to a chair. After we were seated, he cleared his throat. "You said on the phone that Mickie was in serious trouble." He glanced at Michelle, then back at me. "What kind of trouble?"

"Have you watched the news on TV this morning?" The explosion had happened too late to be in the morning newspapers.

"We don't watch TV at breakfast. That's family time."

"This morning you should make an exception." I scanned the dining room—no television, of course. I remembered where

I had seen one the previous day. "Let's move this meeting to the breakfast table and watch the local news."

I found the remote on the kitchen counter and flicked on the TV.

A female announcer sat at a news desk with an orange and red fireball frozen on the wall-sized screen behind her. The tag line on the back screen said *Bridge Bombing*. "—at 11:30 last night, as the freight train approached the Seeti River Bridge. Here is footage from a nearby security camera. I warn you, these images are graphic and disturbing." The picture switched to a dark, grainy image of the automatic railroad bridge. A headlight from a diesel locomotive flared in the background, oscillating as it approached the camera. Suddenly the bridge was lit from below by an orange light an instant before it flew into the sky in three giant pieces of twisted steel. The orange and red fireball expanded and morphed into a cloud of smoke and debris. The engine's oscillating headlight flashed on the smoke cloud, then disappeared as the diesel roared into the cloud and plunged off the track into the river. Three more railroad cars followed and piled on top of the engine, their rear ends jutting above the water.

The female announcer was back in the picture. "Authorities are looking for three persons of interest that were captured in this security video." The screen featured a still image from the video with three lighter circles highlighting three people standing on the south side of the bridge as the fireball was frozen in mid-explosion. I could make out the three figures and the banner as a black rectangle backlit by the fireball. "We'll have a report from Oscar Reynosa at the scene."

Three, I thought. *The security video showed three people at the scene.* I couldn't believe we'd been so lucky. Where was the fourth person? Even if one of the three in the video was Michelle, if I could deliver Wallace, Shamanski, and Ponder, maybe I could keep Michelle out of this.

I clicked off the television.

John frowned at his daughter. "Michelle Teresa Babcock, what on earth have you gotten yourself into?"

I raised a hand. "Don't answer that."

John stood and confronted me, disbelief written on his face. "What is this, Chuck? I'm the client, not Michelle."

"Sit down and I'll explain."

John clenched his fist. "Mickie is my daughter, dammit. I hired you to find her. I have a right to know what she's involved in."

"Yes, you do, John. If you'll sit down, I'll explain the situation." I waited.

Penny tugged his sleeve. "Sit down, John. Let him talk."

John scowled at Penny, then Michelle, then me. He made a sound between a moan and a growl, but he sat.

"John," I said. "I told Michelle not to talk to you or Penny about what happened last night. She can talk to you both about anything else in her life, but not last night."

He started to stand again, and I made a *stop* gesture. "This is to protect both of you and Michelle. The police, the FBI—even Homeland Security—may interview any or all of you. It is a federal crime to lie to a federal official, even if they haven't given you a Miranda warning and even if you're not under oath. You and Penny should tell the absolute truth to any official who comes here. You truthfully say that you don't know what happened last night or what Michelle did or where she was. But if they ask, you tell them I told you that she was at James Ponder's house last night. That's the truth, and they'll find that out anyway."

"How?" John asked.

"They'll track the cellphones of everyone involved."

"Involved in what, for God's sake?"

"I can't tell you."

"I've seen that cellphone tracking thingy on NCIS," Penny said. "I didn't think it was real."

"It is," I told her. "Most smartphones have GPS built in. Unless you turn it off, the cops can locate your phone to within three feet. Even with no GPS, they can triangulate with cell phone tower signals to within about thirty yards. So, if anyone asks, I told you Michelle was at Ponder's last night, and that's all you know until I arrived with her this morning. And that's the truth."

I handed Michelle the burner phone I'd bought and activated in the store. "Here's your new cellphone, Michelle. The only people—and I mean the *only* people—who are to have this number are your parents, your grandparents, and your attorney."

Michelle pivoted to her father. "Do we have an attorney, Daddy?"

I raised my hand again. "We'll get to that in a minute. You are not to give your new phone number to anyone else, no friends, no cousins, no school buddies, nobody. Is that clear?"

John frowned again. "A new cellphone. I don't understand. What's wrong with her old one?"

"I can't tell you. Please make a note of her new number."

John started to object, but Penny laid a hand on his arm. "Dear, let's let Chuck handle this. He was a police detective, and he knows how these things work; we don't." She nodded at me. "How can we help, Chuck?"

"Moral support and money—a lot of both."

Penny's mouth stretched into a wan smile. "Thank God we have an ample supply of both. Where does that support begin?"

"Do you and John know a good criminal defense attorney?"

"I certainly don't know one." Penny gave John a questioning look.

He shook his head. "We've never needed one."

"I know a good one and I always carry his business cards." I fished a card from my pocket and handed it to Michelle. "After I leave, call this number and ask for either Abe Weisman or Diane Toklas. You don't have to write that down. Both of their names are on the card."

I rotated to her parents. "You'll have to pay them, but don't be surprised when they won't discuss Michelle's case with either of you. Michelle is of legal age and she'll be the client, so any conversation the attorneys have with either of you about her case would not be privileged."

"We understand," Penny replied. "What else can we do?"

"Let's make my relationship clear. First, my assignment was to find Michelle and make sure she was safe. I did that yesterday and I reported to you both last night on that assignment." I waited for John to acknowledge me.

He waved a hand. "Yeah, yeah. Go on."

"That assignment is finished and I'll send you a bill for that after I get to my office. So that's over now; Michelle is back home safe. Agreed?"

John waved a hand dismissively. "Agreed." He made a *get on with it* gesture.

"I won't tell you how I know this, but Michelle has a problem of her own. She wants to hire me to help her solve this problem. I can't tell you what this problem is, but solving it will require all my skills, contacts, resources, and a lot of luck—if I can solve it at all."

John frowned. "So, Mickie wants to be your client. So?"

"She's a college student without a job, living at home. She can't afford me."

Penny made a funny expression, not quite a smile, like she had gotten a joke. Penny's father was Hank Hickham, Port City's legendary owner of Hank's Bar & Grill & Bodacious Ribs. Tourists from all over the world lined up to eat at the waterfront icon. The restaurant churned out over a million dollars a year in profits, and she had been raised in a life of privilege. Hank was a good friend of mine and an occasional client.

She said, "You need us to pay you, but you work for Michelle. This means you don't answer to us anymore than the attorneys do. You answer to Michelle. Is that it?"

I spread my hands and shrugged. "I don't care who pays me. You and John are the logical ones. Next to Michelle, you have the most at stake. It could be Hank or the Mayor of East Muleshoe, as long as I get paid. I have to make a living."

Penny slid a checkbook from a drawer under the kitchen counter. "How much do you need to start? If you need much more than thirty thousand, I'll have to transfer funds."

"Twenty thousand is okay for the first week or two."

John stood up. "Now wait a minute, both of you. I don't mind paying, but I've got to know what's going on. Otherwise, it ain't gonna happen." He posed like he was confronting a bully.

Penny found a pen in the drawer. "Who do I make this out to, Chuck?"

"Wait a damn minute." John stalked over to the counter. "I said we're not paying until I know what's going on."

Penny smiled at John. "I know, dear. I heard you." She patted him on the arm, then eyed me. "Will you excuse us for a moment?"

Penny positioned the check and pen side by side on the counter. "John dear, may I speak with you privately?" She walked from the room without a backward glance. John grunted, but he followed.

I gazed at Michelle. "What do you think will happen?"

She smiled. "Daddy will cave like a sand castle as the tide comes in. He'll come back and make out the check himself, and he'll act like it's his idea. All my life, Grandpa Hank has smiled at Grandma Lorene and said 'Happy wife, happy life.' I know Daddy got the message." She grinned at me and appeared about twelve years old.

Ten minutes later, Michelle's parents came back. John slipped a Montblanc pen from his shirt pocket and picked up the check Penny had laid on the counter. "Why don't I include what we owe you for yesterday? How much is that?"

I did a quick mental calculation, added five hundred dollars for the fight with Ponder. "Three thousand will cover yesterday."

John handed the check over. "Chuck, I don't know you like Hank does, but he swears you're the greatest detective since Sherlock Holmes. Take care of our girl."

"I will." I pocketed the check. "Someone may come by here looking for Michelle. That person may intend to hurt her."

"Who? How? Why? You've got to tell us," said John.

"Sorry. The FBI might ask you about it, and you'd have to answer. Remember: Any stranger and anyone you don't personally know to be a family friend is a potential danger. Don't tell anyone where Michelle is, and don't let anyone in to visit her. Drive her to Hank and Lorene's ASAP. Leave her car here. Hide her away for a few days, maybe a couple of weeks.

Get Hank or Lorene to drive her to Mango Island and keep her under wraps until I give you the all-clear."

"But what about school? Penny asked. "It starts next Monday."

"Her life is more important than school."

Chapter 13

JAMES PONDER'S HANDS TREMBLED as he punched the cellphone keys. It didn't help that he was coming down off the Oxycodone Michelle had given him the previous night. He had dreaded making this call ever since Michelle freaked out beside the railroad tracks and ran into the night. *She's a true believer like me, isn't she? I even told her that you can't make an omelet without breaking eggs. She agreed with me. How could I have figured her so wrong?*

He had made his way home from the railroad track and collapsed on the bed, but he hadn't slept. He smelled Michelle's fragrance on the bed from the previous day and night. He was simultaneously aroused and appalled that he was thinking about sex. Especially now that both their lives were subject to Redwood's "repercussions." He rubbed the stub where his little finger had been amputated. *What the hell will Redwood do to me now?*

Redwood had said to call him at eight a.m. It was unthinkable not to follow his orders. Ponder glanced at his phone. It was 9:02; 8:02 where Redwood was. He breathed deeply and pressed the *call* button.

Redwood answered the phone on the first ring. "What happened, Lamp Post? The package was supposed to be stopped, not destroyed. Why didn't you deliver the present the way I instructed?"

"That was Stev—that was Skylight's fault. He had the trigger. He waited too long to pull it."

"I shall deal with Skylight. Is there anything else you wish to tell me?"

Ponder paused. "There's been a… complication."

Again, that unnerving silence.

"The girl…" Ponder had to force himself to say it. "The girl… she freaked out when we delivered the present… she ran away."

Redwood's voice was so quiet that Ponder strained to hear him. "And where is she now?"

"I… I don't know. I haven't seen her since the explo—the present was delivered."

"This person can identify all of you, and you three idiots can identify me. She is the weak link. In fact, she is a broken link. She was your mistake, your responsibility. You must be the one to remove her from the chain."

"If I talk to her… explain why we did what we did… I'm sure she'll come around. She can be a valuable team member. We don't want to waste an asset like that." *Or a piece of ass that good.* "Let me talk to her first."

"Listen to me, you addicted piece of garbage," Redwood said, "I shall say this once. If you delay, she has time to go to the authorities." His tone sounded like every word was in capital letters.

"But she's involved. She can't go to the cops."

"She'll make a deal to testify against you, Kinetic, and Skylight. You will find her and eliminate her. And, since I no longer trust your judgment, send me everything you know about her—and I mean everything—by encrypted email in case I have to do this myself."

Chapter 14

SNOOP PROPPED HIS FEET ON MY COFFEE TABLE and opened a manila folder. "It's early days yet but here's what I have so far. Steven Michael Wallace, PhD, tenured professor of environmental studies at UAC. Forty-two years old. Albany, New York native. Bachelor's degree from the University of Albany, Master's and PhD from Yale. Member of the American Association of Atheists, registered Democrat, vice-president of the UAC teachers' union, and member of the Ad Hoc Committee on Climate Change, whatever the heck that is. He writes lots of articles and editorials for several left-leaning political websites on the dangers of global warming and the use of fossil fuels and the desirability of renewable energy sources. He's had thirteen letters to the editor printed in the *Port City Press-Journal*, all related to global warming, opposition to fossil fuels, and Port City Power and its coal-burning power plant. I copied them all, but I haven't read them yet."

I sipped my coffee that was getting cold. "Don't bother. I get the idea about his motivations. Anything on possible affairs with female students?"

Snoop lifted a manila folder from the table. "Yeah, when he was a PhD candidate at Yale, a freshman coed charged him with date-rape. It was a 'he said/she said' thing and nothing could be proven one way or the other. There was nothing about it in his student file at Yale since they couldn't prove him guilty."

"Then how did you find it?"

"I hit it lucky on a Google search. His name came up several times in the *Yale Daily News*, so I searched the online edition. Pretty sensational stuff. There were women's lib pickets at his student conduct hearings and arrests at the demonstrations."

"Anything here at UAC?"

"Nothing on a Google search. He's either kept his nose clean, or else he's been more careful."

"Okay. What else do you have?"

Snoop flipped over a page in the folder. "Wallace has been arrested a few times. Most recently for handcuffing himself to the railroad fence gate at the Port City Power generating plant. It's the gate where the trains bring in the coal."

"Who else was involved in that?"

"None of our persons of interest. A dozen other people, students mostly. One little sidebar—none of the protesters was from Florida. They were all from out of state—mainly from the Northeast. I can get you their names if it's important. It happened several years ago. Not relevant, except that the arrests mean that Wallace's fingerprints are in the system."

"I concur. Forget the others. What else?"

"Wallace makes a large outside income from government grants to research the effects of global warming or climate change." He flipped through the sheets of paper and whistled. "Whoa. The guy has scored over three million dollars in taxpayer money in the last five years."

"So, he has a financial interest in global warming. So do a lot of other people. Anything else?"

Snoop slapped down the manila folder. "I only had two hours to work on this. How about we continue after lunch?"

"Okay. Keep working here while I'm gone."

"You're not eating lunch?"

"I'll buy a sandwich on the way to the Port City Police HQ. I'm going to ask what the cops have on the bombing so far."

Chapter 15

FROM BEHIND HIS DESK, JORGE CASTELLANO GREETED ME in Spanish. "Sit down, Chuck. Anything to get a break from this paperwork. Ever since they made me lieutenant, I don't have time to be a real detective anymore." He thrust a pile of paperwork to one side.

I deposited a box of Krispy Kreme donuts on his desk and plopped into a chair.

Jorge's scoffed. "I just finished lunch. How am I going to find room for donuts?"

I continued in Spanish. "There's always room for donuts. You'll find a way."

He tore open the box and selected one with multi-colored sprinkles. "So, what have you been up to, *amigo*?"

"Same old, same old. Slaying dragons, rescuing fair maidens. Tote that barge and lift that bale." I snagged a chocolate-covered one.

Jorge washed the donut bite down with coffee. "What do you hear from Bob Martinez?"

"Last week he sent me an email with a picture of a Tahiti beach. He was drinking something with an umbrella in it under a grass hut with a girl in a bikini."

"Where do things stand with Martinez and Graciela? I worry about that girl."

"I had dinner recently with her friend, Miyoki Takashi. Miyo said Graciela was in rehab again somewhere in upstate New York."

"Such a beautiful girl; such a tormented soul." *Tormented soul* sounded beautiful in Spanish: *alma atormentada*. Of course, most things sound beautiful in Spanish. After all, *garbage dump* is *botadero de basura*.

"Drugs, what can I say? Once you get involved with them, it's hard to get loose."

He leaned over the box and inspected the donuts. "Whaddya think that one is?"

"A jelly-filled."

"I know that, smart ass. I meant what flavor?"

"Want me to sample it for you?"

"Not hardly." He bit off a chunk. "Raspberry. You bring me donuts when you want a favor."

"You detective lieutenants don't miss much, do you? Who's working the railroad bombing case?"

"It happened last night, and it's not our kind of case," said Jorge. "The FBI hogs stuff like that, along with Homeland Security. Those two agencies are probably duking it out right now and getting in each other's way. I'd rather stand aside instead of spinning our wheels attempting to work with those three-letter agencies."

"There are state crimes involved. Won't you have a liaison?"

"It happened late last night, *amigo*. The dust hasn't even settled yet. I'll assign Kelly Contreras and Bigs Bigelow, but I'll tell them not to get bent out of shape about it. I'd bet a steak dinner against one of these donuts that the Feebs won't cooperate with them even if they ask. Besides, Kelly and Bigs are kind of busy with homicides. You do know we do that sort of thing around here, right?"

"The train's engineer and conductor were killed. That's two homicides."

"Okay, big guy, it's obvious you want a pipeline to the investigation—unofficially of course. Tell me what's going on."

"Off the record?"

Jorge spread his hands. "You know me, *amigo*. You've always trusted my judgment. Now spill it."

I laced my fingers across my stomach. "Hypothetically, suppose I have a client who was in the wrong place at the wrong time and might have witnessed the explosion and might be guilty of felony murder. But he or she didn't intend to commit a felony or to hurt anybody. He or she didn't know there was a bomb. I need to get my client out of this mess. Hypothetically."

I bit off another chunk of donut while he digested my hypothetical.

Jorge stroked his chin. He drummed his fingers on his desk. He gazed in my direction without seeing me. I could practically hear the wheels spin in his mind as he debated with himself. "What do you intend to do with this information? Hypothetically."

"Find out who's responsible for the bombing, collect the evidence to convict them, and deliver it to the Feds in exchange for them keeping my client out of it. Hypothetically."

"Okay. I'll call Kelly and Bigs. By the time you get wherever they are, they'll know to expect you." He held a finger up. "Don't tell them what you told me. They might not be as discreet as I am. In fact, I know that Kelly wouldn't be. In spite of the fact that she has the hots for you—or maybe because of it—she won't cut you any slack. She arrested you before, and she'll do it again if she thinks you're obstructing justice."

I shook my best friend's hand. "Saying thanks isn't enough."

"Don't forget—you gave me Krispy Kremes." He grinned as I walked to the door. "I hope you haven't wasted them."

"Krispy Kremes are never wasted."

"Next time bring *pastelitos*."

DRIVING TO THE NORTH SHORE PRECINCT HQ, I thought about Jorge's throwaway remark that Kelly Contreras had the hots for me. If she did, it was news to me. Still… I pushed the thought aside. I had a client problem to solve.

Kelly was on the phone as I walked through the door of the squad room. She waved me into a chair. "We'll be there at nine o'clock tomorrow, Gene. See you then."

She extended her hand for me to shake. *Did she grasp my hand a little too long?* I shoved the question aside.

"Hi. Did Jorge call you?"

"The lieutenant said I should cooperate with you, but off the record. Tell me what's going on."

I paused for a beat to telegraph that the answer would be no. "I'd love to, but I can't. But Jorge wants to help my… project. Is that enough for you?"

Kelly patted my hand. "It'll have to be. So, what can I do for you?" Kelly always places her hands on me somewhere, but that's the way she is with everybody. *She's a toucher, right?*

"I need you to find out everything about the railroad bombing last night. What do the Feds know, where are they looking, who do they suspect, everything." I shut up and waited.

"Wow, you don't ask for much, do you?" She scrutinized my face for a moment.

I studied her in return. I'd asked her to do something that was against her training—maybe even illegal. She would weigh the issue like she did most decisions: the interests of justice, friendship, duty, boss's request, legal issues, what her partner would think. She tapped her chin with one manicured finger. "Okay. Bigs and I will see the Special-Agent-In-Charge tomorrow morning."

"Anybody I know?"

"Gene Lopez. You know him?"

"Yeah, we worked together a year ago. He wouldn't remember me though."

"Oh, he'll remember you, Chuck. Everyone remembers you."

I APPROACHED THE FEDERAL BUILDING SECURITY STATION carrying two cappuccinos. "If I can lay these on your table, I'll show you my PI license. There's a pistol in my shoulder holster that I have a license to carry. I'm here to visit the FBI office." I set the two cups on the wooden table next to the metal detector. One of the guards stepped back and positioned his hand on the butt of his pistol.

"You'll have to check your weapon with us," said the other guard.

"What if someone tries to mug me in the Federal Building?" I showed him my license.

The second guard smiled and relaxed. The first guard didn't get the joke; he seemed nervous.

I smiled. "Shall I hand you my weapon, or would you rather remove it yourself?"

The second guard stepped toward me. "You can hand it to us, sir."

"You think I'll be safe without it?"

The second guard accepted my holstered gun when I unclipped it from my belt. "Who knows? You'll have to take your chances with the rest of us. FBI is on the sixth floor."

SAIC EUGENIO LOPEZ SQUINTED AT ME. "Don't tell me… the Simonetti case last year."

"Right." I plunked the cappuccinos on his desk. "You still drink cappuccino?"

He snapped his fingers. "You have a good memory. McCrary, wasn't it?"

I responded in Spanish. "Still is. Carlos McCrary. Good memory yourself. Call me Chuck. Good to see you again, Agent Lopez."

"Call me Gene and speak English. A few of the guys get their panties in a wad if I do business in Spanish. Makes them feel excluded because they can't eavesdrop." He grinned. "Sit down, Chuck." He picked up the cappuccino. "This isn't an official call or you wouldn't attempt to bribe a federal agent with one lousy cappuccino."

"Yeah, my Port City cop friends demand a dozen Krispy Kremes."

"They have higher standards than I do. I'll roll over for a cappuccino any time. What do you need?"

"Who's working the railroad bombing from last night?"

"I am. Or at least my team is. Why'd you ask? You got information?"

"No, but I thought I might be able to help."

"How?"

"As a consultant, a sounding board, and an independent pair of eyes on the case."

"What's your interest in the case?" He grabbed a notepad and pen.

I shrugged. "This is the first domestic terrorism case in Port City. You know I was Special Forces, right?"

"Yeah. You earned a Bronze Star in Iraq."

"It was Afghanistan. All I got in Iraq was my first Purple Heart and two scars. But that's not important. This bombing… it offends me deeply. I want to help catch the bad guys."

"Not good enough, Chuck. I think you have a dog in this fight. What's your interest, really?"

"The television news said you have three persons of interest shown on the security video. You think three people were enough to pull this off?"

"Chuck, you know the drill. I can't comment on an ongoing investigation. I'm the one asking questions. Do you know anything I should know?"

I spread my hands, palms up. "Maybe I could learn something on the street, unofficially, that you couldn't learn officially. The guys you use for informants hate you. The guys I use may not love me, but at least they don't hate me. They're less likely to lie to me than they are to you. What do you say? We work together?"

"The Bureau's job is to suck up information like a vacuum cleaner. We don't share information with outsiders."

"I've got another advantage you official guys don't. I'm a private citizen. I don't worry about due process and search warrants and such." I leaned back in my chair. "Sometimes I hear things on the street. But before I can help, I need information to evaluate any rumors that I hear. How many perps are we looking for?"

Lopez carefully positioned the pen and aligned the notepad with the edges of the desk. He moved his cappuccino to one side and propped both hands on the desk. It was like watching a professional athlete put on his game face. He sat straight as a flagpole—and as expressionless. "This is a Federal investigation. I am a Federal agent." I could hear the capital F as he said it. "If you know something, you are required by law to be forthcoming or you'll be guilty of obstructing justice. What do you know about this, *Mister* McCrary?" He waited.

"So, I'm not 'Chuck' anymore. I merely asked how many perps you think were involved. The television said three. How many is it, Gene?"

"McCrary, I'll arrest you if you spit on the sidewalk. Tell me what you know forthwith, or I'll bury you *under* the jail."

"Wow, now I'm not even a 'mister,' merely a last-name lowlife 'McCrary.' You must be the bad cop. No, Gene, that's not the way to do bad cop, although 'forthwith' is a great word choice. If you're gonna be bad cop, you need a good cop in here too. That way you soften me up by using words like 'forthwith' and the good cop gets the information because I'm scared out of my wits."

He started to reach for his intercom.

"Gene, before you call for backup—which isn't necessary since I'm unarmed and won't resist arrest—let's think this through. If you arrest me, what then? My lawyer knows I'm here and she will be down here in thirty-five minutes if I don't call her and tell her I'm okay. Then she'll file a writ of *habeas corpus* and bring a suit for wrongful arrest and maybe false imprisonment and kidnapping—she goes a little overboard sometimes. Just between us, I think she's a drama queen. She'll hold a news conference on the steps of the Federal Building and point a finger at your office window. Everybody will waste time and get their bowels in an uproar over nothing." I leaned back in the chair. "And I will still say that I don't know anything and I merely wanted to help."

I laced my fingers across my stomach again. "Or… you can level with me and maybe I can help you find your bombers. I get paid by the hour, so it doesn't matter much to me either way. Which way you want to go?"

I had told Lopez something important if he was sharp enough to hear the words I hadn't said. A client was paying me to find out about the bombing. Lopez should realize I did know something. He also couldn't prove that I was withholding evidence. The only way he could find out what I knew was to cooperate.

He relaxed. "One guy could do this. It's not rocket science. Remember the Federal Building in Oklahoma City, the Boston Marathon bombs. One or two nuts is all it takes. We saw three on the security video."

"On television, it seemed like the bomb was below the bridge. Did they use a boat?"

"Yeah, but the current swept the debris into Seeti Bay. We're collecting every scrap of floating crap we can skim off the bay." He shrugged. "Maybe we'll get lucky." He picked up his cappuccino and leaned back.

"Unless they rowed, there will be a motor on the river bottom. You can get serial numbers off it and trace the boat."

"We've had divers in the river since sunup."

"How did they set off the bomb?" I asked. "If I were doing it, I'd use remote detonation. A timer wouldn't work to catch the engine on the bridge if the train were even one minute late or early."

"One perp on the security tape held his hand up, like maybe he used a cellphone to do it."

"Yeah, that would do it. I'd buy a burner phone, wipe it clean, drop it in the river or in a shopping center dumpster a mile away. You'd never find it. But you could trace the cellphone pings off the tower. Any luck there?"

Lopez shook his head. "There are several high-rise condos along the river and on the bay shore. There are hundreds of cellphones within a mile of the blast site—maybe thousands. We're running the cellphone signals but it's a needle in a haystack."

Chapter 16

SNOOP WAS SITTING AT MY DESK when I returned to the office, having dodged the wrath of Special Agent Eugenio Lopez. At least for now. If Lopez had a Christmas card list, I wasn't on it. Snoop started to stand when I opened the door.

"Stay there. I'll sit over here. What've you got?"

He settled back in the chair. "Ponder is James Kennedy Ponder, twenty-nine years old, graduate teaching assistant in environmental studies. Born in Macon, Georgia. Bachelor of Science in Chemistry and a Master's in Public Policy from the University of Georgia."

"Where would he learn to build a bomb in a boat? Do they teach that at UGA?"

Snoop smiled. "You can find virtually anything on the internet. If nothing else, then on a jihadist website. And Ponder has a BS in Chemistry. Maybe he learned enough to build a bomb. Even those two yahoos who did the Oklahoma City bomb had less education than that."

"Good point."

"He's working on a PhD at UAC. President of a tree-hugger student club called Defenders of the Earth." Snoop squinted one eye. "Isn't that a cartoon show my kids used to watch when they were younger?"

"Yeah, but no one on the TV program has complained about the name."

"I examined their website—the tree-huggers, not the cartoon—and they have their panties in a knot over various real and imagined threats to Mother Earth. The website has links to various ecoterrorism sites that teach things like how to disable logging or construction equipment, commit arson on housing developments, blow up pipelines, and other fun stuff like tree spiking."

"Tree spiking? That sounds familiar."

Snoop recited from a notebook on my desk. "Tree spiking is done to discourage logging a forest. The tree spiker drives a six-inch nail, available at any hardware store, into the bottom of a tree to break the logger's chainsaw blade. The logger can replace the blade in five minutes, so the spiker is supposed to use lots of nails in each tree."

"Can a broken chainsaw kill someone?"

"Not any I've found. There have been a few minor injuries. Chainsaws have built-in safety features." He flipped through the notebook. "One guy in a saw mill was injured by a spike driven farther up the tree. That breaks the blade in the saw mill when they try to cut it into lumber."

"Doesn't spiking it hurt the tree?" I asked.

"Not as much as being cut down."

"How do the tree-spikers expect people to build houses if they can't use lumber?"

Snoop shrugged. "Maybe they expect everyone to use bricks. Or maybe they care more for trees than they do for people."

I shook my head. "Go on."

He flipped a page in the notebook. "One linked site claimed that nature was being *despoiled*—is that even a word? They blamed *capitalism, patriarchal society, and the Judeo-Christian tradition*." Snoop peered up from his notes. "So, they don't like free enterprise, the traditional family, or most religions."

"Nice guys."

"The tree spiking site said to avoid imported spikes because they are cheaper construction and might bend as you hammer the spike into the tree. Then it said…" Snoop referred to his notes. "…*Stick to the U.S.A. or Canadian brands (No, I'm not a patriot.)*"

"There's no law against providing links to radical websites," I said. "We need something criminal to stick these three with."

"Maybe I got that too, bud. While Ponder was at UGA working on his master's degree, he was arrested for arson and murder. He burned down a housing construction site where a night watchman was killed. Cops didn't get a proper warrant before they searched his apartment and his car. The DA dropped the charges after the judge threw out the evidence, but there's no doubt that he started the fire. He got away with murder —literally. Maybe we can resurrect that charge."

"Contact the detective in Georgia who had the case. Find out everything about the fire and about the evidence that was excluded. Maybe we can help out. Anything else on Ponder?"

Snoop said, "He works for Wallace on the environmental studies grants."

"Who funds the grants?"

"Who else? Uncle Sugar."

"So, Ponder is on the public teat for global warming too? How much does Wallace pay him?"

Snoop said, "Not shown. I think he's like Wallace's employee or sub-contractor. He's mentioned as a contributor in several of Wallace's grant reports."

"Okay. What do you have on Shamanski?"

Snoop held the notebook on his lap and tilted the desk chair back. "Katherine Shamanski, age twenty-three, senior working on a Bachelor's degree in environmental studies. Vice-president of Defenders of the Earth. She's chair of the Democratic Party precinct that includes the University. Active in various left-wing organizations and projects. Pro-choice, wants to legalize marijuana, supports LGBT causes—all the politically correct stuff. Worked for both Obama campaigns, though she was too young to vote for him the first time."

"My brother-in-law voted for Obama. So did millions of people. Nothing wrong with that."

Snoop continued. "Both her parents are lawyers in Chicago. Her mother is a hot-shot personal injury lawyer, and her father is too, but with a different firm. They're not partners. They both invest in several government-subsidized green energy companies—solar panels, battery technology, wind turbines, and such. All a matter of public record and all with their hands in the government's pocket."

"Everything on the up-and-up?"

"It smells funny, but I didn't find any criminal indictments anywhere, so I guess it's legit. I saved reports on the perps and everybody else on your hard drive in a folder called *environment*." Snoop stood up. "I don't feel comfortable on this side of your desk when you're here. Let's go to the conference room." He carried the notebook in one hand and his coffee in the other. "Get the door, will you?"

After we were seated in the conference room, I said. "Wallace and Ponder have their fingerprints on file because of prior arrests. What about Shamanski?"

"I don't think so," said Snoop. "Did they wear gloves on the boat?"

"Let's ask Michelle."

Chapter 17

"WHY ARE WE MEETING HERE instead of on Mango Island?" I asked.

Michelle scanned the area to make sure no one in Java Jenny's sat near us. I had picked the last outdoor table for that reason. Traffic noise masked our conversation.

She shrugged. "I haven't gone to the island yet. Don't worry, I'm staying with Grandpa and Grandma like you said."

"That's not what I told you to do. I said for you to stay at their condo on Mango Island. After we finish here, Snoop will follow you until you're safely on the ferry."

She crossed her arms. "What about my clothes?"

"Michelle, what part of 'your life is in danger' isn't clear to you? Your grandparents can fetch your clothes for you."

I watched her expression. "Michelle, if you don't listen to me and treat this situation as life-and-death serious, I swear to God I'll quit and leave you on your own."

"You don't have to get mad." She stuck out her lower lip.

"Kid, this job is hard enough without you making me swim with weights on. To do this, I need your complete, sincere, one hundred percent cooperation. You understand?"

She stared into her cappuccino. "I understand."

"Okay. Did you four wear gloves on the boat?"

She leaned close to my ear. "Katherine handed us each a pair of gloves before we got on the boat. I thought that was kinda strange. We never wore gloves before on our other protests. I asked her why we had to wear gloves, and she said, 'You never know. Despite the best intentions, sometimes people get hurt.' Now I know why."

"What kind of gloves were they?"

"You know, rubber."

"Good. What type of rubber gloves?"

"Like, hello-o-o, *rubber* gloves. What more do you want me to say?"

"Were they like the gloves on the doctor dramas on television, or the kind you wear to work the garden, or like the gloves you wear to clean an oven?" Snoop asked.

She stared at Snoop as if he had asked a stupid question. "How should I know? I've never cleaned an oven or worked in a garden."

"Were they thin or thick?" I asked.

She bit her lower lip. "Thin-ish, I guess."

"Were they white or colored? Could you see your hands through them?"

"It was nighttime. I didn't notice."

"Close your eyes."

She stared at me. "Why?"

"It's a memory trick. We did this before, remember. Close your eyes."

"Okay."

"Now, in your mind, scan around the parking lot and *see* Katherine pass out the gloves… Watch yourself pull them on… Examine your hands… Examine the gloves."

She opened her eyes. "I could sort of make out my nail polish through the gloves. They must have been white-ish."

I searched for *surgical gloves* on the internet and twisted the screen toward her. "Were they like any of these pictures?"

"Yeah. That one, I suppose."

"Good, we're making progress." I gave her a lined pad and a pen. "Draw me a diagram of the boat."

She made no effort to pick up the pen. "It was a boat."

"What kind of boat?"

"I don't know… a *motor* boat."

"Describe the motor." It was like playing twenty questions, except it was fifty questions, maybe a hundred. I coaxed each fact out of her, question after question, digging out information she didn't know was buried in her mind.

We used my laptop to research various boating websites. We concluded that the boat was a Boston Whaler. It had twin outboard engines, so it was at least twenty-five feet long, but shorter than thirty-five based on her vague description. That meant it was a 280 or a 320 Outrage outboard boat.

"Like that." She pointed at the screen. "Or maybe that." She pointed at another boat. "Oh… I don't remember." She began to gawk over my shoulder and her attention wandered.

"Patience, Michelle. It takes as long as it takes. Would you like a cookie?"

Snoop went to buy us a round of chocolate chip cookies.

She frowned. "I don't see why it's so freakin' important what kind of boat it was. Who cares? The boat's in a zillion pieces. It was a *boat*." She seemed as if she were about to cry, then realized where she was and glanced around, embarrassed.

"Michelle, I don't have the luxury of time for you to play drama queen. This is not a teenage game you and I are playing. You could serve a life sentence in a federal prison. Stop screwing around and second-guessing me. Your freedom is in my hands. If I can't do this, the next person you'll be asking for help is a criminal defense attorney. You got that?"

Her lower lip quivered.

"If I'm going to keep you out of prison, you have to help me. When I say 'jump,' you say 'how high?' Got it?"

"All right, already."

Snoop produced a tray with a platter of cookies and three fresh drinks—coffees for Snoop and me and cappuccino for Michelle.

"No more games," I continued, "Draw me a diagram where each of the four of you sat in the boat."

She did, without complaint. A good sign.

Chapter 18

I PLUNKED A BOX OF *PASTELITOS* and a stack of napkins on Jorge's desk. He raised his eyebrows. "What? You actually paid attention to me for a change?"

"I figured I'd keep you close to your Cuban heritage. If these are not up to your standards, I'll take the box with me." I pretended to reach for the flaky pastries.

He snatched the box. "No complaints. I figured you for more of a *pan dulce, ¡Viva Mexico!* kind of guy." He selected a jelly-filled.

"You've heard of pan-Asian cuisine; I'm a fan of pan-Hispanic pastry plus bagels. And donuts." I slid the box over and surveyed the pastries. One doesn't rush decisions like that. "How's the paperwork going? You know that stuff would go faster if you'd learn how to read."

"I started lieutenant-style delegating. I assigned reports to the sergeants involved. I'm going out later and do real detecting." He dragged the box back and selected another pastry. "I keep up this delegating stuff and they're gonna make me a captain for sure."

"How do you like that guava-filled one?" I asked. "It any good?"

"The worst *pastelito* I ever had was still pretty good. These are keepers. Here, have one; you'll like it."

Jorge was right; they were keepers.

"What brings you around here, friend? Did you meet with Kelly and Bigs?"

"Bigs wasn't there. Kelly said she and Bigs would meet Gene Lopez at the FBI this morning. She'll keep me looped in." I wiped my hands on a napkin. "I need another favor. Anybody report a Boston Whaler stolen in the last couple of weeks?"

"This got anything to do with the bombing?"

"I have a hunch."

"Let me punch it up." He wiped his fingers on a napkin and tapped the keyboard. "Prime Marina. One of their customers keeps a 280 Outrage stored there. Reported it missing yesterday."

"Any idea when it was stolen?"

Jorge examined the screen. "Reporting officer said the owner hadn't used it in three weeks. Came down yesterday and found it gone. It could have been stolen any time in the last three weeks."

"Where's the marina?" I stepped around his desk.

He rotated the monitor my direction. "Right there, three miles upriver from the bay."

It was two-and-a-half miles from the railroad bridge and closer than that to McKinley Park.

PRIME MARINA WAS ANYTHING BUT. The phone number on the marina sign had the old area code for Port City that had changed ten years before as the city grew and its area code spun off from Fort Lauderdale. The parking lot was cracked and potholed. The stripes had worn off long ago. The rusted hurricane fence had gaps where the mounting wires were gone. Snoop shrugged. "I hope the security cameras work."

"And that they kept the footage," I added.

We headed toward the office. It was a little more modern inside. My hopes rose.

"Come in, gentlemen. I'm Eddie Terrazo, the manager. Lieutenant Castellano from the Port City police called and said you were coming about our missing boat. Have you found it?"

"Carlos McCrary. Everybody calls me Chuck." I handed him a business card, one without a lightning bolt and Captain America shield. "And this is my associate Raymond Snopolski."

"Call me Snoop."

The manager shook hands with both of us. "You found our stolen boat?"

"We're private investigators, not cops. We have something else to ask you about."

Eddie shrugged. "Sure. How can I help?"

"Maybe we can do something for you, Eddie. I'd like for Snoop here to review your security video for the last three weeks to get a handle on how the Boston Whaler was stolen. Maybe we'll find something to keep your insurance premiums from going up."

"Knock yourself out. Use that desk and monitor over there." He pivoted to a woman working at another desk. "Carla, this here's Snoop. Help him out if he has any questions, will you?"

"Sure thing, Eddie." She smiled at Snoop. "You want coffee?"

I asked Eddie, "Can you show me where the boat was stored before it disappeared?"

"It was in dry storage at the back of the rack. Follow me." He led me out the back door of the office and down the courtesy dock. The dock surface was mildewed and uneven. Boards were warped and worn. Some were missing screws. The supporting pilings had settled over the years and the dock surface was wavy and uneven. A rusty island freighter chugged down the Seetiweekifenokee River past the dock. The freighter's small wake made the dock creak and sway beneath our feet.

"This here's the launching slip, thirty feet wide by fifty feet long," the manager boasted. "We can handle any size boat you got." The dock made a right-angle bend away from the river and a U around three sides of the slip before returning to the riverside. On the far side and end, a large concrete apron filled the area between the water and the storage building. "We launch the dry storage boats down here when the owners are coming to use them."

Fifty yards farther, Eddie stopped at the entrance to a giant steel storage building. Its paint was once white but had aged to a dingy gray, peeled on the west side, punished by the Florida sun. The twin sliding doors angled crookedly on their tracks. A large padlock hung open through the hasp on one door.

"This here is our enclosed dry storage area." Twin rows of giant galvanized steel cubbyholes faced each other from both sides of the ancient building. Each of the four levels held row after row of boats stacked on twin rails inside each cubbyhole. Two huge forklifts waited against the back wall, their padded arms stretching empty, waiting to be summoned to lift boats off the racks.

"Which, uh, garage was the Outrage stolen from?"

"We call them 'slips.' Third row up, left side, nearly to the back. Let me show you." Terrazo strode off toward the rear of the cavernous space. He stopped twenty feet from the back wall. "Right there." He gestured to an empty slip.

"How do I get up there?"

"There's stairs at each end of the rack. Walk between the wall and the rack, right back there."

"Yeah, thanks." The galvanized metal steps clanged as I climbed them two at a time. A catwalk ran behind each row of slips. I sidestepped down the catwalk behind the two boats at the rear of the building until I reached the empty slip.

"Careful," Eddie called from the floor. "Don't want you falling through or nothing. That could ruin your whole day." He laughed.

"Thanks. I'll hang on."

The empty slip had twin steel I-beams stretching thirty-five feet from the catwalk to the front of the rack. Slabs of hard rubber were wrapped around the beams and held in position every foot by plastic straps to protect the fiberglass boat hulls from scratches. Here and there, straps had snapped and the rubber had broken into pieces and fallen off, exposing the steel beam. The boats on either side of the empty slip had no padlocks, no chains around the rails or motors to secure the boats, only gravity and their own weight. Anyone with access to the forklifts could steal any boat if the sliding doors at the front were unlocked at night.

I snapped pictures with my cellphone and made my way down to the ground. I walked over to the forklifts. Keys dangled from both ignitions. The marina owners must have figured no one would be stupid enough to steal a forklift big enough to carry a twenty-thousand-pound boat. They were right. The thief hadn't stolen the forklift, merely borrowed it long enough to lift the boat out of dry storage and launch it on the Seeti River.

I scanned for security cameras as I walked back to the office. There were none in the dry storage building, but I spotted two at the ends of the courtesy dock.

Snoop gazed up as we walked into the marina office. "It didn't take long to find the theft. There are two security cameras and they snap one frame per second. Watch this."

The manager and I stood behind Snoop and peered over his shoulder at the monitor. "It was ten days ago, early Saturday morning."

The monitor displayed the courtesy dock from the north end facing south. The security lights made the picture plenty bright. The dock dwindled toward a vanishing point near the top of the screen. The launching slip was a thin black line cutting the dock in two pieces near the top of the picture. The dry storage building doors were closed.

"I adjusted it for real time. It will display one frame per second like it was recorded. It's 2:18 a.m. Watch the dock." Snoop tapped a key and a figure appeared at the far end of the dock and jumped six or eight feet toward the camera with each second. Then it jumped its way around the launching slip. "I can calculate his speed based on how long he took to walk around the slip. Carla said the slip is 30 x 50, so he walked 130 feet to get around it, maybe a skosh more. He did it in twenty seconds. That guy walked fast, more than four miles per hour. He's not running; that might attract attention. But he's walking real fast."

The figure curved toward the dry storage building and stopped at the locked doors. Snoop froze the picture. "Notice anything unusual about that guy, Chuck?"

"Besides the long beard? He's wearing a hoodie and a baseball hat on a warm, muggy night."

Eddie leaned closer to the monitor. "No way you make out a face from this distance behind that hoodie and hat. Oldest trick in the book, wearing a fake beard. Heck, it might be a woman, trying to throw us off."

I winked at Snoop behind Eddie's back. "Yeah, that's a bogus disguise."

"I'll zoom it." Snoop enlarged the image, but the pixels became large squares and the resolution was insufficient to print a mug shot. But the hat had a red bill and a big script *A* on the black crown that looked like the Atlanta Braves or maybe the University of Alabama. Ponder attended the University of Georgia, so it was probably the Atlanta Braves. I made a note.

Snoop played the video again, and the figure bent over the lock and stayed that way for a minute. "He didn't have a key or he could've opened it sooner. He must've picked it." The figure straightened up and slid the left door open a foot. He slipped sideways through the opening and the door slid closed again.

Snoop touched the keyboard. "Nothing happens for six minutes. I'll skip ahead." The monitor displayed 2:26 a.m. and the left door slid open. A figure crossed the opening to the right door and slid it back halfway. He disappeared inside the building. Seconds later the nose of a boat, concealed under a blue boat cover, eased through the door. The body of the forklift emerged, bounced over the track of the sliding doors, and rolled onto the pavement.

The forklift glided toward the launching slip. "Snoop, notice how smoothly he made the turn. This ain't his first rodeo. That guy knows how to operate a forklift."

"Yeah, but Carla said he doesn't know squat about launching the boat. Watch." The forklift stopped on the near side of the launching slip and the boat jerked and bounced on the outstretched arms.

"That's not the way we do it," Eddie said. "You gotta haul it around to the end."

The forklift stopped, and its arms bounced up and down with the boat's weight. The boat elevated six feet and stopped, bouncing again. After it stopped, the forklift backed up, spun, and moved to the rear of the launching slip.

Eddie nodded his approval. "Now he's figured out how to do it."

The man lowered the boat into the water, grasped a line, and tugged it off the submerged forklift arms. He tied the boat and returned the forklift to the storage building, relocked the doors. Within five minutes, he had eased the boat into the main channel and powered upstream. He slammed the throttles forward and the Outrage leaped ahead, throwing him back against his seat. The prop wash swirled the peaceful river into choppy turbulence in his wake. In seconds the boat climbed the bow wave up on plane and charged upstream. Its wake splashed and rebounded against the docks and seawalls on both sides as the boat disappeared around a bend in the river. The monitor displayed 2:45 a.m.

Eddie said, "He sure made it look easy, didn't he?"

"Can I copy the video, Eddie?"

"I gave Snoop a copy on a stick drive," said Carla.

"Any suggestions to improve our security?" Eddie asked.

I spread my hands. "A couple. First, I would lock the forklift keys in the office every night. Then I'd get a better padlock for the doors. Buy a lock that can't be picked in thirty seconds. I'd get four cameras for inside the dry storage building, one in each corner, and a couple for your parking lot. If you had a parking lot camera, we might have known what kind of car the thief used. Maybe even his license plate. Good cameras don't cost much anymore."

We said our goodbyes.

Snoop waited until we were in our car in the Prime Marina parking lot. "That guy on the security video matched your description of James Ponder. We need to ask Michelle to describe the baseball hat Ponder wore that night."

I cranked the van. "I'm ninety percent sure he was the thief."

"Ninety percent, my ass. How many skinny guys have a Taliban beard? Remember Rule Three: *There's no such thing as a coincidence.* He's a prime suspect until proven otherwise. And he's from Georgia—could be a Braves fan."

"Right. I'd like to know where he learned to handle a forklift."

Chapter 19

I HANDED SNOOP A SUB SANDWICH and dropped into a chair. Four months before, Java Jenny had expanded to the adjoining space and added a sandwich and pizza shop. We sat at the same end table where we'd interviewed Michelle that morning. Were things really moving that fast?

He unwrapped the sandwich. "Ponder had a summer job during his undergraduate days working at a Home Depot. I found it on his Facebook page. My guess is that's where he learned to drive a forklift." He tasted his sandwich. "Too much mayo."

"I'm buying, so don't complain."

"You mean Michelle Babcock's parents are buying." He tore open a bag of tortilla chips. "You want me to tail Ponder? He knows you."

"No. We've got the dirt on Ponder. I'll get Frank Bennet to follow Shamanski and see what he comes up with." Frank Bennett was a young Port City cop I used from time to time when he was off duty. "I'll follow Wallace; he doesn't know me from Adam." I had kept the paper from Monday with Wallace's address on it. I punched it into my tablet, then switched to Google Street View. "Something strange about Wallace's address. He shouldn't be living in a cheap apartment."

Snoop's mouth was full, but that didn't stop him from talking. "How so?"

I handed the tablet to Snoop. "Wallace is a tenured professor. That means he makes a six-figure income. And with his government grants, he's gotta pull down a half-million a year, net. I examined the photos on his Facebook page. He wears expensive clothes, and he drives a Tesla. Not surprising, given his views on fossil fuels. But this apartment—" I tapped the table beside the tablet. "That's a blue-collar flat in a blue-collar neighborhood. That's inconsistent with the upscale car and expensive clothes."

"So maybe he's a man of the people," said Snoop.

"I don't think so. His apartment complex has open parking lots—no private garages."

Snoop sipped his iced tea. "So what?"

"So, he has no location for a charging station for his Tesla."

"You don't buy an electric car without somewhere to charge it."

"Michelle is tight with Wallace. I'll call her." I did. "Michelle, Wallace drives a Tesla, right?"

"That's right. Why? Are you following him?"

"Not yet. How does he charge it?"

"There's a public parking lot a block away with a free charging station and free parking for electric cars."

"Yeah, yeah. I remember an article in the *Pee-Jay*." In a public seizure of political correctness, the City Council of Port City had chosen to buy an electric car charging station for one spot in each downtown parking lot. The *Port City Press-Journal*, which locals call the *Pee-Jay*, reported that the charging station was free to electric car owners. The fossil-fuel burning cars that parked elsewhere in the lots had to pay.

"His Tesla is good for a week or so without a charge. When it gets low, he parks it overnight in that public charging spot."

"Thanks, Michelle. One other thing: Describe the baseball hat Ponder wore."

"It was black and red."

"Good. Which part was red?"

"The part over your eyes. I don't know what you call it."

"The bill," I said.

"Yeah, the bill. The round part that goes on your head—what's that called?"

"The crown."

"Yeah, the crown. It was black. Oh, and it had a white capital *A* embroidered on the hat."

"Thanks."

"So, can you tell me anything?"

"Ponder is a Braves fan."

"Anything else you can tell me?"

"I'd rather not talk about it over the phone. We're making progress. We'll get together soon to talk. Stay hidden."

Chapter 20

I FOUND WALLACE'S TESLA right where Michelle told me it would be—in a public parking lot one block from his apartment.

This parking arrangement made him more difficult to follow. Normally, I stake out a target by parking my white minivan nearby and following them after they drive away. Americans are supposed to drive everywhere; it's the American way. Most Americans won't use public transit if they can afford any other way to get around.

But Wallace wasn't a typical American; he didn't always drive. Michelle said he often walked since he lived on the outskirts of downtown. Sometimes he rode the Port City Hopper, a public bus line. I couldn't wait near his Tesla either, since he might take the Hopper or walk, and right now his car was charging in the public lot.

I compromised by sticking a GPS tracker underneath the Tesla's rear bumper—illegal of course—and parked my minivan on the other side of the lot from the Tesla. I walked the block to his apartment and staked it out on foot. If he walked to his destination, I could follow at a discreet distance. If he drove his Tesla, I'd follow him to the charging station and tail the Tesla in my van using the GPS tracker. Routine surveillance, unless he rode the bus. That would cause a whole other array of problems. I crossed my fingers and hoped for the best.

Wallace's apartment was one of four similar buildings forming a square courtyard with a swimming pool in the middle.

That meant I couldn't watch his door from the parking lot. There were exits from the courtyard between each building. To keep tabs on him, I would have to hang out in the courtyard where someone would eventually notice I was a stranger.

I didn't have a choice. I hung out and walked around, on and off, all afternoon. With schools on spring break, a horde of shouting kids cavorted in the pool. I blended in among the stay-at-home moms and dads watching them play.

My cellphone rang. John Babcock's name shined on the screen. "Yes, John."

"That James Ponder character came here and wanted to talk to Michelle."

"To your house? How'd he get past the guard house?"

"He didn't. The guard called me and said Ponder was at the gate. I had the guard tell him that Michelle was gone for the week. I thought you'd want to know."

"Thanks. You did the right thing to send him away and the right thing to call me."

Wallace emerged from his apartment.

"John, I hate to rush, but I've got to go."

Wallace about-faced on his porch and locked a deadbolt from outside. This class of apartments usually has a cheap lock in the doorknob. He must've installed his own deadbolt for extra security. Did he have something to hide inside? Maybe he had expensive furniture and electronics to protect.

He walked off without a glance around him. Not a care in the world. He wasn't headed toward his car. I let him get around the corner before I followed.

Five blocks later, he stopped at a door with a ½ address in a three-story concrete block and stucco building. There are a million like it all over Florida. It was a plain steel door opening to a stairway that climbed to the second and third floors. It was sandwiched between Gino's Pizza on the right and Sal's Easy

Pawn on the left. This had to be the building where the three perps plus Michelle had met to plan the so-called protest. I was a half-block behind and across the street. I zoomed my phone camera and photographed him standing at the door. He didn't knock or ring a bell. He punched a code in the electronic pad and walked in like he went there every day.

I needed to know what was behind that door. Rule One: *When in doubt, ask questions.*

The choice of which neighbor to visit was easy. In that neighborhood, Sal's Easy Pawn would have a steel mesh cage above the counter to protect the owner from robberies. Sal would be suspicious of a stranger; pawnbrokers often were. Gino's Pizza would welcome strangers. Plus, Michelle had eaten pizza Monday night before the bombing—maybe from Gino's.

It was late afternoon and I was hungry. The door rang a small bell as I opened it. It was early for the dinner crowd, so I was one of two customers. An old man at the counter nursed a beer.

"You Gino?" I asked the middle-aged man behind the counter.

He grinned. "*Nah.* Gino's the guy what started the pizza parlor twenty years ago. I'm his son, Vinny." He wore disposable food handler gloves, so he didn't offer to shake hands. "Vincenzo Carpaccio to be exact, but everybody calls me Vinny."

"Chuck McCrary."

"What can I get you, Chuck?"

"Small pepperoni, mushrooms, jalapenos, and olives."

"What are you, a revolutionary? You don't mix no jalapenos with no olives."

"No? What would you recommend?"

"The pepperoni, mushroom, and olives is okay, but don't add no jalapenos; they'll fight with the olives, y'know?"

"You're the chef. I bow to your expertise."

"You'll thank me. What you want to drink?"

"Port City Amber."

"Good choice. That's my favorite." Vinny yanked off the flimsy gloves, dropped them in the trash, and reached in the cooler for a bottle. He used a bar towel to twist off the cap. "Here you go, Chuck." He wrote an order ticket and laid it on the counter. He slipped on another pair of gloves, grabbed a dough ball, and rolled it out.

"Vinny, I've lived in Port City for years and I never heard of your shop. And I love local restaurants. You've been here for twenty years?" I sipped my beer.

"Not the whole time, at least, not me personally. I bought the parlor from Dad five or six years ago. He retired." Vinny poured a ring of extra virgin olive oil on the dough and spread it with a pastry brush.

"What'd he do, move to Florida?"

"Ha. That's a good one, Chuck. *Nah*, Dad got kinda old. He moved in with my sister and her husband in West Palm Beach." He ladled tomato sauce on the dough and spread it with the bowl of the ladle. "Since this is your first time here, I'll let you in on what makes my pizzas so special." He picked up a log of white cheese a little smaller than a brick and positioned it on a slicer. "First secret is *Asadero* cheese from Mexico, not that imitation Mozzarella like most cooks use." He sliced the cheese log and covered the tomato sauce with the white slices. He applied the pepperoni slices with a practiced motion that was so fast I could hardly follow it. He sprinkled the mushrooms expertly, then the olives. "I grate my own Parmesan cheese each morning." He heaped a handful of grated cheese from a plastic container in the middle and spread it with the edge of his hand. "Here's my other special touch, Chuck. I sprinkle a little chopped sweet basil on top."

The old man at the counter lifted his beer bottle in my direction. "Vinny's right. Best pizza I ever had."

Vinny smiled at the old man. "Thanks, Freddy. Hey, you want another beer?"

"I'm good."

"Okay. Let me know if you need anything." Vinny focused back to me. "Wait 'til you taste it. You'll think you've died and gone to heaven, I swear to God." He slid the pizza into the oven, closed the door, and twisted a timer. He placed the timer on my ticket. "I guarantee you won't find another pizza like this nowhere in Port City."

"I can hardly wait." I dragged up a stool and sat at the counter, observing the street in the mirror behind the food prep station. "You know Sal next door?"

"Yeah, that crazy old geezer," he said with affection. "Sal, he orders the same thing for lunch every day, small plain cheese pizza, y'know. I walk it over and slide it through the slot in his cage, and he slides the money back. He don't never seem to leave the shop 'til closing time. He'll probably come out soon. He knocks on the window and waves before he goes home."

In the mirror, I watched a young couple on the sidewalk. The bell over the door rang as they came in.

Vinny waved. "Hey there, Tyler and Megan, my favorite customers. How's it goin'? You want the usual?"

The man spoke up. "Yeah, and two Diet Cokes." The young couple sat at a table at the window.

"You got it, folks." Vinny stripped off his gloves and dragged two silver cans from the cooler. He dried them with a towel and carried them to the couple.

After he returned, I said, "You must know everybody in the neighborhood."

He grinned. "Everybody loves my pizza." He lowered his voice like he was telling a state secret. "It's the Asadero and the basil." He wrote another ticket, donned fresh gloves, and started on the young couple's order.

"Who lives upstairs?"

Vinny peered at the oven timer before he replied. "Tough question. It was vacant a long time—years it seems like—before they rented it. I seen different people come and go for the last couple of years. But nobody's like... like a *regular*, y'know? I don't think nobody lives there. I think maybe it's more like a small club, or maybe a meeting place. They got one of them fancy electronic locks on the door."

I displayed James Ponder's picture. "You ever notice this guy go in there?"

Vinny leaned back. "What are you, some kinda cop? I don't want to get nobody in trouble." He finished the order wordlessly and slid it into the pizza oven. He set a second oven timer and placed it on their ticket.

"I'm not a cop, at least not anymore. These days I'm a private investigator." I laid a business card on the counter, one without the logo of the Sherlock Holmes deerstalker cap and the magnifying glass. "You ever see this guy?"

Vinny held the picture at arm's length and squinted. His pupils dilated and he dipped his head so faintly that I knew it was an unconscious act. "What's he done?"

He'd taken the bait; he recognized Ponder. Now I needed to reel him in. "How do you feel about a man who would beat up a woman?"

"This guy beat up a woman?"

"That's confidential. How long since you saw him here?"

"I don't look out the window when we're busy or I'm working by myself like now. But I seen him a few times." He tapped the picture with his other hand. "I mean, with a beard like that, who'd forget him? Y'know, he kinda looks like a wife-beater, don't he?"

"When's the last time you noticed him?"

"Lemme think… last weekend maybe… yeah, last Saturday night, right before closing. I remember I was nearly out of dough balls, and I didn't want to make no more because we're closed on Sunday and they won't last over two nights. This guy comes in and orders a large pizza to go." He handed the picture back to me.

"How about this guy?" I handed him Steven Wallace's picture I had downloaded from the internet.

Vinny's eyes narrowed again. "You followed him here, didn't you? You came in here right after he went upstairs." He frowned. "What's *this* guy done? Another wife-beater, I suppose." The friendly gaze had grown cold.

"No, Vinny. I'm not supposed to tell you this, but it's this guy's wife that the bearded guy beat up."

Vinny leaned close, friendly once more. "No shit?"

"This is her." I showed him a picture of Katherine Shamanski, also from the internet.

"Holy crap. I seen her go up there with her husband late Monday afternoon. They came down around eight o'clock, right at closing. They ordered two large pizzas to go. Lousy tippers—all three of them."

I killed time with Vinny until Wallace came out. He came into Gino's, ordered a medium pepperoni to go. He paid me no attention. I followed him home about six o'clock. He was in for the night with his pizza. I still had time to make my date with Miyo.

Chapter 21

"WELL, HELLO-O-O, HANDSOME. Come on in." Miyoki Takashi had drawn her hair into a ponytail. She wore pink, raw silk shorts and a matching sleeveless top with a bare midriff. She held my hand and led me into her apartment.

I kicked the door closed behind us as she wrapped her arms around my waist, holding me hard against her body. "I missed you, big guy. Three days is a long time… without a Margarita."

"They serve Margaritas in New York City," I said.

"Not the same without my bay view. I love the sunsets."

Miyo had been in New York City at another gallery exhibition. We had Skyped every night, but nothing replaces flesh and blood. She gazed up at me as if she were studying my face for the first time. She kissed me slowly, giving me her full attention.

I remembered the first time Miyo kissed me—I mean *really* kissed me. "Where did you learn to kiss like that?" I had managed to ask after I caught my breath.

She had giggled like a school girl. "I bet you never kissed a saxophone player before."

"You play the saxophone?"

"Not anymore, but I played tenor sax in high school."

"I didn't know that. One more of your many talents. But what does playing a saxophone have to do with kissing?"

"Before you play the instrument, you have to moisten the reed. You do that by tonguing the reed—a lot. It's like sucking a Popsicle. Would you like me to demonstrate again?"

"Yes, please. Early and often." And she had.

We'd dated for two months, ever since she'd asked me over to enjoy the sunset from her balcony. Whenever she kissed me, it still made my knees weak.

Miyo gave me a squeeze before letting go. "The Margaritas are on the balcony. I think they're lonesome."

We had begun dating right after the Super Bowl. The relationship was new and we were feeling each other out around the edges.

I wanted to know Miyo a lot better because I was pushing thirty and looking for a wife. In my family, men and women typically marry by the time they're twenty-five and have kids before they're thirty. My grandparents doted on their great-grandchildren and hinted that I should step up to the plate and start a family. My parents understood my situation, and they were patient and understanding. I had delayed the family tradition when I joined the Army after high school and served several tours in Iraq and Afghanistan before attending the University of Florida. My father and mother had met in college, but I had no such luck because I was shy around women.

My older siblings were all married and I had seven nieces and nephews. Lots of men nowadays think that thirty is not old to marry. So far, Miyo ticked all the boxes. She loved children, for example. We had not reached the point of exclusivity though I had not been with another woman since we began to date. Even Vicky Ramirez, my occasional friend with benefits, had not been able to jump my bones for a few weeks.

Every time I saw Miyo, I thought we could have beautiful children together. But it was too soon to speak of that. All in good time. I didn't want to scare her off.

It was a glorious spring day in south Florida and Miyo had opened her balcony doors. The sun was dropping toward the horizon and the gold reflections danced across Seeti Bay.

"Candles on the table?" I said. "It's still light."

"Candles are romantic any time. Besides, I like them."

"Excellent. I'll remember that later when you come to my condo."

"Now make yourself useful and mix more Margaritas."

I inverted the cocktail glasses and moistened the rims on the damp towel on the table. "Miyo, do you know anything about global warming?" I dipped the rims in the salt Miyo had poured into a small tray.

"I'm against it. Why do you ask?"

I poured us each a Margarita. "I heard on the radio this afternoon that the cops found a big banner at the site of the train bombing. It said *No more coal-fired plants*. The TV reporter said the bombers had planned a protest against global warming."

Miyo held the glass by the stem. "Doesn't make sense. If they planned to display a banner, why blow up the train? You do one or the other, not both."

"Hmm. You're right." I hadn't thought about that. This was more evidence that Michelle thought the protest would be peaceful. "So, tell me about global warming."

"Don't you watch television and read newspapers? Everybody knows about global warming."

"I peruse the front page, the sports section, and maybe the local news. I don't watch television news." I sipped my Margarita.

"Why not?"

"It's too violent."

Miyo laughed. "Says the man with two tours in Afghanistan under his belt."

"I don't believe that car crashes, gang shootings, and domestic violence are news. That's what most local television news consists of. You know that old saying: *If it bleeds, it leads.*"

"What do you think is news?"

"Sports, extreme weather, and local civic events."

"That's it? What about terrorist attacks, forest fires, politics, and plagues?"

"Those may be news, but they're not relevant to my life." I licked a little salt off the glass. "I don't pay much attention to them."

"Then why the interest in global warming?"

"Merely making conversation. Don't most couples talk about current events, their work, how the day went? Stuff like that? I can't talk about my work like you can—client confidentiality and all that."

Miyo licked an errant speck of salt off her glass. "You said 'most couples.' Are we a couple?"

I sipped my Margarita to stall. "It's a figure of speech, Miyo. I wouldn't presume to characterize our relationship without discussing it with you. For what it's worth, I haven't seen another woman socially since we started dating."

"Hmm. I haven't dated another man either, but that doesn't mean we're a couple."

"No, of course not."

She grinned. "There, we're discussing it. How would you feel if I did date other men?"

I didn't know how to respond without seeming possessive and controlling, so I changed the subject. "Drink that last sip and I'll re-salt the glasses." I made us each another Margarita. "I'm pretty much a one-woman man. Or at least, one woman at a time. Wait, that didn't come out right. Geez, I'm no good at this."

"No good at what?"

"Talking about serious stuff with a woman." I stared down at my hands. "I've had three serious relationships in my whole life, and it wasn't my idea to end any of them."

"Do you want to talk about it?"

I shrugged. "I wouldn't know what to say."

"Tell me about your first relationship."

"Liz Johannes. She was a girl really. It was in Theodore Roosevelt High School. We dated for two years. Then she went to Northwestern University and I joined the army."

"You didn't go to Northwestern to be with her?"

"I would have if she'd given me any encouragement. In hindsight, I realize it was merely a high school romance to her. I wanted something serious; she never did. The day of our senior all-night party she told me she'd been accepted at Northwestern. *Bang*, like that, a bolt from the blue. She never asked my plans before she made hers."

"That must have hurt."

I shrugged again. "I survived. I always survive."

"This kind of conversation calls for more alcohol." She lifted her glass in a toast. "To truth telling." She took a long drink.

"To truth telling." I sipped mine; I had to drive later—unless Miyo invited me to spend the night. *Could happen. There's always a first time.*

"Chuck, you don't have to drive. You can spend the night here."

"You must have read my mind. That's an offer I gladly accept."

She grinned. "I'll make the next batch." She carried the tray into the kitchen.

After she was gone, I watched the sun drop behind the downtown skyline. The sunset colors changed and reflected on Seeti Bay. A handful of boats lazed across the water, spreading wakes that rippled the smooth surface.

I had intended to have this conversation with Miyo, but not this soon. I had rushed things with Terry, my previous girlfriend. She had spooked at the first sign of adversity, when I got arrested for murder. She was a cop. No matter that the charges were later dropped; she hadn't come back. I hadn't seen her since. Since I'd met Miyo, I didn't think of Terry nearly so often.

Miyo carried a fresh tray of Margarita fixings onto the balcony. "Now, fortified with copious quantities of tequila, tell me about the second girl."

"Dotty was a woman. Junior year in Gainesville. We met at a mutual friend's Christmas party where somebody fixed us up. We dated until school let out in May."

"What happened with Dotty?"

"She scored a summer internship in Jacksonville and met another man."

"Ooh... bummer."

"Like I said, I always survive."

"And Terry was the third one?"

I had mentioned Terry to Miyo on our second date. "Yeah. Look, I don't know how to talk about this stuff."

Miyo grinned. "Hell, Chuck, you're practically a virgin compared to me. I've had a dozen relationships."

"How many were serious?"

"All of them—at the time." She held my hand and wrapped my arm around her shoulders. She rubbed her cheek on the back of my hand, then reached across and stroked my chest. "The problem is that I don't think long-term."

"How so?"

"I've been pretty shallow. If I spot a handsome hunk, I go after him like I did with you. Later, after I get to know him better, I learn that his long-term prospects aren't there. Then I dump him and search for the next hunky loser."

"You invited me to spend the night for the first time."

Miyo unbuttoned my shirt. "I don't plan to dump you. Your long-term prospects look pretty good."

Chapter 22

THE NEXT MORNING, I CARRIED OUR BREAKFAST PLATES onto the balcony.

Miyo followed with coffee service on a tray. "Yesterday you asked me about global warming. You still want to know?"

"Everybody takes this stuff seriously, so, yeah, what's the big deal with global warming?"

She poured our coffee. "In a nutshell, when people burn fossil fuels like gasoline, natural gas, coal, and wood, they produce carbon dioxide, which is a greenhouse gas. You know what a greenhouse gas is?"

"A gas that absorbs more heat from the sun than it radiates. Makes the air warmer, right?"

"Right. Water vapor, methane, and ozone are greenhouse gases too. We humans burn more fossil fuels than ever and carbon dioxide in the atmosphere is increasing faster than trees and plants can convert it into oxygen. The carbon dioxide traps heat in the atmosphere and the temperature goes up—global warming."

I added a little milk to my coffee, dashed salt and pepper on the eggs. "That's what the argument is about? The environmentalists want everyone to reduce the burning of fossil fuels?"

"Pretty much. Pass the salsa."

I did. "Then why the big controversy?"

"Fossil fuels are cheap, at least until we run out." She spooned salsa on her eggs. "Wind power and solar energy cost more than coal and natural gas, and they fluctuate with the weather. Battery technology isn't good enough to store the excess power for later when the sun isn't shining or the wind isn't blowing. *Mmm.* These eggs are great."

"Thanks. I must be a great cook."

Miyo punched me on the arm. "What? You think I want you merely for your body?"

"So why would anyone buy alternative energy if it's more expensive?"

"Think long term. We can't sustain an energy-intensive economy like we have now on fossil fuels. Eventually, we'll be forced to convert to renewable sources." She sipped her orange juice. "We have to develop future technology before we need it. And it ain't cheap."

"Where will the money come from?" I asked.

"What, do you live in a cave? The difference has to be paid for by higher utility prices, lower utility company profits, or higher taxes to cover subsidies. Everybody wants everybody else to pay the expense. That's why it's a big political battle."

"What about nuclear energy? I get a newspaper delivered to my cave. Nuclear is much cheaper. We could power more things with electricity and batteries." I thought of Wallace's Tesla automobile.

Miyo shook her head. "Too much danger with nuclear. Remember what happened in Chernobyl. Remember the Japanese tsunami and the problems that caused with the nuclear power plants. Remember Three Mile Island here in America." She tasted her eggs, added more salsa. "Too dangerous."

"Slide the salsa back over here after you're finished. I'm gonna have to eat and run. Got a meeting with Snoop in an hour at my office."

Chapter 23

THE BURNER PHONE BUZZED. Ponder had dreaded this call. He answered anyway. "This is Lamp Post."

"I got your email. It was sketchy. For a man who vouched for her reliability, you know very little about this girl. Have you found her?"

Ponder made sure his bedroom door was closed. "Not yet. Her cellphone goes straight to voice mail. I went by her house or tried to, but it's in a gated community. I couldn't get in."

"You couldn't get in," Redwood mocked. "What does that mean? How did you try?"

"I stopped at the guard house and asked the guard to tell Michelle I needed to talk to her."

"Did you use your own name with the guard?"

Ponder thought, *Oh crap. Was that a mistake?* "What else could I do?" He stood and paced the bedroom like a caged bear.

"Oh, I don't know. You could say you had a flower delivery for a different house in the neighborhood. Or you could rent a panel truck, dress in a khaki uniform, shave your stupid beard, and pretend you worked for the utility company. Or you could climb over the fence after dark. All you had to do was get past the gate, you idiot. It's not rocket science."

Ponder was shaken by the barely contained rage in Redwood's voice. "I… I don't know what to say. What should I do now?"

"I expected you to solve the problem of the girl personally. You failed." Redwood sighed. "But that's the past. We must live and act in the present to gain future benefits." He said it like a mantra. "What else did you try?"

"I called, uh, Kinetic and Skylight. They haven't heard from her either."

"What else have you tried?"

"That's all. In my defense, this is not my line of work. I'm not cut out to be a detective."

"For once, you are entirely accurate. Do you have any other ideas about how you might find her?"

"Maybe she's with that detective," said Ponder.

"What detective? A police detective?"

"No, no. He wasn't a cop, just a private detective who came searching for Michelle—"

"Don't mention any names over the phone, idiot."

"Sorry," said Ponder. "He was merely a guy searching for… the person in question the night before, uh, the package was delivered."

"You didn't mention that in the email. Who was this man?"

"He was a private detective her parents sent to make sure she was okay."

"Why would her parents send a private detective?" asked Redwood.

"I've got his card. He left one here." Ponder dashed to the door.

"Tell me why her parents sent a private investigator after her."

"She'd been sort of, uh, out of touch for a few days. She wasn't answering her phone. We'd been kinda hanging out. She's a freshman—"

"I know that; it was in your email."

"—and I guess her parents were worried about her," he finished lamely. Ponder stepped into the hall and searched for the business card. *Gone. Where the hell could it be?* He dashed to the top of the stairs. *There it is. Must have fallen on the steps.* He climbed a few steps down and snatched up the card. "His name is Carlos McCrary, McCrary Investigations."

Chapter 24

"PONDER STOLE THE BOAT AT 2:45 A.M. two Saturdays ago, and the bomb was onboard at eleven o'clock Monday night when Michelle got to McKinley Park. So, we need to find where the boat was for those nine days." I leaned back and swiveled in my chair. "And it wouldn't hurt to find out who built the bomb, where, and how they got it on the boat."

"The bad news is that Ponder drove the boat upstream," Snoop said. "If he'd gone downstream, we could have searched an area between the marina and the bay. That's two or three miles. But upstream… the Seeti River is navigable to small boats all the way to the Everglades. Could be fifteen miles or more."

"It's actually good news, Snoop. If he'd gone downstream, he wasn't restricted to hiding the boat on the river. We would have had to search the river and Seeti Bay and down to the Keys or up to Palm Beach for that matter. Compared to that, fifteen miles is a stroll on the beach."

I stood up. "What's the nautical equivalent of a road trip? A voyage?"

I FIRED UP MY BOAT, *THE GATOR RAIDER TOO*, while Snoop stowed our drinks and sandwiches in the galley refrigerator. Thirty minutes later, we idled past Bayshore Park and entered the 75-foot-wide Seetiweekifenokee River navigation channel.

The NOAA chart indicated five fixed bridges and twelve bascules along the fifteen nautical miles of navigable water on the Upper Seeti. The bascules all had clearance of eleven feet or more so the *Raider* could pass without waiting for a bridge to open.

"Snoop, you scan the right-hand shore for security cameras. Most docks along the river have a street address or other marker to identify the property. Photograph the security camera first and then the address marker for each camera. That will give us a jpeg file of each in the right order. Write each location on a notepad. I'll do the same for the other shore."

"Why write the locations down if they're gonna be on my camera?"

"Rule Thirteen: *Always have a backup.*"

"Right. You want me to start now? Before we get to the Prime Marina?"

"Snoop, remember Rule Five: *You can never have too much information* and Rule Six: *You never know what you'll need to know.* Catalog every camera we find."

"You could ask the FBI. They must have a database of every security camera on the river. Them or Homeland Security."

"Sometimes I think you're so lazy that you wouldn't breathe if it took any effort."

"I'm not lazy; I crave efficiency of movement. And it's cheaper for the client to ask the Feebs."

"Gene Lopez would want to know why I'm asking. I can't tell him yet." I tapped his arm and pointed. "There's a camera up there. See it?"

Snoop aimed his camera. "Got it… and got the dock marker too." He wrote on his notepad.

We passed the twisted wreckage of the railroad bridge. Huge cranes had hauled out the three locomotives and two coal cars that had plunged into the river. Another gang of cranes, guided by divers, had removed the steel scraps of the bridge from the river. Normal navigation had resumed within forty-eight hours of the explosion.

"They're already removing the old bridge," Snoop said. Steelworkers in protective masks wielded cutting torches on the mangled remnants of the old bridge.

"They've got to remove the damaged part to build the new bridge. The *Pee-Jay* said that all East Carolina & Florida trains have been rerouted to the Florida East Coast tracks and bridge further upriver. According to the newspaper, the coal on the train that Michelle's friends blew up was still delivered to the Everglades Power Plant twenty-eight hours behind schedule, minus the two carloads that fell into the river."

"Life goes on."

We motored up the river for four hours, pulling over for the island freighters wedging their way down the river. The navigable width dropped to sixty feet where the river forked into the Upper Seeti and the Lower Seeti a few miles upstream.

We cruised the Upper Seeti first. From there to the North-South Expressway, we pulled over several times for freighters to pass. West of the expressway, navigation narrowed further to forty-five feet. There were few freighters that far upstream so we made pretty good time. I eased the throttles into neutral, and we glided toward the Florida East Coast Railroad Bridge. "Six feet of clearance there, Snoop. The 280 Outrage needs eight-feet-nine-inches. Ponder couldn't have gone any farther."

I moved the transmissions in opposite directions and the *Raider* rotated in its own length. "Let's survey the Lower Seeti."

As we cruised downstream, we compared our observations of security cameras and found two more that we had missed on the Upper Seeti.

The Lower Seeti navigation stopped at the North-South Expressway so we'd covered about four miles. It took another two hours. By the time we returned to the river's mouth, the shadows had lengthened into twilight and sunset painted the sky with gold and pink. We'd cataloged a hundred seventeen security cameras.

As I lay in bed that night, I pondered how to inspect a hundred seventeen security videos. The only thing I came up with was to ask FBI Special Agent Lopez for help, but I needed to stay beneath his radar. I tossed and squirmed for a couple more hours until I figured out how to cut the work in half—literally. I went right to sleep.

Chapter 25

"YOU GOTTA BE KIDDING, BUD." Snoop waved the sheets of paper at me. "How many freaking cameras are on this freaking list, a hundred?"

"Sixty-two on your list and fifty-five on mine. Rule Eight: *Sometimes there is no substitute for shoe leather.* Don't get antsy on me, Snoop; I pay you by the hour." I unfolded a city map on my desk. "Besides, it'll go quicker than you think. Start here at the 46th Avenue Bridge on the Upper Seeti, six miles upstream from the Prime Marina." I penciled an X on the map. "I'll start on the Lower Seeti at the 52nd Avenue Bridge here." I marked another *X*. "That divides the river into two equal parts. If the boat passes either of these bridges, we narrow it down to half the river from viewing one video on each fork, and we'll know which fork he used. If the boat doesn't pass either bridge, we move halfway toward the marina to the 28th Avenue Bridge here." I marked another *X* on the map. "We'll leapfrog like that, cutting the river in half each time, until we narrow it down to a block or two. Genius, huh?"

"Don't break your arm patting yourself on the back."

AN HOUR LATER, SNOOP AND I CONFERRED BY PHONE. We knew Ponder had not driven the boat under either bridge where we had commenced our search. "What's the first camera you've got east of 28th Avenue, Snoop?"

"Three Isles Dredging. How about you?"

I reviewed the list. "Seeti View Apartments."

"They ought to call it Dredge View Apartments. Okay. I'm on my way to the dredging company."

Luxury condos, rental apartments, and waterfront houses dot the banks of the Seeti, but it's also a working river. The expensive homes often overlook giant steel buildings, rusty barges, and working boats across the river from them. It's marvelously eclectic, often chaotic, and I love it there.

Maritime businesses and distribution companies line the riverbank, jostling for space with the waterfront housing. Half the commerce with the Caribbean and the Bahamas ships on the island freighters that load and unload in South Florida—on the Seeti, the New River in Fort Lauderdale, or the Miami River to the south. Marinas, chandlers, and marine mechanics keep the freighters humming. Also dredges and marine construction companies with floating cranes and pile drivers maintain the river's infrastructure of seawalls, navigation markers, and the channel itself.

I drove tree-lined streets around the canals and tributaries to the peninsula where the Seeti View Apartments stood. As I got closer, the industrial facet of the neighborhood took over the street. By the time I reached the Seeti View at the end, the neighborhood was pure business with hurricane fences topped with barbed wire to guard the outdoor storage and equipment of the maritime industries.

The Seeti View apartment complex was a purebred in a kennel full of mutts. It sat in a forest of Sabal Palms, Royal Palms, and Queen Palms. I counted half a dozen different colors of bougainvilleas. It stood out like a polished diamond in a coal mine.

I glanced in the rearview mirror. The blue Ford sedan bumped into a warehouse parking lot I had passed.

I parked the Avanti in a visitor's spot by the office where a sliding glass door was open to the morning breeze. I didn't notice a spot to knock, so I stepped through the door. "Hello. Anybody here?"

I heard barking and a rapid scratching from the back room before a giant dog barreled around the corner, claws raking the tile floor as it skidded around the curve. The dog slid to a stop four feet from me, snarling like a hound from hell. An indeterminate breed with multicolored straggly fur, his black collar was studded with spikes that matched his personality.

I moved my jacket so I could reach my gun and backed two steps toward the open door. "Easy boy."

The dog advanced in lockstep toward me, his hackles raised.

An old woman puffed around the corner after the dog. "Tuffy, you hush up." She reached down and touched the dog's head. Tuffy dropped to his haunches and quieted to a low growl with teeth bared. His head reached to the woman's waist. I must have encountered a bigger dog somewhere, but I couldn't remember where.

I covered my gun again before the woman noticed it.

She wore turquoise pedal-pushers two sizes too small and a sleeveless pink blouse that let the backs of her arms flop like wet clothes hanging on a line. She had a 'do-rag tied around her dirty gray hair. She wiped the sweat on her forehead with the back of one hand as she considered me suspiciously. "No vacancy. We're full up." Tuffy growled his agreement.

"I'm not looking for an apartment."

"Then whatever you're selling, I ain't buying. Get out of here." Tuffy growled again.

I handed her a business card, one without my SPCA member logo on it. "I'm Chuck McCrary." I did not offer my hand; Tuffy might think it was an appetizer.

She extended her arm full-length and squinted at the card. "Don't have my glasses on. What's it say?"

"It says that I'm a private investigator with McCrary Investigations. I'd like to ask you a couple of questions if I may." *That's me, Mister Smooth.*

She peered at the card again. "Private investigator, eh? Never met one of those. Seen 'em on the TV, but never met one in the flesh. What are you investigating?"

"A stolen boat. I'd like to view the footage from your dock security cameras from Saturday before last from three a.m. to sunrise. It could help me catch the thief."

She eyed my jacket. "You carry a gun?"

"Yes, ma'am."

"You got a license?"

"Yes, ma'am."

"Show me."

I removed my credentials from my jacket pocket and displayed both my concealed weapons permit and my PI license.

"*Hmph.*" She peered at the licenses as if she could read them without her glasses. "That's pretty specific."

I wasn't sure what she meant, but it couldn't hurt to be agreeable. "Yes, ma'am." I stowed my creds away.

She peered over my shoulder. "Is that your Avanti?"

"Yes, ma'am. My grandfather gave it to me for a graduation present. It's been in my family for over fifty years."

"I seen cars like that before at car shows."

"You like car shows?"

"Brings back memories from when I was a girl. You'd never know it to look at me, but thirty years ago, I was pretty hot stuff. Okay, maybe it was forty years ago." She laughed.

"I like car shows too. My Avanti is a collector car to some people."

"But you drive yours."

"Yes, ma'am."

She scratched Tuffy's head. "Did something special happen on our dock between three a.m. and sunrise Saturday before last?"

"Not on your dock, on the river. A stolen boat that might have passed your dock around that time."

"Why you want to know?"

"I've been hired to find the boat." That was almost true.

She wiped her forehead again. She scratched Tuffy behind the ears and he stopped growling. She handed the card back. "Okay. The monitor's in the next room. I'll show you." She patted Tuffy on the head. "Let's go, boy. This fellow's all right. By the way, my name's Becky."

After reviewing the video, I called Snoop. "I got a hit. The boat raced past the Seeti View Apartments at 3:04 a.m. How're you making out over there?"

"I'm not there. I got caught with a bridge up. I'm driving into the parking lot now. I'll call you back in a few."

I slipped the phone back in my pocket and swiveled the chair toward Becky. "Can I copy part of the video to my stick drive?"

"What's that?"

I tugged a stick drive from my pocket. "It's a storage thingy for computer files. I'd like to copy that section of the video to it. It won't hurt your video."

Becky waved a hand. "Knock yourself out."

I copied files from each of the dock cameras, thanked her, and patted Tuffy on the head. He licked my wrist so hard he nearly yanked my watch off.

Waiting in the car for Snoop to call, I spread a city map across the steering wheel and planned our next stop. The river forked at what would have been 39th Avenue, if there had been a 39th Avenue. There was a bridge at 37th Avenue, downstream from the fork, and a pair of bridges at 42nd Avenue, one across each fork.

Snoop called. "Got the boat racing past the dredge company at 3:04 like you said. I copied the video onto a stick drive."

"Great. Let's go to the 42nd Avenue bridges next. You drive the north shore. I'll drive the south side."

I didn't mention the blue Ford. They might have been going to the warehouse. Passing the warehouse entrance, I scanned right. The Ford had parked on the back of the lot. Florida requires license plates only on the rear of a vehicle. Maybe it was a coincidence that this car had backed into a spot, hiding the plate from view. Maybe not. When I reached the top of the street, I checked the mirror again. The blue sedan bounced out of the lot and curved in my direction.

SNOOP AND I EACH STRUCK OUT on both 42nd Avenue bridges, even though we scanned video from 3:04 until sunrise. Ponder never passed under either one. I reviewed the map and my tablet. "Is the Hurricane Host Marina on your list?"

"Yeah. I spotted two cameras there. I can be there in five minutes."

"I'll meet you there in ten. Oh, and a blue Ford sedan is following me. I don't want them to know we're together. You go on into the marina office and wait for me. After we leave, tail them."

"Okay. See you there."

The marina occupied a prime hunk of waterfront west of the 37th Avenue Bridge on North Riverside Drive. The difference between it and the Prime Marina was like comparing a new

Cadillac to a fifteen-year-old rust bucket. Its website said it had 150 wet slips and a shiny white steel building for dry storage. The parking area had been freshly blacktopped and striped. The cast iron fence was shiny with black enamel paint. The office was spotless.

Snoop was inside by the door. A female receptionist smiled from her desk. "May I help you gentlemen?"

"May I speak to your head of security?" I handed her a business card. "We're investigating a stolen boat."

She skimmed my card. "We haven't had a boat stolen in over two years. We have state-of-the-art security here."

"Yes, ma'am. The boat wasn't stolen from here. We think it may show on your security cameras down by the river. May I speak to your head of security?"

She picked up a walkie-talkie. "Mike, two guys here want to talk to you about a stolen boat."

Mike's voice rasped from the speaker. "Emmy, you know that we ain't had a boat stolen in maybe two or three years. Must be another marina."

Emmy shrugged. "It weren't stolen from here, Mike. Can these guys come talk to you? They said it may be on our security video. Where you at?"

"Dry storage on the river side. Send them this way and I'll meet them at my office."

"Roger." Emmy pointed to a giant aerial photograph of the marina on the wall. "Here's where we are… Here's the dry storage where Mike is… And this is his office right here. Walk down the docks here… You'll find Mike in front of his office. He's the guy with the ponytail."

Mike's faded blue baseball hat had a Hurricane Host Marina logo on the front. "Mike Seville." We introduced ourselves. His face was lined from years in the sun. "What's this about a stolen boat?"

"Saturday before last, in the early morning, a 280 Outrage Boston Whaler was stolen from the Prime Marina downstream. The thief drove it upriver. We spotted him on a security camera around 28th Avenue. We'd like to know if he made it this far upstream. I hoped your security cameras recorded him as he passed. *If* he passed," I added.

"Prime Marina," Mike repeated. He scowled. "Their security ain't worth the match to burn it with. No wonder they lost a boat. Guys like that give the industry a bad name. Our security is top-notch. If the thief drove the Outrage past here, you can bet the ranch we got it on video. Come on into my office. I'll fix you up at the monitor." As he spun away, I noticed that his ponytail stuck through the gap in the rear of the hat.

Mike settled us at his desk and briefed us on how to access the six security cameras that covered the river. "If you need me, I'll be outside smoking a cigarette."

"Snoop, begin at 3:04 and play it in real time from the camera furthest downstream."

Snoop tapped the keyboard. "That would be camera one."

We studied the silent river, deserted at that hour. Streetlights on the 37th Avenue Bridge reflected in the water, its surface rippling in a light breeze. Underneath the bridge the camera covered the river for a quarter-mile to where it made a slight curve on its journey to Seeti Bay. Two minutes passed.

"Here it comes," Snoop said. "Still up on plane."

"Freeze that, Snoop." He did. "Zoom in…" Ponder had removed his cap and the wind had flipped his hood back. "Move ahead until he gets closer to the camera… That's perfect. Get a screen shot and let's blow up his face."

I snatched the photo from the printer. "Great job, Snoop. It's definitely James Ponder." I held the photo where Snoop could see. "We've got you, Whiskers. Proof positive that you're the boat-napper." I clapped Snoop on the back. "Forget cameras two to five. Switch to six. Let's watch him pass the marina and find out where he goes."

The picture switched to a northwest view. In the background, the Lower Seeti split off three hundred yards upstream. The Outrage appeared on the screen still on plane. It slowed and yawed as its wake caught up after it came off plane.

"He must be about to dock somewhere near here," said Snoop.

"Or he's planning to take the Lower Seeti." The stolen boat moved up the river and curved into the Lower Seeti at 3:08 a.m. "Let's go grab the guys tailing me in the Ford."

"Then can we grab lunch?"

"One grab at a time."

Chapter 26

THERE'S A STRETCH OF SOUTH RIVER DRIVE where the two-lane street has no crossroads for four hundred yards. Marinas line the river side of the street, and apartments line the dry side. All have gated entrances. The Seeti River may be gentrifying, but it's an iffy neighborhood for burglaries and car thefts.

From the bridge, I curved onto South River Drive and slowed to twenty-five miles per hour. The Ford sedan followed at a distance. I stopped twice like I was searching for an address then idled down the long block. Snoop followed the Ford across the bridge.

My phone rang. "Yeah, Snoop."

"There are three guys in the Ford."

"We have them surrounded."

The sedan stopped on the side of the road two hundred yards behind me.

"Okay, Snoop. Block the road. I'll reason with them."

Snoop angled his car sideways across both lanes behind the Ford with the driver side window toward the Ford. The effect was psychological. The men following could drive onto the grass beside the road and get around his car if they wanted. I figured they would be so intent on me that they wouldn't notice Snoop come up behind until it was too late.

I made a U-turn and headed back up the street toward the Ford. When I got close enough, I crossed the double yellow line and nosed my car up to the Ford's front bumper. I prayed they wouldn't do anything rash to my precious Avanti. I'd had bullet holes in it before and my classic car guy was already miffed at me.

I popped the door and walked around behind my car. I wasn't about to walk between my bumper and the Ford even if I'd left enough room, which I hadn't. The driver could crush my legs if he slammed it in gear. Passing behind the Avanti, I drew my Glock and held it beside my right leg where it wasn't visible from the Ford.

The driver's eyes cut to his rearview mirror. Snoop had his window down and had pointed his pistol at the Ford.

I strolled near the driver's window. My smile was bright enough to melt the glass if I had stood closer. I pointed the Glock at the driver's head. I sidestepped until I lined my pistol up with the front passenger's head too. If I shot the driver, there was a good chance I'd hit the passenger with the same bullet. I stood four feet from his window, smiling, waiting. Mr. Nice Guy with a gun.

The driver grasped the steering wheel with both hands in sight; he'd been stopped by cops before. He twisted his head for a hurried conversation with the man in the front passenger seat. The front passenger stretched his hands to the dashboard. The rear seat passenger grasped the back of the driver's seat with both hands. The driver shouted through the window. "I'm going to use my left hand to lower the window, okay?"

"Everybody keep your hands where I can see them," I said. "Anybody's hands move but the driver's, and you're all dead."

He moved his left hand from the steering wheel toward the door. He paused with his finger extended where I could see it. I nodded, and he moved his finger down below the window. The window purred open. He replaced his hand on the wheel. His knuckles were white.

We stared at each other for a moment. It was hard for him to twist his head that far with both hands grasping the steering wheel.

"If anyone in the car moves, you and the guy beside you get the first bullet. You've noticed that I have both your heads lined up. My colleague behind the car will shoot the man in the rear seat with the second bullet. The whole thing will be over in less than one second. Are you clear on that?"

The driver swallowed hard. "Yeah."

"Remove the keys and drop them through the window." He did. "Tell me who you are and why you're following me."

"I'm not following you."

I shot out the front tire and re-aimed the Glock at the driver before he could react. "Try that answer again."

"Whaddya want from me?"

"Who are you and why are you following me?"

"I don't know what you're talking about."

I didn't dare move my Glock a second time. I raised my voice. "Snoop, shoot out the back tire." He did.

I asked again. "Who are you and why are you following me?"

The driver's sunglasses pointed in my direction. "Let's get real, McCrary. You're a law-abiding PI. You ain't gonna shoot nobody. This here's a public street in broad daylight. There's gotta be surveillance cameras recording us right now."

One car and a truck had stopped behind Snoop. Another car approached from the other direction. Someone would call the cops soon if they hadn't already. "Lower all the windows." He did. I stuck the Glock in his ear and reached into his jacket. I drew out a Browning .380 pistol and stuck it in my pocket. I reached back into the jacket, found his wallet, and pocketed it. "Left hand, give me your cellphone."

He handed me a flip phone. "Now you in the front passenger seat, slowly, using your left hand, drop your piece out the window." He did and I heard the clunk on the asphalt. "Now toss your wallet and cellphone onto the grass." I didn't want the cellphone to break when it hit the pavement. I stepped to the back door and stuck my pistol in the rear passenger's ear. He wasn't wearing a jacket. "Where's your piece?"

"Belt on the left side, butt forward."

I reached inside the window, removed his gun, and dropped it onto the street. "Now hand me your cellphone and drop your wallet out the window. Left hand, slow." He handed me another flip phone and dropped his wallet on the pavement.

I stepped back. "Snoop, you got their plate number?"

"Do the swallows return to Capistrano?"

I drew the driver's Browning from my pocket with my left hand. I pointed both guns into the car. "Snoop, pick up their guns, wallets, and phones, then move your car."

I kept the three men covered while Snoop collected our trophies. "Don't anyone get out of the car until we're gone."

Snoop backed onto the shoulder. The backed-up traffic cleared. The Ford wasn't going anywhere.

Snoop leaned out his window. "Now can we please have lunch?"

Chapter 27

I SHOVED MY LUNCH DISHES ASIDE and spread the city map on the table. "Right there would be a perfect spot for a camera to pick up Ponder making the curve. What cameras did we find near there?"

Snoop flipped pages. "Several. Best view would be from the River View Terrace on the south side." He pointed to the map. "Right there."

I punched up Google Earth on my tablet for an overhead shot of the River View Terrace. "They have a perfect view." I switched to Street View for a quick familiarization of the area. The apartments were fifteen stories tall. They had a dozen or more units on each floor—plenty large enough to have security cameras, probably in good working order. "You're right, Snoop. You want to ride with me?"

"We'll need two cars if the trail forks again and we have to split up. Plus, we haven't seen the last of those three guys. Two cars seems like a good idea."

###

A CONTRACTOR WAS BUILDING A CONCRETE BLOCK WALL along the sidewalk at the River View Terrace. The new wall had already replaced half the old wrought-iron fence I'd noticed in Google Street View. A large plastic banner fastened on the completed end of the new wall announced *Under New*

Management. The new management had added an attended guardhouse and a sliding security gate at the entrance. I looked in the rearview mirror and called Snoop. "New wall, new gate. The complex seems a little small to afford a full-time guarded entrance. They must have security problems."

"Let's hope so, bud. That should mean their security cameras are the latest model."

The entrance pylon at the gate was brand new and painted in the rainbow colors of a gay pride flag. It announced *River Oaks Apartments.* Another neat sign heralded the new management. I stopped at the guardhouse where a uniformed, armed guard stepped out and waited for me to lower the window.

"How can I help you, sir?"

"I'd like to speak to your manager. And the man in the car behind is with me."

The guard smiled. "You want to rent an apartment?"

"No."

The guard's smile faded a little.

"We'd like to view your security videos from two Saturdays ago."

"May I inquire what this is in regards to, sir?"

"We're tracking a stolen boat that passed behind your apartments early two Saturday mornings ago. We hope your security cameras got a picture of the driver."

"May I make a copy of your driver's license, please?"

I handed it to him. "Have you had security issues here? I notice the new guardhouse and the new wall."

The guard smiled again. "No, sir. The new management is renovating and upgrading the facilities for our new clientele."

A dozen live oak trees were newly planted and braced with two-by-fours on the edges of the parking lot. The new management was adding the trees to go with the new name. A landscaping crew was planting another.

I waited beside my car while Snoop had his driver's license copied and then parked beside me in the visitors' lot. Two well-dressed men walked through the lot and got into a red Corvette.

Snoop locked his car. "Maybe you and I should hold hands as we walk into the office. We might fit in better."

"Control your so-called sense of humor, Snoop. Don't piss anybody off. We have a job to do. Would you rather wait out here?"

"I swear that guard leered at me when I came in."

"You're ugly as a muddy mole and you're old enough to be that's guy's father."

"What's that got to do with anything?" He clapped me on the shoulder and laughed. "Don't worry, bud, I won't embarrass you. I was yanking your chain."

I opened the office door and led the way inside. The name plate on the desk said *Kevin*. He looked like a Kevin. A twenty-something man wearing a pink Polo shirt and white pants. Of course, if the name plate had said *Stanley*, I would have thought he looked like a Stanley. Kevin's bleached hair was gelled and spiked in a way that some folks would consider fashionable. The faint aroma of a men's fragrance (isn't that what they call it when a man wears perfume?) filled the room. I knew it wasn't after-shave because the guy had a week's growth of beard, also considered fashionable by some people.

I handed him a business card that he dropped on the desk without reading. "We're tracking a stolen boat that passed on the river behind the River Oaks Apartments between three and four a.m. two Saturdays ago. We'd like to review your dockside security videos for that time, if we may."

Kevin eyed my jacket where the Glock made the bulge. He jumped up and stalked around his desk. He stood between me and the rear door that led to the rest of the office. He crossed his arms and stuck his chin out. "You're wasting your time, officer. Our security videos are confidential unless you have a warrant." He was six inches shorter than me and sixty pounds lighter. His attitude was so assertive that a person less polite than I might have called it bellicose. He hadn't even said "I'm sorry" before telling me to buzz off.

I had to admire Kevin's courage, standing up to two armed strangers. "I don't need to view any interior videos, not even the ones around the pool. We want to survey the dock and river from 3:10 a.m. to 4:00 a.m. two Saturdays ago. And the dock was probably deserted at that time of night."

Kevin seemed unmoved.

"We're trying to catch a criminal here. We could use your help."

"Let me see your search warrant."

"We're not cops; we don't have a warrant. We're asking for a little help from a fellow public-minded citizen."

Kevin's eyebrows went up. He uncrossed his arms. "You're not cops?"

"No, we're private investigators." I didn't add *like it says on my business card which you didn't read*. No point in being petty. "The insurance company hired us to recover the stolen boat."

Kevin's attitude warmed a little. "You're not here to hassle us?"

"We're here tracking a stolen boat. That's the sole item on our agenda. Could you help us please, as one private citizen to another?" I spread my hands in a gesture of supplication. Give Kevin the power.

Kevin stroked his chin. "I don't see what it would hurt, but I don't know how to operate the system. Somebody from the security company comes in once a week and does maintenance or something. Do you know how those things work?"

"I'm familiar with a lot of security systems. If you'll show us your monitors and keyboard, we'll take it from there. Feel free to observe us if you like. We merely want to look at the time frame I told you about."

Kevin waved a hand. "Oh, don't worry about that. I thought you guys were cops. We've had bad experiences with cops. You understand."

"I know the kind of cops you mean." There weren't many of them still in the Port City Police Department, but a handful remained to be weeded out.

Kevin led us to a small security alcove at the rear of the office suite. Snoop sat at the monitor and I rolled a chair over next to him.

Kevin stepped toward the door. "I made a fresh pot of coffee. Would you guys like some?"

Snoop said, "Sounds good. I drink mine black."

"And I like a little creamer, no sugar. Thanks very much," I added.

Snoop flicked switches from camera to camera, searching for the right view. "Something wrong here, Chuck. I see two cameras on the dock, but the rest are different exterior shots. Nothing covers the river."

"Show me." The two cameras focused on the dock were mounted high on the wall and pointed at the dock and the boats moored there. The angle of vision did not include the river itself. "Show me the view at 3:08 a.m."

"Won't do any good, Chuck. All you'll see is the boats tied up at the dock and maybe a couple feet of river. The cameras are too high and aimed down to video the rest."

"Just do it, Snoop. 3:08 a.m."

Snoop punched the keyboard. The monitor displayed the eight-foot wide dock and two boats below. The only motion on the screen was the time indicator ticking over in the corner. The rest could have been a snapshot, unmoving.

I watched for a while. "The boat on the right is twenty-five feet long; the one on the left is thirty-one."

"How can you tell?"

"Count the dock boards. Six inches per board. Notice the reflection of the boat on the right?"

"What reflection?"

"Its hull. You can see about a foot of the underneath side of the bow reflected in the surface of the river. It's lit by the dock lights."

"Yeah, I see it. So?"

"Study the reflection. If I'm right, you'll see something interesting soon."

We waited.

"I see it," Snoop said. "The reflection moved."

I jotted down the time. "That was the stolen boat's wake as it passed in the middle of the river. Switch to the other camera and watch the effect of the wake hitting the boats at the other end of the dock."

Snoop punched the keyboard and another unmoving image filled the screen. One boat moored at the dock was a sailboat, the other a sport fisherman. "Camera angle's no good, Chuck. Can't see the reflections of the hulls."

"We don't need reflections, Snoop. Based on the length of the sailboat, I'd estimate the mast is forty feet tall. If the wake is the same size as the first one, the mast will rock about two feet back and forth. The sport fisherman's outriggers will move about a foot." Sure enough, a minute later the sailboat mast moved. But it was six or seven inches. The sport fisherman didn't move at all.

Snoop froze the picture. "That's impossible. We had a good wake on the first boats, a small one for the sailboat and none on the sport fisherman. Can't be."

I loaded Google Earth. "There's a canal lined with houses across the river. Ponder must have piloted the boat up the canal. We're getting closer."

Chapter 28

KELLY ANSWERED ON THE FIRST RING. "Hey, Chuck."

"Hello, Kel. When do you get off?"

"In five minutes. Why?"

"I need a favor. Then I'll buy you dinner if you're free."

Kelly paused before she replied. "Is this like a dinner… date?"

I realized I'd said the wrong thing. "No, no, no. I want an update on the matter we were discussing."

"What's the favor?"

I hauled out the three driver's licenses I'd collected from the gunmen in the Ford. "I need reports on three guys from Chicago." I recited the names, Chicago addresses, and Illinois driver's license numbers. "And I need a trace on a license plate. I think it's a rental, so I need to know who rented it." I read her the license plate.

"Give me a half hour. Where you want to meet?"

"I'll meet you at Barney's." That was a cop joint near the North Shore Precinct where Kelly worked.

"How about the Rusty Pelican instead? If I'm gonna work for free, you ought to give me fringe benefits." The Rusty Pelican was a swanky restaurant on an island in Seeti Bay with a million-dollar view of the Port City skyline and prices to match.

"I'd love to, but we'd never get a table on Friday afternoon at six o'clock without waiting in the bar for an hour. The lawyers, bankers, and hedge fund managers will have the good tables. Besides, this is a working dinner, not a social event. I'll treat you to the Rusty Pelican after this is over."

"I'll hold you to that. For today, should I bring Bigs if he's free?"

I nearly said yes, then changed my mind. "No."

After I hung up, I wondered why I'd wanted to see her alone.

I SPOTTED KELLY AT A BACK BOOTH. A pitcher of dark beer and two mugs sat on the table. She waved and poured me a beer as I crossed the crowded restaurant and bar. "You like Port City Amber, Chuck?" She shoved the mug across the table.

"You better know it." I slid into the bench across from her. I clinked my mug against hers. "*Salud.*"

Barney walked over in his trademark long white apron over his khaki slacks and Port City Pelicans tee-shirt. "Welcome back. You folks want a menu?"

Kelly smiled at Barney. "I'd like a grilled chicken Caesar salad, no croutons, please."

Barney entered her order on a tablet computer. "You, Chuck?"

"Chicken-fried steak, gravy on the side, coleslaw, and a sweet potato, naked. And corn bread."

"I'll turn your order in. Sheryl will be your server. I'm helping out during the rush. See you both later maybe. Enjoy." He about-faced and walked away.

Kelly wore a cream-colored silk blouse with a dark gold silk neck scarf and a heavy gold chain necklace. Below the scarf, three buttons were undone, flaunting the necklace between the twin swells of her breasts.

"I'm glad you picked a back booth. More private." This was where I should have asked for her report—correction, reports. But I didn't. She had brown eyes, the same shade as Miyo's. And dark, dark brown hair like Miyo's.

She smiled. "Aren't you going to ask me about the three thugs from Chicago and the rental car? And what about the train bomb investigation?"

I cleared my throat. "To tell you the truth, I find your, uh, cleavage distracting."

"Your honesty is refreshing—I guess. If you're going to be direct, I will too. It's supposed to distract you. That's why women do it." She grinned. "When I'm on duty, I button it to the top. More businesslike. I'm off duty now."

"That's for sure. I've never seen you off duty before. At least not this way."

"You've never seen me off duty before—period. Would you like me to button up?"

"God, no. I like the view so long as you don't mind if I leer."

"Like I said, that's why I did it."

I dragged my gaze up to her face. "Okay. Let's get the business out of the way." *Out of the way of what? This is supposed to be a business dinner.*

Kelly flipped open a large leather purse sitting beside her on the bench seat. She drew out several sheets of paper and unfolded them. "Rap sheets for the three thugs." She handed them across. "They're muscle for Adam Wolenski, a mobster in Chicago. Gofers and strong-arm guys."

I perused the sheets. "Any hired killers among them?"

"Hard to say. Most of their arrests are for assault and battery, one had an attempted murder eight years ago, charges dropped. Murder wouldn't surprise me though. These are bad actors."

"Thanks." I folded the papers and stuck them in a pocket. "How about the car?"

She handed me another sheet. "Like you thought. They rented it at the airport last night. The driver's license address was phony and different from any of the driver's licenses you read me."

"Did you trace the credit card?"

"Dead end. The card was issued by McKinley Travers Bank & Trust Company, chartered in Liechtenstein. Liechtenstein bank confidentiality laws are tighter than Switzerland's."

I stuck the new sheet next to the other ones. "Thanks for the help. How goes the train bomb investigation?"

"Not so fast, hotshot. When I ran the license plate, it showed up in another report. A driver on South River Drive called 9-1-1 this morning to report an altercation between persons in an Avanti, a Toyota, and a Ford. The helpful citizen watches cop shows on TV and gave us the license numbers for all three vehicles. He reported two shots fired. When our patrol car arrived, the only thing at the scene was the abandoned Ford with two tires shot out."

Kelly held her mug in both hands. She leaned toward me and her breasts thrust their way over the edge of the tabletop. She lowered her voice. "Tell me what's going on."

I temporized. "Are you doing that because you want me to look down your blouse?"

She glanced down at her chest, fingered her gold necklace, and leaned back. She smiled as if she was about to speak then changed her mind. "Don't change the subject. What's going on with those three guys?"

"It has to do with the project I cleared with Jorge."

She studied me for a moment. "Well… no one was hurt. I'll let it pass… for now." She sipped her beer.

"These are the three guys' phones." I tugged them from my pocket and pushed them across the table.

Kelly eyed the phones but didn't touch them. "How'd you get those?"

I removed the three driver's licenses from another pocket and slapped them on the table. "The same way I got these Illinois driver's licenses. I asked nicely and said please."

"Of course you did." She stuffed the phones and licenses into her voluminous purse. "What do you want me to do with these?"

"Each of the four phones lists three contacts: the names of the other two guys, plus a third contact named *Redwood*. I'd like you to ping all four of them and trace their calls for the last two weeks."

"And you want all this off the books?"

"If it'll make you feel better, ask Jorge."

"This'll cost you dinner at the Rusty Pelican plus a brunch on Mango Island."

"I'm not a member of Mango Island."

Kelly scoffed. "Puh-leeze. Everyone on the force knows about your connection to Hank Hickham. He'll get you a guest pass."

That was uncomfortably close to the truth about my history on Mango Island. I decided to quit while I was ahead. "Deal."

We clinked our beer mugs. "Now tell me about the bridge bombing investigation."

"That Gene Lopez can be a real prick sometimes, you know?"

I laughed and clinked my mug against hers. "Has the FBI found the boat?"

"Yes and no. The boat's in a million pieces, most of which floated away down the river or sank to the bottom. They found one piece with a partial on the FL number. But they did recover two outboard engines from the river bottom. The serial numbers belong to a Boston Whaler."

"What model?"

"I think it was a 280 Outrage. Why?"

I shrugged. "Just in the interest of completeness. Go on."

She flipped open the purse again and slid out a palm-sized spiral notebook. As she leaned over, her blouse gaped open and flashed a glimpse of pink lace. "Yeah, it was a 280 Outrage. The boat was delivered to a dealer here in Port City six years ago. The dealer is out of business, so they don't know who he sold it to. All the dealer's records were lost."

"How will they find out who owns the boat?"

"They're running the partial FL registration number against the state records. That will take a while."

"What about security videos from along the river?" I asked.

"They reviewed them all. They confirm it was an Outrage, but the quality wasn't good enough to get the FL number. Oh, on one video there was a fourth person in the boat."

"What do they know about the bomb?"

She referred to the notebook again. "Ammonium nitrate, liquid nitromethane, set off by Tovex. Approximately fifteen hundred pounds."

"*Umm.* The first two are pretty easy to get; the Tovex is regulated." I drew out my notepad and wrote down the ingredients.

Sheryl arrived with a serving tray balanced on one hand and a wooden stand hooked over her elbow. She flipped open the stand with a practiced move and positioned the tray on it. She studied the collection of plates crowded on the tray. "Who had the chicken fried steak, gravy on the side?"

I refilled our mugs while Sheryl served. "Anything else I can get you folks? No? Holler if you need anything."

I spooned a little gravy on my steak. "How far up the river did they trace the boat?"

"How did you know the boat came from upriver? It could have come from downriver."

I shrugged. "Best case, it was fifty-fifty they came downriver. What's your point?"

"You know more than you're telling me." She moved her salad to one side. "What aren't you telling me?"

I spread my hands in a surrender gesture. "It's nothing. I figured they came downriver since it's what I would have done. There are lots of spots to hide a boat on the river. Not nearly as many on the bay shore. Remember, they had to construct a bomb onboard. That might take days. They had to plan things several days ahead. Plus, the perps had to worry about bad weather if they came across the bay. And they would have been recorded on the coastal radar. There wouldn't be many boats on the bay in the middle of the night. It would be easy to track them back to their point of origin. They would stand out like a skunk at a Persian cat convention. Why'd you make such a point of it? Did they come from downriver?"

"No. They came from upriver," she said.

"So how far upriver did Gene trace the boat?"

"About two miles. They lost the trail south of McKinley Park. You know where that is?"

"On the east side, right? How could they lose them? I assume there would be security cameras all up and down the river."

"There are, but for a quarter mile below McKinley there is a big development of new condos on each side of the river. The construction site videos cover the construction sites, not the river in front."

"What about the park? Surely it has security cameras."

"Atlantic County budget cuts. Those cameras were vandalized two weeks ago. They're supposed to be replaced or repaired in the next fiscal year."

I ate a bite of coleslaw, chased it with beer. "If I were you, I'd tell Gene Lopez to examine the river cameras further upstream from McKinley Park, but in the daylight."

Kelly frowned. "I have that feeling again that you know more than you're telling me."

"You'll have to trust my judgment. I offered to consult with Gene on the bombing, and he basically told me to take a long walk on a short pier. Gene is so smart that he doesn't need my help. But I'm thinking like the bad guys here. If I wanted to bomb a train, I'd put those park cameras out of commission and I'd use the park for a staging area. I would bring the boat to the park ahead of time in the daylight when lots of boats are launching and retrieving. I'd blend in with the afternoon crowd and then wait until nighttime to load my crew."

I stabbed another bite of steak. "I presume the bomb was concealed by a tarp or some such?"

"Yeah. They saw that in the videos."

"Did they survey the cellphone records from the neighborhood around the bridge?"

"There are over three thousand cellphone customers within a mile of the crime scene," she said. "Over two thousand phones were on the network at the time of the explosion. That's a lot of data to review. Even with the importance of this case, there are limits to the manpower they can throw at it. Gene thinks it could require three or four weeks to run down two thousand phones."

"I don't suppose the Feds have found the cellphone used to set off the bomb, have they?"

Kelly cut her grilled chicken into smaller pieces and tossed them in her salad. "They emptied every dumpster within a mile of the crime scene. They examined every storm sewer and trash bag. The divers raked the muck on the river bottom in case the perp threw it into the water. *Nada.*"

I cut into the sweet potato, stripped the peeling off. "If they haven't found the phone by now, they're not gonna. Unless the perp was stupid and didn't throw it away."

"No one would be that stupid." She sipped her beer, wiped the foam off her lip with a napkin.

I forked a bite of sweet potato. Delicious. "How about the three perps? What have they got on them?"

"Two men and a woman. They enhanced the video and one man had a full beard. Another one held up the phone to set off the bomb. They analyzed the images six ways from Sunday and determined that one walked like a woman and was five-foot-five or five-foot-six. The other two were men, both five-foot-ten."

She forked another bite of salad. "Oh, yeah. The one with the beard is a Braves fan."

Chapter 29

MICHELLE LOOKED VERY HOLLYWOOD as she sat down with her sunglasses on. We had a table at the Coconut Corral Café on Mango Island, but it was in the shadows since the sun hadn't climbed over the high-rise luxury condos. Palm trees and bougainvilleas decorated one side of the outdoor tables, opposite the blue water of Seeti Bay.

"You want breakfast, Michelle?"

"I'll have a cappuccino. I don't eat breakfast."

"You'll attract more attention wearing sunglasses at eight o'clock in the morning than you would without them. Why don't you slip them in your bag?"

She scanned the other tables. "I never thought of that. I'm not used to sneaking around." She stowed the sunglasses.

"It's necessary for a while. But you should act like nothing has happened. Remember, as far as you know, nothing did happen. You were miles away from… anywhere. You got that? I've kept you out of this so far. But you have to stay away from the other three musketeers."

"Why? They're my friends."

"They may want to kill you."

She acted like I'd slapped her. "I can't believe they'd do anything like that. Katherine's a pacifist, for God's sake."

"Three thugs from Chicago with big guns followed me yesterday. They think I'll lead them to you."

Michelle said, "Katherine's from Chicago."

"But the only one of your friends who was aware that you knew me was Whiskers."

"Whiskers? You mean James?"

"Sorry," I said. "Snoop and I call him 'Whiskers.' James Ponder."

"How do you even know they were from Chicago?"

"I trapped them on a lonely road, held them at gunpoint, and stole their wallets. A contact with the Port City police ran their rap sheets for me. They're soldiers for an organized crime family in Chicago."

I waved at a server. "Two cappuccinos and I'll have a Western omelet with hash browns and whole wheat toast with peanut butter. Thanks."

I waited until the server left. "And that's why you need to stay hidden."

"Okay, I guess."

I patted her hand. "We're making progress. We know where Ponder stole the boat and we can prove it. I can give that information to the authorities whenever I choose. They can nail him for stealing a boat, even if we can't tie that specific boat to the bombing."

"But that's the boat we were in."

"Yes, but you'd have to testify as a witness. Remember, I want to keep you out of this. Don't worry; the FBI is searching the bay for scraps of the boat. And they recovered the engines from the river. They'll match the serial numbers from them and match that to the boat. The FBI is good at that sort of thing. For now, I'm keeping the information on Ponder under my hat until I have a package to give to the Feds. Patience is a virtue."

The server arrived with our cappuccinos. "I'll have your omelet out in two minutes."

"Thanks."

I would have preferred coffee, but Michelle liked cappuccino. So did Gene Lopez; there's no accounting for taste. I can't complain; Snoop drinks his coffee black and thinks I'm a sissy because I use a little creamer. "I still need to tackle Shamanski and Wallace to prove their involvement. What more can you tell me about Shamanski?"

"She's rich. I think her father is a high-powered entrepreneur in Chicago and owns a bunch of companies. He bought a luxury condo for her near campus. And I know she has no student loans, so he must pay her out-of-state tuition."

"What does he invest in?" I asked.

"I don't know. I do know that he pays for all her college expenses."

"What's his name?"

"I'm sorry," Michelle said. "Katherine calls him 'Daddy.'"

"Don't worry about it. With a name like 'Shamanski' it won't be hard to track him down. What about her mother?"

"She's a lawyer and a community activist for environmental issues. Or maybe she's a lobbyist or something. Katherine told me that her mother spends so much time in Washington that she owns an apartment there."

"What's her mother's name?"

"Sorry, I don't know that either. But I know her last name is different from Katherine's. She kept her maiden name after she got married."

"How do you know that?"

"Katherine said that when she first came to UAC, she considered registering with a hyphenated last name. You know, combining the names of her father and mother."

"You mean like if you called yourself 'Michelle Babcock-Hickham'?"

"Yeah, like that. But Katherine said that Shamanski plus the other name was too long, and she didn't want to write them both for the rest of her life." She made a clicking sound with her tongue. "I remember now. Katherine said her name would have been Shamanski-McAllister."

"Great." I noted that for my researcher. "What else can you tell me?"

"Chuck, I know so much about her that I could talk for a long time. But it might be a waste of energy since I don't know what's important and what's not. I mean, she likes Indian food for example. But that's not important, is it?"

. "Good point. Tell me the courses she takes and what her class schedule is."

Michelle thought about that and managed to give me a pretty good list. "I remember something that might be important. She changed her major. As a freshman, she enrolled in the College of Engineering and worked toward a BS in Environmental Engineering. After her sophomore year, she switched to the College of Agricultural and Life Sciences. Now she wants a BA in Environmental Science."

"Why did she change?"

Michelle scoffed. "She *says* it's because the BA involves studying more Humanities and people-oriented subjects, but I think it's because engineering was too much homework. You can tap-dance your way around the urban planning and political science stuff, but you can't fake chemistry and calculus." She leaned back. "And Katherine is la-a-azy."

That was interesting. "So, she took chemistry?"

"Oh yeah. I'm taking it this semester; it's required."

"Did you know that Ponder has a Bachelor of Science in Chemistry?"

"Sure. Remember I told you that's the main reason I sleep with him. He's for sure not much of a lover; I think it's all the drugs. Anyway, he's a pretty good tutor when he's not high."

"Would he and Shamanski know enough chemistry to build a bomb?"

Michelle's eyebrows shot toward her hairline. "Omigod, yes."

Chapter 30

BACK IN THE OFFICE, I CALLED MY RESEARCHER. I don't know his real name, but his handle is Flamer. I know: It's a term that some gays find insulting. I do know that Flamer is gay, so maybe he's taking ownership of the slur. Flamer is not your ordinary human. Sometimes I think he has computer superpowers.

"Flamer, I'd like to know about global warming and/or climate change."

"This a paid assignment?"

"Yeah."

"First thing to know is that the two terms do not mean the same thing, though the idiot media uses them interchangeably. But then, the idiot media screws up even the simplest facts." Flamer always calls the regular newspapers and network news the "idiot media."

"What's the difference between global warming and climate change?" I asked.

"Global warming is the theory that humans are causing a rise in global temperatures by the increasing use of fossil fuels."

"Yeah, my girlfriend said fossil fuels produce lots of CO2, which is a greenhouse gas."

"That's right as far as it goes," Flamer said, "but the global warming theory is mostly claptrap spread by a bunch of opportunists with a political agenda that lets them get their hands on government grants."

"How so?"

"Because of climate change. Climate change is the natural change in global temperatures that occurs over time spans of years and centuries—like ice ages. Climate has always changed, and it always will. You sure you want to hear this junk? It can be pretty boring to anyone who's not a science nerd."

"I've got a fresh cup of coffee. I'll tell you if it gets too boring. Go on." Flamer could expound at great length when he chose to. I peered out the window at the traffic on Bayfront Boulevard. Another Ford, white this time, cruised by and parked in the lot across the street. Maybe a rental, and it had three people in it. Was it the same three guys?

"You're paying, Chuck. Yes, the idiot media are right that the earth is warmer today than it was at the end of the last Ice Age. But it's also lots colder than it was 1,000 years ago. Did you know that when the first Vikings settled Greenland, it really was green?"

"I thought that was medieval bait-and-switch advertising. They named it Greenland to attract settlers."

"Nope. God's honest truth. The Vikings grew grain there for a long time. Climatologists call it the Medieval Warm Period, and it lasted from about 950AD to 1250AD. Look it up. It was followed by a Little Ice Age from about 1350 to about 1850. That's when the Viking settlements probably failed."

I wrote that down. I didn't need to know that for the case, but writing things down helps me remember them. "So, the warming today is part of the natural process of climate change. I didn't cause it by driving my Avanti and living in an air-conditioned apartment."

"Mostly, yeah. And it's not clear whether the global temperature has gotten warmer over the last few years. For example, a recent analysis of ice cores in northern Greenland proved it was warmer there from 1920 to 1940 than it is today."

"So what causes climate change, if it's not me driving my Avanti?"

"The biggest influence is variation in the amount of radiation the earth gets from the sun."

"The sun's radiation changes?"

"Yep. The earth is sending one-tenth of one percent more radiation our way than it did a hundred years ago."

"Doesn't sound like much."

"It isn't, but it doesn't take much variation to cause changes in the earth's weather. The closest correlation to solar radiation is sunspot activity—more sunspots, more solar radiation. Sunspots vary on approximately an eleven-year cycle. There are also longer cycles that last hundreds of years."

"So, it's not human activity."

"Yes and no. It's inconceivable that seven billion humans producing energy would have no effect on the climate. The problem is that no one knows—no one *can* know—how much is human activity and how much is natural."

"So why is the public worked up about this?" I asked.

"You know who H. L. Mencken was?" Flamer asked.

"The name's familiar, but I can't place him."

"Mencken was a journalist and satirist. He said, 'The politicians aim to keep the voters alarmed so they will clamor for the politicians to lead them to safety. They menace the populace with an endless series of hobgoblins, all of them imaginary.' And then the politicians get more power and the bureaucrats get more money."

"So, you believe people are upset because the politicians and the news media want them to be upset."

"The *idiot* media; they're not *news* media any more. They don't give you the real news; they publish pre-digested pap for the benefit of their masters."

Don't ever get Flamer started on his conspiracy theories. I take everything political that he says with a spoonful of salt and a heap of skepticism. But he's a great researcher, in spite of his political views, or maybe because of them. Nobody's perfect.

"That's a pretty cynical view of society, Flamer."

"Just because you're paranoid, doesn't mean they're not out to get you. This whole change in the catch phrase from 'global warming' to 'climate change' demonstrates how silly this so-called issue is. The politicians and the idiot media paint the normal course of climate change as evidence of doomsday."

"Why would the media go along with this?"

"Why not? Disasters make big headlines. They sell lots of newspapers to idiots who watch lots of commercials on television's so-called news. Idiots who pander to other idiots."

Chapter 31

A BOMB BIG ENOUGH TO OBLITERATE A STEEL RAILROAD BRIDGE. The FBI estimated fifteen hundred pounds. That would be mostly ammonium nitrate. The Oklahoma City bombing spurred many attempts to regulate the sales and use of ammonium nitrate, but it was years before effective laws were passed and regulations issued. And enforcement was spotty. Still, thinking like a bad guy, if I wanted to buy fifteen hundred pounds of ammonium nitrate, how would I do it? I'd do it one fifty-pound bag of fertilizer at a time. That's thirty bags and I would scatter the purchases over several states—none in South Florida.

I called Michelle. "This is Chuck. Did any of your four musketeers leave town several times this year for any reason?"

"Katherine goes home to Chicago most weekends to visit her parents. She claims she hasn't been laid this entire semester because she's gone so much. But I know for a fact that she's been sleeping with Steven. Why do you ask?"

"Just gathering facts. Never know what might be important to know. Anyone else travel much?" Outside, the white Ford with the three Chicago hoods was still parked across the street.

"Steven makes speeches at environmental rallies, mostly in Washington or Tallahassee or other state capitals."

"How often does he do that?"

"Maybe once a month or so."

"What about James Ponder?"

"*Nah*, he's pretty much a homebody. I've never heard him mention any family."

"Thanks."

I called Flamer. "I need everything you can get on Katherine Shamanski and her parents."

"Katherine with a *C* or a *K*?"

"A *K*. Last name S-H-A-M-A-N-S-K-I. Her father is an investor and maybe a personal injury lawyer, lives in Chicago, maybe a suburb, and invests in green energy projects and companies. Her mother's last name is McAllister. She may be a personal injury attorney in Chicago also. She is not in partnership with her husband. She owns a house or condo in the Washington, D.C. area. She's an environmental activist or lobbyist or some such. That's why the house in Washington."

"How deep you want to go?"

"To the center of the earth. Cover the last five years—no, make it six years. I need financials, politics, social activities. You know the drill. His and her friends, their business associates, where they vacation. Same thing for the daughter. Oh, yeah, find out if Katherine has any siblings. If so, get the same info on them."

"Anything else?"

"That's it."

The line went dead. Flamer once told me that saying goodbye wastes his valuable time. Like I said, he's peculiar, but he's the best researcher in fifty-seven states.

Chapter 32

"ROAD TRIP, SNOOP."

"Where to?"

"Athens," I retorted.

"You gotta be kidding."

"Georgia."

"Oh, yeah. Ponder's arrest for that arson, right? I talked to Jake Andrews last Wednesday. He's a detective in Robbery, Homicide & Forensics. He's a real good ol' boy."

"Call him and get an appointment for tomorrow morning."

I wished I could see the expressions on the guys in the white Ford when they followed my Avanti to the Port City airport.

SNOOP AND I ARRIVED at the Robbery, Homicide & Forensics office of the Athens-Clarke County Police Department at eight o'clock Monday morning. Andrews had told Snoop on the telephone that we had to meet with his boss, Lieutenant Ed Howard first. We waited for Howard to arrive. We introduced ourselves and I handed him a box of bagels.

He smiled. "You boys must need a favor."

"Of course. But regardless, we were both detectives in Port City before we became PIs. I remember how much we appreciated an occasional bagel when we were on the job."

Howard stood. "Let's carry this to the break room. Share it with the other folks."

After we took a table in the break room, Howard held his coffee cup in both hands and stared at me over the rim. "What can I do for you folks?"

"We're investigating a man named James Kennedy Ponder. Y'all arrested him for arson and homicide a few years ago. He torched an apartment construction site where a night watchman was killed. Jake Andrews worked the case. When we called Jake for an appointment, he said we should talk to you before meeting with him."

"I recall something about that case. How can we help?"

"We believe Ponder was guilty, even though the case was dismissed. We want to get him on a second murder."

"Then why aren't the Port City police detectives up here instead of you two private investigators?"

"Good question. Lieutenant Jorge Castellano in Port City Robbery/Homicide can answer that. Here's his number." I handed one of Jorge's business cards to Howard.

He stuck the card in his pocket. "Let's go to my office. Bring your coffee." He snagged another bagel as he led the way from the break room.

"Lieutenant Castellano?" he said into his office phone, "This is Lieutenant Ed Howard of the Athens-Clarke County Police Department... Yeah, they're here in my office." He smiled. "Yeah, they brought bagels. Okay, stand by." He punched a button on the base of his phone and returned the handset to its cradle. "I have you on speaker, Lieutenant."

Jorge's voice squawked from the small speaker. "Call me Jorge. Ed, we're working another case in Port City involving James Kennedy Ponder. Our investigation has not progressed to the point where my captain will approve the expense of me sending two detectives to Athens on what might be a wild goose chase, what with our budget pressures. You follow me?"

Howard chuckled. "I got a captain like that too. He's tight as a pair of two-dollar shoes."

"Budgets are the same the world over. Fortunately, Chuck McCrary has a case that involves Ponder. Chuck owes me a favor and his client has deep pockets. By the way, he and Snoop are both former Port City police detectives. I used to work with both of them. I asked Chuck to review Ponder's prior case in Athens, providing you approve. It would be a big help to me and our departmental budget if you would extend Chuck and Snoop the same professional courtesy you would me if I visited Athens."

Howard glanced at Snoop then at me. "Sure, why not?"

"Thanks, Ed. I owe you one."

Howard punched off the phone. "That file is in the East Precinct office; that's where the fire was, and that's where Jake Andrews is stationed. I'll call Jake and tell him you're coming."

As we left his office, he added, "While I appreciate the bagels, it wouldn't hurt if you picked up a box of donuts for the East Precinct. We Southern boys usually eat donuts, not bagels."

DETECTIVE JAKE ANDREWS SHOVED THE FILE FOLDER across the table toward me. "I remember that case." He reached in the box and came out with a chocolate-covered donut. "That investigation was a monumental screw-up from the get-go."

"How so?" Snoop asked, snagging a glazed donut.

I opened the *Hillside Pines Apartments* folder and reviewed the file. Snoop continued the interview.

"We don't normally discuss our cases with civilians—even civilians that used to be cops. What's your interest in this case?"

"Jake, you look like you're pretty close to retirement."

"Yeah, twenty-eight years in, two to go. So?"

"I retired with thirty years on the job. I had a pretty good closing percentage."

"Yeah, so?"

Snoop lowered his voice. "So, a couple of evildoers got away. Perps who I knew were guilty as sin, but cases I couldn't close because of a technicality, or because someone else in another department screwed something up. There were a couple of cases where I'd have given my left nut to find a way to get the perps. You ever have one like that?"

Andrews stared at the wall behind Snoop without seeing it. "Every cop has cases like that, and the Ponder case comes mighty close."

Snoop said, "Right. This yo-yo shouldn't get away with murder. You told me last week that your department found proof of Ponder's guilt, but the judge threw out the evidence because of an improper warrant."

I thumbed through the file and listened with half a mind.

Andrews rapped the table with his knuckles. "The warrant was not improper; it was non-existent." He shook his head. "We're pretty peaceable around here for a city our size. Academic atmosphere, university town, and so on, y'know?" He bit off a quarter of the donut.

Snoop was getting on well with Andrews, so I let him continue the interview.

Andrews waved the donut. "Most of our homicides are pretty ordinary. Drunken bar fight, abusive spouse, jealous ex-boyfriend. Heck, most of our fires are pretty ordinary, y'know? It was the arson investigator what screwed up the case."

I gazed up from the file and waited for him to continue.

"At first everyone thought the fire was an accident. The night watchman died from smoke inhalation in the construction trailer where he was stationed." He bit off another precise quarter of his donut, chewed twice, and talked around the wad of dough. "I thought the poor guy was maybe sneaking a nap when he should have been patrolling, y'know?"

Snoop nodded. "Been there, done that."

"Winston Taylor was his name, retired civil servant, married to the same woman for forty-seven years. He left a widow, four children, three grandchildren." Andrews picked up his cup again. "My department, we don't investigate fires unless the fire department determines that there's been a crime. Oh, sure, we send a patrol car to every fire call to help with traffic control, but we don't get involved in the investigation. The fire department has trained people who investigate the causes of fires, y'see?"

"Sure," Snoop said. "The Port City PD is the same way."

"That case was a major screw-up," Andrews said. "After that Chicago shyster got Ponder's case booted, we reorganized how we handle fire investigations."

"What happened?" Snoop asked.

"The ME's autopsy determined that the watchman was unconscious before the fire started. He died from smoke inhalation after being whacked on the head with a blunt object, maybe a tire iron. Blood from the wound had congealed a little—maybe fifteen or twenty minutes' worth of scabbing. Murder, plain as a hand-painted sign." He moved the box of donuts my way.

I took another to be sociable. I didn't want a third donut, even a Krispy Kreme. The sugar and the caffeine could make me jumpy. "Sounds like it. What happened to screw the case?"

"The arson investigator—Wallace Covey was his name. He was suspicious about the fire. He reviewed security footage around the construction site and found a clear shot of Ponder walking away with something in his hand that resembled a tire iron. This was at the time the fire started."

"How'd Covey identify him?" Snoop asked.

"From Ponder's car. Security video captured one car other than the watchman's parked near the site. Video showed a partial license plate and a bumper sticker that said 'There is no Planet B.' Actually, it was kinda clever." He leaned over the donut box. "Y'all gonna have another donut?"

"I'm good with this one." Snoop nudged the box across the table.

Andrews selected a powdered sugar and waved it as he spoke. "Anyway, Covey, he's hanging around the autopsy suite like a kid waiting for the candy store to open, when the ME discovers the skull fracture. *Boom*, the ME mentions the fracture to him—unofficially, of course." Powdered sugar floated in the air and settled on the table. Andrews bit off a quarter of his donut, licked the sugar off his lips. "Covey was new with the fire department, right out of training school. Not much experience, but full of piss and vinegar like all these young studs. He calls my department, tells us to get a warrant, and runs over to Ponder's apartment like his pants was on fire—which, I guess, they sorta were."

Snoop swallowed his donut. "Let me guess—Covey went in before you got there with the warrant."

Andrews smacked the table with the flat of his hand, sending a mist of powdered sugar into the air. "It was worse than that. Covey talks to the wrong guy in my department. He talks to the desk sergeant and he says, 'We've got to get a warrant to the hippie's car and house.' We record all calls to the desk sergeant, so I remember that that's exactly what he said." He pivoted back to Snoop. "The sergeant, he ain't sure what Covey wants. I mean, who does *we* refer to? *We've* got to get a warrant. What kind of message is that? And who's *the hippie*? So, the sergeant sticks a message in the box for Charlie Thomas to sort it out. Charlie handled crowd control while the firemen fought the fire."

Snoop said, "So I'll bet that Charlie didn't get the message until he came off patrol and looks in the box at the end of his shift."

Andrews popped the remainder of the donut in his mouth and washed it down with coffee. "Right. Charlie had been a patrolman for fifteen years at that time, but he don't act like he'd had fifteen years of experience; he acts like he's had one year of experience fifteen times. He ain't the sharpest knife in the drawer."

I grunted.

"That's why he's still a patrolman," Andrews continued. "Hell, it's five years later, and Charlie has had his one year of experience *twenty* times." Andrews smiled at his own cleverness. "Charlie don't know what to do with the message so he stuffs it in his pocket. Figures he'll bring it up with the sergeant at the next morning's muster."

"So, what happened the next morning?" I finished the last of my coffee.

"Nothing. Not a damned thing." Andrews winced. "Charlie sticks the note in his uniform pocket and drops the shirt in the dirty clothes hamper at home." Andrews pounded the table again. "We never got a warrant—never. Every bit of evidence that the idiot Covey collected— Ponder's cellphone, computer, his clothes with the guard's blood spatter on them—even the tire iron he found in the perp's trunk—every piece of evidence was ruled inadmissible." His shoulders slumped. "With no evidence, the case couldn't proceed."

I set my empty cup aside. "You might've discovered that evidence with your normal police investigation. Didn't the DA argue for the inevitable discovery exception to the exclusionary rule?"

Andrews eyed my cup. "I'm out of coffee too. Let's get more. Wash down the rest of those donuts." He fetched the coffee pot and poured for the three of us.

For a guy who didn't discuss cases with civilians, Andrews was talking a lot. I decided not to ask for creamer for the coffee.

Snoop said, "We were talking about y'all arguing for inevitable discovery."

Andrew took the folder and flipped toward the back. He stabbed a sheet of paper with a stiff forefinger. "Eliazar—yeah, that was the scumball's name, Walter Eliazar. I couldn't remember the shyster's name. Fancy-pants, high-powered Chicago lawyer comes in here, and our DA is outmatched. I remember this sleazy shyster, this Walter Eliazar guy. Me and the DA called him 'Wally the Weasel'. Less than twenty-four hours after we arrest Ponder, Wally appears like a magician."

I hadn't gotten far enough back in reviewing the folder to learn the lawyer's name. "That's unusual, a Chicago attorney representing a college student in Athens, Georgia. How did Ponder come to be represented by a Chicago lawyer? Was there any previous connection between him and Eliazar?"

"Beats me. The hippie must have had this jerk on speed-dial. Wally the Weasel swoops in here with a whole stack of motions already printed out. He files them with the court within an hour of meeting with the hippie the first time."

"So what happened next?" Snoop asked.

Andrews squinted one eye at me. "The Weasel gets the evidence tossed, gets the evidence returned to Ponder, and gets the charges dropped." He handed the file across the table. "By the time we get another warrant to search Ponder's car and house, the evidence is gone. *Poof.* Ponder reports his car stolen; when we found it, it had been set on fire. Whatever evidence might have been in the trunk went up in smoke. His apartment had been cleaned like a hospital operating room. The tire iron is probably at the bottom of a lake somewhere. We never found one shred of evidence. Case is still open but inactive. We got nothing to work."

I opened the folder and thumbed to another page I had noticed earlier. "Jake, is this the inventory of what was missing from the construction site?"

He glanced at the upside-down page. "Yeah, why?"

"Two twenty-five kilo cases of Tovex water gel explosive."

Chapter 33

SNOOP DROVE ON THE WAY TO THE ATLANTA AIRPORT so I could call my researcher. "Flamer, I got more info on Ponder." I told him about the Chicago attorney.

"I'll investigate the attorney after I email my report on Katherine Shamanski and family. Check your email in ten minutes." The line went dead.

I looked at Snoop behind the wheel. "Flamer is emailing me a report on the Shamanski family. Can you come to my office first thing tomorrow to go over it with me?"

Snoop shook his head. "I'm working another case for an attorney. I stalled him to go on this road trip with you. I can't put him off any longer. I'll be all day. Try to figure out something by yourself, without my years of experience and sagacity."

"*Sagacity?*"

"Yeah, an eight-letter word meaning 'keen perception.'"

"Then I shall persevere without you," I said.

"*Persevere?*"

"If you can be sagacious, I can persevere."

###

I SLID A COPY OF FLAMER'S SHAMANSKI REPORT across the table
to Snoop. "Study this while I get another coffee. It's pretty
disturbing."

I got my coffee and came back. "What do you think?"

"Give me your analysis first."

I leaned back in my chair. "Here's how this thing works:
Morris Shamanski is a personal injury attorney. So is his wife,
Virginia McAllister, although they're not partners. He makes a
ton of money suing corporations and insurance companies and
invests it in various companies, some of which the corporate
department of his firm does the legal work for. So, the firm
makes money that way too. Most of the companies he invests in
are involved in green businesses."

Snoop said, "The solar energy and environmental stuff."

"Right. Flamer says that Virginia McAllister donates
buckets of money to politicians. The government regulators
reciprocate with loan guarantees and subsidies to the companies
that Morris Shamanski invests in. One hand washes the other.
Lots of people don't make the connection between McAllister's
political contributions and Morris Shamanski's subsidies
because they have different last names."

"You do remember that Flamer's a dyed-in-the-wool
libertarian. He's opposed to all government programs, right?"

"Yeah, so?"

"So maybe he shaded this report a little." Snoop tapped on
the report. "Everything in here made legal sense to somebody or
the Feds wouldn't have handed over the money. And I didn't
read in here where anybody went to jail. So, there's nothing
criminal here."

"*Hmm.* Maybe."

"And even if it's true, what's it got to do with the price of
eggs?"

"Michelle thought Katherine's father was an entrepreneur, but that's an outgrowth of his personal injury law practice. They're from Chicago and Walter Eliazar, the lawyer that got Ponder off on that Athens arson and murder, is from Chicago. Find out if there's any connection."

Chapter 34

I CALLED FLAMER.

"If you're calling about the rest of the report on Katherine Shamanski, it's ready. I'm emailing it now."

"I called to talk to you about your report on Morris Shamanski and Virginia McAllister."

"So talk."

"You made it sound like what they did was criminal. I did my own research on this. No one's gone to jail over any of her political contributions or his investment subsidies. *The New York Times* even called one scandal that you included a 'phony scandal.'"

"Everything in that report is a verifiable fact I teased out of dozens of reports filed with the Federal Election Commission and other federal government open-record websites. You can interpret the cause and effect yourself. I stand by my report. Who you gonna believe, me or the idiot media *New York Times*?"

"Good point."

Flamer hung up without a word.

"Flamer is sending the rest of his report on Katherine Shamanski. We need a wall map of the Southeast United States. Trot over to a book store and pick one up, will you?"

"How about I drive over to the book store? I don't trot unless someone is shooting at me. Then I run like hell."

Flamer's email report arrived seconds after Snoop left the office. As I suspected, Shamanski had not visited her parents in Chicago every weekend. Credit card charges confirmed that she'd flown to Chicago about once a month. The other weekends for each of the last three months, she had made credit card charges for gasoline and motels several places around north Florida and in Alabama, Georgia, and South Carolina.

Snoop walked in with a cup of coffee in one hand and a map tucked under his arm. "Where you want the map?"

"Tape it on the corkboard. There's masking tape in the supply closet." I finished my first pass through Flamer's report.

After Snoop mounted the map, I found a yellow highlighter in the desk drawer.

"How much does a bag of ammonium nitrate fertilizer sell for?"

Snoop tapped the keyboard. "About a hundred bucks online, plus or minus, for a fifty-pound bag, more at a small-town garden store. Say a hundred ten plus tax—a hundred twenty to be safe."

"If she picked up, say, four bags, she'd need five hundred dollars cash before she left town. I don't think she'd withdraw five hundred dollars at one time. That would be pretty rich for a college student, even one with wealthy parents."

"Unless she was stupid and used ATMs along the way, maybe in towns where she bought fertilizer. Then she could make more frequent, but smaller withdrawals."

"Stupid or careless. Either one would help." I scanned Katherine's travel charges. "First out-of-town charge is Ocala, Florida on Friday, January 13 at a Cumberland Farms. From the amount, it has to be for gas. Ocala is about a tank full from Port City. She rented a room at a Holiday Inn Express." I marked the highway from Port City to Ocala. "Then she charged lunch in

Quakerville, Georgia at a local café and drove through Valdosta. Quakerville's twenty miles from Valdosta." I extended the line to Valdosta and Quakerville. "She made a larger charge, maybe dinner, in Cairo, Georgia. Then another Holiday Inn Express charge in Thomasville." I drew the line to Cairo, back to Thomasville. "Okay, Snoop, what's the distance from Quakerville to Cairo?"

"A little over forty miles. That's not much distance between lunch and dinner."

"Unless she made stops, maybe in small towns in southern Georgia. Probably looped around Thomasville, stopping to buy fertilizer." I peered in my coffee cup. It was empty. "Let's think like she did. If I'm going to buy bomb-making material, I'd want to buy it in a small town in the next state, where I won't be noticed."

"I don't think so, bud. She's more likely to be remembered in a small town than in a large city."

"Yeah, but the big city stores would be more computerized. They'd have security cameras and maybe more regulations regarding ammonium nitrate fertilizer sales. On a practical note, it's easier to visit stores in smaller towns. If she bought in a bigger city like Thomasville or Valdosta, we'd have two chances of finding where she bought it—slim and none."

"And slim left town," Snoop finished. "Okay, we assume she started in Quakerville." He punched the keyboard. "Two fertilizer stores in Quakerville."

"Assume she bought her first bag in Quakerville. She stows it in her trunk. She's excited about constructing her big bomb. What does she do next? She finds another fertilizer store in a small town near Quakerville. I need more coffee. Helps me think. I'll be right back."

I headed to the break room and hit paydirt. Another tenant in the office suite had abandoned a half-box of croissants on the counter. And they weren't too stale. I carried one back for Snoop.

Snoop sampled it. "It's more or less fresh, thanks. While you were refueling your stomach and your coffee cup, I've been working like a draft horse. Next small town with a fertilizer store is Barton, sixteen miles from Quakerville."

I extended the line to Barton. "So, she buys another bag there. She gets stoked; she's on a roll. Where would she go next?"

"Coleridge, Georgia, fifteen miles."

"Great." I marked the line. "Then where?"

"Meade, twenty miles."

I highlighted the route. "So, we have Quakerville... Barton... Coleridge... then Meade. But we know she ate dinner in Cairo. How far from Meade to Cairo?"

"Sixteen miles."

"Hmm. That would be five stops... No, I don't think so."

"What do you mean?"

"That's a bridge too far," I replied. "She wouldn't buy five bags; that's too many for a clandestine shopping trip. No, it's one or two stops too many." I drank coffee and thought. "Maybe one store she stopped at didn't feel right. Maybe it had an obvious security camera, or maybe a cop car drove by and spooked her. Whatever, she bypassed it. Or maybe one store didn't carry ammonium nitrate. That would explain the extra stop."

"Yeah, or maybe one store wasn't open on Saturday, or it closed by the time she got there. Or maybe ammonium nitrate is a seasonal fertilizer and the stores wouldn't carry it in the winter. Remember, it was January."

"Good points. Also, by the time she drove to Cairo, it would have been dark in January. And she had to drive to Thomasville to rent a hotel." I reviewed the credit card charges again. "Sunday, January 15, there's a car rental in Valdosta, Georgia. Doesn't make sense. Oh, wait. It was charged to her card when she returned it. She rented a car to have Georgia license plates when she bought the fertilizer."

Snoop said, "That means she went back to Valdosta to retrieve her own car and transfer the fertilizer from the trunk of the rental."

"Yeah, on Sunday, she bought gas again north of the Florida line at the last stop in Georgia."

I sat in a visitor's chair across from Snoop and read Flamer's report. "She withdrew four hundred dollars from a Port City ATM on Friday before she left. That wouldn't buy four bags of fertilizer after you allow for sales tax and maybe paying a little more than a hundred bucks a bag."

"So, she bought three bags," Snoop said.

"Or she got more money from another ATM. I'll keep checking. Nope. Of course, she might have had cash on hand before the ATM withdrawal."

"So, she bought a max of four bags. How many did they need in all?"

"Lopez said fifteen hundred pounds of explosive. That would be at least fourteen hundred pounds of ammonium nitrate—minimum of twenty-eight bags, maybe thirty—plus other ingredients and a blasting cap or other ignition device."

"Like the Tovex that Ponder stole in Athens Georgia?" Snoop asked.

"Exactly like that," I responded.

Chapter 35

THE SOUTH GEORGIA AG & CHEMICAL COMPANY occupied two acres surrounded by a six-foot chain link fence topped by barbed wire. A twenty-foot electric sliding gate was open, allowing access to the graveled parking lot and the steel buildings inside. A red on white sign fastened beside the gate advised us to *Please stop by the front office for a delivery ticket before entering the warehouse.* Three pickup trucks with Georgia plates were parked at the one-story office that squatted beside a drive-on truck scale. An assortment of steel buildings and huge cylindrical tanks were scattered across the rear. Two pieces of heavy equipment with chipped yellow paint nosed up against the left fence.

Snoop snapped photos of the site through the windshield as I bumped my Dodge Caravan across the gate track. I had hidden in the rear of the van the previous morning while Snoop drove us out of the condo garage. The three stooges from Chicago sat in their white Ford and paid no mind to the van. They must not know that I owned the van, and Snoop aroused no suspicion because he'd been parked behind them when we had trapped them the previous week. I doubt they saw his face. We had driven to Valdosta and spent the night. Today we were hot on the trail of Katherine Shamanski.

"If I were Shamanski, this is the last place I would hope to buy fertilizer and not be noticed. Cute girl like that, she'd stand out like a strobe light in a candelabra."

"You're right, Snoop. Still, we came all the way to Quakerville, we may as well ask."

There were four ill-defined parking spots for the office and the three pickups managed to occupy them all. I U-turned on the gravel lot and parked against the front fence. Dust swirled around our shoes when we walked to the door.

"Can I help y'all?" the man behind the desk said. He wore a battered straw cowboy hat, a short-sleeved plaid shirt and denim overalls.

"I'm Chuck McCrary. This is my associate Ray Snopolski."

"Charlie Wheeler." He stuck his hand across the desk. "Pleased to meet you." We shook hands. He gestured at two wooden office chairs with frayed seat pads that sat near his desk. "Set if you like."

"Thanks, Mr. Wheeler." I slid Shamanski's photo from my pocket. "We'd like to know if this woman purchased any ammonium nitrate fertilizer from your company last January."

"She's a looker, I'll say that. I'm pretty sure I'd remember if a pretty girl like that came in here. Mostly it's farmers and such." He looked to his left. "Hey, Will, Zack. Either of y'all sell any ammonium nitrate to this girl last January?" He held the photo where the two men could see it.

"Nope, I'd remember her. She's a real looker, ain't she?"

Wheeler handed the photo back. "Sorry, fellas."

Snoop and I returned to the van and crunched our way across the lot back to the two-lane county road we had come in on. Snoop said, "Southern Pines Farmers Co-op is on this same road, two miles to the left."

I waited for an eighteen-wheeler to pass and followed it. The road's center stripe soon dissolved into a ghostly shadow where the yellow paint had been applied decades before. The paving degenerated so gradually that I couldn't tell where the asphalt ended and the gravel began. I dropped back from the truck to avoid the rocks thrown up by its rear wheels.

"Looks like the truck's headed the same place," Snoop said. He consulted his phone. "No point trying to pass; we're only a mile away."

We passed a group of one-story brick houses with weed-filled yards that sat abandoned behind another of the ubiquitous chain-link fences. A half-mile farther a well-tended cemetery nosed up to the road. The cemetery ended at an intersection with a four-way stop.

The eighteen-wheeler lurched through its gears as it passed the stop sign and rumbled another quarter-mile. Brakes lights flashed as it eased through the gate at the Co-op. We waited for it to back up to the loading dock before entering the parking area.

Snoop opened the passenger door. "This looks like another spot a pretty girl wouldn't come to buy fertilizer."

"I know. Still… we gotta ask."

We did and got the same answer as before. On to Barton, population 386, where Southern Pines Farmers Co-op had another location.

WE PASSED TEN MILES OF PECAN ORCHARDS and another ten of peach orchards along the highway to Barton. A few blocks before we reached the center of town, the two-lane county road widened to accommodate three blocks of downtown stores, now mostly shuttered.

It felt like driving onto a western movie set. On the south side of Main Street, corrugated steel awnings leaned out from the storefronts and shaded the sidewalks like a John Wayne town. The north side had a few tin awnings too, coupled with a one-story frame antique store next to the concrete-block post office. A sedan and two pickups were parked in its adjoining parking lot. A dog lay sleeping on one side of the lot.

Two pickups were parked at the co-op, so I parked in front of the Downtown Grill, which served, according to its sign, *The Best BBQ in Georgia.*

Snoop inhaled as we exited the van. "Ah, southern barbecue. Let's eat lunch first."

"Sounds like a plan, Snoop."

The barbecue was excellent.

A corroded Coke cooler sat against the front of the co-op in the shade of the awning. "How about a root beer, Snoop?" I selected two from the icy water and handed him one. We opened the bottles on the opener on the front of the cooler.

I held the co-op door for a gray-haired man in a straw cowboy hat exiting carrying a box with six quarts of motor oil.

"Thanks, young fellow."

"My pleasure, sir." I walked over to the cashier. A teenage girl in a red Barton High School Volleyball tee-shirt perched on a high stool behind the counter.

I lifted my root beer. "Is this where I pay for the drinks?"

"Yes, sir. That'll be two dollars and twelve cents."

I fished money from my pocket. "Snoop, you got two pennies? Thanks. Here you are, young lady." I handed her correct change. "Who would I ask about buying fertilizer?"

"That would be my daddy." She leaned toward the rear of the building. "Daddy," she screeched, "someone up here wants you." She turned to me and smiled. "Daddy will be here quick as anything." She eyed me up and down, then Snoop. "Y'all don't look like no farmers."

"That's because we're not. We want to know if this woman bought any fertilizer here last January." I handed her the photo of Shamanski.

She studied the picture. "Are y'all detectives, or something?"

"We're private investigators. Have you seen this woman?"

"Oh, sure. I remember her. I never seen her before nor since, but I sure do remember her."

"Oh?"

"She was driving a brand new red Jeep Grand Cherokee. Parked it right out there in front." She pointed. "I been wanting me one of them ever since forever. Daddy promised to get me one, soon as I get my license and graduate high school. 'Course, mine'll be used." She handed me back the photo as a middle-aged man walked over.

He stuck out his hand. "I'm Jeff Wilkins. Can I help you folks?"

We introduced ourselves. I handed him Shamanski's picture. "Your daughter was telling me that this woman was here last January."

Wilkins studied the picture. "Yeah, she seems sorta familiar. Can't be sure though." He handed the picture back.

The girl said, "Sure you remember her, Daddy. She's the one was driving that red Cherokee. Like the one you promised to give me for a graduation present."

Wilkins frowned. "I never promised, Melissa. I said if you keep your grades up and make at least a B-plus average."

"I'm carrying a low A right now, Daddy."

Wilkins focused back to me. "Yeah, she was here. If you say it was January, then it was. Don't recollect exactly. I do remember that it was cold as a blizzard with no snow when I loaded her bag in the Jeep. Why you asking? You a cop?"

"Private investigators. Do you remember what she bought?"

"Yeah, now that Melissa reminded me. It was real strange. She sure weren't no farmer. But she wanted a bag of fertilizer."

"What kind?"

"Ammonium nitrate, why?"

IN COLERIDGE, WE VISITED THREE STORES before we found where Shamanski had bought her second bag. And in Meade, we struck out at both stores. In Cairo, we hit a gold mine. The second store we called on had security cameras and even archived their footage. We copied the security video of her loading the ammonium nitrate in the Jeep.

"Let's eat dinner where Shamanski ate, Snoop. Maybe they'll remember her."

"Or have video."

No such luck. It was five hundred miles back to Port City, so we rented two rooms in Cairo.

I fell asleep that night thinking we'd made good progress.

My cellphone rang while Snoop and I were at breakfast. I peered at the screen. *Why would John Babcock call me at 8:05 on a Saturday morning? This can't be good.*

Chapter 36

JOHN BABCOCK'S STOMACH TURNED CARTWHEELS. Chuck had warned him this might happen. He had said, "Eventualities tend to eventuate; therefore, we plan for them." Chuck rehearsed this situation with him and Penny. Penny was the strong one. It had been almost two weeks and nothing bad had happened. *Well, that weirdo Ponder tried to talk to Mickie, but that's all*. John had relaxed and let his emotional guard down. And now this. Penny handled these things better than he did, but she had gone out for a jog, and John was alone. *Keep calm*, he commanded himself. *Do this like you rehearsed it with Chuck. Keep calm. And smile, dammit!*

John smiled through the screen door at the two people on his porch. The man wore a dark suit, white shirt, and striped tie. The woman was in a tan pants suit with matching low-heeled closed toed shoes. Her short hair didn't reach to the collar of her off-white silk blouse.

Swallowing hard to keep his breakfast down, he unlatched the screen door and held it open. The visitors on the porch stepped back to make room. John stepped onto the front porch and closed the door behind him. "I'm confused why the FBI would appear at my house out of the blue. What's this about?"

"May we come in?"

"The house is a mess. What's this about?"

"We'd like to talk to Michelle Babcock. Is she here?"

"Why do you want to talk with my daughter? Is she in trouble?"

"We're not at liberty to discuss that. May we talk to Michelle?"

"I think I should call my counsel." He was careful to say *counsel* instead of *lawyer*, like Chuck had told him. John punched up his cellphone and stared at Chuck's picture on the screen while he waited to connect. He held the phone to his ear.

"Good morning, John. This is Chuck. What's going on?"

John faced away from the unwelcome visitors. "There are two FBI agents at the front door. They want to talk to Michelle."

"Are they with you now? Can they hear what you're saying?"

"The three of us are on the front porch."

"Remember what we practiced: Be friendly and smile. Tell the agents that you're confused by this sudden visit. Ask them to excuse you while you step inside to talk to your counsel. Tell them you'll talk to them when you finish this call. They might agree to that. They may insist on coming inside or you staying outside with them. They may not want to let you out of their sight. If they do let you go inside, leave the door open so they can see you. We don't want them to think you intend to run."

John held the phone to his chest and regarded the two agents. "I'm confused. Would you folks excuse me for a minute while I talk to my counsel inside? After I finish talking to him, I'll invite you both inside. Okay?"

The lead agent leaned toward her colleague and said something John couldn't make out. She switched back to John. "Sorry, sir, we have to keep you in sight. Bureau regulations. You can finish the call out here or we'll need to come inside."

"Hang on, Chuck." He held the screen door open while the two agents stepped inside. "How about if I finish the call in the powder room here?" He opened a door off the foyer.

The male agent reached through the doorway and switched on the light. He peeked behind the door then nodded to the other agent.

"That'll be fine, sir."

John closed the powder room door behind him. "Okay, I'm alone."

"Do they have a warrant?"

"I don't know. Should I ask?"

"No. If they had an arrest warrant or a search warrant, they would have said so, and they wouldn't agree to let you close the door. Is Michelle where she was last weekend?"

"No, she's at Hank and Lorene's condo on Mango Island."

"Good. Is Penny with you?"

"She went for a jog. She should be back any time."

"Okay. After we hang up, I'll call Abe Weisman's office and tell them to expect a call from you. Invite the agents in, offer them coffee, do the whole *good host* thing. Then call Abe or Diane. It's okay to call right in front of the agents. In fact, it's better if they hear you call. If Penny comes home while the agents are there, tell her in the presence of the agents that you called me and that you called Abe. She knows what to do like we rehearsed. They won't ask you any questions after you tell them you are represented by counsel. But if they do, do you remember how to respond?"

"I say, 'My wife and I will be happy to talk to you with our attorney present.' We say that no matter what they ask." He breathed with an effort.

"John, I know this freaks you out a bit, but you'll get through this okay. You haven't broken any laws and, if you do what we practiced, you'll be okay. I know you can do this. Keep saying 'My wife and I will be happy to talk to you with our attorney present.' Keep saying that until they give up and leave. Are you going to be okay?"

John's stomach churned again. "Where are you, Chuck? How long for you to get here?"

"I'm in Georgia. I'm driving back after Snoop and I finish breakfast, but I won't be back until late this afternoon. Remember: If they ask to look around, tell them you have to ask your attorney. If they don't have a warrant, they can search only if you give them permission, and you won't do that. You and I both know you have nothing to hide—nothing to be afraid of. Don't answer any other questions. Call Abe and stonewall them until they leave."

John's throat tightened up. He forced the words out. "What are you doing in Georgia?"

"What you're paying me to do—investigate for Michelle. That's all I can tell you."

John thought about Chuck being hundreds of miles away. And Penny wasn't here. He was alone, confronting two FBI agents. His body shook. "Gotta go, Chuck."

He dropped to his knees at the toilet, retching. The whole world was coming up his throat. Not merely his breakfast, but maybe even last night's dinner. He hoped the FBI agents couldn't hear him. He vomited until he had the dry heaves. He hauled himself to his feet and washed his face. Cupping his hands under the water, he rinsed his mouth. He assessed his reflection in the mirror and smoothed his hair down with his wet hands. He pulled a paper cup from the dispenser. This time he drank the water to have something in his stomach.

You can do this, he thought. *What would Penny do?* He surveyed the half-bath, cleaned the toilet rim with a wad of toilet paper, and lowered the lid. He straightened the contour mat around the base of the toilet, fluffed up the hand towel, and took a deep breath. *Into the valley of the shadow of death. Do it for Mickie.*

Chapter 37

Special Agent Emily Fuller set her coffee cup in the center of the saucer. "We'd like to speak to Michelle Babcock. Is she here?"

John sipped his own coffee before replying. *What is keeping Penny?* "No, she's gone away for the weekend."

"Where is she?"

"Before we go any further, I think I'd better call my attorney."

"Didn't you call him while we waited on the porch?"

"This is a different person I need to call." He scrolled through the contacts on his cellphone. He picked up a landline and punched in a number. "Abe Weisman, please... John Babcock... Okay, I'll speak to her... Hello, Diane... Diane, there are two FBI agents here... Are you sure?... Okay." He punched a button on the handset and laid it on the coffee table.

A too loud voice came from the phone. "This is Diane Toklas with the law offices of Abe Weisman. Our firm represents the Babcock family. To whom am I speaking?"

Agent Fuller sat up straighter and adjusted her jacket unconsciously. "FBI Special Agents Emily Fuller and Hector Marsalis."

"Agents, would you please tell me the nature of this unannounced visit?"

"We'd like to interview Michelle Babcock."

"In connection with what?"

"We're not at liberty to say."

"Do you have any type of warrant?"

"No, ma'am. We want to interview Ms. Babcock."

"Fine. I will make Ms. Babcock available to meet with you in our office Monday afternoon at one o'clock."

Agent Marsalis lifted a notepad. "Please spell your name, Ms. Toklas."

She spelled both names. "Would you like the address of my office?"

Agent Fuller said, "Yes, please."

Diane gave her the address. Agent Marsalis wrote it down.

"And now, agents, I am instructing my client to say nothing else. John, are you there?"

John picked up the handset. "Yes, Diane. I took it off speaker... Are you sure? Okay." He switched the handset back on speaker and positioned it in the center of the table.

Diane's too loud voice said, "John, the agents will be leaving now. You have my permission to tell them goodbye. Say nothing else."

Chapter 38

WE STOPPED THE MINIVAN IN THE PORT CITY SUBURBS and I hid in the rear while Snoop drove us back to my condo garage. "Yeah, the three stooges are on duty in your guest parking lot. They must want Michelle pretty bad to go to this much trouble. Or maybe they want you." I felt the van pause while the garage gate rose.

"*Nah*. They sent only three shooters after me. It's practically an insult."

Snoop drove up the ramp. "You joke, but how do you know they don't intend to hit you? Maybe this has nothing to do with Michelle."

I sat up in the rear seat. "If they wanted to hit me, they'd use a sniper from another high-rise with a view of my balcony. It wouldn't be a difficult shot, maybe a hundred yards."

"Chuck, they know you live in these condos by following you. But this is a big building, and they don't know which apartment is yours since you own it in a Florida Land Trust. No one can find out who owns it."

"Sure they can. The utilities are in my name, and the security on the utility company can't be that great. A little bribe to someone in the water department office and they get the address."

Snoop scoffed and drove the van into a parking spot next to his car. "Okay, smart guy. The stooges are from Chicago. Wally the Weasel, who defended Ponder, is from Chicago. He's a criminal lawyer, probably has lots of mob contacts, even if he's not a mob lawyer. I'll bet you that Walter Eliazar is involved in this somewhere."

I slid open the passenger door and stood between my van and Snoop's car. "Maybe you're right, Snoop. But I think they're after Michelle, and I'm their best lead because I told her parents to stay in their house for a few days. And they may not figure out that Michelle's grandparents are Hank and Lorene Hickham."

Snoop exited the van. "God help us if they do find out. Or rather, God help Hank and Lorene."

I said, "I'll warn them tonight to stay in their Mango Island condo until I clean up this mess."

"They'll be safe there. No way could the stooges get to her on Mango Island. Island security is too good."

"You forget Vicente Vidali? Nobody could get to him on Mango Island either—supposedly. I don't want the three stooges to know that there's anybody on Mango Island. They're sure to follow the Avanti when I leave. You park your car near the north entrance to the Port City Outlet Mall. I'll park at the east entrance and lose them in the mall. I'll meet you at the north entrance and drive your car to Mango Island."

"You want me to drive the Avanti back to my house?"

"*Nah*. Leave it. Call Uber for a ride home."

The white Ford did follow me when I drove away in the Avanti. They might not know that I owned the van since I bought it in the name of an LLC and registered it at a blind post office box. I wanted to keep it that way. They trailed me to the outlet mall and two of them followed me inside, where I lost them. I wondered if they would stake out my car until the mall closed.

MICHELLE CUT HER EYES BACK AND FORTH between Hank and Lorene Hickham. Then she settled on me. "How did the FBI find me?"

The four of us sat at a quiet table eating dinner in the posh Mango Island Caribbean Club restaurant—although adding *posh* to anything about Mango Island was redundant. The last time I'd been in the Caribbean Club was at a Super Bowl party before I'd confronted Vicente Vidali on his home turf. Even on a crowded Saturday night, the rich upholstery and drapes swallowed the sounds. The private island for mega millionaires, movie stars, and mobsters was the plushest neighborhood in Florida. Hank Hickham fit the mega millionaire category. His penthouse condo on Mango Island wasn't his main house. He used it for fun and the occasional guest. Right now, he had hidden Michelle there.

"Michelle, you and I have a confidential relationship. That means I can't discuss this with anyone but you." I glanced at her grandparents. "Hank, you and Lorene understand."

"Sure thing, Chuck," Hank said. "Why don't you and Michelle stroll outside while me and Lorene pour us another glass of wine. We'll wait here 'til you get back." He reached for the wine bottle and laughed. "But don't expect any wine to be left."

Michelle and I walked through the French doors onto the patio. We wove our way through the outdoor tables and down the coral steps. Soon we reached the landscaped garden, dimly lit by the lights from the patio. I led us across the garden and swiveled 360 degrees. We were alone. "Over there."

I led Michelle to a marble bench near the beach. Frogs croaked in the quiet night. Soft waves lapped the beach every few seconds. Scattered puffy clouds were visible from the reflected lights of Port City. A good location to deliver bad news.

Michelle pressed her knees close together. She stared at her hands clasped in her lap. "How'd they find me?" she said in a small voice.

"Agent Lopez must have traced my cellphone's location and calls back to when the bridge exploded. They would have found out that I received a phone call from you in the middle of the night and that I was in the Day and Night Diner early the next morning. They would know your phone was there too. They traced your phone back and discovered you were in the same house with Ponder. And they know I was there too. I'd bet that they Googled Ponder, noticed his beard like the guy in the video, and made the connection. You're their lead to their main suspect."

"Why don't they go to James's house?"

"I'm sure they did. But Ponder is no fool; he must be hiding out. He's a person of interest in two murders."

Michelle gave me a deer-in-the-headlights expression. "What am I supposed to do now?"

"You stay in hiding until Monday afternoon. Snoop will bring you to Diane Toklas's office. I'll be there too. When you meet with the FBI in her office, you let her do the talking. She'll handle everything."

Her lower lip quivered. "Why don't you come pick me up?"

"Because I'm being followed."

"Followed? I don't understand."

"Three armed men have followed me for the last few days. That's why I drove here in Snoop's car and I'm sending Snoop to get you on Monday." I let that sink in.

The deer-in-the-headlights expression returned. "Can't you call the cops? Make them stop?"

"It doesn't work that way. The cops would want to know who these people are and why they're following me. I can't tell them that. That's why it's important for you to stay hidden."

Michelle bit her lower lip. "Who are they? What do they want?"

"They work for an organized crime family in Chicago. As for what they want, I believe they think I'll lead them to you."

"Why do they want me? Omigod, do they want to kill me?"

"Don't worry; I won't let them."

"Don't worry," she repeated. "You're one man, Chuck. You said they have three men."

"That's why I asked Hank and Lorene to hide you over here. You'll be fine."

"I'll be fine. I'll be fine," she mocked. Michelle jumped to her feet. "For the rest of my freaking life? I can't live like that." She paced back and forth, wringing her hands.

I remained seated. "I promise you it won't be forever. We're making real progress. This will be over soon."

She stopped pacing. "What kind of progress? How soon?"

"I can prove that Katherine bought the materials to make the bomb. I can prove that James has the knowledge to help make the bomb and that he stole the boat. I'm working on proving that Steven Wallace was the ringleader. After I have that, I'll deliver the evidence against the three of them to the FBI without involving you. Then you can go home. Give me a few more days."

"I guess I can do that."

I put my arm around her shoulder. "I know this is scary because I've been there."

"You've been where?"

"Didn't Hank or Lorene tell you I was arrested for murder once? Two of my own cop friends arrested me. It can get pretty scary." I gave her a hug. "You won't be arrested, and you won't go to jail—not even for a little while. That's why I had you hire Abe Weisman's firm. They're the same ones who helped me.

There's nobody better anywhere." I released her shoulder. "There's one other thing you need to know."

"What?"

"More bad news, I'm afraid.

I sat and patted the bench beside me. "You'd better sit down."

Her shoulders slumped. "What's worse than someone trying to kill me?" She sat on the bench.

"If these three gangsters find out who your grandparents are, they might use them to get to you."

"Omigod. Did you tell Grandpa and Grandma?"

"Not yet. That's why I asked them to meet us here on the island. I'll tell them now, and ask them to stay on the island with you for a while. Let's go back and talk to them."

Chapter 39

EARLY SUNDAY MORNING is a good time for breaking and entering an empty building. When I left my condo before dawn, there was no sign of the three stooges. Maybe they figured I would sleep in on Sunday. If so, they weren't hired for their brains.

My target was the unit above Gino's Pizza where Wallace went when I followed him. Gino's was closed on Sunday and that part of Uptown was deserted at dawn.

There was no point testing the front door. Electronic locks are tricky, plus it was on a public street. I parked the van a block away at a discount furniture store that would have a variety of cars coming and going after it opened. One more anonymous white minivan, as noticeable as a pebble in a gravel pit. I wandered up the alley, another homeless person with my worldly goods in a ratty backpack, searching for treasure in the debris behind the stores. I poked around the dumpsters and worked my way to the fire escape behind Gino's Pizza.

The fire escape ladder screeched from disuse when I hauled it down. Inevitably, a homeless person or two would be sleeping somewhere in the alley, but they wouldn't pay attention to the racket or to me. I was merely one more unexplained phenomenon in a world they didn't understand. I climbed to the steel platform. The corrosion on the pulley kept the ladder's counterweight from heaving it back up. I left it down; the odds were that no one would notice it. Besides, I would need it when I left.

The steel fire escape platform served two second-story windows, both of which had burglar alarm sensors. An opaque curtain made it impossible to see in the first window. The other window had no curtain. It held empty cardboard boxes, an old-fashioned wooden office chair with a missing wheel, and a plastic chair mat.

I opened my pack and removed two suction handles like the ones glaziers use to carry sheets of plate glass. Using them and a glass cutter, I removed a section from the center of the window and entered the room.

My first step on the thread-bare carpet made the floor creak loudly in the Sunday morning silence. I froze and listened. Nothing. I sidestepped along the wall where the floor was less likely to creak. Easing the door open, I shined the Maglite both ways down the hall.

To the left, the hall opened into a large room. I inspected the three rooms to the right. Empty.

The room with the opaque curtain was furnished with castoff motel furniture. A safe house maybe?

The door across opened to a room like the one I'd broken into. A 1993 calendar hung on the wall, flipped to November.

I moved to the large room.

A six-foot catering table with a chipped laminate top was jammed against the wall. At the table's other end stood a four-drawer metal file cabinet with scratched green paint. All four windows had burglar alarm sensors. Two more catering tables were jammed together in the center, with two newish folding chairs at each side. A modern classroom-style whiteboard on a stand stood six feet from the two tables.

The third floor was abandoned, but each window was burglar alarmed. Whoever leased the space didn't want intruders, but I hadn't seen anything worth stealing. Why were they so security conscious?

As if responding to my thought, police sirens, more than one, screamed on the street outside. I froze. *Did I trigger a silent alarm? Maybe a pressure sensitive spot under the threadbare carpet in the first room?* I held my breath until the sirens moved past. Their haunting whine diminished and faded away.

I descended the stairs to the street entrance. A new burglar alarm panel was mounted inside the front door. The red light glowed; the system was armed. I opened the access door and photographed it. The installation date was three years earlier. Maybe Flamer could tell something from the alarm permit or from the make and model that would be useful. You never regret the picture you do snap, just the one you didn't.

I returned to the second floor and opened the file cabinet. *Bingo*. Inside was the treasure the security system was all about.

Chapter 40

MANILA FILE FOLDERS WITH COMPANY NAMES on the tabs filled the top two drawers—over a hundred files I guessed. I scanned the company names for anything familiar. The first name that caught my eye was HILLSIDE PINES APARTMENTS, ATHENS, GA. I pulled it for closer examination.

Data in the file was a matter of public record available under the Freedom of Information Act. Transcripts of meetings of the Athens Planning Commission. A topographic map showing where the developers intended to blast the hillside for parking lots, swimming pools, and foundations. The annual report of the corporate developer, 4Square Properties, listed on the New York Stock Exchange. Newspaper clippings about protests at the construction site and the developer's headquarters in Cincinnati. Clippings about the fire, the night watchman's death, Ponder's arrest, and subsequent release.

There was a chart of 4Square Properties' stock price for the fifty-two weeks that ended a week after the fire. Why was Wallace interested in the developer's stock price?

There was nothing criminal in the file. Any good defense attorney could explain everything in the file as legitimate fodder for protests.

I photographed the stock chart and the topographic map.

The next familiar name was *Port City Power*. The file contents were similar. One article included a photo of Wallace chained to the gate of the plant entrance. Someone had circled his face with yellow highlighter.

A fifty-two-week chart of the stock price ending the week after the gate-chaining protest was in the file. A second chart covered the fifty-two weeks ended last Tuesday, the day after the railroad bombing. There were clippings of articles from the *Port City Press-Journal* on the bombing and investigation, one dating to last Wednesday's *Pee-Jay*. Maybe that's why Wallace came here Wednesday afternoon, to add the clipping and stock chart to the file.

In the second file drawer, I scanned the tabs and one name caught my attention, *Great Southeast Forest Products*. I had read the company name in the website about tree spiking that Snoop had found. The file contained newspaper articles on protests of logging in seven different states in the Southeast and the Pacific Northwest. But there had been no tragedy involving Great Southeast that I was aware of. Was that Wallace's next target? There was no stock price chart, so perhaps an attack was not imminent.

I selected three other files at random. Two had stock charts and one did not. I photographed the stock charts. What did the stock prices mean?

I knew who could tell me.

Chapter 41

"TANK, I NEED TO SEE YOU ASAP."

"Your semi-annual portfolio review isn't due for another two months."

"Something's come up. I need your advice on another matter. It doesn't involve me."

"Chuck, you do remember that April seventeenth is one week away, right?"

"What's so special about April seventeenth?"

"April fifteenth is on a weekend this year, so income taxes are due the following Monday, which is April seventeenth." Thomas Tyler—known in his football days as "Tank"—was my CPA and investment advisor. My modest portfolio must have been his smallest client.

"So? You already finished my tax return. I mailed it to the IRS a week ago."

"I know you act like you're my only client sometimes—like right now, but I'm kinda busy for the next few days, pal. Can it wait till next week?"

"Tank, I won't say it's a matter of life and death because two people are already dead. But it's really important. Delay could keep a young lady in danger."

"How about Thursday at seven?"

"You get into the office that early?"

"I meant seven p.m., buddy."

"How about this morning?"

"Chuck, I'm swamped this morning. I have appointments scheduled all day. You're an early riser. How about seven tomorrow morning?"

"Thanks, Tank. I'll meet you at your office."

"Remember, I moved. Don't go to the old office."

"I remember, Tank. Say, will I need an oxygen mask on the sixty-first floor?"

###

DIANE TOKLAS MET ME IN THE FIRM'S RECEPTION. "Come in, Chuck. Abe is in court making his magic, but this FBI thing is a pretty routine life-and-death matter. I've done these a dozen times." Diane smiled and her blue eyes sparkled. "It's always life-and-death to the client, but you and I know better."

I didn't agree with Diane that this wasn't life-and-death, but I didn't argue. I admired the view of her professional pantsuit from the rear as she led me down the hall. Diane was married, and I would never mess with a married woman. Didn't keep me from appreciating beauty though. Short blonde hair, thirtyish. Every time I saw her, she reminded me of a picture I had seen of Hillary Clinton when she was young.

She ushered me into the conference room. Seeti Bay sparkled through the window. A file folder with a big red *Confidential* stamp across the cover lay on one end of the polished walnut table. A giant Chinese lacquered tray holding a coffee set with service for six was in the middle and two deli sandwiches. "I ordered you a corned beef sandwich. Is that okay? Today, we'll make you an honorary Jew."

"I love corned beef. Thanks. Otherwise I wouldn't have had any lunch today."

"We're expecting two FBI agents, Michelle, and Snoop. With you and me, that makes six. Did I count that right?" Diane sat at the head of the table and picked up a sandwich.

"Sounds good." I grabbed a cup off the tray and sat with my back to the window. I loved the view, but I didn't want the distraction. I lifted the insulated silver carafe and poured. Steam rose from the cup. I pushed the carafe toward Diane and unwrapped my corned beef.

She opened the file and handed me a check. "This is for ten dollars, payable to McCrary Investigations. We retained you and Snoop as our investigators on behalf of Michelle Babcock. Actually, we retained you when you first discussed the case with Abe. We're late paying you." She smiled. "Documentation in case we're ever questioned. Everything you and Snoop discuss with Abe and me is privileged."

I pocketed the check. "Thanks. Not that it's likely, but what would happen if a conflict of interest developed between Michelle and her parents?"

"We would resign from representing her parents and continue to represent Michelle. She has the more serious legal exposure, obviously."

"Good. How much did Abe tell you?"

"Everything, of course, but only up to the time the Babcocks hired us." Diane poured her coffee. "A lot has happened in the last two weeks. Bring me up to date."

Between bites of corned beef, I told Diane about our trip to Athens and the road trip around South Georgia. When I got to the part about breaking into the building above Gino's Pizza, she stopped making notes.

"No point in writing that down," she said. "Other than the cut-out window, is there any evidence that you were there?"

I winked.

She smiled. "Of course not. Go on."

I told her about the three stooges who had been following me whenever they could.

"Why don't you tell the police about them?"

"A Port City detective ran rap sheets for me—unofficially. If I make an official complaint, the police will want to know why someone would follow me. Same thing with the FBI. I want to keep the Feds in the dark about my pipeline into the Port City cops and about the three hoods who are following me. Too easy to trace back to Michelle."

Diane blew on her coffee. "I understand. From what you said on the phone, they may know only that she met you at the Day and Night Diner."

"The Feds must know more than that. If they found out about the meeting, they would trace Michelle's phone back to when she was at Ponder's house. She and Ponder probably have smartphones with GPS built in, so the Feds will know the exact address. And Michelle called Ponder, Shamanski, and Wallace frequently. They could get those in seconds." I handed her a picture of Ponder. "If the Feds do a simple Google search for Ponder, they'll find this picture. I downloaded it from his Facebook page. Any idiot can see that he's the bearded man in the train bombing video."

"You said the three men following you are from Chicago. Why the Chicago connection?" Diane cleaned her fingers with a wet-nap from the deli and threw her lunch trash into a wastebasket.

"That's not clear. Lots of clues lead to Chicago though. Katherine Shamanski is from Chicago. Both her parents are personal injury attorneys in Chicago, and Walter Eliazar, the guy who defended Ponder on the Hillside Pines arson, is from Chicago. One of them might be the Chicago connection."

"Which one?"

"Don't know yet," I replied. "I haven't found the connection between Eliazar and Katherine's parents, if any."

Diane asked me a lot of questions. I filled her in on every detail of the investigation. Everything I did, every theory I formed. While she caught up with her note-taking, I finished up my corn chips, cleaned my hands with the wet-nap, and disposed of my trash.

The intercom dinged. "Ms. Toklas, Special Agents Emily Fuller and Hector Marsalis are here for a one o'clock appointment."

"Thanks. I'll be right out. Have you heard from Raymond Snopolski or Michelle Babcock?"

"No, ma'am."

Diane stood up. "You call Snoop while I fetch the agents." She winked. "I'll walk slowly."

Snoop's phone rang several times and went to voicemail. *That's strange.*

Chapter 42

SNOOP FIRST NOTICED THE BLACK SUBURBAN as it glided into the Mango Island ferry terminal parking lot two cars after he did. He lined up his Toyota in the boarding lane to fetch Michelle for their appointment at the lawyers' office. *Hope we don't have to wait too long for the ferry.*

The Suburban didn't join the boarding line; it parked across the lot where the employees parked their cars. Snoop drummed his fingers on the steering wheel for the ten minutes he waited to board the ferry, but no one emerged from the Suburban. He filed that information in the back of his mind. *Suspicious, but not definitive.*

An hour later, he and Michelle returned from Mango Island, and the black Suburban was still lurking in the lot. The huge vehicle stood out like a giant among pygmies with its windows open in the Florida heat. Snoop made out the silhouettes of three men inside who waited with the engine off. The SUV shivered as the engine rumbled to life. Its windows rolled up as the ferry glided to its berth at the dock.

Snoop studied the SUV as he exited the ferry, watched it in his rearview mirror as he rolled east onto the Beachline Causeway. The SUV let two cars in between, and then followed. "I don't want you to worry unnecessarily, Michelle, but someone is following us."

"Omigod. Do you think it's the same guys who followed you and Chuck the other day?"

"Don't worry about it; I'm gonna lose them." He slowed at the Azalea Island Drive traffic light, waiting for it to turn. *Slower...* The car behind him honked. *Wait for it...* The light flicked from green to yellow. Snoop hesitated two more seconds then stomped the accelerator. His Toyota leapt across the intersection with squealing tires as the light cycled to red.

Snoop's phone was sitting in the dashboard cup-holder. It played *The Mexican Hat Dance*. The screen flashed with Chuck's picture. Snoop cut his eyes to a split-second peek in the rearview mirror at the black Suburban lurking two cars behind him.

"Want me to answer that, Snoop?" Michelle asked.

"No. It's Chuck wanting to know why we've been delayed. I don't need the distraction. Oh, geez, they're gonna run it." The SUV drove onto the shoulder, passed the two cars, and ran the red light. Black smoke rose from its tires as it dodged across the intersection, narrowly missing the cross traffic. Cars turning onto Azalea Island Drive honked and brakes squealed. *The Mexican Hat Dance* kept playing.

The Suburban dodged the last of the cross traffic and sped into the left lane, gaining on Snoop's Toyota. Snoop and Michelle were nearly to the next traffic light at Poinciana Island Drive when the windows on the right side of the SUV rolled down. Two black gun barrels stuck through the openings.

"Those are AK-47s," Snoop shouted. "Get on the floor." Michelle unbuckled and squeezed into the foot well, curling into a ball.

The SUV closed on the Toyota. The gunmen raked the rear of Snoop's sedan with a burst of automatic gunfire. His rear windshield and windows shattered under the fusillade.

Snoop slammed on the brakes and jerked the wheel as another *br-a-a-ap* of bullets raked the Toyota's rear door. He slammed his left rear door against the right front fender of the pursuing vehicle. The SUV driver fought for control, the Suburban rocking from side to side as he fought the skid into the oncoming traffic waiting to curve onto Poinciana Island Drive. Snoop straightened out, stomped harder on the accelerator, and willed his Toyota to give him a little more speed. Behind him the SUV skidded sideways and slammed into a traffic barricade.

Chapter 43

I DIDN'T HAVE TIME TO WORRY ABOUT SNOOP not answering his phone because Diane brought the FBI agents into the conference room. Slowly. She was stalling until Snoop and Michelle arrived.

She raised an eyebrow.

I shrugged.

Special Agents Emily Fuller and Hector Marsalis introduced themselves. It was obvious that Fuller was the senior agent. Her gray pinstriped pants suit and yellow scarf reeked of authority. She wore matching low-heeled gray pumps. Marsalis wore a gray pin-striped suit with a yellow tie that in years past was called a *power tie*. I was tempted to ask if they coordinated their outfits, like twins. Cooler heads prevailed.

We shook hands all around and Diane gestured them into chairs. "Would you like coffee? We also have decaf, water, and soft drinks."

Fuller responded for them both. "Regular coffee is fine, thank you."

Diane poured the coffee. Slowly. "My client will be here shortly."

Agent Fuller tugged a tape recorder from her pocket. "I'd like to record this meeting." She deposited it in the center of the table.

"Of course." Diane selected a small device from her briefcase and positioned it beside Fuller's. "I will too." She smiled a saccharine smile. "We wouldn't want there to be any… misunderstanding about who said what."

Fuller jerked her head back a fraction of an inch. "Of course," she said coldly. Fuller switched on the recorder and recited the names of those in attendance, the location, and the time and date. "Ms. Toklas, you told us on the phone last Saturday, April eighth that you would have your client available for an interview at one o'clock, Monday, April tenth. It's one o'clock now."

"Yes, it is," Diane agreed. "My client has been unavoidably detained. Perhaps I can answer questions before she arrives. What did you wish to ask?"

Fuller and Marsalis both pulled out notebooks. Fuller said, "Michelle Babcock met with Carlos McCrary on Monday morning, March 27 at approximately seven a.m., at the Day and Night Diner."

Diane stared at Fuller, expressionless.

Fuller asked, "Well?"

Diane waited before responding. "Well what? I haven't heard a question."

Fuller's face became pink. "Did that meeting occur?"

"Yes."

"So, you're admitting that Michelle Babcock met with Carlos McCrary?"

"Agent Fuller, even though I charge my client by the hour, let's not waste my time or her money. If you intend to repeat every question and ask me to answer twice, this meeting will take much longer than necessary. Do you have any more questions?"

Fuller's face became redder. "What was the substance of that meeting?"

"That's privileged."

Fuller faced me. "Mr. McCrary, are you Michelle Babcock's attorney?"

"I'm not anybody's attorney. I'm a private investigator."

Fuller smirked. "Then your conversation with Ms. Babcock is not privileged."

Diane cleared her throat. "Agent Fuller, please address your questions, comments—or legal opinions—to me. If I want Mr. McCrary to respond, I will tell him so. But, for the record, my firm retained McCrary Investigations to help us with our representation of Ms. Babcock. Therefore, his conversations with Ms. Babcock are in his capacity as our agent and are covered by our attorney-client privilege."

Marsalis had scribbled in his notebook the whole time.

Fuller's lips compressed into a straight line. "When did Ms. Babcock retain your law firm?"

"At five a.m. Monday, March 27," Diane responded.

"Ms. Toklas, were you at that meeting at the Day and Night Diner?"

"The substance of that meeting, including the people in attendance, is privileged."

The intercom dinged. "Ms. Toklas, Ms. Babcock and Mr. Snopolski are here."

Diane spoke to the intercom. "Bring them in, please." She focused back to Agent Fuller. "We'll wait."

Agent Marsalis spent the uncomfortable silence staring out the window and sipping his coffee. Agent Fuller spent the time glaring at the blonde attorney.

Diane refilled her cup. "You want more, Chuck?"

"Thanks."

She poured, then smiled at Agent Fuller. "More coffee, Agents?"

Fuller shook her head. Marsalis answered, "I'm good."

The door opened and Snoop walked in, followed by Michelle. I said, "Sit here, Michelle." I gestured to the chair between Diane and me. I wanted Michelle to feel sheltered between two allies.

Snoop sat at the other end, opposite Diane. "Sorry we're late, Diane."

Diane waved a hand dismissively. "You're here now. Ms. Babcock, these are Special Agents Fuller and Marsalis from the FBI. They are recording this meeting. So am I." She gestured at the two recorders. "It is a federal crime to lie to federal agents, even if you're not under oath, so I want you to answer truthfully. Agent Fuller—and possibly Agent Marsalis—have questions for you. You are not to answer any question until I tell you it is okay to answer. Are we clear on that?"

Michelle twirled her braid in her hand. She bobbed her head once.

Fuller sat up straighter. "For the benefit of the recording, Michelle Babcock and Raymond Snopolski have joined the meeting. Michelle—may I call you Michelle?"

Michelle cut her eyes to Diane, who nodded.

"Yeah, sure." She twirled her braid more.

"Michelle, we are recording this meeting as Ms. Toklas told you, but I am required to tell you also."

"Okay."

"Michelle, did you meet with Carlos McCrary at the Day and Night Diner the morning of Monday, March 27th?"

Diane made a *stop* gesture. "Agent Fuller, that question has been asked and answered. Please move on."

"Ms. Toklas, this is not a courtroom. I would like to hear Michelle's answer."

Diane considered that. "No. Any other questions for Ms. Babcock?"

If I had special glasses, I could have seen the lightning flash from Fuller's eyes. She tugged her jacket straighter and cleared her throat. "Do you know James Ponder?"

Michelle cut her eyes to Diane before she spoke. "Yes."

"What is the nature of your relationship?"

Diane said, "Don't answer that." She confronted Fuller. "That's too ambiguous to answer factually. Please be more specific, perhaps asking a question that can be answered yes or no."

Fuller nudged a wayward strand of hair behind her ear. "How long have you known James Ponder?"

Diane nodded permission to Michelle, who twirled her braid. She bit her lower lip. "Since last Halloween."

"Do you consider Mr. Ponder a friend?"

Diane said, "You can answer."

"Yes."

"Are you romantically involved?"

Michelle asked Diane, "What does that mean?"

Diane smiled. "Are you dating James Ponder?"

"Yes."

"Have you been intimate?"

Diane raised a hand. "Don't answer that." She said to Fuller, "I fail to see the relevance of that question; she told you that Ponder is a friend and that they are dating. You may draw your own conclusions from that."

Fuller cleared her throat. "Do you know Steven Wallace?"

Diane said, "You can answer."

"Yes."

"And how long have you known Mr. Wallace?"

"It's *Doctor* Wallace, and I've known him since, uh, since this semester commenced. The second week in January, I think."

"Do you take any classes from *Doctor* Wallace?"

"Yes, *Introduction to Environmental Science.*"

"What about Katharine Shamanski?"

Michelle started to answer, and Diane grasped her arm. "What about her?"

"Do you know Ms. Shamanski?"

Diane released Michelle's arm. "You may answer."

"Yes," said Michelle.

"How long have you known Ms. Shamanski?"

"Since I enrolled at UAC last August. We're—"

Diane touched Michelle's arm. "Answer the question factually. You don't have to say any more than that."

Michelle frowned. "Sorry."

Diane patted her on the arm. "That's all right, dear." Diane was maybe ten years older than Michelle. I smiled at the maternal "dear."

Fuller asked voluminous questions covering Michelle's interactions, on and off campus, with Ponder, Wallace, and Shamanski. Diane intervened several times to keep the questions specific and to cut off Michelle when she volunteered information. The meeting dragged on for another hour and Diane's secretary brought in another carafe of coffee and several bottles of water.

After what Fuller euphemistically called a "comfort break," Fuller resumed the interview. "Michelle, where were you the night of Monday, March 27?"

"At James Ponder's house."

"Did you have a date with Mr. Ponder?"

"*Nah*, we were just, you know, hanging out."

"What time did you leave Mr. Ponder's house?"

Diane said, "That's enough, agents. This is a fishing expedition. You won't tell me what you're investigating or who, and that's your right. My client has the right not to have her personal life paraded for strangers. You've been at this for two hours and, to my way of thinking, have not elicited any information you could not have found from other sources. I'm not going to allow any more questions. This meeting is over."

Chapter 44

DIANE LEFT THE CONFERENCE WITH THE FBI AGENTS. I waited until she closed the door behind her. "Okay, Snoop, why were you late?"

Snoop blew air out between his lips. "It's my fault. Three guys in a black Suburban followed my car to the Mango Island ferry terminal. I didn't spot them until they drove into the ferry parking lot after I did. Otherwise, I would have kept driving toward the beach until I lost them. Now they know that Michelle is staying on Mango Island."

"No sense crying over spilt milk. That's not all the bad news. The white Ford sedan that's been shadowing me followed me here. I thought that the white Ford was the three stooges, but if the stooges were following you and Michelle, then they must have sent for reinforcements. There must be a second team following me. Tell me what happened."

Snoop squeezed his coffee cup with both hands. "They waited in the parking lot blending in with a bunch of employee cars while I ferried across to fetch Michelle. They followed us onto Beachline Causeway. I slowed at the Azalea Island traffic light to lose them. You know the intersection."

Snoop lifted his cup but didn't drink. He took the carafe for a refill. "I keep this up and I'm gonna need another one of Agent Fuller's 'comfort breaks.' The evildoers ran the red light when I tried to lose them."

"Was it the three stooges?"

"I had assumed so, but with more guys following you, who knows? I do know that they've increased their firepower. I spotted two gunmen with AK-47s. I recognized the barrels, of course."

"They must have copied your license plate when you blocked their first Ford on South River Drive. They ran your plate to find out where you live. Oh shit. The white Ford is a second team. If they were surveilling you on Saturday, they followed your car from my apartment to the mall. Even after I lost the three stooges in the mall, the second team watched me get in your car. They would have followed me to the Mango Island Ferry. They already knew that Mango Island was involved in this somehow. Did you get the license number of the SUV that ambushed you?"

"No, I never saw the back bumper. But they abandoned their vehicle anyway."

"Oh?"

Snoop smiled. "They drove into the left lane and came up to hit us with AK-47s. I ran them into a traffic barricade at Poinciana Island." He held his hands like a steering wheel and jerked them to his left.

"You and Michelle okay?"

"Yeah, but they shot out my windows and punched bullet holes in a door and fender," Snoop said. "You owe me serious body work on the Toyota. And, of course, Janet will be furious with me." Janet is Snoop's wife.

"I'm glad that nobody was hurt." I gestured at Michelle. "You okay?"

She twirled her braid again.

I patted her shoulder. "This must have been frightening for you."

Michelle's lip trembled. She stopped twirling the braid and covered her face with both hands. She sobbed and rocked back and forth.

I waited for her to finish crying. Finally, she said in a small voice, "I peed my pants when those men shot at us. They're navy blue and no one noticed, but it feels really *icky*."

"That I can fix." I punched the intercom.

"Yes, Mr. McCrary. This is Janine, Ms. Toklas's assistant."

"Janine, Ms. Babcock needs assistance in the conference room. Can you come in?"

In seconds the door opened and Diane walked in. "I sent the agents on their way." She smiled at Michelle. "Janine said you need assistance?"

"Michelle needs a new pair of pants and underwear," I said. "Here's my credit card. Please find out what size and style she wants and send someone to the hotel shop next door to buy them, if you don't mind. And buy her a gray non-descript hoodie and big dark sunglasses. I'm going to disguise her when she leaves here."

Michelle stood up. "I can do that. I have my own credit card."

I made a *stop* motion. "Sorry, Michelle, it's too dangerous. You can't use a credit card anyway. The bad guys could find you from your card charges. You'd best not even carry a credit card with you until I give you the all clear. That's why you need the disguise. You're not the only one who was followed. A car full of men followed me here from my condo. They'll be waiting for me when I leave. Even if the men who tried to kill you earlier are out of the way now, they'll get back on the trail soon. And these other people have joined the search for you. You need to stick close to me, okay?" I smiled, comfortingly I hoped.

Diane accepted my credit card and huddled with Michelle for a minute. They both giggled. Diane used the intercom to summon Janine and sent her away with the credit card. Michelle

remained standing at the window. No more sitting in her icky pants. She twirled her braid and stared out the window.

I gestured to Snoop. "Tell Diane what you told me."

After he finished, I said, "The rented Ford followed me here from my condo. I couldn't tell how many were in it because they stayed too far back. It's safer to assume they have three or more in the new Ford." I stood and paced. "Traffic cameras will have filmed both intersections on the Beachline Causeway. You need to get to the PCPD to report the incident, before they come searching for you. Your car drivable?"

"Surprisingly, yes. The damage is to the back half, and they missed the tires and gas tank. I parked in the garage downstairs."

"I want to be with you when you give your statement to the cops. I can't leave Michelle unprotected, and I won't expose her any more than necessary." I pivoted to Diane. "Can we ask the cops to come here?"

"Sure. Use this conference room. I don't have to be here for that. Michelle, let's go to my office."

Chapter 45

KELLY CONTRERAS AND BIGS BIGELOW ARRIVED WITHIN THE HOUR. Kelly, the senior detective of the pair, entered first. "I smelled coffee in the hall on the way here. I'm dying here, big guy. Can I have a cup?"

I grinned at her. "I'll see what I can do." I peered over her shoulder at Janine, standing in the hallway.

Janine had heard the conversation. "I'll bring coffee for four. Or will Ms. Toklas be rejoining you?"

"Just us four, Janine. Thanks."

Bigs was right behind Kelly. He could barely fit through the conference room door. A former NFL defensive lineman, Bigs became a Port City police detective after he retired from a Hall-of-Fame career with the Port City Pelicans of the NFL. "Hey, Chuck, it's good to see you." His massive hand made mine look like a child's.

"Bigs, thanks for coming." I gestured at the conference table. "Sit down."

Snoop related the essential details of the attack, omitting any mention of Michelle being in the car. He paused when Janine returned with the same Chinese tray I'd noticed earlier. Either that or its twin.

During the pause, Kelly opened a laptop and accessed the traffic camera footage. After Janine left, Snoop continued his statement. Kelly and Bigs asked questions to clarify a few points. Kelly said, "After these guys tried to kill you, Snoop, they carjacked a Lexus stopped at the same traffic light where the perps totaled their vehicle. They pistol-whipped the driver, an old man, and sent him to the hospital. He'll live. They escaped in his Lexus eastbound on the Beachline. We're combing Port City Beach right now."

"Oh, geez," Snoop said.

"Why did they want to kill you, Snoop?"

Snoop spread his hands. "It's in connection with a case we're working that I can't tell you about."

Bigs smacked the table with a hand the size of a catcher's mitt. The floor shook. "Cut the crap, Snoop. There was a carjacking and automatic rifle fire. An old man is in the hospital, and he could have been killed. More innocent people could have been hurt by the gunfire. You both were cops. Remember 'serve and protect'? What the hell's going on?"

"Kelly," I interrupted, "these may be the same three guys I asked you to run the background checks on a couple of days ago. They've followed me ever since."

"Did your traffic cams catch the carjackers' faces?" Snoop asked.

"Let me check." She tapped the keys and swiveled the screen toward Snoop. "Hit the play button there on top."

Snoop viewed the video. He rotated the computer back toward Kelly. "That's the three guys that Chuck and I call the three stooges. They're the ones who followed Chuck originally."

She gave me a hard expression. "I think it's time you tell us what's going on."

"They think I'll lead them to a client whom I'm protecting."

"You won't tell me who the client is, so I won't ask." Kelly turned to Bigs. "Let's watch the feed from the Azalea Island camera again." They studied the screen for a moment, ran the video forward and backward. "Snoop, there's someone in the front seat with you in the Azalea Island footage. And they're not there in the footage from the Poinciana Island camera."

"I told... the person to hide on the floor when I spotted the gun barrels sticking through the windows."

"Looks like a woman, Snoop. Is that the client you're protecting?"

Snoop didn't say anything.

Kelly slapped the table top with both hands. "That's it. We can't do this anymore, Chuck. Jorge said to cut you some slack, to look the other way a little, and we did. But none of us anticipated that would include ignoring automatic gunfire on a crowded street or carjacking and pistol-whipping an old man. You asked me to trust you when you first tangled with these three, and I did since no one got hurt. Now you don't trust Bigs and me enough to tell us the whole truth? Trust is a two-way street, *amigo*. You either tell us what's happening right now, or I call the lieutenant and tell him we're off the case." She sat back in her chair and crossed her arms.

Snoop shrugged.

Bigs's deep voice rumbled, "That's the way it is, Chuck."

I said to Kelly, "If you and Bigs promise not to make any notes on this, I'll tell you what I'm doing. Hypothetically."

They agreed and I told them. They drank their coffee while I talked, occasionally interrupting with a question. I laid everything out except Michelle's identity. "And hypothetically, I uncovered evidence that the train bridge bomb and the arson at the Hillside Pines Apartments were planned by Steven Wallace. He has two drawers full of files I didn't even peek at. They could be about other eco-terrorism they've perpetrated, or stuff they're planning to do. I don't have the resources to investigate all the other files."

Kelly leaned back in her chair, holding her cup in two hands. "Okay, we're in. How can we help?"

"Where did the three stooges get the black Suburban? I stole their driver's licenses and their wallets with their credit cards."

"You did that on March 31," she said. "They had plenty of time to get replacements. Their black Suburban was a rental. The address on the driver's license was the same phony address they used before and they used the same dead-end credit card."

"But you confirmed the addresses on their driver's licenses that I confiscated. They were real. They must carry another license just to rent cars. It must have been in the Ford's glove compartment instead of the driver's wallet. That's why I didn't get it. Any luck on the highjacked car's GPS?"

"They abandoned it in a parking lot of a hotel on the Beach. Could have taken a cab from there."

"Did you and Bigs drive an unmarked car here?"

"Yeah."

"Good. I need you to drive a woman to the Mango Island Lodge. I won't tell you her name, and don't ask her either."

"And how do we find this unidentified woman?"

"She's in Diane Toklas's office."

Kelly smiled. "That's simple enough. Anything else?"

"Pursue the three carjackers as if it were a random drive-by shooting at Snoop, and a carjacking of the old man. Try to get them off the street without involving my client."

"We're doing that anyway," she said. "I'll have the police lab haul Snoop's car to the crime lab for evidence. Where is it, Snoop?"

"Garage downstairs." He handed her a slip of paper. "Here's my parking ticket. I wrote the floor and parking spot number on the back."

Kelly stared straight at me. Bigs sat to her right. She winked her left eye, the one Bigs couldn't see. "You owe me big time for this."

Chapter 46

REDWOOD SNAPPED THE FLIP PHONE SHUT and slipped it into his pocket. *Mango Island? What on Earth is that silly girl doing on Mango Island? Wait a minute. That idiot Ponder said she was rich. Could she be Mango Island rich? Even I would be hard pressed to afford a condo on Mango Island.* He slid over a keyboard and opened a web browser.

Father is John Babcock. Nothing special about him. Corporate executive. Redwood searched the Atlantic County property tax records. *His home is in a gated community, but the idiot Ponder told me that. And it's not on Mango Island. No other property listed. Maybe it's in his wife's name. I can't remember if Florida is a community property state.*

He tapped the keyboard again. *Mother is Penelope Faith Hickham Babcock. Maiden name is Hickham. Something familiar there.* He Googled "Penelope Faith Babcock," then "Penelope Babcock," and finally "Penelope Hickham." *Good Lord. Hank Hickham. That's where the money is, and it's a boatload too.*

Redwood searched the Atlantic County tax records again. *Nothing under Hickham. That's funny. He has to own his own home, probably a mansion. Probably has it under a corporate name or a trust like I do.*

He swiveled his desk chair and flipped through an old-fashioned Rolodex on his credenza. *P... Q... R.* He found the business card stapled to a slotted card in the Rolodex. He punched in a number.

"EDWARD TAYLOR HERE. Yes, I specialize in real estate. You heard me speak at a bar convention? Thank you for saying that, you're very kind. How can I help you? Hickham probably owns his home in a Florida Land Trust. That keeps the actual ownership confidential. No, even I can't find out who the real owners are. Why do you need the information? That's all? If you want to serve him notice, you don't need to know where Hank Hickham lives, my friend. Drop by his restaurant. Everybody in Port City knows that he's down there practically every afternoon. Don't mention it. Consider it a professional courtesy to a fellow lawyer who enjoyed my presentation. Good day, Mr....?"

The line went dead.

Chapter 47

HANK HICKHAM ANSWERED ON THE SECOND RING. "Hey, Chuck. Any news?"

"We had a little hiccup with the Michelle situation." I paced Diane's conference room, nervous energy needing an outlet. I was forming a plan in the back of my mind; action was coming soon.

"What happened?"

"Three thugs followed her and Snoop when they left the ferry today. They tried to gun them down. Michelle's okay. Snoop out-maneuvered the bad guys and got her safely to Diane Toklas's office. The bad news is that the bad guys have learned that Michelle's staying somewhere on Mango Island. It's possible—even likely—that they will learn she's your granddaughter. If so, they could find out which condo is yours."

"Actually, they couldn't, Chuck. I own all my stuff in one of them land trusts that my lawyer whipped up to keep my stuff private-like." Hank laughed. "Chuck, you know we have great security on Mango Island. We're safe here."

I stared out the window at a cruise ship leaving the Port City Cruise Terminal. "Have you forgotten Vicente Vidali? He thought the Mango Island security was great too."

"But the newspaper said his own men killed him, didn't they?"

The cruise ship glided down the ship channel toward the Atlantic. Beside the channel, rush hour traffic on the Beachline Causeway headed home from their downtown jobs.

"Hank, don't believe everything you read in the papers. Humor me and move Michelle to the Mango Island Lodge. It's for her own safety. Register her under the name Dolores Calderone." I spelled both names.

Snoop smiled when he recognized my *abuelita's* name.

"Okay, Chuck. I'll get over there after we hang up. In fact, I forget that I'm on a cellphone. I'm walking that way right now."

"Good. Then call Michelle's cellphone and tell her the name to use. The people she's riding with will let her off at the Lodge."

Hank asked, "You mean she's not with you?"

"Two of my cop friends will give her a lift. You can't be any safer than that." We said goodbye.

Flashing red and blue lights from a Port City Marine Patrol boat caught my attention as it sped across the channel behind the cruise ship and headed toward the Beachline Causeway shore. Two black-and-whites bounced onto the causeway shoulder, lights flashing. A crime scene truck bumped in between them. Behind them, traffic backed up with gapers' block.

Snoop sat at the table, sipping his third cup of coffee. I touched his shoulder to get his attention and pointed to the scene on the causeway. He stood and walked to the window.

"What do you make of that, Snoop?"

He squinted. "Too far to make out without binoculars."

Diane opened the door. "You guys still here? Hey, it's after five. Time to go home."

I pointed my thumb over my shoulder. "Look out the window."

She did. "Yeah, so?"

"What do you think that is?"

She leaned toward the window. "Last time I saw something like that, a body had washed up on the rip-rap."

"That's what I was thinking. Too bad we don't have binoculars."

"We keep binoculars in the drawer for clients to look out the window." She stepped to the walnut credenza and opened a drawer. "Here."

I adjusted the optics. "There it is on the rip-rap. It's a body like you said."

"I've seen that a couple of times in the three years that we've officed here."

I handed the binoculars to Snoop. He waved them away. "*Nah*. You get to be my age, Chuck, you'll have seen too many bodies too."

Diane returned the binoculars to the drawer. "Do you fellows need anything else before you leave? Hint, hint." She softened the message with a smile.

Snoop asked, "You got any to-go cups?"

"Sure. I'll get you one from the kitchen on our way out."

Snoop carried the carafe and followed Diane out the door. I brought up the rear.

I waited until the elevator doors closed. "The Port City cops are searching for the three stooges. Another car full of hoods must be following me in the white Ford."

"You got something in mind?"

"The gloves came off when they drew guns on you and Michelle. No more Mr. Nice Guy."

Snoop smirked. "As if you were ever Mr. Nice Guy with evildoers."

Chapter 48

THE HOTEL WHERE JANINE HAD BOUGHT MICHELLE'S CLOTHES had a car rental office on site that was open until six o'clock. The rental agent had her keys out and was about to lock the door. She seemed ticked off when Snoop and I walked in five minutes before closing. Maybe she had a date and wanted to sneak out early. I made sure she had the right kind of car available for Snoop before leaving. My parting words to Snoop: "Take the insurance; you never know."

I rode the parking elevator to the fourth floor. The garage echoed with emptiness as I opened the steel door. I figured the hoods wouldn't make a run at me in the garage because of potential witnesses, but I held the Glock by my right leg as I walked to the Avanti, alert for any movement. When I'd come in at noon, they couldn't have known that I'd be this late leaving. I figured they would wait in their car near an exit ramp on a lower floor to follow me. There was one down ramp and one up ramp. On the first floor, the down ramp branched to two exits, one for Fourth Street and one for Bayshore Boulevard. The bad guys couldn't know which exit I'd use, so they would wait on the second floor for me to pass. At least, that's how I had it figured.

Sure enough, that's where they were.

I'd used binoculars from my condo balcony the previous day to read their license plate in the visitors' parking lot. Today I spotted their car on the last ramp on the second floor. There were no heads visible through the rear window; they had to be bent over in the seats—however many "they" were. I watched their car out of sight and it never moved, so they weren't afraid of losing me. They must have hidden a tracking device on my car. That's what I would do if our positions were reversed.

We had one hour before sunset. With rush hour traffic, the timing would be tight.

I was two blocks along Bayshore Boulevard before they exited the parking garage. I led them up the entrance ramp to I-795 headed toward the Everglades. I lowered the visor against the setting sun and sped up to sixty miles per hour. Sixteen minutes later the freeway ended at Florida Highway 888, a four-lane divided road. I slowed to fifty. South Florida is flat and the roads are straight. I watched the white Ford a mile behind me in the sparse traffic. I passed a new housing development where the highway became Atlantic County Road 888a, dropping to two lanes with a wide shoulder. I slowed to forty. The Ford began to close the gap. Two miles later the shoulder disappeared where the sugar cane fields nudged nearly to the edge of the pavement, green stalks towering ten and twelve feet high. The homes and apartments disappeared behind us. I slowed to thirty. The sedan closed to two hundred yards.

I grabbed the breathing mask from the passenger seat and slipped in on, adjusting the straps with one hand. The goggles restricted my peripheral vision, but I wouldn't need that. I only had to watch straight ahead. The sun had dropped to an awkward angle on my left. I slapped on a Pilots baseball hat to shade my eyes.

I hit the brakes so the men following would notice the flash of the brake lights, then I sped up to seventy-five on the flat deserted road. I hoped to mimic a panic-stricken man who had noticed that someone was following him. Green walls of sugar cane blurred on either side. The white Ford knew that I knew they were following me. They sped up.

Ahead lay the Everglades, a desolate spot where they could kill me with no witnesses.

Or vice versa.

The sugar cane fields ended at a drainage canal and earthen berm marking the edge of the Everglades. I hit the brakes where the road ramped up over the berm. The white Ford closed the distance. I bumped down the berm and the pavement ended. I stomped the accelerator and shot down the sandy road, heading for the three giant white sand hills ahead. Abandoned retention ponds of milky green water lined both sides of the sandy road for a quarter of a mile.

Dust billowed behind me, shrouding the Ford from sight. I couldn't see them but they couldn't see me either. I knew the road; they didn't. They would have to follow the dust cloud and, in order to do that, they would have to slow down.

I gunned it to generate the maximum dust cloud. Just past the first sand hill, I slammed on the brakes and drifted into the turn, kicking up more dust. I drove between the two hills on the left and slid behind the second hill, parking out of sight. I patted my pockets by habit, feeling the two extra magazines inside. I got out, rolling my shoulders to release tension as I jogged around the sand hill to the northwestern side, glad that I was wearing the breathing mask in the heavy dust cloud.

The sun was behind me until the clouds blocked it.

The old phosphate mine had closed long before I came to Port City. A friend with a swamp buggy had driven me out here the year before. Abandoned machinery posed like monsters from a horror movie as the vines stretched from the surrounding sand to reclaim their territory on the rusted steel. The sandy ground was covered in spots with wild grasses and vines that flew in on the wind or were carried on the feet of birds. Mother Nature was recycling the machinery.

I selected a spot behind the shoulder of the sand hill and assumed a prone firing position. I breathed deeply and felt my heart rate slow down.

Any second now.

Chapter 49

AS I WAITED, CLOUDS MOVED OVER THE SUN. Dusk deepened to twilight. I heard the Ford's engine long before it came into view. The slight breeze swept the dust cloud south. The white sedan crawled into view, emerging from the billowing gloom into the dusky evening.

The Ford coasted to a stop in the middle of the three sand hills, dimly visible in the dusty air. I heard the gears lock into park; the engine die. The croak of a distant sandhill crane carried through the gathering dusk. All four windows hummed down. Nothing moved for a minute. The dome light flicked on as the doors opened.

Two men got out on each side, all four crouching to make smaller targets. The two from the rear seat carried Kalashnikov AK-47s. *Oh, well,* I thought, *that's why I carry extra magazines.*

Showtime. "You're surrounded. Drop your weapons and keep your hands where we can see them."

All four jerked their heads toward the sound of my voice. The two on my side swung their guns toward the sound of my voice.

I planted two bullets in the chest of the man aiming the AK-47. The other three scattered from the car like rats from a burning ship. Snoop dropped the one who had been seated on the right front, opposite the driver. The other two returned fire in my direction. The *br-a-a-ap* of the remaining Kalashnikov sprayed gritty geysers into the air on the right, pelting my goggles with sand, grass, and vines. I rolled behind the hill and ran counterclockwise around the mound. I rounded the other side of the hill behind the other two gunmen who stood back to back, straining to scan all directions. I slammed two bullets in the center mass of the nearest one. His Kalashnikov sprayed another *br-a-a-ap* in the air before it thumped to the sand. The last man looked toward the sound of my gun and leapt behind the open rear passenger door. Snoop couldn't see him from his angle either.

I noticed his legs below the open door, but nothing through the window. He had to be bent almost double.

"Don't shoot! I surrender. Do you hear me? Don't shoot."

"I hear you," I replied. "You're surrounded. Toss your gun out."

He did. Dust puffed up where his pistol hit the sand.

"Now the other one."

"That's all. I swear."

If he hadn't sworn, I might have believed him. "I can shoot right through the door, you know. And I'm going to do that on the count of three. One... two..."

"Okay, okay, you win." A smaller handgun followed the first one, scooting across the sand.

Snoop emerged from behind the sand hill on the other side of the car, his gun pointed in a two-hand grip while he surveyed the scene.

"Hands on your head, fingers interlaced." I waited for the shooter to comply. The sun was a bright spot in the cloud bank.

He stood and followed my instructions.

Snoop walked around the car's front, pistol aimed at the shooter's chest. "Take three giant steps away from the car and drop to your knees. Keep your hands on your head."

The man jumped at the sound of Snoop's voice. He tried to twist his head toward the sound, but the hands on his head made that difficult.

"You heard me, dog breath," Snoop repeated. "Three steps." He gestured with his Glock.

The man made three giant steps like he was playing Simon Says and dropped to his knees in the dust. I moved to within six feet, Glock aimed at his head. "Pretend you're a statue and you can survive tonight."

Snoop holstered his weapon and frisked the prisoner. He handed me the shooter's wallet, two key rings, and two cellphones: one smartphone and one flip phone. *Fool me once, but you can't fool me twice.* I remembered the three stooges surrendering their flip phones. We already knew those were burner phones. They must have had personal phones with them too, but I hadn't thought to look for them. Rookie mistake. *Note to self: If they give you a flip phone, always search for the smartphone.*

I stuck both cellphones in my jacket pocket. "Why two sets of keys?"

"The one with the company logo is for the rent car. The other bunch is my personal set."

I slipped the rental's keyfob in my jacket pocket and tossed the personal keys to the ground inches from the kneeling man. I confiscated the money and driver's license from his wallet and tossed the wallet near the keys. "Do what I say and you can live to use those keys and credit cards again." I pocketed the money and read his driver's license in the fading light. "Arthur Caprese?"

He stared at me and said nothing.

I smacked him on the side of the head with my gun barrel hard enough to get his attention. "Are you the Arthur Caprese whose picture is on this license I removed from the wallet I found in your pocket? It's not a hard question." Once a prisoner says something, anything, it's easier to get them to keep talking. I waved the gun barrel at him.

"Yeah," he grunted.

"That's better. You're from Chicago. Hey, Snoop, another goombah from Chicago." I pocketed the license and stuck the Glock under his chin. "You work for Wolenski too?"

Caprese lifted his chin. "Don't know nobody by that name."

I slapped him with my left hand. "We do this easy, or we do this hard. It's up to you, pal. Do you work for Wolenski?"

He shook his head.

"So, who do you work for if not Wolenski?"

"I don't work for nobody."

I made sure Snoop had a gun trained on Caprese. I holstered the Glock then slapped him three times, left-right-left. Sometimes humiliation works where brute force won't.

"You're too dumb to be self-employed, Caprese." I dragged one of the dead men's bodies to the base of the nearest sand hill, a dozen feet away. I frisked the corpse, removing his wallet, two cellphones same as Caprese, keys, and an ankle-holster with a Browning .380 in it. I dropped the ankle-holster with the pistol to one side. I extracted the driver's license and money and tossed the wallet and keys onto the body. "He won't need those anymore." I stuck the license and money in my pants pocket. I dropped the cellphones in my jacket pocket. "Why did he carry two cellphones?"

Caprese glared at me.

I shrugged and seized the next body beside the fallen AK-47 and dragged it over by the first. I found the dead man's wallet, two cellphones, and car keys. I dropped the cellphones in my jacket pocket where they clunked against the other four. The pocket was getting heavy. I stuffed the money in my pants along with the driver's license. I tossed the wallet and car keys onto the body.

I dragged the last man and stacked his body on the other two, removing another wallet, two more cellphones, and a pistol from a shoulder holster. "No car keys for him?" I tossed the pistol near the other one. I would retrieve them later.

Caprese spit on the ground.

"Oh, I get it," I said, "He caught a ride to the airport with you. Huh, goombah?" Same drill with the money, cellphones, and driver license. I had quite a collection going. "Watch this, Caprese." I drew my weapon again to cover him and waved to Snoop. "You know what to do."

Snoop disappeared. Seconds later a powerful engine *varoomed*. Snoop drove a Jeep into view and paused at the base of the hill near the three bodies. He shifted the Jeep into four-wheel drive and climbed up the hill. Clumps of sand held together by the sparse grass and vines cascaded down the slope from the front wheels, crowding toward the three bodies.

Snoop ran the Jeep farther up the slope. The sandy avalanche covered the feet of the nearest body, and I motioned him to stop. "Caprese, if my friend drives farther up that hill—say, to the top and down the other side—the sand will cascade down and bury your three friends in an unmarked grave. Did any of them have families?"

He stared at the three bodies.

"You may as well tell me, Caprese. I'll get the information from their cellphones and driver's licenses. Everything's on the internet these days."

"Deuce and Al have wives and kids. Yank has a fiancée—*had* a fiancée."

"That's better. You know, Caprese, if I drag your dead body over there and pitch it on top of theirs, the sand will bury you too. There will be no evidence that any of you ever lived. None of you will have a funeral. Your families will have no graves to visit. They won't know what happened to you because your bodies will never be found out here. Not ever. This phosphate mine has been abandoned for years. I'll roll your rent car into that old retention pond over there. It's thirty feet deep. Did you know that? The car will never be found either. It will be like the four of you never existed."

Caprese swallowed hard, sweat beading on his forehead, barely visible in the dim light. I didn't think it was from the heat. He collapsed back on his heels and bent at the waist. His shoulders shook.

"Now I'm going to count to three. At three, I'll put a bullet in your ear unless you talk. One... two..."

"Wolenski."

"I can't hear you, Caprese."

"We work for Wolenski."

"Why have you been following me?"

"Hey, my knees is killing me, man. Can I, like, stand up or something?"

"Sit cross-legged. Place both hands on the ground behind you and lean back on them."

He dropped his hands to the ground in front of him and rocked on his hands and knees. But instead of rolling over to his backside, he lunged sideways towards the AK-47 lying ten feet away.

I shot him in the knee. "Don't make me kill you."

He kept scrambling and grasped the Kalashnikov in both hands. He rolled over, swinging the barrel toward me. My first bullet ricocheted off the Kalashnikov, sending sparks into the twilight like fireworks and spoiling his aim. The second bullet hit the ground beside him, kicking up a geyser of sand. The third bullet hit him in the shoulder. It was the shoulder shot that made him miss me. The fourth bullet ripped into his stomach. A gut shot makes the body relax reflexively. The AK-47 *br-a-a-apped* a burst of automatic gunfire into the air as it fell from his limp fingers. I kicked it out of reach.

He hugged his midsection with both hands. Blood bubbled from his lips.

I lifted my phone to call 9-1-1. I tapped in the number then noticed there was no signal in the Everglades. I knelt beside the fallen man. "Why, Caprese, why? A few years in prison is better than dying. Why?"

"You was gonna kill me anyways."

"No, I intended to give you to the Port City police. Now I can't even call an ambulance."

"It don't matter none, McCrary. Yeah, I know who you are. It don't matter none, 'cause I'm gut shot." He grimaced and groaned. "Finish it, McCrary."

"I can't."

"McCrary, I'm a dead man. I'm in a lot of pain, dude. Finish it, for crissakes."

"I can't do that, Arthur."

Snoop had backed the Jeep off the hill when Caprese commenced to talk. Snoop walked toward us. "Bud, you go inspect the Ford. I'll stay with Arthur."

I walked to the rental car. As I slid into the passenger seat, a gunshot shattered the silence of the Everglades. I peered at Snoop, holstering his weapon. He gazed back through the tears in his eyes. "Had to be done, bud. It was the humane thing to do."

Chapter 50

I FOUND A FOLDED SHEET OF PAPER in the glove compartment. It was a printed email sent Tuesday, March 28 at 9:04 a.m. to an email address that started with *deuce* followed by five digits @gmail.com. The sender's address was a jumble of letters and numbers, also @gmail.com, obviously an account used the one time. The email had a good quality portrait of Michelle from her Facebook page, along with her name, home address, and Ponder's address, with the notation *Boyfriend*.

"Check this out, Snoop. It was sent the morning after the bombing. Whoever sent this knew of Michelle's involvement and knew she was in a relationship with Ponder. Obviously these four guys were working with the three stooges."

Snoop peered at the photo. "That's fast action. One of Michelle's other three perps sent it, or talked to someone else who sent it to the three stooges."

"Then the stooges gave it to these four. Wallace may be a bomb-thrower, but he has no connection in Chicago that I know of and probably no mob connections either. More likely the tip on Michelle came from Shamanski. If her father is an attorney, it's likely that he knows someone like Wolenski who could send a bunch of killers on an airplane on short notice."

I pocketed the email and found another pair of folded pages in the glove compartment. "Here's another email to this *deuce* address from a different random address sent Thursday, March 30 at 9:32 a.m. This one added my name and office address above Michelle's picture on the first page." I handed the sheet to Snoop.

"They added you to the hit list. But why no picture?"

"I'm not on Facebook and there's no picture of me on the McCrary Investigations website," I said. "All the sender had was my name and office address. They must have tailed me from my office Friday morning. I'm slipping. I didn't make them until three hours later."

"Is this the spot where I say *I told you so?*"

"This is that exact spot."

"Okay, I told you so. They had a contract on you."

"Before you get too smug, O Great Detective, consider this second sheet where they added James Ponder as a target. And look at the handwritten note at the bottom."

Snoop read the email. "That's my license plate number and home address." He held the sheet closer to the dome light. "They're written in different pens. The three stooges must have read my license plate when I blocked them in on South River Drive. They got my home address from the license plate and added it. That's why they followed me to Mango Island this morning. I must be slipping too."

Chapter 51

I DROVE TEN MINUTES BACK TOWARD PORT CITY before I found a cell signal. I parked on the shoulder and found the GPS tracker that Caprese or one of his dead friends had stuck under my rear bumper. I threw it in a canal beside the highway and called Kelly. "I'd like to report that four men attempted to kill me earlier, right about sunset."

"You in the hospital?"

"No, I'm parked on the shoulder of County Road 888a. This is me, good citizen that I am, calling the cops to report a crime."

"Obviously, they didn't succeed."

"Yeah, and I'd like to report four dead bodies too."

"Where?"

"The old phosphate mine at the end of 888a."

"Who are they?"

"The shooters." I read from the driver's licenses. "Arthur Caprese, Lawrence R. Lambert, Jr., Alberto A. Echeverria, and William J. Yankelowicz."

"You realize that I got off duty at seven p.m., right? It's... ten now. You ruined my afternoon. You gonna ruin my evening too?"

I stuck the licenses in my shirt pocket. "You don't seem concerned for my welfare."

"I know you too well," said Kelly. "Did you kill four of them yourself, or was Snoop with you?"

"Snoop was with me. I sent him home; he's had a rough day."

She sighed. "Okay. Meet Bigs and me at the crime scene."

"I have an early appointment tomorrow. How about I meet you where I-795 ends and becomes Florida 888. You know that Denny's on the north side of the street?"

"Yeah."

"I'll be there eating dinner."

KELLY SLID INTO THE BOOTH BESIDE ME. Bigs filled a whole bench by himself.

The server came over with an order pad. "Y'all want a menu?"

Kelly smiled at her. "Just coffee. It's gonna be a long night. How about you, Bigs?"

"Three-egg western omelet, grits, and coffee."

After the server left, Kelly asked, "What you got?"

"Here are the dead men's licenses." I fished them from my shirt pocket. "And here are the keys to their rented Ford. Snoop and I locked the guns and their other personal effects like wallets and cellphones in the trunk."

She handed the licenses and keyfob to Bigs. "When can we get statements from you and Snoop?"

"How about tomorrow morning late, after you've run the call logs from the phones? Each man carried a flip phone and a smartphone. We can meet you at the North Shore Precinct."

The server delivered two cups of coffee. "I'll be right back with your omelet, officer. You want a refill, Chuck?"

"I'm good, Ruby."

Kelly slurped her coffee. "Where are the guns you and Snoop used?"

"They're in my car. I didn't want to bring them in here. Might freak somebody out."

Chapter 52

EVERY OFFICE DEVELOPER WHO ADDS ANOTHER GLASS TOWER to the Port City skyline thinks they need to build the new one taller than the last one. Tank Tyler had moved into the newest and tallest marble monument early in January. I hadn't had occasion to visit him since then and I looked forward to seeing both his new offices and the new building.

My ears popped as the high-speed elevator rushed to the sixty-first floor in less than a minute. Tank's offices had double mahogany entrance doors at the end of the hall. *Impressive.* A discreet brass plaque on one door said *Thomas Tyler Asset Management LLC.* The other door had a similar plaque announcing *Investments/Estate Planning/Tax Planning.*

A soft musical chime rang as I opened the door. I spent the first few seconds rubber-necking at Tank's reception room. Mahogany paneling matched the reception desk. Silver Berber carpet, Knoll chairs, glass-topped coffee table and original artwork on the walls.

He opened the mahogany door behind the reception desk. "Susan doesn't come in until eight. That's why I switched the chime on." We shook hands.

I gestured at the reception area. "On the weekends, do you remove the furniture and play Jai Alai in here?"

He smiled. "It's not that big, not quite anyway. C'mon, I want to show you the new kitchen." He led the way down a mahogany paneled hallway.

"Are there any mahogany trees still standing in Madagascar or wherever?"

He grinned and his teeth gleamed in his chocolate-colored face. "Honduras. You like it?"

"Between the silver padded carpet and the wooden walls all around, I feel like I'm in the world's largest coffin."

"Ha. That's a good one. Here we are." He opened a door on the right and led me into the kitchen. "First class all the way. That's a Sub-Zero three-door refrigerator freezer. Restaurant-size ice-maker over there. Dishwasher here. A Gaggenau oven and range, not merely a microwave and a toaster-oven like the old office. And a professional coffee maker and espresso machine." He spread his arms wide and bowed. "Ta-da."

"And mahogany cabinets."

"What can I say, Chuck? My decorator likes mahogany. What do you think?"

"It's the kind of kitchen Rachel Ray would buy if she had the money."

"Let me pour you a coffee in one of my new gold-trimmed China mugs." He opened a cabinet and selected a bone China mug with the *TT* logo on it. He stuck it under the spigot and pressed a button. The machine hissed to life and shot precisely the right amount of steaming coffee into the mug. He handed it to me and moved toward the door.

"Aren't you having any?"

"I've been here for an hour. My cup's on my desk. Doctor it up anyway you like. Half-and-half's in the fridge."

I added a little half-and-half. "Tank, how much of this machinery do you know how to operate, really?"

He grinned. "I only use the coffee machine, but my people use this stuff to make cappuccinos and lattes, crap like that. One analyst cooks her lunch occasionally. It's a fringe benefit. Come on, let me show you my office."

Tank was once a defensive end for the Port City Pelicans. Even so, the big guy fairly skipped down the hall to another pair of double doors. His playing weight had been north of 350 pounds. You can carry that much weight when you're six-foot-six and anchor the right end of the Bigs Brigade, which is what the sportswriters called the Pelicans front four when Tank, Bigs Bigelow, and two other defensive linemen had dominated the AFC. Tank dropped the better part of a hundred pounds after he retired from the Pelicans and founded his CPA and money management firm, but he was still a giant of a man in more ways than one.

He stepped to one side as he entered his corner office, letting me appreciate the full effect of the two window walls that overlooked Seeti Bay. The rising sun glared through the windows.

"On a clear day, can you see Bimini?"

"Not quite, the horizon's thirty miles away. Oh, you were joking."

The opposite wall—mahogany, of course—featured his CPA certificate, a master's degree from the University of Atlantic County, a photo of the UAC Falcons national championship team from years earlier with Tank on the back row, and an autographed photo of the Bigs Brigade posing with the AFC Championship trophy the Pelicans won the year before he retired. They had lost the Super Bowl in overtime.

I flopped down in one of four matching client chairs. "You've come a long way from Alabama, Tank."

He punched a button beside the window and a sun shade whirred down. "It's way too bright until about ten o'clock, but I wanted you to appreciate the great view." He sat down behind an L-shaped mahogany desk that was six feet on the base and nine feet on the long side where I sat. "I have a full appointment book ahead of me, pal. You said you needed advice on something important. How can I help?"

I opened my briefcase on the next chair and found three of the photographs I'd printed from Steven Wallace's files the previous Sunday. I handed them over.

He perused the first one, flipped it facedown. The second took another couple of seconds. The third one he hardly considered. "Stock price charts for fifty-two weeks displaying daily high, low, and closing prices, along with trading volume."

"Hell, Tank, an old country boy from Adams Creek knew that. Read the notes handwritten on the charts." I pointed to the circled area on the first photo and the arrow leading down to a series of cryptic figures. "Are these a code? What do they mean?"

He laid the three photos side by side and studied them. "*Hmm.*" He swiveled ninety degrees to the short side of his desk and slid out a keyboard tray mounted under the desktop. He positioned the first photo between the keyboard and monitor. His fingers danced across the keys. "*Hmm.*" He hauled a legal pad from a drawer and made notes. He brought over the second photo and did the same drill. Another "*Hmm.*" Same routine with the third photo. "*Hmm,*" again.

"This is good coffee, Tank."

"For three thousand dollars, it better be."

"You paid three grand for a coffee machine?"

Tank spread his hands. "What can I say? It's the best."

"I'd say you got your money's worth." I tasted the coffee again. "Did you figure out what this code means?"

"Yeah. It's quite clever. Diabolical even." He twisted the computer monitor so we could both see. "This is the fifty-two-week chart of 4Square Properties for the same period in your photo there."

I compared the photo to the screen. "Yeah, the graphs have the same shape."

"This circle here..." he tapped the photo, "covers one week, five trading days from Monday to Friday." He sipped coffee while I studied the photo.

"I'm with you."

"On Monday, 4Square traded from a $42.15 high to a $41.87 low, and closed at $41.96. That means that the day's last price before the market closed was $41.96." He zoomed in on the graph to make the week fill the whole screen.

"I can see that."

He tapped the photograph. "This first group of letters and numbers is the symbol for the $42.00 put option on 4Square stock that expired three weeks later."

"Say that again, but this time in English."

"Do you know what a 'put option' is?"

"Not a clue. I'm the world's greatest private investigator, not a financial genius like you."

"Very funny, Sherlock Holmes. A put option is a bet that the stock price will go down. An investor who thinks a stock will go down buys a put option on that stock. If the stock goes down, he wins the bet."

"Is that legal?"

"It's not merely legal, pal, it has the federal government's blessing. The guys who buy and sell these options pay a ton of taxes on them. There are even option exchanges that are like stock exchanges, except they don't trade stock; they trade the *options* on the stocks. Billions of dollars change hands every day on these option exchanges."

"Anytime there are billions of dollars sloshing around, somebody crooked will scam some. Is that what's going on here?"

"You got it, cowboy."

"All these notations are about bets that 4Square stock will go down?"

"They are bets on both 4Square and also Port City Power & Light." He touched the other photos. "All the big corporations have options traded on their shares. Literally hundreds of stocks."

"So, lots of people think these stocks are going to go down?"

"No, no. Not just down; there are options for investors to bet that a stock will go up too. Those are *call* options. They are the opposite of the *put* options." He noticed my frown. "For our purposes, let's concentrate on 4Square Properties and Port City Power. Read this first line." He pointed a finger big as a bratwurst. "This guy bought the $42.00 put option for $1.60 on Monday. Note the date written here. And see this '1.60' here?"

"Yeah. What's the second line?"

"It's another date code—that's Friday. During the week the stock dropped $2.00. See here? It opened at $39.85 on Friday. That's about two bucks less than it sold for on Monday. That's a good-sized drop in four trading days, but not so much that the security regulators would think something was fishy. Notice this '2.00' on this line? Write a dollar sign in front. It means that he sold the put option for $2.00 on Friday."

I referred to the photo again. "And this third line is his profit of $.40. Right?"

He reached across and gave me a fist bump. "Right on. He made a profit of forty cents per share on the option."

"There's gotta be more to it than this, Tank. You can't buy a jawbreaker from a gumball machine for forty cents."

"Keep your shirt on, pal. I don't want to overload you. Your brain could explode. Look at Port City Power." He handed the next photo to me. "This first circle covers two days' prices, a

Wednesday and Thursday." He tapped the keyboard and zoomed in on the picture of the two days' trades.

"Okay, let me see if I can figure this out." I compared the screen to the photo from Wallace's file.

"Stock traded in a range of $54.52 high to $53.93 low on Wednesday and closed at $53.99."

When Tank smiled, it seemed bigger than when other people smiled. "I'll make a financier out of you yet, Chuck."

"Not on your life, buddy. I'd never get a chance to rescue beautiful princesses and chase bad guys." I peered closer at the monitor. "The stock opened on Thursday at $51.85 and closed at $52.23."

"That's a drop of about four percent. That is a big drop overnight, often caused by bad news involving the company."

I read the cryptic notes in the bottom of the photo. "Does this first line mean that he bought the $55.00 put option for $.90 on Wednesday?"

"You're a quick study."

"And this next line means that he sold it for $3.10 on Thursday."

"Right again. Profit of $2.20, over 200 percent in one day." Tank grinned like I was his prize pupil. Right now, I was his only pupil.

I studied the final photo. "Next chart shows Port City Power ten months later, right up to a week ago. Pull up the chart like you did before and zoom it for me. Let me track this, now that you explained how it works."

His fingers flew and the monitor switched views. "Okay, Chuck, lead me through this trade."

I ran my finger across the photo. "Monday, March 27, the stock traded in a range of $64.63 high to $63.89 low and closed at $63.92… Whoa. The stock opened the next morning at $59.85 and closed at $61.23."

"That's a drop of six and a half percent—a huge drop. That was right after the railroad bridge bombing hit the news. Very bad for the company."

"Not to mention the two dead railroad employees and their families. This first line means he bought the $65.00 put option for $1.30 on Monday the twenty-seventh."

Tank nodded. "And the next line…"

"The next line means he sold it for $5.10 the next day." I stared at the stock chart. "Profit of $3.80 in one day. That's a lot better than the forty cents he made on 4Square in one week." I drank the last of my coffee. "Tell me how a guy makes a killing, both financially and literally, with a measly $3.80 profit."

"Here's where I drop the other shoe, Chuck. Each option contract is for one hundred shares."

"Still just forty bucks on the first trade, big guy. You can't take a girl to dinner for forty bucks. And the last trade gained… three hundred eighty dollars. There's got to be more."

"I'm not finished. Notice this number here?" He pointed to a note on the 4Square Properties stock chart.

"It says '1K' on the line beside the profit per share." The light went on. "One thousand? He bought options on a thousand shares. One thousand times forty cents a share is four hundred bucks profit. Better, but not worth breaking the law."

He shook his head. "The '1K' means one thousand option *contracts*. It covers one hundred thousand shares."

The light went on again and flashed like a neon sign. "Geez. He made $40,000 profit on the 4Square deal." I reviewed the first Port City Power trade. "It says '5K.' Five thousand contracts. That's five hundred thousand shares… times $2.20 is… $1,100,000. In one day."

Tank waved his legal pad. "Read the third trade, Chuck."

I flipped to the final photo, the one that displayed the profit of $3.80 per share. "It says '10K.' That's a million shares. This bastard cleared $3,800,000 by murdering two railroad employees."

My stomach churned when I remembered that Wallace's file cabinet had two drawers filled with similar files.

Chapter 53

"WE COME BEARING GIFTS." I deposited a box of *pan dulces* on the conference table.

Kelly stifled a yawn. "You jokers had a good night's sleep, didn't you? That's why you're cheerful this morning. Gimme a *pan dulce* and forget the diet for now." She ripped open the box, snagged a pastry, and passed the box to Bigs. "I didn't get to bed until four this morning. Don't expect me to be little Miss Sunshine." She gulped her coffee.

Snoop and I sat across the table from the two police detectives.

"You find anything interesting on the cellphones we found on the dead men?" I asked.

"We have someone working on that. First, let's take your statements about last night's shootout."

That lasted an hour and a half.

After we finished, Kelly said, "What made you two *estupidos* think you could take on four gunmen—especially after the earlier attack on Snoop? You knew they carried automatic weapons."

I shrugged. "It is what it is. We offered them a chance to surrender. We won; they lost."

"That's the kind of macho bravado that could get you both killed," said Bigs.

"Don't be wishy-washy, Bigs," I said. "Go ahead and tell us what you really think."

Kelly shook her head. "Let me ask if Terry's finished analyzing the phone records." She left the room.

My heart flipped. *How many cops named Terry can there be? It could be a man named Terence. Or a woman named Teresa Kovacs. She's stationed at the North Shore Precinct. She's a patrol cop. Of course, that was last year. Maybe she's been promoted to detective.*

Kelly came back. "She's right behind me. Let's move where we can all see the whiteboard."

Terry walked in.

It was her; it was *my* Terry. I hadn't seen her in months, but I remembered her scent, the feel of her skin, the sound of her voice as if it were yesterday—or last night. "Hello, Terry. It's good to see you again." Understatement of the year. The sight of her made my heart ache.

She set her coffee cup and her notebook on the conference table and stuck out her hand. "Hey, Chuck, how are you?"

I shook her hand. "Are you a detective now?"

She blushed. "I'm working on it. I'm training to analyze evidence. That's what I've been doing since sunup." She shook hands with Snoop, who stood up when she came into the room. Such a gentleman. "How are you?"

"Fine, Terry." He sat back down.

Kelly frowned. She was in no mood for chivalry this morning. "I understand you have a report for us."

Terry handed us each a sheet of paper. "This is a printout of my findings. There are eleven hoodlums in Port City on three different teams."

Eleven bad guys, not seven. My stomach felt queasy.

"There were four flip phones and four smartphones in the trunk of the Ford. The smartphones were their personal phones—pictures of the kids, the wife, and so forth. Nothing of interest there."

"That's what Snoop and I figured."

Terry smiled. "I analyzed the phone contacts and call logs. I pinged the numbers on the call logs and traced their locations back a minimum of two weeks or to their activation dates. The four flip phones had substantially identical address books. Each phone had the other three phones in their contacts along with eight other numbers, a total of twelve entries in all, since no phone had its own name in its contact list."

She picked up her copy of the printout. "All entries are first names, except there are two *Johnnies*, a *Johnny J.* and a *Johnny R.* The four phones I analyzed belonged to *Al, Artie, Deuce,* and *Yank.*"

Terry perused the colored markers in the whiteboard tray and selected a black one. She wrote the four names in a column on the board, then drew a bracket beside them. "It was easy to determine that *Al* was Alberto A. Echeverria." She added the name beside her first entry. "*Artie* was Arthur Caprese, *Deuce* was Lawrence R. Lambert, Jr., and *Yank* was William J. Yankelowicz." She added each name to the list. "Let's call those four men *Team Dead.*" She drew a line across the board above and below the four names.

She wrote *Team Dead* next to the bracket. "These sheets summarize the findings on each of the twelve phone numbers. Seven of the other eight entries were also first names, except, as I said, for the two *Johnnies.*" She leaned over and peered in the box of *pan dulces*, but didn't say anything. "The next seven contact list entries: *Johnny J, Ted,* and *Forte…*" She wrote the names in the space below Team Dead and continued down the board. "…*Harry, Johnny R, Lou,* and *Willy.*"

I said, "That's a total of eleven names. What about the twelfth name?"

"Ah, yes, the twelfth name." She smiled. "I'll explain that one in a minute."

She drew a bracket beside *Johnny J, Ted,* and *Forte* and wrote *Team Two* in the margin. She peered into the pastry box again.

"Terry, would you care for a *pan dulce*?" I asked.

"Don't mind if I do." There were two left. "Thanks." Then there was one.

Kelly gestured with her chin at the board. She mouthed the words "Team Two."

I walked to the whiteboard and picked up a blue marker. "May I?"

Terry's mouth was full, so she gestured her assent.

I drew a line through *Team Two* and wrote *Three Stooges.* "Terry, your *Team Two* names match the driver's licenses and contacts entries on three phones that Snoop and I lifted from three guys who followed me on Friday, March 31. They're not very smart, so we call them the three stooges. Kelly has their full names for your list."

Kelly removed the three licenses from an evidence bag and shoved them across the table.

Terry seemed puzzled. She didn't have a clue what I was talking about. All she knew about was last night's gunfight. Kelly and Bigs had kept my confidence. "The three stooges followed you?"

"Snoop and I got the drop on them and confiscated their driver's licenses, cellphones, and guns."

"Is that the incident report I read on those shots fired on South River Drive?" She regarded Kelly. "Why didn't you tell me about this?" Terry smirked. "Those are the three guys that you ran rap sheets on last Friday and didn't list in the evidence log, aren't they?" She wagged a finger at Kelly. "You've been holding out on me."

"Terry, there was no paperwork on the three guys following Chuck. Bigs and I are working the case off the books with Chuck and Snoop—with Lieutenant Castellano's blessing, I might add. You okay with that?"

"Sure, sure. If the LT says it's okay, it's okay." Terry blinked. "Wow, that explains something that had me scratching my head. When I pinged the twelve phone numbers on the list and traced them back to when they were activated, I discovered that all three phones for the three stooges were bought at a local Walmart on Friday, March 31 at 4:52 p.m. and activated at the same time." She paused for another bite of pastry. "Wait a second. Three guys tried to kill Snoop yesterday. Was that the three stooges too?"

"The same," Snoop answered.

Terry scooped up the three licenses and added the names to the whiteboard.

"What about the other four names?" Kelly asked. "The ones at the bottom."

I spread my hands. "The names don't mean anything to me. But it means that there are four more gunmen out there that we didn't know about. Call them *Team Three* for now."

Terry bracketed the names and wrote *Team Three.*

Snoop addressed Terry, who was finishing off her *pan dulce.* "What did you find when you pinged the phones?"

She wiped her fingers on a napkin. "All eight phones for Team Dead and Team Three were bought and activated at a discount electronics store in Chicago on Thursday, March 30 at around ten a.m."

"What about the odd one?" I asked.

"It was bought and activated at a different Chicago electronics store on Tuesday, March 28. The funny thing is, that store sold and activated four phones at the same time, but we haven't found the other three. Are those the ones you took from the three stooges?"

"Probably."

Kelly pulled out another evidence bag. "Here they are. Chuck confiscated these phones from the stooges on March 31. Their contact lists each have three names. Each phone has the other two phones plus one other name, *Redwood.*"

Snoop stood. "This calls for more coffee."

"Bring the pot," Kelly said. "What do you think about that, Chuck?"

"The name *Johnny J.* on Terry's list is in these earlier phones as *Johnny.* I'd bet a Porsche to a pogo-stick that the three phones I confiscated on March 31 are the three phones you're missing. Kelly pinged them unofficially. *Redwood* is listed in all seven phones we've found. We'll assume that he's listed in Team Three's phones too. Where have you pinged Redwood's number?"

"It never left the Chicago area, and the phone went off the grid at 8:30 last night."

"That agrees with what I found when I pinged the number a couple of days ago," Kelly said. "Always in Chicago or a suburb."

Snoop came back with a fresh pot of coffee.

"Snoop, you remember that Redwood entry we found on the first three phones?"

Snoop refilled our cups. "Yeah, what about it?"

"It went off the grid last night. Right after we killed those four shooters."

"Sure," Snoop said, "In fact, Terry, I predict you'll find that all twelve numbers dropped off the grid. Redwood's the boss. When Team Dead didn't touch base, the boss dumped his phone. It's at the bottom of Lake Michigan by now. But first I'd bet he texted the three stooges and Team Three to dump their phones in Seeti Bay."

Terry said, "How come you said Redwood dumped his phone in Lake Michigan instead of Seeti Bay. I never told you where that phone was pinged. You were out getting coffee."

"You didn't have to tell me," Snoop retorted. "Everybody in this whole freaking mess is from Chicago."

I dumped a packet of non-dairy creamer in my coffee. "Two of the first three phones said *Johnny* instead of *Johnny J.* but it's the same guy. That tells me that the three stooges were the first team sent down to find Michelle. They were the guys that Redwood sent on that Tuesday. The stooges must have been lurking around getting nowhere. By Thursday, Redwood gets serious and sends Team Dead and Team Three for reinforcements. One of the new guys was *Johnny R.* When the stooges bought new phones to replace the ones we confiscated, they added *Johnny R* to their address books to distinguish him from *Johnny J*, and those three stooges are still out there."

I moved to the whiteboard and picked up a red marker. "We have to deal with Team Three: Harry, Johnny R, Lou, and Willy." I wrote a name at the top of list. "Plus their boss, Redwood."

Chapter 54

REDWOOD FISHED THE FLIP PHONE FROM HIS POCKET. "Yes."

"This is Johnny R., Mr. Redwood. We been staking out the restaurant like you said. By the way, those ribs are the best I ever ate. All the guys think so."

"Let's be perfectly clear on one thing, Johnny. You and I do not have a social relationship; I am your employer. If you felt you needed to eat at the restaurant as part of your mission, then I applaud your initiative. You do not, however, owe me a restaurant review."

"Sorry, boss."

"Now tell me: What have you learned?"

"The news ain't good, Mr. Redwood. I asked our waitress if I could meet the chef and pay him our compliments. We did that and I asked the guy if I could also thank the owner for having such a fine establishment. He said he ain't seen the guy in a week or so. His office manager says he's on vacation. She don't know when he's coming back. Said he's in Europe or someplace like that. What you want us to do now?"

"Get back on Wallace. He's your top priority. If you encounter McCrary or Snopolski, be careful; you know what happened to the other four men I sent."

Chapter 55

JORGE CASTELLANO OPENED THE CONFERENCE ROOM DOOR. "I got news. You remember the body that washed up on the Beachline yesterday afternoon?"

"Yeah. Snoop and I were in Diane Toklas's conference room yesterday when they recovered the body. We watched through the window."

"We've identified the victim. It's James Ponder."

"This must tie into the railroad bombing. When do we tell the FBI what we know?" Bigs asked.

"Jorge, come in and close the door." I waited while he did. "You got a time of death on Ponder?"

"Ten a.m. to noon, Sunday."

That explained why no one was on duty to follow me Sunday morning. All three teams had been focused on Ponder. "Did Terry tell you about Redwood and the guys he sent down here to Port City?"

"Yeah. She let me read her report while she waited for Kelly and Bigs to finish taking your statements. What about them?"

I needed coffee. I returned to the table for my cup. "*Amigo*, we need you to join this meeting. We have tough decisions to make. You need to be in on them."

"Sure thing, Chuck." Jorge snatched the last *pan dulce* and sat at the head of the table.

"Redwood sent killers after Michelle and after me," I said. "He was after Michelle because she could identify Ponder, Wallace, and Shamanski. He was after me because he thought I'd lead him to Michelle. That didn't work, so he sent down two more teams to search for her." I sipped coffee and felt the caffeine hit my bloodstream.

"What's your point?" Jorge asked.

"Redwood is tying up loose ends, targeting anyone who knows anything about the bombing. He intends to eliminate anyone who can identify him. He's already killed James Ponder. Maybe Steven Wallace and Katharine Shamanski can identify him. If so, they could be his next targets."

Jorge chewed his *pan dulce*, swallowed. "We don't know that Shamanski and Wallace can identify him. Maybe Ponder was the only link."

"If that were the case, he would have called off all three teams after they killed Ponder. Remember, Ponder was dead yesterday before they shot up Snoop's car on Beachline Causeway and followed me to the phosphate mine."

"Good point, but it's not proof that Redwood is after them." Jorge finished his pastry.

Terry frowned. "Lieutenant, if we have reasonable suspicion that Redwood might target Wallace and Shamanski, shouldn't we place them in protective custody?"

I scanned around the table. "Shamanski helped Ponder build the bomb, and Wallace set the thing off, killing two railroad workers. They're both guilty of capital murder. *If* you bring them to justice, they'll get life in prison. And if they both testify against Redwood, the real ringleader, they'll do a lot less time in prison. Like you said, *amigo*, we don't *know* that Redwood is after Shamanski and Wallace. Why not leave them out there to let nature take its course? Sort of poetic justice."

Terry jumped to her feet. "I may be the most junior cop in the room, but legally Shamanski and Wallace are innocent until proven guilty. We can't leave them exposed."

"Terry," I said, "there is the law and there is justice. Usually law and justice work side by side, moving law officers in the same direction. But not always. Sometimes the law doesn't move in the direction of justice. It doesn't move in the opposite direction from justice, but it pulls cops in a different direction. Justice sometimes gets lost in the shuffle."

Jorge said, "Terry, you remember that I was arrested for a murder I didn't commit. That was legal, but it wasn't justice. If it hadn't been for Chuck…"

"That's one reason I'm no longer a cop," I added. "If I'd been a cop and subject to a cop's restrictions, then I couldn't have found the real killer. I intend to find Redwood, but I may have to cut corners to do it."

I glanced around the table. "This must be a unanimous decision. To find out who Redwood is, I need unofficial access to police resources. I've got to know that I won't be hung out to dry."

Jorge gestured toward Kelly first.

Her lips compressed into a straight line. "Why not?"

Jorge glanced at Bigs, who nodded.

Lastly, he faced Terry. He didn't say a word.

Terry frowned. "What should I do, Lieutenant?"

"Your choice," he said.

"I'm in." she said.

I stood up. "Good. Kelly, did you or Bigs have anything else you wanted to ask Snoop or me about the shootout last night? No? Great. Jorge, thanks for sitting in on the meeting. Snoop and I are going to meet privately with Terry now. We'll let you nice folks get on with your day." I waited until they were gone.

"Terry, I need to know where those twelve phones were when they went dark. Where's the best area to work?"

"My desk computer. Let's go." She led us to her work station.

I knew that Redwood's phone went dark in Chicago. "I need a specific street address where he made each of his calls."

"Can't do that, Chuck," Terry said. "These are cheap phones without the built-in GPS. I can give you the cell tower locations and the times the mobile system handed off the phone to the next tower. I might be able to narrow it down to about thirty meters, say, a half-block."

"Okay, let's go with that."

Terry tapped her keyboard. "The calls originated from the two cell towers on the Willis Tower or else towers near Kenilworth, Skokie, and Winnetka, Illinois. Those are all suburbs of Chicago. See this section here where the signal is handed off from one tower to the next?" She pointed to a line on her computer monitor. "It's at 5:48 p.m. local time. Probably commuting home. He must live in the high-rent district and work in or near the Willis Tower."

I had a glimmer of an idea. "Snoop, call Flamer and have him find out where Walter Eliazar's office is. Also, where Katharine Shamanski's father's office is and her mother's office too."

Snoop carried his phone across the room where it was quieter.

I faced Terry. "After I confiscated the three stooges' flip phones, they went to the nearest Walmart and bought replacements. They must have gotten the money from one of the other teams, because I pocketed their cash and credit cards. Maybe they did that again after they went dark with the new phones last night. Where did they go dark?"

She did her magic on her computer again. "They were on the Mango Island cell tower. Looks like in the ferry terminal parking lot again."

"They staked out Mango Island, waiting for Snoop or me to visit Michelle or else bring her off the island again. Find the Walmart nearest the Mango Island terminal."

"South Beach."

"Let's go."

Twenty minutes later, Terry flashed her badge and the store manager at the South Beach Walmart gave us access to their security camera recordings. Like tugging a string and unraveling a sweater, we got their new cellphone numbers. By the next morning, Terry would have a warrant to tap the new phones. The next time they touched base with Redwood and Team Three, we would learn the rest of the new phone numbers, maybe capture a recording of somebody talking to Redwood. The miracle of modern technology.

But they might wait until the next night to check in with Redwood.

There was nothing I could do but wait.

Chapter 56

THE NEXT MORNING, SNOOP AND I CRUISED THE STREETS around Steven Wallace's apartment in the invisible minivan. Team Three's cellphones had gone dark from the cell tower near Wallace's apartment. I expected the three stooges to stake out the Mango Island ferry again and Team Three to search for Wallace and Shamanski. I called Terry. "Where are the three stooges?"

"Wait a sec... Mango Island cell tower. They're hanging around the ferry parking lot again."

"Have you picked up Team Three's new phone numbers yet?"

"Yeah. Got them early this morning. All four are near Wallace's apartment."

Funny that one team wasn't staking out Katherine Shamanski at her apartment near the UAC campus. If Redwood was killing off the loose ends, why wasn't he after Shamanski too? Could Redwood be Morris Shamanski, her father? That would explain him not sending a hit squad after her.

Terry pinged Wallace's phone, and I knew he was in a hotel near the beach in Hollywood—Florida, not California. Wallace's smartphone was an older model and didn't have the GPS locator chip. He'd gone to ground after he heard about Ponder's death. Jorge agreed not to execute a search warrant on Wallace. The hoodlums had staked out Wallace's apartment. If cops showed up with a warrant, they would know we were onto Wallace.

I needed to pinpoint the locations of the remaining four gunmen.

There were four entrances to the central courtyard in front of Wallace's apartment. Snoop and I spotted Team Three's rented Ford parked a block away on a side street in a two-hour parking zone. I stuck a GPS tracker under the empty car's bumper and texted the license plate to Terry. Team Three had the manpower to stake out all four courtyard accesses from the surrounding streets. I had not had that luxury when I first followed Wallace.

I spotted the first three easily. They stood out like skunks at a black cat convention. The fourth one was tougher. "Snoop, he has to be where he can spot Wallace if he walks through the gap between those two buildings. All I see is dads, moms, and kids."

"He's gotta be posing as a dad, Chuck."

"But all of them are with little kids. Holy crap."

"What? What did you see?" Snoop asked.

"It's not what I see; it's what I don't see. Or, rather, what I didn't notice until now. Three of the four names on Team Three could be women's names. *Harry* is a nickname for Harriett. *Lou* is short for Louise or Louisa or Luella. *Willy* could be Willamina. There she is—the one reading a book on the park bench next to the stroller." I zoomed in and snapped her picture.

"But she's with a kid."

"No, she's with a stroller, but it must be empty. It's a brilliant disguise, really. She probably keeps her weapon in the stroller under a blanket. Okay, we've tagged all of Team Three. I'll email their photos to Terry to try to identify them."

Wallace's Tesla was parked at the electric charging station. How did he get to Hollywood Beach?

I called Terry. "Call Uber and the taxi companies and ask if they picked up Steven Wallace in the last couple of days and where they dropped him. Check Uber first; Michelle told me Wallace has an Uber app on his phone. If that doesn't work, call Lyft."

###

UBER HAD DRIVEN WALLACE TO THE REYNOLDS BEACHSIDE HOTEL a block off A1A. Built in the forties, the sand-colored Art Deco motel was well maintained. Rounded turrets bulged toward the street at each end of the flat-roofed building. They enclosed three sides of a grassy courtyard with a swimming pool, lounges, and umbrellas. Concrete staircases with steps painted terra-cotta curved around the turrets up to the second floor, where a balcony stretched from one side of the motel to the other. A sign visible from Surf Road said *Rooms $49 and up* and *Kitchenettes available*. It was three hundred yards from the beach.

We walked around to the rear parking lot. "No rear exits from the upstairs rooms, Snoop. Even the windows have air conditioning units in them."

Snoop said, "Not the bathroom windows, but they're kinda small to climb out of."

"Notice there's no fire escape."

"Building was grandfathered on the fire codes. Must have been built in the thirties or forties."

"So, if he's on the second floor," I said, "the front door is the only way in and out."

Snoop pointed up. "Unless he crawls out the bathroom window."

"Unless that. If he does that, I ain't jumping after him."

"Me neither."

"Some ground floor units have back doors."

Snoop scanned the back wall of the motel. "Probably the larger units. Sign said they have kitchenettes; those could be them."

The rear doors had unit numbers mounted beside the doors. "I'll go around and knock on 117."

"Odds are that's not his room."

"We have to start somewhere. Maybe we'll get lucky. You wait here and catch him if he runs out this way."

I returned to the front grassy lawn and studied the layout. I had to do something before the manager noticed two strangers poking around. I climbed the first of three terra-cotta colored steps for Unit 117 and knocked on the door. I waited and knocked again. The twin front windows were draped so I couldn't see inside. The window closest to the door had an air conditioner whirring in the muggy heat.

I moved to Unit 115 and knocked. Same result. I called Snoop's cellphone. "I'm going to touch base with the manager. Wait there."

A small bell mounted above the door rang when I walked into the office. The living room of the manager's apartment was visible through the door behind the counter. A fiftyish woman entered through that door. "How can I help you?"

I gave her my hundred-watt smile. "I'm Chuck McCrary. I came here to treat my friend Steve Wallace to lunch, but he's not in his room. I wondered if maybe he left a message for me."

"He's not in his room? He doesn't have a car, so he can't have gone far. Maybe he's at the beach."

"Steve said to pick him up at 11:45 and it's that time now. I knocked on 117 and he didn't answer. You sure he didn't leave a message for Chuck McCrary?"

"You got the wrong room, mister. Mr. Wallace is in room 107, not 117."

I thanked her, went back to the grass lawn, and called Snoop. "He's in room 107. Does it have a back door?"

"Yeah. You knock; I'll wait here in case he rabbits."

I stood on the bottom step and knocked. The drape above the window a/c unit moved and an eye peeked out. I smiled and waved. Just folks. The drape closed again. Nothing happened. I counted to ten and knocked again. "Steve, it's Chuck McCrary. I'm here to treat you to lunch." No answer.

Michelle had given me his phone number, so I called it. I heard it ringing behind the door, but he didn't answer. When it went to voicemail, I hung up.

I stepped back on the grass and called Snoop's cellphone. "Anything happening back there?"

"Nope. You want me to knock too?"

"May as well. You couldn't do any worse than I'm doing."

The front door opened a crack, held by the safety chain. "What do you want?" The room behind him was dark as a cave.

I stepped to the bottom of the steps, four feet from the door and a foot lower. "I told you; I'm here to buy you lunch."

"I don't know you. I don't know you at all actually."

"Chuck McCrary. The guy who knocked on the back door is Snoop Snopolski. We're friends of Michelle Babcock."

Wallace's eyes gazed over my head at nothing in particular. They darted back and forth for a second. He nodded, perhaps to himself. He frowned. "Wait... wait here." He closed the door. The noise from the a/c unit was so loud I couldn't hear if he was sliding the safety chain off. I hoped so. Nothing happened, then I heard his voice from inside. "Come in."

I opened the door and stepped into the apartment. After the bright sunshine, I could barely see. Dim light squeezed around the heavy drapes in the front windows. All the other lights were off. The kitchenette at the rear of the unit had a small frosted glass window that added a little light, but not enough to read a newspaper.

It was so dark I could scarcely make out Wallace standing on the far side the bed, a revolver in his hand. Pointed at me.

Chapter 57

"RAISE YOUR HANDS UP, McCRARY. Hands up." He held the revolver in two shaky hands. He shifted his weight, dancing from one foot to the other.

"That's not necessary, Steve. You don't have to point a gun at me. I'm here to help you."

"Never call me Steve. Never call me Steve. You don't have the right to call me Steve. You don't have that right, McCrary. I've earned the right to be called *Dr. Wallace.*" He waved the gun up and down to emphasize his point. "I sometimes let dear friends call me Steven. Yes I do, I do actually. But you are not a dear friend; I don't know you."

I make it a policy never to argue with people who are pointing a gun at me. Especially nervous, twitchy, crazy people. "Sorry, Dr. Wallace. It's okay for you to call me Chuck though. Everyone does." I smiled. "I'm here to help you."

Wallace relaxed a smidgeon. On a ten-point scale, the tension in the room declined from 9.9 to maybe 9.5, or maybe that was just me. I didn't raise my hands, but I kept them where he could see them.

Wallace waved the revolver. "How can you help me? I don't need any help. I'm fine actually. I especially don't need *your* help, McCrary. How can you help me?"

"Redwood…" I watched to notice if his eyes widened. They did and I continued. "Redwood sent eleven people to kill you, James Ponder, Michelle Babcock, and Katharine Shamanski." His eyes widened more. "Three of them are waiting to catch and kill Michelle Babcock, and four of them are waiting near your apartment as we speak. They came down from Chicago to kill you all. They already found and killed James Ponder. I came here to save you from them."

"I don't need saving. I'm fine actually. I'm just fine. Redwood would never kill me; I'm central to the operation. Central." He smiled as if he loved hearing his own words. "Central to the operation. James was merely a pawn. A pawn and a dupe, McCrary. He's no great loss. No loss at all actually."

"Please call me Chuck, Dr. Wallace. Everyone calls me Chuck. May I sit down? We need to talk."

"Sit down? Sit down?"

I pointed at the ancient Formica and chrome dinette suite with its two matching chairs. It could have been an original from the 1940s. "I can make us coffee or tea and we can talk. How about that? Do you have coffee or tea?" If he had coffee, I prayed it was decaf. I didn't want to make this nutcase any more nervous than he already was.

Wallace wobbled two jerky steps toward me, waving the gun as he advanced. "I have tea, McCrary. I have tea. Do you know how to make tea?"

"Sure, Dr. Wallace. I'll get the teapot." I moved sideways toward the kitchen; Wallace moved sideways toward the front door like we were twirling in a slow dance.

He kept the gun aimed at me, but I had moved ten feet farther away.

"I'll make tea, and you and I can sit at this dinette near the front door and talk about things." I backed into the kitchen, and Wallace sidestepped toward the dinette. "Why don't you relax in that chair by the front door while I make the tea?" The farther away from me he was, the more likely he would miss if he did shoot.

As I lifted the teapot with one hand, I reached behind with the other and unlocked the back door. Couldn't hurt. "Where are the tea bags, Dr. Wallace?"

He let go of the gun with one hand and pointed. "First cabinet."

As I filled the teapot, I noticed two used cups filled with water in the sink. I positioned the pot on the burner and switched it on. "Thank you, Dr. Wallace." I opened the cabinet and found a box of teabags. "And the cups?"

He pointed again. "Second cabinet."

"Thank you, Dr. Wallace. Why don't you have a seat by the front door and I'll sit across from you while we wait for the water to boil. I'll fix us a nice cup of tea."

Wallace shuffled one more step sideways. His leg bumped the chair.

"Dr. Wallace, since you're standing beside the chair, why don't you sit down and I'll fix the tea?" The teapot whistled.

He glanced away, and the revolver wavered. "Maybe I will sit down." The pistol wobbled again. "I've not been sleeping well actually. Not well at all."

"Then relax; have a seat." I waited for my chance.

As Wallace twisted to move the chair, I opened the back door.

"Now Snoop." I jumped out the back, slammed the door behind me, and rolled out of the line of fire as Wallace fired a single time. The bullet shattered the frosted glass window. I reached into my side pocket for my cellphone, which had been on the whole time. "You got him, Snoop?"

"I've got him. We're clear."

It's a funny thing about one gunshot. Most people who hear one gunshot don't recognize that it's gunfire. If they're of a certain age, they think it's a car backfiring, forgetting that modern cars virtually never backfire. If they're younger, they think someone slammed a door, or dropped a heavy trunk—almost anything but a gunshot. It's when they hear two or more shots that they realize what they are and call the police. I wasn't worried. If the cops did come, I was on the side of the angels this time.

I opened the back door and switched the stove off. Snoop was standing across the room from Wallace holding the professor's revolver. I breathed again. "Good work, Snoop. You want tea?"

"*Nah*, I got too hot standing in the sun listening to you and Dr. Looney Tunes here enjoy yourselves in this lovely air-conditioned room."

I poured a cup of water for Wallace and carried it and a tea bag to the dinette. "Here you are, Dr. Wallace." I gave him the cup and tea bag and dragged the other chair across the room in case he decided to throw boiling water at me.

He dipped his tea bag up and down, up and down, up and down. "I could use a nice cup of tea actually, McCrary."

Snoop sat on the bed. I spun the chair around and straddled the back. "Dr. Wallace, tell me about Redwood."

"Redwood would never kill me. Never kill me actually. I'm central to the operation. Central."

I pulled out the sheet of paper that Terry had prepared for our meeting the previous day and slid it in front of Wallace. "Do you know what this is?"

He peered at the paper with interest. The tea had calmed him. "No. What is it?"

"That's a list of the code names and phone numbers of the people Redwood sent to kill you."

His eyes cut to me then back to the list.

"You notice Redwood's name at the top," I said. "We know all about him."

"I'm central to the operation actually."

"Not any more, Dr. Wallace. In Redwood's opinion, you are no longer an asset. You have become a liability. Ever since you blew up that railroad bridge and killed two men. That was a bridge too far." I couldn't resist making the reference to the old war movie.

Wallace's bottom lip trembled as he brought the cup to his lips and blew on it. He was staring at something far, far away.

"The names below Redwood's name are designated Team One."

He wrenched his focus to the list again. "Team One?"

"Yes."

"*Johnny J, Ted,* and *Forte.* Those are the three gunmen from Chicago that Redwood sent to ambush Michelle Babcock."

He stared at the list.

"Do you see Team Two?" I asked.

Wallace grunted.

"The first name, *Al* was Alberto A. Echeverria. I say 'was' since Al is dead."

"Dead?" He blew on his tea then sipped.

"Redwood sent Team Two to kill me and then to kill you. You and I are on the same side; Redwood wants us both dead. But I killed Al Monday night." I observed his reaction. There was none, so I continued. "*Artie* was Arthur Caprese. I killed him Monday night too. *Deuce* was Lawrence R. Lambert, Jr. My friend Snoop over there, he killed Deuce on Monday night. Snoop's on your side too, because Redwood tried to kill him twice."

Wallace's gaze darted like pin balls in an arcade, the tea forgotten.

"Last was *Yank*, William J. Yankelowicz. I killed him too. All of them are dead. But Redwood sent them to kill you, me, Michelle, and Snoop." The tea was now cool enough for me to slide the chair over to the table. I showed Wallace a picture of the four bodies. "This is the crime scene after Snoop and I finished with them."

Wallace snatched the phone and zoomed the picture. "I've never seen these men."

"Of course not. You weren't meant to see them until it was too late." I tapped the paper. "Consider this Team One." He did. "They're still out there. *Johnny J.* is John L. Janowicki, *Ted* is Theodore V. Bonham, and *Forte* is Forte Fortunato. Two hours ago, they were parked at the Mango Island ferry terminal waiting for Michelle to arrive so they could kill her.

"And then there's Team Three: Harry, Johnny R., Lou, and Willy. We don't know their full names, but I have their pictures." I found the photos I'd snapped near his apartment and scrolled them where he could see. "You'll notice that one killer is a woman. You might never suspect her. But the stroller is a prop. It's empty. She keeps her gun in there." I didn't know that, but it was what I would do if I were her. It sounded good too.

I found the next picture on my phone. "Dr. Wallace, Redwood sent these people to kill you and anyone else who might be able to identify him. Here's what James Ponder looked like the last time I saw him." I showed him the crime scene photo of Ponder's body after the Port City Marine Patrol dragged it from the ship channel.

Wallace's eyes grew big as silver dollars. "That's... that's horrible. James was a pawn, but he didn't deserve that."

I didn't mention that he'd murdered a night watchman with a tire iron and helped murder two railroad workers. "Redwood is your enemy. Even if I stop the remaining seven killers, he'll keep sending more until... You. Are. Dead."

"But... but... why? I'm central to the operation. Central actually."

I wagged a finger at him. "Not any more, you aren't. Now that we know about it, Dr. Wallace, there is no more operation. There will be no more put options. No more sucking money from the stock market like a vampire."

That struck a chord. He flinched.

"Yes, I know all about the put option scam. That operation is finished, *kaput*, over. You and Katherine Shamanski are the two people still alive who can identify Redwood. That's why you have to help me stop him. It's the best way to save your own life." I waited for his reaction.

"But we were doing so well," said Wallace. "We were doing so much good. Redwood donated to so many progressive causes and progressive campaigns. He funded so many environmental programs. We were making the world a better place. A much better place actually."

I spread my hands. "Not any more. It's over. You're a dead man walking, unless you help me take Redwood down."

Wallace picked up the paper with the killers' names and phone numbers on it. He crumpled it in his hands, hid his face, and sobbed loud and long.

Snoop and I glanced at each other, waiting for the catharsis to end.

Wallace whimpered. It occurred to me that he probably had stayed in that room for two days and had had nothing to eat. The sobbing grew fainter and faded into silence. He breathed deeply and let it out. Fumbling with the list of killers, he struggled to straighten the creases he'd made, rubbing it repeatedly with the side of his hand. He thrust it away and dropped both hands to his lap.

"Does Redwood actually intend to kill me?"

Chapter 58

SPECIAL AGENT IN CHARGE EUGENIO LOPEZ didn't appear happy as he gazed up from his desk. "You can keep your stinking cappuccino, McCrary. It's bad enough you call me down here on a Saturday morning, but you hide a person of interest in the case."

I set a cappuccino in front of anyway. "I hid a POI? I don't understand."

"The girl, Michelle Babcock. Her father hid her under a rock somewhere, but you told him to do it."

That wasn't a question, so I said nothing. I couldn't deny it, although technically it was her grandparents who hid her.

"What do you say to that?"

"I have nothing to say to that, Gene. This is America. You're entitled to your opinion on anything, even if it's wrong. That's the beauty of America, the land of the free and the home of the brave. We can agree to disagree."

"Stop waving the flag and cut the crap. Tell me why you called me down here. What's so damned important that you spoiled my Saturday?"

"I thought the Bureau never slept when they were on a case."

"That's a load of bull and you know it. We put our pants on one leg at a time like everybody else."

I sat down. "I'll make you glad you came down on the weekend. I'll answer your questions now."

"Where's Michelle Babcock?"

"Wrong question. Ask me who the bombers are."

"Okay, you win. Who are the bombers?" He finally picked up the cappuccino.

I dropped Wallace's picture on the desk. "This is Steven Wallace, PhD, professor of environmental studies at UAC, the ring leader of the other two perps, and, I might add, a real nutcase."

"He was already a person of interest. We asked Babcock about him, remember?" He pulled a legal pad from a drawer and wrote on it.

I lined up Ponder's picture beside Wallace's. "The late James Ponder, PhD candidate, formerly taking environmental studies under Wallace. He was the bearded guy from the video."

"We had figured that out too."

"Ponder had a Bachelor of Science in Chemistry and he probably helped build the bomb. He stole the boat used to transport the bomb."

"We knew about the BS in chemistry; we did not know about him stealing the boat." He wrote more on his notepad.

I tossed a stick drive onto the desk. "These are videos of Ponder stealing the boat and driving it up the Seeti River to wherever they hid it while they made the bomb. I can tell you what canal the house was on where they built the bomb, but you'll need to pin it down to the specific house. You folks are good at that. There may be another co-conspirator or fellow-traveler connected to the house."

Lopez wrote what I had said. "I don't suppose you know who the third perp is, do you?"

I lined up the third picture beside the other two. "She was on your radar also. Katherine Shamanski, senior at UAC, working toward a Bachelor of Science in Environmental Studies. She majored in chemistry for two years before she switched to environmental studies. She helped Ponder build the bomb."

"Where is she now?"

"She went into hiding after the bombing. I've had an operative searching for her without success. I suspect she's back with her parents in Chicago, but I don't know that for a fact. She's not in her apartment and her car is gone. Maybe she drove to Illinois. Y'all will have to find her, but you're good at that too."

Lopez wrote that down. "You got more?"

"I can prove Ponder stole a boat but not that it's the boat the bomb was in. By the way, he wore gloves to steal the boat and to drive it to the railroad bridge a few days later. Even if you found the remains of the boat, there wouldn't be any fingerprints on it. You'll have to prove it's the same boat that blew up the train. But y'all are good at that sort of thing too."

Lopez made more notes.

"Shamanski bought the bomb materials a little at a time in various stores in Georgia, South Carolina, and maybe Alabama. I can prove she bought 150 pounds of ammonium nitrate on one trip to Georgia. We inferred the other purchases from her credit card activity." I tossed another stick drive onto his desk. "This is the video of her purchasing one bag. Also, a list of her credit card charges on the other buying trips."

Lopez lifted the new stick drive. "Are you an anonymous source on these drives?"

"If you like, I'll wipe my prints off them and mail them to you."

"*Nah.*" Lopez used a tissue to wipe the stick drives. "I think I came to my office on Monday morning and found them lying on my desk. I have no idea how they got there. Maybe somebody on the cleaning crew got paid to leave them there. No way to tell."

"Works for me. You should claim inevitable discovery. We got the videos with old-fashioned shoe leather. No warrants required."

"How did you get Shamanski's credit card history?"

When someone asks a politician a question they don't want to answer, they answer a question they do want to answer. I did the same thing. "You could get the same information with a warrant based on the purchase video I gave you. Inevitable discovery."

"But how did you get the credit card information in the first place?"

"An anonymous source."

Lopez shrugged. "I had to ask."

I tapped the first picture. "You know that Wallace is the faculty advisor for a UAC club called Defenders of the Earth." Lopez started to speak. "Yes, I know. The TV program either doesn't know about the club or doesn't care. The other two perps are club members. They're a sort of an inner circle. They call themselves the Three Musketeers. He's Shamanski's faculty advisor, and I think he's sleeping with her too, but I haven't devoted any of my limited resources to prove it. You may want to consider that in your quest for a motive."

"What makes you think he's sleeping with her?" He drank more cappuccino.

"As a PhD candidate at Yale, Wallace was accused of date rape of a freshman woman. He was in his late thirties at the time, so we know he likes younger women. I have an anonymous source who claims that Shamanski is sleeping with him, and that he sleeps with one of his female undergraduate students currently."

"Your source reliable?"

I rocked my hand from side to side. "Don't know. Up to you whether to check it out."

Lopez scribbled more notes.

"Wallace is an ardent progressive and environmentalist. Nothing wrong with that. He receives millions of dollars in government grants to study global warming. Nothing illegal about that. He's been arrested for several illegal and violent protests. Apparently the people who dole out the government grants think there's nothing wrong with that either. Wallace paid Ponder over a hundred thousand dollars a year to work on his government grant projects. That means he had financial influence over Ponder as well as being his faculty advisor on his PhD program."

"Ponder lived one small step above a slum. He didn't make that kind of money."

I shrugged. "He was a junkie. Most of his money went up his nose or into his veins. Read the Medical Examiner's autopsy report. Ponder had a serious drug addiction."

"How did you discover this?"

"Underneath my shirt I wear a bright blue leotard with a big red *S* on it. Also, I have turned Steven Wallace; he agreed to cooperate."

"We'll need to interview Wallace," the FBI agent said.

"No problem. Snoop's babysitting him in a safe house until you pick him up."

"Where is he?"

I waved a hand. "Not so fast. Wallace's location is my hole card. We have to make a deal first."

"Wallace set off the bomb. He doesn't get any deal."

"I'm not talking about Wallace. I have a different deal for another person to work out. Can you get a U.S. Attorney in here on short notice?"

"Why would I do that?"

"Because Wallace was the head of the three people who blew up the railroad bridge, but he's not the big boss. There's another guy above Wallace who wasn't even a blip on your radar. A man who's pulled the others' strings for years. He called the shots, not merely for the railroad bombing, but for at least six other violent environmental protests that injured or killed innocent people. I've already established four more murders with this guy's fingerprints all over them."

Lopez sat up a little straighter. "Literal fingerprints?"

I shook my head. "Figurative. He called the plays, the others executed them. In effect, this guy is a serial killer with an environmentalist theme song. And I have evidence he's planning another attack on Great Southeast Forest Products. They've got operations is a dozen states, and you have the resources to prevent the attack."

"Who is the big guy?"

"I'll get to that. You'll need to bring a U.S. Attorney down here to cut a deal with another person. A semi-innocent person in the wrong place at the wrong time."

Lopez sipped his cappuccino. "I'm interested."

I waited.

"Can you deliver this serial killer?"

I shrugged. "That may be a problem, Gene."

"How so?"

"He's 'connected' in both meanings of the term." I made air quotes.

"Oh?"

"He's politically connected and also connected to the mob, although he hides that so well you'd never prove it."

"Then how did you find out?"

I shrugged again. "Gene, I'm a private investigator; you're a federal cop. Seven of eleven guys we identified in three hit squads hail from Chicago and work for a mobster named Adam Wolenski, but I can't prove it in court. You have a legal obligation to prove everything you know; I don't. Sometimes I just *know*."

Lopez made a *go on* gesture.

"This top dog's code name is *Redwood*. According to Wallace, Redwood has political connections all the way to the top of the Justice Department. He's the kind of guy who's invited to Presidential Inaugural Balls. To top it off, he has more money than Oprah, and he's a sharp attorney. I spent the last two days researching files on the case and all I come up with is circumstantial evidence. Some evidence is indirect—smoke but no fire. It might be so hard to prove the case that he could persuade a friendly Attorney General to let it slide."

"So why should we make a deal?"

"The deal I want is unrelated to this serial killer. It's for a semi-innocent bystander in the wrong place. This person deserves a break. After you hear the whole story, you'll think so too."

"You want Michelle Babcock to skate on felony murder in exchange for telling us where you stashed Steven Wallace?"

"I never said it was Michelle Babcock."

"You didn't have to. You're not the only one investigating this case." Lopez grinned. "We found the fourth person when we enhanced the security video footage of the bombing. It fits Babcock's description like a glove. We investigated her. She's a sweet, naïve kid who got in over her head with some bad actors." He held up a hand. "You don't need to confirm or deny."

"In return, I'll give you Wallace and bring down Redwood, the serial killer, one way or another."

"You'll bring down Redwood," he repeated. "Interesting choice of words, 'bring down.' Could mean a lot of things."

"After you hear the whole story on this gangster, you'll agree he needs to be dealt with. If you don't agree, I'll walk away and the bad guy will too. You're the law, so it's your call. Cut my client a deal, and I'll tell you the whole story."

Lopez twirled his cappuccino cup in the hands. "You said the U.S. Attorney might not be able to prove a case against him."

"One way or another, Redwood needs to be brought to justice. He's caused a lot of deaths—six capital murders that I know of—and he'll cause a lot more if someone doesn't stop him. But if you can't bring him to trial…" I fell silent and waited for Lopez to consider his options.

He leaned his chair back and stared at the ceiling. He laced his fingers across his stomach.

I waited.

He hummed a tuneless ditty, then stopped and spoke in a voice so soft I could barely hear it. "My former boss, George W., said 'We'll bring the 9-11 evildoers to justice, or we'll bring justice to them.' I had finished training in Quantico. I remember him speaking on television like it was yesterday." He stood, walked to the window, his back to me. "Maybe an anonymous tipster will accidentally find Redwood's burner phone and send it to us."

"Or a burglar might steal Redwood's computer from his home, intending to sell it for drug money. But he discovers that the guy whose computer he stole is involved in bad stuff."

"So, in an attack of conscience, he sends it to us, the good old FBI?"

I shrugged. "Could happen."

"But if none of this evidence shows up?" I asked.

"This Redwood could slip on a banana peel, or accidentally fall in front of a train, or choke on a hotdog."

"Or get hit by a dump truck," I said, "or struck by lightning, or smashed by a falling meteorite."

"Or he could have a heart attack," Lopez countered, "or slip and fall in his bathtub and break his freakin' neck."

"The world can be a dangerous place, even for dangerous people."

A small smile creased his lips. "When can your client give her statement?"

"His or her statement," I amended. Abe Weisman would not want to meet on the Jewish Sabbath if at all possible. His associate Diane Toklas is observant but not orthodox; she'd told me she'd meet if necessary. "My client and my client's attorney are both waiting for my call. They can be here in twenty minutes."

"The U.S. Attorney may not be available on short notice. Could be tomorrow."

I shrugged. "Anytime, anyplace."

Lopez reached for his phone. "I'll make a call."

Chapter 59

IT WAS SUNDAY MORNING before Lopez could get the players together, so neither Diane nor Abe had any ethical dilemmas. The meet was scheduled in the Miami office of Harding Louis Jefferies, the U.S. Attorney for the Southern District of Florida. Lopez told me he'd asked Jefferies to come to the FBI office in Port City, but Jefferies and he played "who's got the bigger dick?" and Jefferies won.

Assistant District Attorney Tomás Estacado attended to put Atlantic County's oar in the water on behalf of Michelle's numerous state crimes.

I arrived early with a bag of bagels and a pint of lox and cream cheese spread I'd bought at a kosher deli near my condo. Estacado, Lopez, and I had coffee and bagels and chit-chatted in the conference room about the price of eggs in Omaha or something equally important until the real players arrived. Estacado knew that Harding Louis Jefferies was the eight-hundred-pound gorilla. Whatever the U. S. Attorney wanted, the U.S. Attorney got.

Jefferies and Abe Weisman, Diane Toklas's boss, walked in together. Jefferies wore a navy-blue blazer, a button-down cotton shirt with no tie, khaki slacks, and scuffed boat shoes with no socks. It was Sunday after all. Jefferies held the door for Abe, who wore a black satin yarmulke, a dark gray, three-piece pinstriped suit with a starched white shirt and a red and blue striped tie, his Allen Edmonds shoes burnished to a gleaming shine. Score one for Abe.

Jefferies sat at one end of the table, Abe at the other, Estacado across from me. You could never say that Abe sat at the foot of any table. He had a presence, a *gravitas* that made wherever he was the center of the action. Estacado and Lopez each wore a suit and tie, as did I. Score tied for the supporting cast.

Coffee and introductions were like the referee giving the pre-fight instructions to the boxers. I witnessed the fight from a ringside seat.

Abe and Jefferies bobbed and weaved. They threw punches and counterpunches, raised their guard and lowered it. They quoted scripture—or was it case law? Estacado threw in an occasional point so the big dogs didn't forget he was in the room. It was like the legal fight of the decade as they negotiated the terms of Michelle's deal. If I'd been an attorney, it might have been fascinating. As it was, after twenty minutes, it was like listening to two people argue in Mandarin. It continued over two hours. I drank three cups of coffee and took frequent bathroom breaks to stay awake.

At the end Abe, Jefferies, and Estacado shook hands. Michelle would plead guilty to a federal crime that I didn't even understand in return for a suspended sentence and five years' probation. The State of Florida agreed to drop all charges. She agreed to testify against any and all of the other conspirators at their trials. *If any of them are still alive*, I thought.

I handed Lopez a piece of paper. "Here's the address where Snoop is holding Wallace."

He read it, stuck it in his pocket. "I'll send two agents to collect him."

"I'll text Snoop that they're coming."

We broke for lunch, agreeing to reconvene at 1:30 for Michelle to give her statement. Abe and I stopped on the steps outside the Federal Building.

"I'll call Diane to bring Michelle down," Abe said. "She'll represent Michelle while she's giving her statement. Don't worry. Diane is young, but she's well qualified to handle this."

"I wasn't worried, Abe. In fact, I was surprised to see you in the meeting this morning instead of Diane. I even brought bagels, lox, and cream cheese from a kosher deli."

"Harding Louis Jefferies and I go back a long way. If I sent a cute thirty-year-old blonde like Diane to go up against him, he would feel disrespected. He thinks he's the smartest guy in the room—any room. He would be insulted if the other side didn't send their best. It's *gadles* on his part." He noted my expression. "Sorry, *gadles* is Yiddish for arrogance or conceit."

WE RECONVENED AFTER LUNCH, and Diane escorted Michelle into the room. Estacado, Kelly, and Bigs joined the meeting because the attempted murders of Snoop and Michelle by the three stooges were state crimes. I understood this part of the meeting since I took statements often when I was a police detective. In fact, I participated in two more hours of interviews, helping with questions, answers, and clarifications. Finally, the lawyers and cops had wrung Michelle out like a sponge and were ready to cut her loose.

Estacado referred to his notes. "We charge the three stooges with attempted murder, grand theft auto, carjacking, and reckless endangerment. Maybe a couple more I'll think of later. The four guys in Team Three—"

"Three guys and a woman," I corrected.

"Yeah, yeah," he said. "The four *persons* in Team Three, we can charge with conspiracy and illegal parking—maybe jaywalking too. It's pretty thin."

"The ballistics on the bullet that killed Ponder did not match any of the weapons from Team Dead," said Kelly. "The guy who pulled the trigger was either from the three stooges or Team

Three. We won't know who the triggerman was until we collar them. If we're lucky, it will be a member of Team Three and you'll be able to charge the remaining three as accessories."

"I'll like you to hold back on the collars," I said. "Terry Kovacs is tapping the phones of the three stooges and Team Three. We'd like to record Redwood's voice when they call him. Maybe we could do something with a voiceprint."

Kelly gave me a puzzled expression. "They haven't called every day?"

"Sort of. They report by text," I said, "and then with innocuous code words. Terry wants to record his voice. I think we should give it two or three days."

Concerned for Michelle's safety, I asked Kelly and Bigs to drive Michelle back to Mango Island. They left and the rest of us took a break and refilled our coffee.

Diane produced her own tape recorder and switched it on. She announced the date, time, location, and persons in attendance. "I represent Carlos Andres McCrary. Everything he is about to tell you is speculation. He does not represent that anything he says is a fact, so he is not lying to any federal agent. Are we clear on that?"

"I agree," Lopez said.

"I agree," Jefferies echoed.

Diane waved to me. "Go ahead, Chuck."

"Five years ago, an unknown person known as Redwood heard Steven Wallace speak at the World Economic Forum Annual Meeting in Davos, Switzerland on the threat of global warming and what corporations should do to combat it. Redwood agreed with Wallace's views and became an admirer."

"Where did you learn this?" Jefferies asked.

"Wallace told me. I was able to confirm that Wallace was, in fact, on the Davos program that year."

"So, Redwood attended the WEF meeting in Davos?"

"Yes, but Redwood didn't meet Wallace in person. He told Wallace that he wanted to remain 'an anonymous admirer.'" I made air quotes.

Jefferies asked, "How did Redwood make contact?"

"A week after the conference he sent Wallace an email from an anonymous account. Later they communicated by burner cellphone, with Redwood's phone number changed every month or so."

"Wallace has never met Redwood in person?"

"That's right. In the initial email, Redwood told Wallace that the shares of the companies that Wallace excoriated in his Davos speech declined big time the next day. Redwood did more research and noticed that bad publicity from a speech or a violent protest against a company often causes the company's stock to dive. Sometimes a big dive. Remember the effect of the Deepwater Horizon oil spill in the Gulf of Mexico in 2010. BP's stock tanked big time."

Jefferies was making notes. Lopez had heard this the previous afternoon.

"Redwood proposed that Wallace inform him in advance when Wallace's followers intended to protest or when Wallace himself was scheduled to attack a corporation in a major speech. Redwood would buy put options on the company's stock before the protest or the speech, betting that the stock would go down. After the stock tanked the next day, Redwood would sell the options at a quick profit and split the money with Wallace."

"How did he send the money to Wallace?" asked Jefferies.

"By wire transfer from a numbered account at McKinley Travers Bank & Trust Company in Liechtenstein," said Lopez. "I already checked yesterday; it's a dead end."

"Too bad," said Jefferies. "Wallace agreed to the scheme?"

"Wallace insisted that Redwood donate a portion of the profits to various progressive politicians and environmental causes that they both supported anyway. Redwood agreed, and they commenced to skim millions from the option market. They both made a pot full of money and kept most of it for themselves."

"Pretty ingenious actually," Jefferies said.

"Wait 'til you hear what Wallace did with the money."

"Wallace donated a little of his share of the loot to various left-wing Political Action Committees and environmental groups in order to maintain and increase his influence with them. Many environmentalist groups are legitimate, like the Sierra Club and the National Wildlife Federation, but Wallace supported groups that advocate civil disobedience and violence against law-abiding companies that they thought hadn't done their part to help combat global warming or otherwise help the environment. The bulk of the loot, he kept and invested. He lives modestly, so he's pretty wealthy."

"How wealthy?" asked Jefferies.

"Nine million and change in a brokerage account. He invested his share in what he called 'socially responsible mutual funds.'"

Lopez nodded to Jefferies. "We'll seize that for reparations. Make it part of the deal so he doesn't get the death penalty."

Jefferies made more notes. "Go on, Chuck."

"Redwood started small to learn if the scheme worked in the real world. It worked over two-thirds of the time, but not always. Sometimes a stock didn't tank and Redwood lost money. But, overall, he and Wallace made big scores—hundreds of thousands of dollars at first. Then Redwood stepped it up. He risked bigger purchases, gambled more money, and made bigger killings." I leaned back in the chair.

"The railroad bombing alone made him over three million dollars," said Lopez. "He's been doing that a half dozen times a year."

"And how do you know this?" asked Jefferies.

"Yesterday afternoon Chuck drove me to a covert office where Wallace keeps a cabinet full of files on the companies he's harassed over the last few years. We spent the afternoon reviewing the evidence. It's the real McCoy on how the scheme worked."

"Tell him the bad news, Gene," I said.

"We can't touch Redwood—legally."

"The arm of the Justice Department is long," Jefferies said. "We can touch anyone we need to."

I shook my head. "Wallace and Redwood are kindred spirits about global warming. They've talked on the phone for years now. Wallace said they're virtually friends. Based on things Redwood let slip over the phone, Wallace says that Redwood is on the U.S. Attorney General's Christmas card list, literally. Wallace knows for a fact that Redwood is on the White House Christmas card list, but that doesn't mean anything because thousands of people are. Redwood has at least the Cabinet Secretaries of the Department of Energy and the Department of the Interior on speed-dial, maybe others. He's tight with the Administrator of the Environmental Protection Agency. Redwood's loot on this scheme has financed large campaign contributions to environmentally conscious politicos for at least the last five years."

"I don't think we can touch him in court," Lopez said.

Jefferies sighed. "Chuck, Diane, can you give Special Agent Lopez and me the room for a minute?"

I stood. "Diane, it's time for a break. Let's get coffee."

Jefferies picked up Diane's tape recorder. "Take this with you and wait for us in the kitchen please."

No one else was in the office late on a Sunday afternoon. Nevertheless, I closed the door to the coffee room. Diane sat at a small table near the kitchen counter. "What do you think they're talking about, Chuck?"

"Discussing justice for Redwood."

"Justice for Redwood?" she echoed. "What does that even mean?"

"Everyone in that room today knows that Redwood has committed several capital crimes. Gene's an attorney, like Jefferies. They speak the same language. He'll explain to Jefferies why they don't have enough evidence to bring Redwood to trial, and he'll tell him that they'll probably never have enough evidence legally. Maybe they'll even discuss whether I can help them bring Redwood to justice... another way."

Diane's eyes widened. "That's what you've been angling for? You want them to engage your services to investigate Redwood so you can prove their impossible case for them?"

"The FBI doesn't hire outside investigators, Diane. They think they're the smartest guys in the room. Gene is typical of them. It's *gadles*, but that's the way they think."

"Where did you learn about *gadles*?"

I grinned. "Abe said it this morning. Did I pronounce it right?"

"Close enough. You have to be Jewish to get it right." She smiled. "So, if they won't hire you as an investigator, what do you expect from them? Are you going to find Redwood and burgle his home or office and send the evidence to the FBI as an anonymous tip like you did with Katharine Shamanski?"

I shrugged. "It's a shame the bagels are gone."

"Don't change the subject, Chuck. Surely you don't expect them to send you off as a... a hired killer, do you?"

I stared at Diane and didn't say anything. We both knew there was no legal way to stop Redwood. *She may be my attorney and our conversations may be privileged, but I draw the line at discussing my plans with her.*

"You're out of your mind if you think the U.S. Attorney and a Special Agent of the FBI will turn you loose as a sanctioned executioner."

That wasn't a question, so I said nothing. A Florida attorney is ethically obligated to blow the whistle if he or she knows that a client intends to commit a crime—any crime. *Even if the target deserves to get hit, she'll feel she needs to report my intention. Then she'll feel guilty if she does report me and equally guilty if she doesn't. I won't snag Diane on the horns of an ethical dilemma.*

"Well?" Diane asked.

I gave Diane my most sincere expression. "Diane, you are a wonderful criminal defense attorney. I value your opinion and Abe's on criminal matters. You both saved me from a life sentence for a murder I didn't commit."

"Thanks, and all that, but what do you have to say about this 'sanctioned kill' thing?" She made air quotes.

"You're a great attorney, but you don't know doodly squat about how the real world operates. Let's wait and see what they say."

The kitchen door opened and Lopez came in. "Will you join us in the conference room?"

Jefferies stood when Diane walked in. "Diane, you don't need to switch the recorder back on."

After we were seated, Jefferies flattened his hands on the table and moved them from side to side like he was smoothing an invisible tablecloth. "As you know, most FBI agents are educated as attorneys or CPAs. Special Agent Lopez has a Juris Doctor degree. He appreciates the, uh, difficulties sometimes of proving a case beyond a reasonable doubt..." He glanced at Lopez. "...even in the presence of moral certainty."

Jefferies stood and slid his notepad back in his briefcase. "This meeting is over." He shook hands around and left.

Diane appeared stunned. "What happened here?"

Lopez smiled. "The meeting is over. Michelle gets her deal. I have two guys assigned to pick up Wallace. Chuck has not committed any crime. Everybody's happy. Good job, counselor." He stood up. "Chuck and I will walk you out."

Diane and I stopped on the steps where Abe and I had stood earlier. Lopez walked to the bottom and waited out of earshot.

"What are you going to do about Redwood?"

"I have your phone numbers, Diane. I'll call you if I need you. Enjoy the rest of your weekend."

She squeezed my arm. "You're on thin ice here, Chuck. You shouldn't talk to the FBI without representation."

"Gene and I have things to discuss."

Diane started to object.

"Diane, I don't need counsel for this, uh, discussion. Gene said I've committed no crime. Enjoy the win, Diane."

Chapter 60

LOPEZ SHOVED HIS PLATE ASIDE AND RUBBED HIS STOMACH. "Man, that was good." He washed his banana cream pie down with more milk.

We had met at the Day and Night Diner. Veraleesa didn't work Sundays, but the pie was still good. This was where the case had opened when I met with Michelle. Was it less than three weeks ago?

I finished the last bite of my pecan pie. "What did you tell Jefferies to get him to come around?"

"I told him the truth: We would never pin anything on Redwood. The evidence wasn't there beyond a reasonable doubt. I told him I reviewed Wallace's files on the companies they attacked, that I interviewed him over the phone yesterday to clarify the elements and events of the scheme, and that Redwood was a powerful, twisted man who would find another poor schlub like Wallace to do his dirty work. I also told him that Great Southeast Forest Products has dozens of locations that could be the next target for violent protests or, worst case, eco-terrorism. Lives are at risk; he understood the urgency."

"I meant 'How did you get Jefferies to agree to a plea bargain for Michelle?' We both know you'll never call her to testify against Redwood, and Wallace has already turned State's evidence. What's the consideration for letting Michelle off easy?"

"Officially, Michelle agrees to testify in Redwood's trial, and there's always Katherine Shamanski for Michelle to testify against too. That's plenty of consideration for offering the plea deal." He pushed his milk glass to one side. "Between us, I think that Michelle was criminally foolish in the protest banner fiasco. She'll pay a small price in probation for the Justice Department to have plausible deniability concerning Redwood's future. The Department can demonstrate their intent to prosecute Redwood. We know Wallace will plead out. Any good criminal defense attorney will convince the Shamanski woman to plead out too. We located the house on the canal where the bomb was built. By the time our forensic guys finish processing it, we'll have plenty of evidence that Shamanski helped build the bomb."

Lopez handed me a piece of paper. "This is the personal cellphone number for Andy Cabela, an agent in the Chicago field office. He's also a friend. I told him about you. If you need any resources or logistics, you call him. Naturally, I never gave you this number."

"Of course not." I entered the name and number in my phone's contact list. "You want me to eat this piece of paper, Gene?"

"Let me have it." He tore the paper slip into tiny pieces and dropped them onto his dirty plate. "Godspeed."

AT ONE TIME, THE WILLIS TOWER CLAIMED TO BE NORTH AMERICA'S TALLEST BUILDING. Whether that's true or not, it is gigantic. I shivered on the sidewalk in the raw April wind with my overcoat collar turned up and rubber-necked straight up at 110 stories of glass and steel. Thousands of people worked there. It's a small city. The internet said that dozens of law firms with hundreds of attorneys officed in the building. Most buildings within five hundred yards also used a Willis Tower cellphone tower.

Wallace had assured me that Redwood was an attorney and that he had a raspy voice. He sounded perpetually hoarse. I called Terry. "Any luck recording Redwood's voice yet?"

"Last night he called the leaders of both teams. I'll play you the recording of his call to John L. Janowicki. Johnny J. must be the leader of the three stooges. I'll hold the speaker up to my phone."

Redwood's voice was creepy. It sounded ominous, methodical, and cadenced. Little more than a whisper, the raspy words sounded like someone reading an obituary. Something is wrong; it is too quiet. *Wallace has not been seen at his home or on campus, Michelle is somewhere on Mango Island, and we don't know where McCrary is. If you don't see any action by tomorrow's check-in, call it off and come home.*

I couldn't call and ask to speak to hundreds of attorneys until I heard the creepy voice. There must have been a hundred or more attorneys living on the north side who officed in or near the Willis Tower. The search field was too broad. I had to narrow the parameters somehow.

I remembered my conversation with Diane Toklas in her office before Michelle's interview with the FBI agents. I told Diane I needed to find the connection between Walter Eliazar and Katherine Shamanski's parents. I felt at a bone-deep level that there was a connection somewhere. Then I had forgotten about it in the rush of the following days. Dumb mistake. I was glad Snoop wasn't in Chicago to bust my chops.

I went for coffee in the Willis Tower Starbucks and used their Wi-Fi to research suspects on my tablet. I punched up Morris Shamanski, Katharine's father. He officed at 233 South Wacker Drive, in the very Willis Tower where I sat. Walter Eliazar officed across the street from the Willis Tower. It couldn't be that easy. I plugged in earbuds and tried YouTube for video clips of Eliazar or Shamanski. I found an interview Eliazar had given after a trial. His voice sounded normal. Not Redwood. There were no video clips of Shamanski. I Googled Morris Shamanski's home address, not listed. Figured as much.

I called Flamer. "I need the home address of Morris Bertram Shamanski in the Chicago area. There's no listing on Google."

"This guy is Katherine Shamanski's father?"

"Yes."

Flamer hung up without saying goodbye.

Two minutes later, my email dinged. Flamer sent me Morris Shamanski's home address. It was in Kenilworth, the right neighborhood. If Morris Shamanski was Redwood, it explained why he hadn't sent a kill squad after his own daughter. I did a little research on Shamanski's law practice then called his office. "I'd like to speak with Mr. Shamanski, please."

"One moment and I'll connect you."

It couldn't be this easy. It never is.

"Mr. Shamanski's office."

"I'd like to speak to Mr. Shamanski, please."

"Mr. Shamanski is with someone. May I take a message?"

"This is Walter McNeil. I'm a neighbor of Bob and Elaine Fineman. The Finemans said that Mr. Shamanski got them over a million dollars from that fellow who ran the red light and hit their car." I had learned that on Shamanski's website.

"Yes, Mr. McNeil. Do you have a similar problem?"

"I sure do. My wife got T-boned by some idiot and damn near died. She recently got out of the hospital. I want to sue that son-of-a-bitch for everything he's got, and, believe you me, he's got plenty. That jerk drove a brand-new Cadillac Esplanade, so I know he's got money." I recited the number of the burner phone I bought that morning at a discount store near my hotel.

"I'll make sure Mr. Shamanski gets your message, Mr. McNeil. Thanks for calling."

I went back to the hotel and waited. I was close to the target.

Two hours later, Morris Shamanski returned the call. When he said "This is Morris Shamanski," I knew he wasn't Redwood. Dead end. I blew a little smoke up his skirt and hung up.

I called Flamer and explained the situation. "There's a connection between Walter Eliazar and Morris Shamanski or his wife, Virginia McAllister. Find it."

"I already looked. Not a to-the-ends-of-the-earth search, but pretty deep. What if there isn't a connection?"

"Then I've wasted my money and I'll think of something else. There is a connection; find it." ·

I called Lopez's colleague in Chicago.

"Andy Cabela here."

"Do you know who this is?"

"I recognize your number. Our mutual friend said you might call."

"Can we meet?"

"Give me ten minutes. I'm kinda in the middle of something."

"I'm in the Willis Tower. You're a twenty-minute cab ride away."

"You know where I am?"

"Our mutual friend gave me full contact particulars."

SECURITY WAS TIGHT AT THE FEDERAL BUILDING. I checked my weapon with the guards and waited for Agent Cabela to come downstairs.

"Let's go to my office." Cabela's office was on the tenth floor with a view of the federal parking garage across the street.

"Gene said you were on a special project and I should help you any way I can, but off the record."

"Thanks." I gave Cabela a full rundown of what I knew about Redwood, including the particulars of the people whose deaths he had caused. I wanted Cabela firmly on my side. I handed him a paper with Redwood's current cellphone number. "Can you give me any addresses on the north side, maybe near Kenilworth or Winnetka, where this number made phone calls from?"

Cabela punched up the number on his computer. "We can't give you an exact street address because this cheap phone doesn't have built-in GPS. I can get the location of the cell tower it used. Right now, for example, it's pinging off the Willis Tower. He's probably in his office. Thousands of phones use that tower, as I'm sure you know." He hit more keys. "This phone made a half-dozen evening voice calls and over twenty texts from these towers here on the north side." He touched the monitor that displayed the cell tower maps. "From the distribution of the towers used, I'd bet he lives in Kenilworth." He leaned back. "That's as close as I can get. Is that any help?"

"Not much. I knew he commuted from the Kenilworth/Winnetka area." I stood. "Thanks for trying."

"You have my number. Gene Lopez said this guy Redwood is a second-hand serial killer with another target already picked out. You need to find him—and sooner rather than later. If you come up with any more leads, no matter how far-fetched, you call me. We need to stop this guy before he kills more people."

"I will. Is there a cab stand downstairs?"

"You'll never get a cab out here. It's not like in the Loop. You'd better call Uber or Lyft."

###

A HALF-HOUR LATER, I WAS IN MY HOTEL ROOM scratching my head about what to do next when Flamer called. "Chuck, repeat after me."

"Huh? Okay."

"Flamer, you are a freakin' genius."

"Not until you show me the genius."

"I found the connection between Eliazar and Morris Shamanski. You would never find this on your own."

"Okay, let's hear it."

"I sent you an email. Call it up on your monitor. I'll wait."

I did. "It's on the screen."

"Shamanski's law firm incorporated SAVY Energy LLC seven years ago," Flamer said. "The S is for Shamanski, of course. V is Victor, one of Shamanski's partners. A and Y are two other investors from New York and L.A., also attorneys. That's why you never would find it. The connection is in L.A."

"I'm reading the list of investors," I said. "Albertson and Young are corporate attorneys; Albertson in New York and Young in Los Angeles. Says here that the four founders invested ten million dollars each, most of which was for research and development for a new type of solar energy collector… yada, yada… applied for a government-guaranteed loan… yada, yada… loan application went nowhere."

"Right," said Flamer. "Scroll down to the next section. One year later, SAVY has run through its initial investment and is about to fold its tent. The company again applies for a government bailout. This time they go big. They ask for a grant instead of a loan. Can you believe this? They don't even have to pay the money back. Free money, courtesy of United States Santa Claus. Notice the amount."

"Geez. Five hundred million dollars."

"They massaged their political connections with the Department of Energy to get the grant. The company struggles along for three more years and burns through the half billion dollars. They go broke, throw several hundred people out of work, and cost the US taxpayers half a billion dollars."

"*Hmph.* Where's the connection between Eliazar and Shamanski?"

"Next section. Read the biographies of the four founders."

I scrolled the page down to the biographies. "You said the connection was Young... there he is, Jason Young. What's the connection?"

"Jason Young graduated from Brown University Law School. Walter Eliazar graduated from Brown the same year."

"Flamer, you're a freakin' genius."

"Told ya."

Chapter 61

IF THE SAVY PARTNERS WERE INVOLVED in the put options scheme, any of them could be Redwood, except for Morris Shamanski, whom I'd already eliminated as a suspect. Redwood commuted from Kenilworth to the Willis Tower. My prime suspect was now Nelson Victor, the V in SAVY, the only other SAVY partner who lived in Chicago. I tried YouTube for any video clips of Nelson Victor. None. I reread the biography section of Flamer's email on SAVY. Victor specialized in environmental law and policy, whatever the heck that meant. I couldn't spoof him into a return phone call since I didn't have a clue what his specialty meant.

I needed to find out where he lived. If it wasn't in or near Kenilworth, I would be at another dead end.

I Googled him. No luck. I used a half dozen other websites that find people. Lots of items on his work and his law firm, but nothing on where he lived. I searched the Cook County Property Appraiser's website for any property he owned. Nothing.

I called Andy Cabela again. "It's me again."

"Sure, fire away."

"Not over the phone. Where can I meet you?"

"There's a coffee shop near here called A Cup of Kindness." He gave me the address. "Meet me there in twenty minutes."

###

I BOUGHT A LARGE CHOCOLATE CHIP COOKIE and coffee and joined Cabela at a table in the back. After pleasantries, I asked the favor. "Nelson Montgomery Victor, attorney-at-law. He offices in the Willis Tower. He's Morris Shamanski's law partner." I paused while he wrote that down.

"Okay, got that. What about him?"

"I need his personal cellphone number and home address, residential phone number, along with a description and license plates on his cars."

"You think he's Redwood?"

"Maybe. I want you to ping his personal cell and back trace it to March 27. Find if his personal phone pinged the same towers at the same time as Redwood's phone. I have the number Redwood used before the current one." I handed him a paper slip with the number.

"Give me ten minutes." He stepped out onto the sidewalk.

I texted Flamer:

Find me everything on Nelson Victor, especially political connections.

Cabela came back in twenty minutes. He leaned in closer to my ear and lowered his voice. "It's him. I've emailed you the back traces on the phones so you can read them yourself, but it's him. Nelson Victor is Redwood."

Chapter 62

I CLICKED ON THE COOK COUNTY PROPERTY APPRAISER'S WEBSITE AGAIN, using the street address Andy Cabela had given me. Victor's house was owned by Trust Number 672. The official mailing address to receive Cook County property tax notices was in Liechtenstein. I dug deeper on Trust Number 672; the trustee was McKinley Travers Bank & Trust Company.

Rule Seven: *There is no such thing as a coincidence—except when there is.* Not likely this time. There it was—a possible key to finding the evidence to make a successful prosecution against Redwood.

I read it twice to make sure I had the information right. The three stooges had rented their car with a credit card issued by McKinley Travers Bank. Wallace's share of the option loot had been wired from McKinley Travers Bank. McKinley Travers Bank owned Nelson Victor's house. I recalled one of my favorite lines from *Goldfinger*: "Once is happenstance; twice is coincidence; three times is enemy action."

I emailed Gene Lopez this additional information about the offshore bank. My phone rang immediately. "It's seven o'clock in Port City, Gene. I didn't expect you to still be at the office."

"The Bureau never sleeps when we're on a case. I researched McKinley Travers Bank in our files. Other FBI offices are working three cases involving this bank. None of them knew about the Chicago connection, and none of them had ever heard of Nelson Victor. This link could let us get the evidence to bring Redwood to trial. Maybe he won't need to slip in his bathtub and break his neck. I sent an internal memo to Andy Cabela. Call him and ask if you two can work out a way to get the evidence against this guy—especially since we now know his name and the bank connection. Maybe we can bring him to trial after all."

I called Cabela's cellphone. He was on his way home. He offered to meet me for dinner. It was six o'clock, seven in Port City, and I was hungry. I hadn't worked out for days, so I jogged the mile to the mom-and-pop restaurant he recommended. It featured Chicago soul food, and I ordered smothered pork chops, green beans, fried corn, and candied yams. I lingered over banana pudding and a second cup of coffee.

"I accessed Gene's memo on my phone and made a couple of calls to two other agents before you got here," Cabela said. "Based on what the other agents told me, we can get a warrant on Victor's home and office with this connection to the Liechtenstein bank."

"How long would you need to get the warrants?"

He rubbed his forehead with his fingers. "Couple of days, maybe three. Our SAIC is pretty conservative. He'll make me organize the leads from the other FBI offices and put all our ducks in a row. He's a belt-and-suspenders kind of guy."

I shook my head. "That's way too slow. Victor knows we're one step away from nailing him. He's avoided detection for years—stayed completely below the radar. He's panicking. I think he's retreating into a shell like a turtle with a dog barking at it. We've got to act now—like tonight."

"Why the rush? Victor's not going anywhere. He's lived in Chicago all his life. He owns a multimillion-dollar mansion. He's a partner in a successful law firm. He'll still be there in a few days."

"No, he won't." I shook my head. "His last message to his thugs in Port City said he would shut down the whole Port City operation today if his guys hadn't found me or Michelle by now.

He hasn't found me, obviously, and I've got Michelle buried where he'll never get to her. Redwood intends to cut his losses, dig a hole in the ground for all the evidence, jump in after it, and pull the dirt over his head." I leaned forward. "He'll go missing. With his offshore connections, he's probably amassed a fortune sitting in Liechtenstein. If Wallace has accumulated nine million dollars, you can bet that Victor has ten times more. What he's got in Chicago is chicken feed in comparison. Confronted with life in prison, he'll disappear forever while your SAIC has you jumping through hoops. We need to move now."

Cabela grimaced. "I've worked for the Chicago SAIC for seven years. He won't be rushed; he'll dig in his heels."

"Well, I don't need a search warrant, and I don't worry about due process. Any evidence I find, I can send to you as an anonymous tip. That way, it'll be admissible. What should I collect if I limit it to stuff I can carry at a dead run?"

"Computers, tablets, and cellphones, particularly the burner phone he's using now. The other stuff would be more than you can carry on a dead run: bank statements, files, crap like that. We always drive a van to cart away evidence when we execute a warrant."

"Okay. I need to know what I'll be up against, Andy. You can help. I want to know if Victor is a veteran—in other words, does he have any firearms training. Does he have any gun permits? Assuming that Kenilworth requires burglar alarm permits, what kind of burglar alarm system does his house have? Is it wired direct to the Kenilworth police and fire departments? If he's married, will his wife be home? What about children? What kind of conditions will I find in his house?"

"I can get that info tonight. Say, eight-thirty."

BY THE TIME I RETURNED TO THE HOTEL, Flamer's report on Victor's political connections had arrived. Nelson Victor was supposed to be a hotshot on environmental law and policy. It was natural that he would have arranged to testify before one or two congressional committees. I searched C-SPAN for his name. *Bingo*. I punched up his most recent appearance before the Energy and Commerce Committee hearing on the EPA's proposal to regulate carbon dioxide emissions from power plants. It was from seven years ago, right about the time SAVY Energy had been incorporated. *Why hasn't Victor testified on anything more recently?* I wondered. *Is he avoiding making his distinctive voice accessible?*

I tapped my fingers on the desk in the hotel room while the video, over two hours long, buffered its way to my laptop. I tapped *play*. The camera opened on a shot of the witness table where Nelson Victor waited to be introduced. The chairman took the floor himself to make a five-minute opening statement lauding the EPA and its administrator as a potential savior of the planet that served both the public and the world in general. Every few minutes the view switched to Victor, waiting with practiced patience at the green-draped witness table for his moment in the spotlight. His eyes had the warmth of your average iceberg. Dark blue suit, white broadcloth shirt, striped tie. I couldn't see his shoes, but I would bet he wore Allen Edmonds or equivalent.

The chairman recognized the ranking opposition leader sitting to his right. She read prepared remarks in which she claimed that the EPA's regulatory overreach was wrecking the economy with expensive mandates on the nation's utility companies. The chairman recognized four more representatives, two from each of the political parties, who each needed five minutes to preen and posture for the camera. Occasionally, the C-SPAN camera showed Victor or another committee member. Victor did his best to appear focused and interested in every platitude the committee members uttered. The other members frequently whispered to aides who leaned near them. One dozed. Finally, the chairman introduced Nelson Victor and read his credentials. The camera switched back and forth between the chairman, reading a long *curriculum vitae* and Victor, waiting patiently behind a half-smile. Was it me, or did it seem more like the sneer of an arrogant man? Thirty-nine minutes after he first appeared on the screen, he took the microphone.

Victor's smile for the camera did not reach his eyes. "Mr. Chairman…" The creepy, raspy voice was unmistakable. He was Redwood.

Chapter 63

I WATCHED VICTOR DRONE ON in favor of the EPA regulations, and I imagined what it would feel like if he caught me breaking into his house. If he refused to produce his burner phone and his computers, could I point a gun at him and squeeze the trigger?

I couldn't force myself to shoot an unarmed Arthur Caprese even though he had begged me to. *If I couldn't perform a mercy killing, how will I psyche myself up to kill Nelson Victor in his own home? How will I feel if I witness his blood splatter on the wall behind him? I'll feel guilty as hell; that's how I'll feel.*

This wasn't Afghanistan or Iraq. This wasn't a shootout with well-armed assassins sent to kill me. This was burglarizing a homeowner and gunning down a man in his own home if my plan didn't work.

Could I do it if it came to that?

Then I thought of Winston Taylor, the night watchman at the Hillside Pines Apartments construction site, and of his widow, his children, and his grandchildren. I thought of the two railroad workers who drowned in the Seeti River in the submerged train engine. I thought of what it would feel like to be trapped in a locomotive at the bottom of a river, watching the water rise around your feet, scrambling frantically and unsuccessfully to escape through the mud. What were their last thoughts as the water claimed them?

No, Nelson Montgomery Victor killed those victims as surely as if he started the fire or exploded the bomb with his own hands. Nelson Victor was not an innocent victim; he was the assailant, the killer of innocent people. *If push comes to shove, I'll think of him not as a person, but as a killer—a serial killer.*

It's easy to kill someone. If you're using a handgun, you get within ten yards—five yards is better—then squeeze the trigger. Up close and personal. With a rifle, you shoot from hundreds of yards away. Both a physical and an emotional distance. Line up the crosshairs on the telescopic sight, then squeeze the trigger. The killing is easy; the hard part is getting away with it, leaving no clue to tie you to the crime or the victim.

I muted the sound and observed Victor's body language. He read his notes. He flipped pages in a file. He reached to switch file folders. He looked right and left to regard various committee members as he editorialized in response to questions. I stamped his image and the way he moved indelibly in my mind. I didn't know what conditions I would encounter in his home. It might be pitch dark. His wife might be there, maybe children. If I confronted Victor I had to recognize him instantly.

I also had to ensure that no innocent people died with him. I couldn't shoot if a family member was behind him because a miss could hit an innocent. A through-and-through bullet travels a long way after ripping through a body so I needed to be careful of the area behind him.

I had brought along the Browning .380 that I'd purloined from one of the Team Dead bodies after the gunfight. I didn't know if the Browning was registered or not. The odds were that it had been used in another crime in the Chicago area. If I had to shoot, the ballistics on any bullet recovered from Victor's body would lead to a different Chicago crime and a different Chicago criminal. I slipped on a pair of rubber gloves and thumbed out three cartridges from the magazine. I was in luck. The dead man had loaded his pistol with Federal Premium Personal Defense cartridges. No surprise, since these were the cartridges preferred by most police departments, including mine in Port City. The cartridges would split and mushroom as they hit a target. The odds were that they would not go through his body and come out the other side. If they did, the wall behind would stop the bullet. I held the three cartridges closer to the light. Caprese's fingerprints were visible on the casings. I reloaded the Browning.

My cellphone rang; it was Andy Cabela. "Victor is married. His third wife lives with him and, far as we know, they are both home tonight. He has two adult children from his first marriage, both of whom live elsewhere. He has no military service, but he has a permit for a pistol. I don't know what kind. His burglar alarm is state-of-the-art and it's connected directly to both the Kenilworth police and fire department."

"Bummer. I won't be able to break in. Okay, time for Plan B."

"Which is?"

"You don't want to know."

###

KENILWORTH HAD BEEN DEVELOPED decades before rich people needed guardhouses and gated communities. The streets were public, and anyone could drive anywhere. Multimillion-dollar mansions lined the streets, most of them the better part of a century old and completely exposed to the public.

I punched up Victor's house and neighborhood on Google Earth and Street View. The house reminded me of the White House, but on a smaller scale. *There's no security fence around the grounds. Maybe I can approach from the back.* There was no alley, rather a small forest behind the house. *That guarantees privacy if I approach from behind, but I'd have to park a block away and sneak through a hundred yards of woods. It would take too long to exfiltrate after the mission, especially carrying a sack full of computers and other crap.*

From the Kenilworth Police Department website, I learned they had over a dozen well-trained, full-time sworn officers and a half-dozen part-timers, most of whom had been on the job for over ten years; they knew the town well. There had not been a murder or a robbery in Kenilworth in the last five years. The cops made frequent street patrols. They would notice a strange car parked on the street where the houses had off-street parking, especially at night.

I didn't use the rental car's GPS; that would show up in the device's history. I removed the battery from my phone for the same reason. No point having Victor's home address stored anywhere connected to me. Instead, I overpaid for a Chicago area street map from the hotel gift shop. Convenience costs.

I drove to the long-term parking lot at O'Hare International Airport and spotted a late-model Hyundai with Illinois plates parked in a secluded spot in the crowded parking lot. I circled the aisles. I didn't expect any more arrivals this late at night but you can't be too careful. I parked nearby, made sure I was alone, and switched license plates with the Hyundai.

Fifteen minutes later, I found a Walmart on the way to Kenilworth and bought a bunch of flowers and a vase. I cruised the streets for a two-block radius around Victor's house and found no vehicles parked on the street. I passed one Kenilworth PD patrol car, making its rounds in the chilly night. On my final reconnoiter, I zeroed in on Victor's block. There were three houses on his side of the street. His was the middle one. Three streetlights lit the block—one on each end and another across from his house.

I drove into the circular drive from the left so the driver's door faced the house. I left the engine running and the door open. I lifted the flowers from the passenger seat and climbed the front steps to the double front doors. Ringing the bell, I noticed that the forest green doors were made of steel. On a hunch, I rapped on the doors with my knuckle. *Thunk, thunk.* They sounded like they were bulletproof.

A raspy voice came from a brass-plated speaker discreetly mounted next to the video camera above the doors. "Who's there?"

"Flowers for Mr....," I consulted the clipboard, "Nelson... middle initial looks like an N, or maybe an M... Victor."

"I'm not expecting any flowers."

"Lots of people what get flowers ain't expecting 'em. I'm just the delivery man, boss."

"Who are they from?"

I had anticipated that question and looked up a local flower shop on the internet. "Apollo Blossom Shop in Winnetka," I said.

"I mean, who sent them to me?"

I hadn't counted on Victor being so suspicious, paranoid even. I'd used the phony flower delivery gig lots of times; it had always worked. Until now. I thought fast. I held the flowers up and pretended to read the card. "They're from Virginia McAllister." I figured he'd be intrigued by getting flowers from his partner's wife.

"Leave them on the porch."

Cheapskate doesn't want to tip me, I thought. "I can't. Youse gotta sign for 'em."

"Wait there. I'll be down shortly." *He must be upstairs. Please, God, let his wife stay upstairs.*

Two minutes passed. I felt my heart rate increase. Was he so paranoid that he wouldn't come to the door?

Finally, the door clicked open a couple of inches, secured by an industrial strength safety chain strong enough to tow a car. His right eye appeared in the slot. "I'm Nelson Victor."

I situated the flowers on the porch to one side. "Sign here, please." I held up a clipboard and pen. Victor's gaze swung from side to side as he scrutinized the wedge of his front lawn he could observe behind me. *Oh, crap. What if he thinks this is a trap?* I hadn't anticipated this level of paranoia.

The door closed and I heard the safety chain slide off with a heavy clunk. I transferred the clipboard to my left hand and faced away from the camera. I drew the Browning and held it by my right leg while I waited for him to open the door. I intended to hand him the clipboard. As he signed for the flowers, I would force my way inside and make him lead me to the evidence Cabela told me to get.

The doorknob clicked and the door on the right swung open about two feet. Victor must have been standing behind it, because I didn't see anyone. "Bring the flowers inside," a disembodied, raspy voice said. *This is not good.* I held the clipboard in my left hand and the Browning in my right, hidden in the folds of my overcoat.

"Sure thing, boss," I said. I turned my back and stuck the Browning in my belt, with my overcoat draped over it. He wouldn't notice it, but I couldn't get to it either. I picked up the vase in my right hand and stepped through the open door. The door opened wider; I still couldn't see him.

"Set the flowers on that table." Across the round foyer stood an antique peer mirror above an ornate marble-topped table. Carrying the flowers across the matching marble floor, I glanced in the mirror and saw Victor standing behind the door with a revolver pointed at my back.

Chapter 64

IF NELSON VICTOR INTENDED TO KILL ME, I was already dead. There was no way I could drop the flowers and the clipboard, yank my coat open, turn, and draw the Browning before he could shoot. At this range, he wouldn't miss. Therefore, he didn't intend to kill me; he was merely paranoid. Maybe he was this way with every stranger who appeared at his door; his whole door-opening routine seemed well-rehearsed.

I had no choice but to play it out. I pretended not to notice him standing behind me and kept walking. I positioned the flowers on the table and faced Victor. "Whoa, what the hell? What youse doing, man? You nuts or somethin'?"

I stood like a statue, eyes wide, knees shaking. "What you want, boss? I just want out of here; you don't have to tip me or nothin'." I let my voice break. "You don't even have to sign for nothing'. Let me go, boss. Oh god, don't shoot!" I fell to the floor on my knees, the clipboard skittering across the marble.

"Get up, young man. I'm not going to shoot. I wanted to make sure you were who you said you were. Of course, you'll get your tip. A big one, if you'll stop crying." He lowered the gun a little. It was a Smith & Wesson Model 686 .38 Special. He had jerked the hammer back, which wasn't necessary to cock the double-action revolver, but it made more of a hair trigger.

I climbed to my feet and walked toward the clipboard lying on the floor in front of the open door. It was three feet to his left, where I'd aimed when I tossed it.

"Stop right there." He pointed the gun again. "Don't come any closer."

I froze like a statue, hands at waist level. There was a video monitor built into the wall to the right of the door. My rent car showed in high definition on it. "I was gonna get the clipboard, boss."

He backed away a couple of feet, opening the door wider with his free hand. "Okay, you can pick it up now." He lowered the gun.

The crisp April wind blew through the door, flaring my overcoat. As I moved, I let my coat swirl a bit to let his eye get accustomed to its movement. "Oops," I said. "That's my pen there in the middle of the floor." I whirled again and walked back to the middle of the foyer. I picked up the pen in my right hand and extended it toward Victor. "Here, youse need this to sign."

He backed another foot. "You do it; forge my signature." The gun dropped a fraction more.

I shook my head and spread my hands in an exaggerated shrug. "Whatever you say, boss." I swirled my overcoat and turned toward the open door. I picked up the clipboard with my left hand. "You said somethin' about a tip, boss." I sidestepped once toward the center of the foyer as I turned to him with an expectant smile. I was three feet from him now. If I got the drop on him, I could force him to lead me to the evidence I needed.

"Of course, young man." He stuck his left hand in his pocket and produced a twenty-dollar bill. "Here." As he extended the bill, the revolver drooped a little more.

I grinned as wide as I could. "Hey, boss, thanks." Reaching for the bill, I dropped both my pen and clipboard. His attention flitted toward the falling clipboard, and I shot my free hand out to grab his revolver. I hoped to jam my thumb in the space between the hammer and cartridge to keep him from firing. No such luck.

He jumped to one side and raised the revolver as he staggered backward out of reach. The back of his legs slammed against the marble table in front of the peer mirror, disrupting his aim as he fired.

I whipped my overcoat aside and seized my Browning as Victor yanked the trigger again. As I aimed the Browning, Victor's bullet ripped through my overcoat sleeve, jerking my arm with it. Ears ringing, I dived to the right, following the motion of the overcoat. I raised the Browning as I slid across the marble floor. "Drop the gun, Victor."

Victor fired again. He overcompensated for his first bullet and missed. Chips of marble shattered off the foyer floor.

I rolled onto my back and swung my gun around. "Drop it. I don't want to kill you."

"Fuck you." Victor clutched his revolver in a two-hand grip and swung it toward me.

I shot him twice in the head. The twenty-dollar bill fluttered to the marble floor.

Chapter 65

A WOMAN SCREAMED UPSTAIRS.

I didn't need to feel Victor's pulse; his brains were splattered on the ornate peer mirror and the wall behind him. I closed the door behind me. I dropped the Browning on the welcome mat, walked back to the car, and drove away at two miles per hour under the speed limit.

Four minutes later a fireworks display of flashing red and blue emergency lights lit the sky low in the west. A parade of emergency vehicles rounded a corner and screamed into view, sirens wailing, coming right toward me.

My gut twisted into a knot. I had heard a woman scream, probably Victor's wife. The first thing she would have done was call 9-1-1, probably even before she came downstairs. In fact, the 9-1-1 operator would have told her to stay on the phone and hide in a closet upstairs until the cops arrived. Victor's address would have flashed on the emergency response center's screen before the wife said a word. When she reported hearing gunshots, the center would dispatch an ambulance, a fire truck, and at least one squad car—on a slow night, maybe even two or three. That must be the source of the dazzling light display heading my way.

I stopped at the curb like a good citizen and said a silent prayer that the squad cars weren't after me—yet. Sweat rolled down my temples. I held my breath until three Kenilworth patrol cars, a fire truck, and an ambulance screamed past. Their sirens dopplered to a lower pitch as they faded behind me. I waited for my heart to stop hammering in my chest before pulling away from the curb.

Within three miles, I was on I-94. The pulse in my forehead pounded as the adrenaline coursed through my veins. After-action physiological effects. Traffic was thin and as I drove, I peeled off the bushy mustache glued to my upper lip. I removed the Chicago Cubs watch cap and the skull cap I wore beneath it. At the second exit, I found an all-night McDonalds. Parking in the rear of the lot, I sat there for a moment with the shakes as I continued to recover from the effects of the shooting. I removed the blue contact lenses and peeled off the clear vinyl gloves from both hands. I stuffed everything but the watch cap into a large freezer bag. They barely fit.

I sat in the car while my heart rate slowed. I skinned off the Chicago Cubs sweatshirt I had worn to Victor's door. After locking the car, I dropped the freezer bag into a dumpster in the back. I stuffed the sweatshirt into a trash container in front of the door. After drinking a coffee inside, I abandoned the Cubs watch cap on the bench. Within the hour, someone else's DNA would be on it.

The coffee rebelled in my stomach. I rushed to the men's room and threw up. *Thank God there was no one in the restroom.*

I drove back to O'Hare Airport's long-term parking and switched back the license plates from my rental car to the Hyundai.

I was in bed in my hotel room by three a.m. I didn't sleep well. I kept seeing Nelson Victor's brains splatter on the mirror.

Chapter 66

HANK HICKHAM RAISED HIS GLASS. "To the successful conclusion of a hair-raising few weeks." Hank's wife Lorene and I lifted ours in salute. Michelle stared at her Eggs Benedict, her champagne flute untouched on the table.

After I had informed Michelle's family that Katherine Shamanski and Steven Wallace and the rest of Wolenski's gunmen had been arrested, Hank had insisted on a celebratory brunch at the Mango Island Caribbean Club before I drove Michelle back to her home and her parents. Children played on the nearby beach and splashed in the gentle waves. A Bimini Blue umbrella shaded our waterside table. Flags waved in the gentle breeze, the sun shined between the occasional fluffy clouds, sea birds soared and dived after fish, and boats sailed on Seeti Bay. In this little bubble, at this particular instant, all was right with the world, but not with Michelle.

The three of us clinked glasses and sipped champagne. "What happens now, Chuck?" asked Lorene.

"After brunch, I'll drive Michelle home. She'll appear in court next week to plead guilty to a minor offense. Then she reports to a parole officer periodically for the next five years. After that, she's home free."

Michelle focused on eating her Eggs Benedict, studiously avoiding eye contact with anyone. She must have been embarrassed by being the focus of so much scrutiny for so long.

Lorene glanced at her granddaughter. "What about the drug testing?"

"She'll be tested for drugs every week at first, then every month."

Lorene squeezed Michelle's forearm. "That's not so bad, honey."

Michelle fiddled with her Eggs Benedict.

"The best thing, Lorene," I said, "is that the U.S. Attorney and the District Attorney both agreed to have the judge withhold the adjudication of guilt."

"What the heck does that mean?" Hank asked.

"Technically, the court will agree not to convict Michelle of the crime to which she pleads guilty. She won't lose her civil rights. She can vote, hold office, even own a gun once her parole is over."

Hank smiled at Michelle. "Well, that's fine, honey. If you keep your nose clean for five years, you won't have a criminal record."

Michelle stared at her plate and chased a bite of Eggs Benedict around with her fork.

"Having the adjudication of guilt withheld also means that Michelle can eventually have her criminal record expunged," I added. "Abe Weisman negotiated that."

Michelle dropped her fork on her plate with a clatter, jumped up from the table, and hurried back inside the clubhouse, holding her napkin in front of her face.

Chapter 67

JOHN BABCOCK MET US AT HIS FRONT DOOR, beaming like a new father, which, in some respects, he was. His daughter Michelle was out of danger—at least from the law and from Redwood. She still had life to contend with and a possible drug addiction. He hugged Michelle and kissed her forehead. "Mickie, we've been so worried. I can't tell you how happy we are that this is over."

I stood behind her holding her suitcase.

John grabbed the suitcase. "Come in, come in, Chuck. Come say hello to Penny. I'll take Mickie's suitcase to her room."

We sat at the dining room table. Penny had baked cupcakes which she insisted I sample. "We've decided to send Michelle to rehab," Penny said. "We hope to get her back in school this summer or fall."

Michelle threw her cupcake across the room. "*You've* decided. *You've* decided. What about me? Don't I have any say in my own life?" She jumped to her feet. "For weeks now, everybody has been telling me what to do. Go stay with your grandparents. Now, go to Mango Island. Now, go hide under another name. Don't call your friends. Don't go on Facebook. Keep your head down. Cooperate with the police. Listen to your attorney. Do this; don't do that." She stood and clenched her fists. "I'm an adult. When do I get my life back?"

Her parents stared at her for a long breath.

"Michelle," I said and waited until she looked at me. "Think back to how you felt that first time you called me at home in the middle of the night. Your whole world had exploded, literally. You were panicked and didn't know who to trust. You begged me to get you out of the worst trouble you'd ever been in. Do you remember that feeling?"

Her lip trembled. She nodded.

"With the help of your parents and grandparents, I got you out of that mess. You're safe now."

She sat down.

"You ask when you'll get your life back. You'll get your life back in five years after you finish your parole. At least you'll have a life. Your so-called friends wanted to kill you; now they're all dead or in jail. You could have gone to prison for life; now you won't. All you have to do is pee in a cup once a week for five years and do what any other adult is expected to do—obey the law. Then you can live happily ever after any way you want. That sounds like a pretty good outcome to me."

Michelle sighed. "I'm sorry, Mom. I guess I should be thanking you and Dad for standing by me. Instead I've been blaming you for trouble I caused myself."

Penny grabbed Michelle's hand. "Honey, we'll always stand by you, no matter what you do. That's what parents do."

John grabbed Michelle's other hand. "We'll always be there, Mickie."

Her mom nodded towards the wall across the room. "Why don't you go clean up that cupcake now, honey?"

Michelle grabbed a couple of napkins and walked around the table.

Penny gave me a fake smile. "Let's talk about something more pleasant. How do you like the cupcakes, Chuck?"

"Delicious. Raspberry, aren't they? But I taste something else in there."

She smiled. "Combination raspberry and strawberry. I've never tested that recipe before. I think I'll bake them again. Do you want half-and-half with your coffee?"

"Yes, please."

"I'll have milk with mine," said John.

"Me too," Michelle said from across the dining room.

Penny returned with a pint carton of half-and-half in one hand and a gallon jug of milk in the other. "Now, Chuck, you know we think the world of you, and we can't thank you enough for saving our Michelle. We'll send you a check by return mail when we get your bill."

"Why do I feel like there's a 'but' coming?"

"Don't take this the wrong way," Penny said, "but let's hope that the next time we see you and Snoop again, it is at our Christmas party and Mom and Dad's Super Bowl party."

I lifted my coffee cup. "I'll drink to that."

Chapter 68

MIYO POURED ME A MARGARITA. She sat beside me on the balcony couch and we watched the sun descend once more behind the Port City skyline. "Welcome back. How was your trip out of town?"

"It was… successful."

"You didn't tell me where you were going."

"It was work related." I paused. "That's really all I can say."

"I guess I should be used to that by now. Well, you're home now and I'm glad to see you. What shall we drink to?"

"To Mother Earth—may her children survive the sins her defenders commit in her name."

"Say what?"

"To Mother Earth."

We drank.

Miyo squeezed my hand. "I'll bet there's a story behind that toast, isn't there?"

"You're big on watching the news. Have you been following the arrest of Steven Wallace and Katherine Shamanski for conspiracy and murder in the train bombing?"

"A little. Why?"

"A wise man once said, 'If you don't toot your own horn, there will be no music.' Did you ever hear anyone say that?"

"You're the first," Miyo replied. "Are you going to toot your own horn now?"

"Toot, toot." I beamed at her.

She leaned back. "Did you help with that case?"

"Along with Snoop and the FBI and a whole bunch of Port City cops and Flamer and the District Attorney and the U.S. Attorney and Tank Tyler. Yeah."

"My, aren't we modest."

"Toot, toot." I smirked and swigged my Margarita.

"Was this connected with those four men who tried to murder you in the Everglades?"

"That I can tell you because it was in the newspaper. They were sent down from Chicago by a gangster named Adam Wolenski."

"Was your trip to Chicago?"

"I'll never tell." I handed her a newspaper story I'd printed from the previous morning's online edition of the *Chicago Tribune*.

Miyo set down her Margarita and unfolded the sheet of paper. "This says that a prominent Chicago attorney, Nelson Victor, was gunned down in his own home Tuesday night by an unknown assailant who was delivering flowers. The gun the killer used belonged to Lawrence R. Lambert, Jr., one of Adam Wolenski's gang." Miyo gave me a quizzical expression. "Wasn't that one of the men who tried to kill you?"

I grinned. "Toot, toot."

She continued reading. "Lambert's fingerprints were on the bullets used to kill Victor, but Lambert was already dead here in Port City."

"Strange, isn't it?"

"Who the heck is Nelson Victor? Or can't you tell me?"

"I can tell you because it's a matter of public record. Nelson Victor was a law partner of Katherine Shamanski's father."

"Funniest thing. Okay, let's pull this together." She held up her index finger. "Wolenski sends four guys to kill you. Instead, you and Snoop kill them." She held up her middle finger. "Katherine Shamanski is involved with the train bombing and she gets arrested at her parents' house in Chicago." She added her ring finger. "Her father's law partner is killed with a gun that belongs to one of Wolenski's men." She added the little finger. "And that man is already dead." She ticked her thumb. "And that happens when you are away on business." She handed the printout back to me.

I held the sheet of paper over one of the candles on the table until it caught fire, then walked to the edge of the balcony and held the sheet as it burned, the ashes flying into the void. I dropped the last corner and it floated away.

Miyo joined me at the railing and grabbed my hand. "How do you explain all that?"

"Coincidence."

The end

Enjoy this book?
You can make a difference

REVIEWS ARE THE MOST POWERFUL TOOLS AN INDEPENDENT AUTHOR LIKE ME HAS TO GET ATTENTION FOR MY BOOKS. Much as I'd like to, I don't have the financial muscle of a New York publisher. I can't take out full-page ads in the newspaper or put posters on the subway or bus. (At least not yet, anyway!)

Instead, I have something more powerful and effective than that—something those publishers would kill to get their hands on: I have a committed and loyal bunch of readers.

Honest reviews of my books help bring them to the attention of other readers.

If you enjoyed this story, I would be very grateful if you would spend just two minutes to go to www.amazon.com and www.goodreads.com and write a review (it can be as short as you like) on the book's page.

Your entertainment is the reason I write. I would love to hear from you now that you've finished reading my story. Email me at Dallas@DallasGorham.com. Tell me how you liked my story and what you'd like to see Chuck McCrary do next. Or tell me anything else on your mind.

All the best,

Dallas

CARLOS McCRARY

WILL RETURN

As a writer, I love to build relationships with my readers. I occasionally send newsletters with details on new releases, special offers, and other bits of news relating to my mystery/thriller novels.

If you sign up on my VIP Readers Group email list, I'll send you advanced notice of my new releases (no spam!). Almost always discounted! Also, I'll send you opportunities to WIN cool prizes in special giveaways. Such as free books written by me or by other mystery/thriller authors I recommend and more!

You can get the advanced notices, and access to the special giveaways FOR FREE by signing up at:

www.DallasGorham.com

If you enjoyed *Dangerous Friends*, read on for an exciting preview of *Day of the Tiger*, Book 5 of the Carlos McCrary, Private Investigator, Mystery Thriller series, available in electronic and print editions on Amazon.com. Free to Kindle Unlimited members.

OPPOSITES ATTRACT, RIGHT? Tank Tyler is a wealthy investment manager and Pro Football Hall of Famer. Al Rice, a victim of drugs and self-pity, has been a miserable failure since being kicked off his college football team years ago. The two men share a sordid secret that ruined Al's life and turned Tank's dreams into nightmares for sixteen years, in spite of his success—a secret that still entangles the lives of these polar opposites.

Now Monster Moffett, a sadistic loan shark who mangled Al's hand with a ball-peen hammer when he couldn't repay his loan, again targets Al. Moffett threatens Al's mother, Doraleen Rice. When Doraleen begs Tank Tyler for help, he hires private investigator Chuck McCrary to protect both Doraleen and Al.

Chuck exposes a human sex trafficking ring and forced prostitution in the sleazy world of high-priced "Gentlemen's Clubs"–a world where Chuck will need more than brawn, balls, and bullets to sort out this mess.

With gun in hand, he invades the heavily-armed gang's stronghold alone, but he hasn't counted on facing a knife-wielding African warrior. Now he faces deadly odds of ever seeing the light of day.

Day of the Tiger

A Carlos McCrary, Private Investigator, Mystery Thriller

Tibetan Proverb:

It is better to live for one day as a tiger than to live for a thousand years as a sheep.

Chapter 1

ALFRED RICE CRINGED as the man in black raised the ball-peen hammer above his left hand. "No, for God's sake, Monster! I paid you the interest. I'll pay you the rest, I swear." He struggled to free his arms. Panic rose in his throat like bile.

"Crummy forty thousand dollars. That pays the interest to last month, you moocher. I told you I want the whole two hundred grand. I don't trust you no more." The man in black, Montgomery "Monster" Moffett, raised the hammer again. The industrial fluorescent lights high above the table cast multiple shadows across Rice's arm. "You're thirty days past due. This is the late fee."

"Monster, I need both hands to work," Rice pleaded.

"Hold him steady." Moffett's men jammed Rice's forearm tight against the table. Moffett's eyes blazed and his breath came quicker as he smashed the back of Rice's hand with the hammer, shattering the fourth metacarpal bone. The blow crushed the veins and capillaries surrounding the bone. Skin ripped at the ragged edges of the ugly crater in Rice's brown skin. Subcutaneous bleeding oozed into the crater, filled it, and spilled across the back of his hand like red lava spreading across a brown mountainside. Moffett licked his lips as he got a whiff of blood.

Rice shrieked like a banshee. His vision blurred as pain dominated his senses and became the focus of his universe.

"You don't work, loser; you hang out in strip clubs when you could be making money to pay me back." Moffett swung the hammer again.

Rice's scream echoed off the concrete block walls as his second metacarpal bone splintered. He stared wide-eyed at the second crater that the hammer gouged. Blood pooled, escaped, and mingled with the flow from the first wound. The red stream dripped off the back of Rice's hand. A red slick began to spread across the table top. Sobbing, he pleaded with Monster. "I swear on my mother's life I'll pay you the rest, Monster. I'll pay you, I swear."

"You should've thought of that before you tried to welsh on a debt." Moffett swung the hammer again and pounded a third crater between the first two. "You owe me two hundred large. You're past due. You got two weeks."

Rice's vision turned to red. He slumped to one side.

Moffett swirled the bloody pool with the hammer, smearing streaks across the Formica. He laid the gruesome hammer head on Rice's wrist. He grabbed the frightened man's ear and twisted it savagely. "You hear me, loser? You listening to me? Huh?"

Rice mumbled through the bubbles that formed on his lips. He tried to nod, but it hurt his ear.

Moffett tapped the victim's wrist with the side of the hammer, leaving a red smear. "In two weeks' time, I turn Teddy loose on you with his knife. He'll carve you a reminder to pay your debts. Two weeks after that, I break both arms. Two weeks after that... Well, you did swear on your mother's life, didn't you?"

Rice tried to turn his face toward Moffett. "That's not what I meant. You can't—"

Moffitt twisted Rice's ear again. "You don't tell me what I can't do, loser. You understand me?" He waved at the other two men, who stepped away from Rice.

Moffett released Rice's ear and shoved his head away, knocking him off the metal chair.

Rice peered up from the concrete floor. "You stay away from my mother. Just stay away. Do whatever you want with me. Maybe I deserve whatever I get, but not my mother." His eyes narrowed. "Not my mother. You touch a hair on her head and I'll kill you if it's the last thing I ever do."

Moffett kicked him in the stomach. "Yeah, and I'm the Tooth Fairy." He laughed when Rice vomited.

Rice collapsed in a heap, sobbing as he cradled his ruined hand in the crook of his other arm.

"Throw this bum out."

Chapter 2

"I OWE AL RICE A DEBT I CAN'T REPAY." Tank Tyler paused to see if I was listening.

I was looking east out the window of Tank's sixty-first floor office in Port City's newest skyscraper, admiring the view of Seeti Bay. The sea breeze had scrubbed the late afternoon air to a clean, crisp blue beyond the window wall. The knife edge of the horizon beyond Port City Beach appeared to be at arm's-length. "Can you see all the way to Bimini?"

"Not quite. Look, Chuck, I didn't ask you here to admire the view. I have a friend who needs help." He paused. "Earth to McCrary. Earth to McCrary. Come in, McCrary. Hey, you're the McCrary of McCrary Investigations. I said I have a friend who needs your professional services. Did you even hear me?"

I turned from the window. "I don't have to read your lips to hear you, *amigo*. You owe Al Rice a debt you can't repay, yada, yada. I got it. Tank, you have more money than Tom Cruise. I would've said you have more than you can count, but you're a Certified freakin' Public Accountant with a computer for a brain. If you owe this Rice guy a debt, write him a check for crissakes."

He sighed. "Some debts can't be paid with money. God knows I've tried."

"How so?" I sipped Tank's expensive beer.

He waved the question off. "That's personal. It's enough for you to know that Al is in big trouble. I hope you can help him, and I'll pay you to try." He lapsed into silence, tilted his glass for the last of the twelve-year-old, single-malt Scotch, then rattled the ice cubes.

I turned the Pilsner glass in my hands while I gazed out the window again. One thing I'll say for Tank: He stocks the best private bar in Port City. "You pay the freight and I'll walk your dog."

He smirked. "Black people don't own dogs."

"Tank, how many times I gotta tell ya? I'm the funny Mexican; you're the studious African American CPA. Besides, you told me you owned a Border Collie when you were a kid." I sipped my beer. "Sure, I'll help your friend. What's his problem?"

"Al has so many problems I don't know where to begin." Tank shrugged. "To start, there's Monty Moffett, otherwise known as 'Monster.'"

Despite me being a tough guy, that sent a frisson down my spine. "Al is involved with Monster Moffett?"

"Yeah. Is that bad?"

I nodded. "What do you know about Monster Moffett?"

"Only what I read in the newspaper. Is he as bad as his nickname?"

"Worse. Moffett is the biggest bookie and loan shark in Port City, both businesswise and physically. This guy is almost as big as you. Must be six-foot-five and outweighs you by fifty pounds. Of course, he's mostly fat and you're all muscle. But even so, he scares the heck out of most people."

"Does he scare you?"

I shrugged. "Maybe he would if I had good sense, but I have more balls than brains."

"I would've said that you have balls *instead* of brains."

"You sure know how to hurt a guy. Especially a guy who is, uh, what's that big word I learned? Intellectually challenged. You forget: I have copious brawn to go with my extraordinary balls."

"So you'll help Al even with Monster Moffett in the picture?"

"You forget: Under this business suit and tie I wear a red cape and a blue leotard with a big red S on it."

"I thought you only wore that when you went clubbing."

I grinned. "The bigger they are... Moffett is ruthless and sadistic, but his nasty temper makes up for it. I'd do the world a favor if I took him down a notch. I suppose Al owes him money?"

"Yeah, and he hasn't got two pennies to rub together. A couple weeks ago Moffett sent two wise guys to haul Al to someplace in the warehouse district. Moffett took a ball-peen hammer to Al's left hand. Poor guy was in surgery for three hours. Over a hundred stitches and God knows how many steel pins. He'll never shuffle a deck of cards again, that's for sure." Tank set down his glass and cracked his knuckles. "Last week Al came to my office with a cast up to his forearm. He told me every agonizing detail."

"If you want me to help him," I asked, "why'd you wait until last night to call me?"

"Frankly, I didn't know what to do. I've bailed him out more times than I can count. It never works. You know that old definition of insanity..."

"Doing the same thing over and over, thinking this time you'll get different results. Yeah, another old joke I tell better than you."

Tank smiled. "Sometimes when you don't know what to do, the best thing to do is nothing."

"That sounds more like a bumper sticker than an excuse."

"In my defense, Moffett did give him two weeks. I knew Al had another week before Moffett came after him."

"So you procrastinated."

Tank stared at his empty glass. "I'm not proud of it."

"What changed?" I asked. "Why did you wait, then call last night in a hurry to see me?"

Tank walked over to the bar. "You ready for another?"

I raised my empty glass. "Last one, I have to drive."

Tank opened the bar refrigerator, slid out another Amstel, and handed it to me. "If I give Al money to pay this loan, Moffett will increase his credit line." He poured a little Scotch and slid a few ice cubes down the side of the glass. "He's done that before. Every time Al gambles or cooks up another hare-brained scheme, he gets deeper in debt to Moffett. When it comes to borrowing money from a loan shark like Moffett, Al's like an alcoholic who can't stop drinking."

I tilted the Pilsner glass and poured the Amstel gently down the slope so as not to bruise it. "How much does Al owe Moffett?"

"Two hundred thousand dollars."

Two hundred thousand dollars was petty cash for Tank, but the way he said it called for a whistle, so I whistled. "What does Al do for a living?"

Tank swirled his drink, rattled the ice. "Anything and nothing. He's full of grandiose schemes. He does an occasional drug deal, he gambles, and he's been arrested twice for shoplifting. He tried to flip houses during the last real estate crash. Lost a bundle, of course."

"Al doesn't sound like the type of guy you'd pick for a friend. In fact, he sounds like the polar opposite of conservative, uptight CPA Thomas Tyler." I poured the remainder of my beer. "How'd you become friends with a man like that?"

"We played football together for the UAC Falcons for two years. Al attended Carver High School here in the City where his mother teaches English and his father was head football coach. Al was a sophomore, a year ahead of me. When I showed up fresh off the farm from Florence, Alabama, he took me under his wing. He drove me to his house for a home-cooked meal." Tank stared out the window, lost in the past. "I was bouncing around like a kid in a hall of mirrors. I'd never seen a city larger than Huntsville, Alabama, except for recruiting trips when I was in high school. Al showed me how things work at a big university in a big city."

"What went wrong with Al?" I asked. "How did he end up such a loser?"

"It was sixteen years ago. Not relevant anymore."

"But he didn't finish college, did he?"

"Nope. Quit after he was kicked off the team in the spring semester of his junior year."

"Why'd he get kicked off?"

"Not important now."

"Could be relevant. Sometimes things like that gnaw on you for years; they color everything you see in the world."

"Drop it, Chuck. It's not important. Trust me on that."

Whenever someone tells me to trust them, it often means they don't know what they're talking about. I tried another tack. "So you two played together for two seasons."

"Yeah."

"What happened to him after he got kicked off the team?"

"He dropped out."

"Why?"

"Not important now."

I shrugged; I would come back to the subject later. "Using my unsurpassed analytical mind, I surmise that, for whatever reason, Al's life went downhill while yours skyrocketed. Consensus All-American your junior year, Bronko Nagurski Award for best defensive lineman in the known universe your senior year, and the UAC Falcons won the National Championship that year."

I pointed to the Falcons team picture on the wall. "And where was Al while all this glory was heaped on you?"

"I lost track of him for a few years."

"But not for long, I'll bet. You were a first round NFL draft choice with a multi-million-dollar contract. It was all over the sports pages. Al had to know about it. Stop me if I get this wrong."

"So far, you're ninety percent right."

"Hurray for me." I lifted my glass and toasted myself. "So Al shows up out of the blue to congratulate his old, but newly-rich friend. You feel guilty about your success—you're rich; he's poor. You're a big football star; he got kicked off the team. How'm I doing so far?"

"A hundred percent."

"Then Al plays the guilt card. He asks you to bail him out of some mischief. You help him out and one thing leads to another. Eventually it becomes a habit for you both. You're a rich man, so why not? I get that. That about right?"

"Yeah, pretty much." Tank stared into his glass.

I threw up my hands. "So why am I here? Why'd you call me last night?"

"Something intervened."

"What is this, big guy, twenty questions? What intervened?"

"More like *who* intervened. Al's mother, Doraleen, called me yesterday afternoon. Moffett showed up at her house and threatened her if Al doesn't pay. Moffett told her that Al swore on her life that he'd pay. He told her Al's two weeks was up tomorrow. She was at her wits end, so she called me. She was so scared she could barely talk. I went out to her home and installed better locks. Then I called you."

I drank Amstel while I decided what to say. "And here we are."

"Yeah, here we are." Tank sighed. "I've fretted over this mess ever since Al's mother called. I'm convinced that throwing money at Al—or at his creditors—is only a short-term solution. I tried that before, and it doesn't make any long-term difference to Al. I want to do something different this time." His eyes were moist. "That's why I called you."

"What am I supposed to do, psychoanalyze him? Read his aura? Adjust his chakras? I'm a poor dumb private investigator with a room-temperature IQ."

"For starters, I want you to help Al's mother."

I inhaled the Amstel's hoppy aroma; at least something in this room was perfect. I made a get-on-with-it gesture to Tank.

"Doraleen was a second mother to me when I attended UAC. I call her Momma Dora. She invited me for Thanksgiving my first year at school. I couldn't afford to fly back to Alabama, and it was too far to drive there and back in four days. After that I spent every holiday but Christmas and Spring Break with Al's family. We became real close."

"Even after Al dropped out?" I asked.

"Even then. Momma Dora said that my ties with Al and her went deeper than football."

"And you stayed in touch all these years."

"Like I said, she's a second mother." Tank's brown face creased in a grin. Sometimes he looks like he has forty-eight teeth. Guy is a real-life toothpaste ad. "Besides, Momma Dora makes the world's best chili." The grin faded. "A stray bullet killed Al's father while we were at UAC. For the last few years, ever since Al became unreliable, I've visited once a month. I help around the house and do a few things she needs a younger person for. I put Christmas decorations on her roof or change a light bulb in a ceiling fixture. Al... he doesn't come to see Momma Dora often enough. Even when he comes, he's not good for much anymore." He sipped his Scotch. "Momma Dora thinks of me as the son who turned out all right."

"What makes Al unreliable? Drugs?"

Tank nodded. "When he can afford them. Alcohol when he can't."

"Al have any brothers or sisters?"

"Momma Dora and her husband William tried to have children for years. They had lost hope when Al came along. She said Al was a gift from God, never repeated."

I pulled a notepad from my jacket. "What's Al's full name? Albert? Alfred? Alexander?"

"Alfred Lord Tennyson Rice."

"For real?"

Tank grinned. "What can I say? Momma Dora's an English teacher.

I scribbled it on my notepad. "Do you have a picture of Al I could borrow?"

"Momma Dora will have one."

"What about on your phone? You have a picture in the contact list?"

"Yeah, I forgot that one."

"Send it to my phone." He did, and I examined the photo. "That's one I can use. Now to the assignment at hand. What should I do about Monster Moffett? Wave a magic wand?

Sprinkle pixie dust? Join hands and sing Kumbaya? My voice sounds best in a large choir where it's drowned out."

Tank stood at the window and spread his hands. When he stood there in his three-pieced, blue pin-striped suit, he looked like the world's largest banker. His bulk blocked the view. "I don't have a clue how to help this family, but I gotta do something even if it's wrong. If Al continues on this path, I guaran-damn-tee you, he'll end up dead. I could live with Al being dead—karma and such. But for Momma Dora... an old woman shouldn't bear a loss like that. I can't let it happen. Not if there's any way under heaven to prevent it."

"From Moffett's reputation, he won't back off unless someone kills him. Then his ghost will haunt you. If that's what you're after, big guy, that ain't gonna happen. I don't do hits, even if the guy deserves it." That was almost true.

"God, no. That's not what I mean. Besides, if Moffett fell into a bottomless pit, Al would find another jerk to gamble with. No, this situation requires a more original approach."

"A personality transplant is outside my area of expertise."

"Nobody likes a smart ass. Come with me to see Momma Dora. She's a wise old bird; heck, she earned a Masters in English Lit. Maybe she'll know what to do."

Chapter 3

DORALEEN RICE TOOK A DEEP BREATH when the doorbell rang. Surely it wasn't that horrible man again. She looked through the peephole and sighed with relief. Tank and a white man, who must be his friend Chuck McCrary, stood at the door. She trembled as she opened the solid oak door. She jumped when it clunked against the brass security bar. "You haven't seen Race Car out there, have you, Tank? I let her out an hour ago. She should be back by now. I'm worried about her, what with that… that gangster making threats yesterday."

Tank scanned the front yard. "No, Momma Dora, I don't see her." He turned to Chuck. "Did you spot a white Persian cat as we walked up?"

"Nope."

Doraleen closed the door to swing the brass security bar open. She reopened it wide enough for the two men to enter. "Come in, come in, boys. Hurry inside."

She slammed the door behind them, threw the two dead bolts, and swung the door guard across the matching knob screwed to the door edge. "I'm not used to this door safety thing, Tank." Standing on tiptoe, she reached her arms as far around Tank's neck as she could and leaned her cheek against his muscular chest. Tank wrapped arms the size of tree trunks around her slender shoulders. She burst into tears.

###

I STOOD NEAR THE DOOR, shifted my weight from one foot to the other, while this tiny woman and my giant friend comforted each other. I felt as out of place as a hooker in church. Glancing around, I noticed the new door guard was expertly installed. One dead bolt was newer than the other. Those must be the extra locks Tank installed.

Tank patted the old woman's shoulder and kissed the top of her head. "There, there, Momma Dora. I'm here. Everything will be all right."

Doraleen looked at my buddy. "I'm frightened, Tank. While I waited for you and your friend to arrive, I kept worrying, 'What if that Moffett man shows up before they get here?' What would I do—what *could* I do?"

She stepped back and smoothed her palms down the front of her brick-red dress. She held out her hand. "I'm Doraleen Rice."

She presented a firm handshake and cold hands. To my eye, she had aged like fine wine with skin as smooth as a burnished oak barrel. The tiny lines that etched the corners of her eyes reminded me of wood grain, not wrinkles. She could have been anywhere from fifty to eighty. Her red dress and salt-and-pepper Afro hairstyle looked like Little Orphan Annie, but all grown up. I handed her a business card, one without the crossed swords on it. "I'm Chuck McCrary. I'm here to help." Instantly I felt stupid. I remembered that old joke: I'm from the government; I'm here to help.

"Let's sit. We have a lot to discuss." She led us into a living room that looked like a set from a 1980s television show. The one modern piece in the room was a huge HD television with a cable box on the table beside it. A bottle of sherry and three stemmed glasses with gold rims sat on the coffee table next to the TV remote.

Mrs. Rice lifted the bottle. "Will you have a sherry, Chuck?"

"No thanks, ma'am, I have to drive." I didn't mention that I don't like sherry. No sense hurting the lady's feelings.

Tank wasn't as tactful as I. "You know I don't drink sherry, Momma Dora." He glanced my way. "Momma Dora puts out a glass for me anyway. She says she wants to be hospitable in case I change my mind." He patted her hand.

"Chuck, I'm old enough to be your mother—maybe your grandmother, but don't make me feel old by calling me 'ma'am.' Please call me Doraleen. Since you don't want sherry, Tank will brew you both fresh coffee while we get acquainted."

I raised an eyebrow at Tank. He grinned. "Don't look surprised, Mr. Gourmet Cook. Despite what you think, I'm not helpless around a kitchen. I know how to brew coffee. You and Momma Dora talk." He took off his suit jacket and draped it across a chair back.

"Thanks, coffee is fine, ma'am. I mean, Doraleen. Just so you know, I call every woman *ma'am* no matter her age, high school English teachers in particular. It's the way I was raised."

Doraleen smiled back, but the smile didn't reach her eyes. She had other things on her mind. She waited until Tank left the room. "Tank is such a good man. He's a second son to me. I don't say it in front of him because it embarrasses him, but I love that boy as much as if I'd borne him myself. How did you and Tank meet?"

"We're both friends with Bigs Bigelow," I answered. "Do you know Bigs?"

"Oh, yes. He and Tank played together on the Pelicans defensive line—the 'Bigs Brigade' the newspapers called them. Bigs is a fine, fine man. Did you know that he retired from football and became a police detective?"

"Yes, ma'am. I met Bigs when I was a police detective."

"So Bigs introduced you to Tank?" She poured herself a sherry.

"Yes, ma'am. I came into a chunk of money a while ago, thanks to a sizable bonus a client paid me. I didn't make millions like Bigs, but I asked him to recommend somebody to keep me from blowing my nest egg on wine, women, and song."

"Bigs got rich playing for the Pelicans," Doraleen said, "but, more important, he *stayed* rich after he retired from football. That's not easy to do."

"I always say 'I can resist anything but temptation.'" If she saw the humor, she didn't let it show. My comedic genius often goes unappreciated. "Tank made sure I resisted temptation," I finished lamely.

Doraleen sipped her sherry. "Many of Tank's friends from professional football wasted their good fortune and wound up destitute. As did my William, God rest his soul. I remind my students that the quality of our decisions determines the course of our lives. My William played two years for the Miami Dolphins and wound up with nothing to show for it but bruises and memories. At least they were good memories. Of course, William made his bad money decisions before I knew him. I would never countenance such nonsense." She leaned toward me. "Tank told me once how William's bad experience inspired him to do better while he was in college. Did you know Tank passed the CPA exam on the first try?"

"No, ma'am, I didn't know, but I'm not surprised."

"Tank is modest, isn't he?"

"Yes, ma'am." If Tank were in the room, I would have said he had much to be modest about. Doraleen would not have found that remark amusing either.

Doraleen's eyes sparkled. "Tank takes his profession seriously; it's almost a mission to him. He says one must respect the money." She leaned back. "So you are Tank's client." It was not a question.

"And friend. We often work out at Jerry's Gym together, and we watch football together."

Doraleen nodded. "Tank tells me you're a private investigator."

"Yes, ma'am. McCrary Investigations."

"Do most private investigators earn enough to require an investment manager such as Tank?"

"Not the ones I know. Most of them make a so-so living like anybody else. I'm the exception. Sometimes, my clients give me a bonus when a case works out better than they expected. I put that bonus money with Tank to invest for me. My account's probably modest compared to his other clients, but I add to it every month." I glanced over my shoulder to see what was keeping Tank. My collar felt a little tight.

"Mighty oaks from little acorns grow, Chuck. Never forget that." She narrowed her eyes. "What makes you exceptional?"

"My strength is as the strength of ten, because my heart is pure." I knew she would recognize that quotation.

Her eyes widened. "You're an Alfred Lord Tennyson fan?"

"All-arm'd I ride, whate'er betide, until I find the Holy Grail."

"*Sir Galahad*, Tennyson's most famous poem. Did you know Al's full name is Alfred Lord Tennyson Rice?"

"Yes, ma'am. Tank told me."

"You see yourself as a knight errant."

"And I have dimples."

Doraleen smiled. Or maybe smirked. "Tank warned me that you fancy yourself a humorist."

"Guilty as charged."

"I'm sure you're quite droll, Chuck, but I don't have a sense of humor."

"You could have fooled me."

"What?" She raised a hand to her chest. "Oh, that was another *bon mot*, wasn't it? It was irony."

"I thought so. Mistakenly, it appears."

"If ever a damsel in distress needed a knight errant like Sir Galahad to gallop in on a white horse, it is I."

I grinned. "Spoken like a true English teacher."

"You shall be my Sir Galahad." Doraleen glanced at the door. "I don't mean to be rude, Chuck, but I'm worried about Race Car. Ever since that horrid man came here yesterday to threaten me, I've felt like a condemned prisoner waiting for the hangman. I think about things I've seen on TV and in the movies... you remember the horse's head scene in *The Godfather*?"

Everyone who'd ever seen that movie remembered the scene.

"That scene scared the heck out of me," I said. My stomach twisted as I remembered another time I'd found a client's dog slaughtered by a mobster with a sadistic streak like Moffett. I forced the dead dog's image from my mind.

"Race Car isn't a prize racehorse, but she is every bit as precious to Al and me. To Tank too, for that matter. We found her when we were walking away from the graveside service at William's funeral. This forlorn, dirty little kitten walks up to us in the middle of that tombstone forest. God knows where she came from. She rubs against Al's leg and he picks her up. She licks his hand and purrs, and Al was smitten. He said, 'It's Dad. He sent this kitten to tell us he's okay.' We looked around the cemetery to see if there was a momma cat anywhere, but it was like the kitten had dropped from the sky—or from Heaven. Al named her Race Car.'"

"Race Car?" I repeated. "An unusual name for a cat."

Doraleen smiled. "When William played wide receiver, he was so fast that his nickname was Race Car Rice. We named her as a tribute to my William. But Race Car's old. There's no telling how much longer she'll live."

"Would you like me to look for her, Doraleen?" I asked.

She set down her sherry and snugged the shawl around her shoulders. "I'll go with you. Race Car can get nervous around strangers. I notice you carry a gun. Even if that… that man is out there, I'll be safe with you." She followed me to the door.

I flipped back the security bar and opened the two dead bolts. "Normally, I'd hold the door for you, Doraleen. In this case, let me go first—for security." I pulled the door open and jerked to a stop in mid-stride, barring Doraleen's path with my arm.

An off-white Persian cat sprawled in macabre repose on the concrete, fluffy fur streaked with crimson splotches. Bloody streaks marked a trail where the pitiful pet had fought her way up the steps and across the porch and collapsed near the door. Ragged stumps were all that remained of her tail and ears. Race Car raised her head and turned her gray eyes toward the door. Her mouth opened in a soundless meow.

Doraleen pushed past my arm with surprising strength. "She's alive!"

Chapter 4

I DREW MY GLOCK AND SCANNED THE STREET AND SIDEWALK; no one was visible in the streetlights. I stuck my head inside the door. "Tank! Get out here—front porch. It's an emergency."

I leapt down the porch steps and ran to the sidewalk where I could see around the Bougainvilleas that sprawled across Doraleen's front yard. A set of taillights sped away a block up the street. The SUV squealed a right turn at the corner and was lost to view. I debated chasing it in my own minivan, but I-95 was two blocks away. The SUV would vanish before I had it in sight.

I holstered the Glock and jogged to the front porch where Tank was cradling Race Car in his arms. Blood stained his shirt sleeves and vest.

Doraleen stood beside him, stroking the cat's back.

"Doraleen," I asked, "do you have a regular vet for Race Car?"

She blinked tears from her eyes. "What...? My vet?" She shook her head as if to clear it. "Yes, yes, of course." She checked her watch. "She might be closed."

"Let's go anyway," I said. "If the clinic is closed, they'll have an emergency contact number on the door. We'll take my van. Tank, you sit in back with Race Car. Doraleen, grab your purse and lock the house."

Doraleen didn't move. She continued to stroke Race Car's matted fur.

I patted the sweet old lady on the shoulder. "Doraleen," I said softly, "we need to take Race Car to the vet. Grab your purse and lock the house. Please."

She kept stroking the cat.

Tank pulled Race Car away from her hand. "Momma Dora, we need to go. Now."

"Okay. I'll be right back." She pushed the door open and went inside.

I thumbed my remote and the rear door of the minivan slid open. I followed Tank to the vehicle, slid the bucket seat back, and waited while my giant friend wedged himself in and slid the door closed. I opened the passenger door as Doraleen hurried down the porch steps. I helped her into the van, closed the door, and trotted around to the driver's seat.

Doraleen clicked her seatbelt. "Head to I-95 and turn south. It's the second exit."

I READ THE VETERINARIAN'S EMERGENCY CONTACT NUMBER by my headlights as I stopped in the clinic's empty parking lot. I punched in the number and handed the phone to Doraleen.

"Dr. Willsey? It's Doraleen Rice… Yes, ma'am. Race Car, a white Persian… Something terrible happened to Race Car. We're parked at your clinic. Can you come down and help her? Someone cut off her ears and tail. Thanks. We'll be waiting."

She handed the phone back to me. "Ten minutes." She wiped the tears from her eyes and twisted where she could reach Race Car in Tank's lap. She stroked the cat's back. "There's a bench on the front porch. I'll take Race Car and wait with her up there."

"You'll get blood on your dress, Momma Dora. I'll hold her. I'm already bloody."

Doraleen opened the passenger door and spoke over her shoulder to Tank. "She'll feel safer in my lap. I don't mind the blood."

I followed both of them to the bench and waited until they sat. "When the vet gets here, I'd like to go back to your street and see if I can locate the place where… that is, the crime scene. Look for evidence."

Doraleen patted Tank's knee. "I'm safe with Tank. You go on. If it rains, it might wash away clues."

I PARKED AT THE CURB in front of Doraleen's house. I pulled on rubber gloves and took a Maglite. Blood drops marked a faint trail on the concrete. The trail led down the sidewalk to Doraleen's next door neighbor. Four more drops and a blood smear clustered on the pavement. I sniffed the air and followed a scent until I knelt on the sidewalk near a plumbago hedge. I sniffed again. Shining the Maglite under the hedge, I spied an empty tuna can. That's how the SOB had attracted Race Car. Any cat within smelling distance would come to him, even one who was nervous around strangers.

I played the beam back and forth under the hedge. A white scrap of fur lay in the mulch. I pulled an evidence bag from my pocket and picked up the white object. A cat's ear. My stomach felt like a fist-sized rock. *Oh, God, that poor cat.* I bagged the ear and found the tail and the other ear nearby. Bagged them too. I wasn't sure what I would do with them. When I found the SOB who did this, maybe I'd make him eat them.

I bagged the tuna can. Maybe I could pull a fingerprint off it.

As I set the evidence bags in the van, a light rain began to fall.

Chapter 5

AL RICE TOOK ANOTHER SWIG OF IRISH WHISKEY, swished it around in his mouth, and stared at the stripper dancing on the stage behind the bar at the Orange Peel Gentlemen's Club. *What was her name? Brandy. Yeah, it's Brandy. Or maybe Amber. What difference does it make?* This might be his last drink in his entire life. He'd never see Jasmine again—even if her name *was* Jennifer now. Tomorrow would be two weeks since Moffett had smashed Al's left hand to smithereens. Moffett had threatened to send Teddy to do even worse if he didn't pay. Teddy, now he was one bad dude. Always playing with that creepy-looking knife. A warrior's weapon, Teddy called it.

And Rice hadn't paid. Two hundred thousand dollars, by God. Moffett might as well demand that Rice pay off the national debt. That was just as likely. What did it matter… it was too late. It was always too late for Al. Too late for something. Too late for anything.

The surgeon who repaired Al's crushed hand had given him a prescription for forty Oxycodone pills for the pain. "Take one every six hours, if needed," he'd said. That was supposed to last ten days. Al filled the prescription and gobbled three pills as soon as he got back to his car. He'd taken eight pills the first day.

Then Cinnamon, another stripper at the Orange Peel, slipped him a note that she wanted to score some Oxycodone. After her shift, Rice met her in the parking lot and sold her the rest of the pills for money and a blow job. The BJ wasn't even good. He was too high to enjoy it. At least the money was good. For the last few days, he'd drunk his way through the cash while he watched Jasmine and the other strippers. *Who says you need Oxycodone for pain? Irish whiskey is almost as good.* Rice's biggest pain was that Jasmine or Jennifer or whatever-the-heck her name was—wouldn't give him the time of day. And why change her name? He had just gotten used to calling her Jasmine.

He took another drink and set the glass on the bar too hard. He waved at the bartender with his right hand. He raised his voice above the music. "Billy! I'll have another."

Billy leaned across the bar. "Pay for the drinks you already drank, Al. You can't run a tab forever."

"How much I owe you?"

"$48.50."

Rice belched. "$48.50. Sure thing, sure thing. I have it here… somewhere." He patted his jacket pockets, then his pants. He stood up from the barstool. Stuffing his right hand into his left front pants pocket, he began to twist around, then tilted and took a staggering step to regain his balance.

A man two stools down peeled his eyes away from the stripper, regarded Rice from the corner of his eye, and carried his drink to an empty table.

Rice lurched into another man at the bar. "Whoa. Sorry, sorry." He grabbed the bar. "Let's see… Aha. Here we go." He tried again, managed to pull a credit card from his pocket, and tossed it on the bar.

The other man frowned, dropped a few bills on the bar, and walked out.

"Al, you're running off my customers." Billy stuck the credit card in a terminal. He punched a few keys, studied the screen for a moment, and scoffed. He slid the card back across the bar. "Declined, Al."

Rice drained the last of the Irish whiskey. *Better enjoy it; it might be the last drink I'll have. Ever.* He reached in another pocket, found another credit card, and pushed it across the bar. "Try this one."

The bartender stuck the card in the terminal. "Declined. You got any cash, Al? You owe me $48.50."

"$48.50," Rice repeated.

The previous night Rice had drunk himself into oblivion at that same bar. He had awoken this morning in his car with no memory of how he got there. Now he wouldn't get enough alcohol to dull the pain of the real world again. How could he enjoy his last night on earth?

He lifted his left hand. "See this cast?" He had trouble saying "cast." It sounded more like "cash."

Billy shouted above the music. "No, but I'd like to see cash."

"No, no, no. Not *cash*. I said, 'See this *cast*.'" He waved the cast.

"Yeah, I seen it lots of times. What about it?"

Rice slid back onto the barstool. "It was a pres… a present."

"Yeah, so what?"

"A present… from Monster Moffett." Rice held the cast in front of his face and studied it with bloodshot eyes. "You know good ol' Monster, don't you, Billy?"

"I seen him around a few times."

"He's gonna kill me tomorrow, y'know. That's why I'm here to enjoy the girls tonight."

"Yeah, right, and I'm gonna be elected president." The bartender shook a finger at Rice. "Listen, Al. Your troubles with Monster Moffett don't mean squat to me. I got troubles of my own. You gonna pay your tab or what?"

"Sure, sure, sure…" Rice slid his hand into his shirt pocket and fished out a clump of crushed bills. He dropped them on the bar and tried to smooth them out with his right hand. "Oops." He pinned a bill under his cast and pressed it out. "Too goddamn dark in here to see what kind this is, Billy. You got a light?"

"If you weren't drunk, you could see." Billy pulled a penlight from his shirt pocket. It was a twenty.

"How much I owe you?" asked Rice.

"$48.50."

Forty… eight fitty," Rice repeated. "I thought that was it." He pushed the twenty across the bar. He pinned another bill under his cast. "Let's see what this one is."

Billy shined the penlight again.

It was another twenty, which Rice laid carefully on the first bill. He pulled another bill out.

A five, and Rice lined it up on the two twenties. "Here you go. Let's call it even." He tried to pick up the remaining bills. "I need something to tip the dancers, Billy."

The bartender grabbed Rice's wrist. "You owe me $48.50, not $45. How much more you got there?" He pried the bills from Rice's fist and counted them. "Four more bucks." He grabbed the bills off the bar. "I'll keep the extra fifty cents as a tip. Sheesh."

Rice nodded. "Okay… Okay… So my tab's paid. How about my other drink?"

"Go home, Al." The bartender walked away.

"You gonna call me a cab?"

The bartender stopped at the far end of the bar. "And just how do you intend to pay for a cab?"

Rice found that uproariously funny. "Just kidding, Billy. Just kidding. I don't need a cab; I have my car. Don't matter none. Got no home to go to. Oops, Momma wouldn't like that.

Lemme rephrase: It doesn't matter, because I have no home to which I could go." He guffawed. "No home to which I could go."

The bartender walked around the bar and grabbed Rice's arm. "Gimme your keys."

Rice stared at him.

The bartender searched Rice's pockets until his found the keys. "I'll keep these until tomorrow. Come back sober and I'll give them to you. Like the song says: *You don't have to go home, but you can't stay here.*" He frog-marched Rice to the door.

Rice stumbled out the door and stopped in the middle of the sidewalk, swaying. He staggered to the wall and leaned on it. Oh, Christ, what would happen to him now? Tomorrow Moffett would send Teddy Ngombo after him. He couldn't go home. He couldn't face Momma like this. He'd been there a couple of days ago. He couldn't bear to see that look on her face again. He should've showered at Momma's. He couldn't remember why he hadn't. God knows, he needed a bath. He hadn't bathed in days, ever since his landlord left his clothes in a plastic garbage bag in front of his apartment. He'd tried the door, but the goddamn landlord changed the lock. That was a week ago, but it seemed like forever. He didn't remember what he did with the clothes.

He slid down the concrete block wall and plunked down on the sidewalk. He belched and then vomited. He leaned to one side and passed out.

Day of the Tiger

a Carlos McCrary, Private Investigator, Mystery Thriller

Book 4,

is available in electronic and print editions on Amazon.com.

Free to Kindle Unlimited members.

Also by Dallas Gorham

I'm No Hero

A special forces suspense thriller short story introducing Carlos McCrary when he was a sergeant in the U.S. Special Forces in Afghanistan. Available (in electronic editions only) at all major internet retailers.

ON A CLEAR NIGHT IN JUNE 2006, Special Forces Operational Detachment Alpha 777, the Triple Seven, gets their mission: Free an Afghan mountain village from a ruthless Taliban blockade that is starving the people to death. The village's crime? They educated girls in the village school.

A courageous young boy from the village sneaks through the hot summer night to escape the Taliban blockade. He runs ten miles barefooted to get help, arriving at an Afghan National Army garrison with bloody feet. He seeks the help of Afghan Major Ibrahim Malik. But Malik knows that his ANA small force is no match for the well-armed Taliban terrorists. Malik and the boy come to the Green Berets of the Triple Seven for help.

The Taliban have a larger force, heavily armed with Kalashnikov AK-47s and rocket-propelled grenades. The Americans must rely on their equipment, their training, and themselves.

This is a story of Sergeant Carlos "Chuck" McCrary, a Mexican-American Green Beret, and his team of soldiers who risk their lives to save two thousand Afghan townspeople they have never even met. Chuck and his fellow Special Forces soldiers live the motto: "We own the night." They set off in the darkness to defeat the Taliban and break the blockade. But when the soldiers of the Triple Seven don their night vision goggles and show up in the dark hours to liberate the village, they are surprised and outnumbered by an ambush of heavily-armed Taliban terrorists.

The soldiers of Team Triple Seven must fight for their lives, or the villagers won't be the only ones the Taliban wipe out.

Six Murders Too Many

Book 1 of the Carlos McCrary Mystery Thriller series, available in electronic and print editions on Amazon.com. Free to Kindle Unlimited members.

The plan was perfect;

all it took was two simple murders...

Then an over-zealous assassin exterminated an extra victim and things got out of hand.

On his first big case as a newly-minted private investigator, Carlos "Chuck" McCrary must untangle a web of fraud, arson, adultery and murder before he becomes its next victim.

A Billionaire's Estate Is Up For Grabs

Ike Simonetti and his model-slim wife, Lorraine, tell Chuck that Ike's stepmother is trying to steal $400 million from Ike's father's estate. But is Ike Simonetti the only surviving heir of billionaire real estate developer Sam Simonetti? Or is there another contender for the fortune-a baby girl born to the dead billionaire's hot young trophy wife six months after Sam's death? The investigation takes Chuck from the sun-splashed beaches of South Florida to the burned-out Cleveland home of two dead daughters.

The Stakes Go Way Up

When mob hitmen ambush Chuck, the case becomes a matter of life and death. To save his own life and that of the supposed infant heiress, Chuck must discover if one of the billionaire's surviving family members is the real puppet master behind the murders.

Double Fake, Double Murder

Book 2 of the Carlos McCrary Mystery Thriller series, available in electronic and print editions on Amazon.com. Free to Kindle Unlimited members.

MOB BOSS GARRISON FRANCO IS GUNNED DOWN IN THE STREET, and the police think they know who did it—Jorge Castellano, one of their own homicide detectives whose wife had been threatened by Franco. Castellano claims he's been framed and pleads with private investigator Chuck McCrary to find the real killer.

Chuck discovers a mysterious teenager who ran away from an abusive foster home who may have witnessed the murder. But the boy doesn't trust anyone and won't tell Chuck what he saw. Chuck must gain the boy's trust before he can solve the crime.

Chuck's prime suspect is Ted Rayburn, a disgraced, former police detective and convicted blackmailer, now out of jail and plying his trade again. With shameful secrets and millions of dollars at stake, three of Rayburn's super rich victims try to hire Chuck to kill Rayburn. He refuses, but days later Rayburn is found shot to death with Chuck's gun. Chuck is arrested for murder.

Now Chuck must not only find out who killed Franco and framed his friend Castellano for the murder, but must solve the new murder or face a lifetime in prison himself.

Chuck must deal with millionaires and billionaires on the one hand and hoodlums and drug dealers on the other.

DALLAS GORHAM SENDS READERS ON A WHITE-KNUCKLE RIDE from the crime-filled streets of a South Florida ghetto to the waterfront mansions and high-rise condos of mega-millionaires in pursuit of the mysterious and elusive killer.

Quarterback Trap

Book 3 of the Carlos McCrary Mystery Thriller series, available in electronic and print editions on Amazon.com. Free to Kindle Unlimited members.

PORT CITY IS EXCITED TO BE HOSTING THE NEW YORK JETS and the Dallas Cowboys in the first Super Bowl in its fabulous, new billion-dollar stadium. Chuck McCrary's old friend from high-school football, Bob Martinez, is starting quarterback for the Jets.

One week before the game, Bob Martinez's supermodel fiancée, Graciela, disappears in the middle of the night from the Super Bowl headquarters hotel. Martinez hires Chuck to find her, but he won't let Chuck involve the police.

That same day the odds on the Super Bowl game change dramatically when someone bets a hundred million dollars that the Cowboys will beat the point spread. Is it Vicente Vidali, the New Jersey casino owner and mob boss? Did he kidnap Graciela?

Chuck discovers that Graciela has a secret that places her life in danger, regardless of the outcome of the game. Was she really kidnapped, or did she run away from her own secret life? Bob Martinez also has a dangerous secret that threatens to destroy his multi-million-dollar career in the NFL.

Chuck's search for the missing supermodel takes him from the dangerous streets and drug dealers of a South Florida ghetto to the waterfront high-rises and private island mansions of billionaires, movie stars, and crime moguls.

Quarterback Trap slices like a scalpel through the hidden world of organized crime, mega-million-dollar scams, and the hidden secrets of an outwardly glamorous world where careers—and lives—can be lost in a heartbeat.

McCrary's Justice

Book 6 of the Carlos McCrary Mystery Thriller series, available in electronic and print editions on Amazon.com. Free to Kindle Unlimited members.

NEBRASKA FARMER WILBUR JENKINS receives a cryptic text message from his missing daughter, Liz, claiming that she is a sex slave in sun-splashed Port City, Florida. Jenkins grabs the next plane and begs the cops to find his daughter. But Liz left home of her own free will, and the texts came from the cellphone of Antonio Crucero, a corrupt diplomat from a Caribbean tropical paradise. Crucero's diplomatic immunity protects him from U.S. law, and he refuses to cooperate.

Police detective Jorge Castellano sends the distraught father to Carlos " Chuck" McCrary.

McCrary is a wisecracking private investigator with a special genius for helping people in trouble. McCrary left the Port City Police so he could do the right thing without worrying about trivialities like *due process* and *probable cause*.

McCrary uncovers a cesspool of sex trafficking and drug smuggling that stretches from South Florida to Switzerland to the Caribbean. And Crucero has his fingers all over the operation.

Crucero's diplomatic status protects him from the reach of U.S. law, but it won't protect him from Carlos McCrary. McCrary has his own brand of justice and sets out to destroy Crucero any way he can—diplomatic immunity be damned.

FROM SOUTH FLORIDA'S GOLDEN BEACHES to a Caribbean vacation paradise, from Coconut Grove to the Florida Everglades, *McCrary's Justice* slashes like a machete through a treacherous jungle of sexual predators, drug cartels, and new and fearsome enemies.

Yesterday's Trouble

Book 7 of the Carlos McCrary Mystery Thriller series, available in electronic and print editions on Amazon.com. Free to Kindle Unlimited members.

YESTERDAY IS DEAD AND GONE. OR IS IT? For Cleo Hennessey, her past threatens to destroy her future.

A young, naïve country singer, Cleo just wants to make music for her thousands of adoring, newfound fans. NBA superstar Marvelous LeMarvis Jones, Cleo's fiancé, bankrolls her first concert tour. Then an unbalanced cyber-stalker takes issue with the couple's interracial relationship.

Cleo won't take the threats seriously, but LeMarvis hires Private Investigator Carlos McCrary to provide security for Cleo's *Summer Fun Concert Tour*. At the tour's first stop, a backup singer with a dangerous past is murdered onstage. Was the bullet meant for Cleo?

Despite Carlos's urging, Cleo refuses to cancel the tour, even as more bodies pile up on the tour's journey across Florida. In Jacksonville, the stakes are raised when the killer tires of Carlos interfering with his quest to do God's work.

What is Cleo hiding? Has the yesterday she thought she'd escaped finally found her?

With the killer outsmarting Carlos and the cops at every turn, has Carlos finally met his match? Will he wind up taking a knife to a gunfight?

Acknowledgments

MY THANKS TO MICHAEL H. HATFIELD of Hatfield & Stack, LLC, Attorneys at Law in Tavares, Florida. Michael has litigated numerous Federal and State jury trials to verdict throughout the State of Florida and United States. He earned a Bachelor of Arts from the University of Florida and a Juris Doctor from Cumberland School of Law, Samford University and is a member of Florida Association of Criminal Trial Attorneys. Michael reviewed my draft for technical accuracy on criminal law and procedure. Any inaccuracies are solely my responsibility.

My thanks to my editor Marsha Butler. She makes me a better writer. Her website is

ButlerInk.com.

About the Author

DALLAS GORHAM IS A SIXTH-GENERATION TEXAN and a proud Texas Longhorn, having earned a Bachelor of Business Administration at the University of Texas at Austin. He graduated in the top three-quarters of his class, maybe.

Dallas (the writer) and his wife moved to Florida years ago to escape Dallas (the city) winters (*Brrr*. Way too cold) and summers (*Whew*. Way too hot). Like his fictional hero, Chuck McCrary, he lives in Florida in a waterfront home where he and his wife watch the sunset over the lake most days and where he has followed his lifelong love of reading mysteries and thrillers into writing them in his home office. He is a member of Mystery Writers of America and the Florida Writers Association.

When not writing fiction, Dallas is frequent (but bad) golfer. He plays about once a week because that is all the abuse he can stand. One of his goals in life is to find more golf balls than he loses. He also is an accomplished liar (is this true?) and defender of down-trodden palm trees.

Dallas is married to his one-and-only wife who treats him far better than he deserves. They have two grown sons whom they are inordinately proud of. They also have seven of the smartest, most handsome, and most beautiful grandchildren in the known universe. Dallas and his wife spend *waaaay* too much money on their love of travel. They have visited all 50 states and over 90 foreign countries, the most recent of which were Indonesia and Malaysia, where their cruise ship stopped at Bali and Kuala Lumpur.

Internet stuff:

Dallas writes an occasional blog you can read at:

DallasGorham.com/blog/

It's sometimes funny, but not nearly as funny as he thinks.

His website

DallasGorham.com

has more information about his books, including the characters, which are recommended for anyone who enjoys action and suspense with a touch of humor and plenty of twists and turns.

If you have too much time on your hands, you can follow him on Twitter at

Twitter.com/DallasGorham

or Facebook at

Facebook.com/Dallas-Gorham-Books-1387561694892999

(Dallas has no clue why you have to have all those numbers; you just do. It might be simpler to go to **Facebook.com** and search for "Dallas Gorham Books.")

His Amazon Author Page is

Amazon.com/Dallas-Gorham/e/B00J4LISCS

Made in the USA
Las Vegas, NV
28 April 2022